THE BESTSELLING NOVELS OF
Tom Clancy

DEBT OF HONOR
It begins with the murder of an American woman in the back streets of Tokyo. It ends in war . . .

"A SHOCKER CLIMAX SO PLAUSIBLE YOU'LL WONDER WHY IT HASN'T YET HAPPENED!"—*Entertainment Weekly*

THE HUNT FOR RED OCTOBER
The smash bestseller that launched Clancy's career—the incredible search for a Soviet defector and the nuclear submarine he commands . . .

"BREATHLESSLY EXCITING!"
—*Washington Post*

RED STORM RISING
The ultimate scenario for World War III—the final battle for global control . . .

"THE ULTIMATE WAR GAME . . . BRILLIANT!"—*Newsweek*

PATRIOT GAMES
CIA analyst Jack Ryan stops an assassination—and incurs the wrath of Irish terrorists . . .

"A HIGH PITCH OF EXCITEMENT!"
—*Wall Street Journal*

continued . . .

P9-DNA-380

THE CARDINAL OF THE KREMLIN
The superpowers race for the ultimate Star Wars missile defense system . . .

"*CARDINAL* EXCITES, ILLUMINATES . . . A REAL PAGE-TURNER!"
—*Los Angeles Daily News*

CLEAR AND PRESENT DANGER
The killing of three U.S. officials in Colombia ignites the American government's explosive, and top secret, response . . .

"A CRACKLING GOOD YARN!"
—*Washington Post*

THE SUM OF ALL FEARS
The disappearance of an Israeli nuclear weapon threatens the balance of power in the Middle East—and around the world . . .

"CLANCY AT HIS BEST . . . NOT TO BE MISSED!"
—*Dallas Morning News*

WITHOUT REMORSE
The Clancy epic fans have been waiting for. His code name is Mr. Clark. And his work for the CIA is brilliant, cold-blooded, and efficient . . . but who is he really?

"HIGHLY ENTERTAINING!"
—*Wall Street Journal*

Tom Clancy's

Op-Center

GAMES OF STATE

Created by Tom Clancy and Steve Pieczenik

BERKLEY BOOKS, NEW YORK

TOM CLANCY'S OP-CENTER: GAMES OF STATE

A Berkley Book / published by arrangement with
Jack Ryan Limited Partnership and S&R Literary, Inc.

PRINTING HISTORY
Berkley edition / June 1996

All rights reserved.
Copyright © 1996 by Jack Ryan Limited Partnership and
S&R Literary, Inc.
This book may not be reproduced in whole or in part,
by mimeograph or any other means, without permission.
For information address: The Berkley Publishing Group,
200 Madison Avenue, New York, New York 10016.

The Putnam Berkley World Wide Web site address is
http://www.berkley.com

ISBN: 0-425-15187-5

BERKLEY®
Berkley Books are published by The Berkley Publishing Group,
200 Madison Avenue, New York, New York 10016.
BERKLEY and the "B" design
are trademarks belonging to Berkley Publishing Corporation.

PRINTED IN THE UNITED STATES OF AMERICA

10   9   8   7   6

Acknowledgments

We would like to thank Jeff Rovin for his creative ideas and his invaluable contributions to the preparation of the manuscript. We would also like to acknowledge the assistance of Martin H. Greenberg, Larry Segriff, Robert Youdelman, Esq., Tom Mallon, Esq., and the wonderful people at The Putnam Berkley Group, including Phyllis Grann, David Shanks, and Elizabeth Beier. As always, we would like to thank Robert Gottlieb of The William Morris Agency, our agent and friend, without whom this book would never have been conceived. But most important, it is for you, our readers, to determine how successful our collective endeavor has been.

—Tom Clancy and Steve Pieczenik

ONE

Thursday, 9:47 A.M., Garbsen, Germany

Until a few days ago, twenty-one-year-old Jody Thompson didn't have a war.

Back in 1991, the young girl had been too preoccupied with boys, phones, and acne to pay much attention to the Persian Gulf War. All she remembered were TV images of white flashes tearing through the green night sky, and hearing about Scud missiles being fired at Israel and Saudi Arabia. She wasn't proud of how little she recalled, but fourteen-year-old girls have fourteen-year-old priorities.

Vietnam belonged to her parents, and all she knew about Korea was that during her junior year of college, the veterans had finally gotten a memorial.

World War II was her grandparents' war. Yet oddly enough, she was coming to know it best of all.

Five days before, Jody had left behind her sobbing parents, her ecstatic little brother, her boyfriend-next-door, and her sad springer spaniel Ruth, and flown from Rockville Centre, Long Island, to Germany, to intern on the feature film *Tirpitz*. Until she sat down on the plane with the script, Jody knew almost nothing about Adolf Hitler, the Third Reich, or the Axis. Occasionally, her grandmother spoke reverently about President Roosevelt, and now and then her grandfather said something respectful about Truman, whose A-bomb saved him from being butchered in a prison camp in Burma. A camp where he'd once bitten the ear of a man who was torturing him. When Jody asked her grandfather why he'd done that, didn't it only make the torture worse, the gentle man had replied, "Sometimes you just have to do what you have to do."

Other than that, the only time Jody encountered the war was on TV, when she flashed past an A&E documentary on her way to MTV.

Now Jody was taking a crash course in the chaos that had engulfed the world. She hated to read; *TV Guide* articles lost her halfway through. Yet she'd been mesmerized by the script of the American/German coproduction. It wasn't just ships and guns, as she'd feared. It was about people. From it, she learned about the hundreds of thousands of sailors who'd served on the icy waters of the Arctic, and the tens of thousands of sailors who'd drowned there. She learned about *Tirpitz*'s sister ship the *Bismarck*, "the terror of the seas." She learned that factories, based on Long Island, had played a large, proud role in building warplanes for the Allies. She learned that many soldiers had been people no older than her boyfriend, and they'd been just as scared as Dennis would have been.

And since she'd come to the set, Jody had seen that powerful script come to life.

Today, by a cottage in Garbsen, outside Hanover, she had watched the cast film scenes in which a disgraced former SA officer leaves his family to exonerate himself on the German battleship. She had seen the gripping special effects footage of the attack by RAF Lancasters that had capsized the battleship in Tromsofjord, Norway, in 1944, entombing one thousand crew members. And here, in the prop trailer, she had touched actual pieces of the war.

Jody still found it difficult to believe that such madness had taken place, even though the evidence was spread on the tables before her. It was an unprecedented array of vintage medals, lanyards, gorgets, cuff-titles, weapons, and memorabilia on loan from private collectors in Europe and the United States. On the shelves were carefully preserved, leather-bound maps, military books, and fountain pens from the library of Generalfeldmarschall von Harbou, on loan from his son. In a file box in the closet were photographs of the *Tirpitz* taken by reconnaissance aircraft and midget submarines. And in a Plexiglass case was a fragment of one of the twelve-thousand-pound Tallboy bombs that had hit the ship. The rusted, six-inch shard was going to be used as a background image for the closing credits crawl.

Oil could stain the relics, so the tall, slender brunette wiped her hands on her School of Visual Arts sweatshirt before picking up the authentic Sturmabteilung dagger she'd come for. Her large, dark eyes shifted from the silver-tipped brown metal sheath to the brown hilt. In a circle near the top were the silver letters SA. Below them were a German eagle and a swastika. Because of the tight fit, she slowly withdrew the nine-inch weapon and examined it.

It was heavy and horrible. Jody wondered how many lives it had ended. How many wives it had widowed. How many mothers had cried because of it.

Jody turned it over. The words *Alles für Deutschland* were etched in black on one side. When Jody had first seen the knife the night before, during rehearsals, a veteran German actor in the cast had told her it meant *All for Germany*.

"To live in Germany back then," the man had said, *"you were required to give everything to Hitler. Your industry, your life, your humanity."* He'd leaned close to her. *"If your lover whispered something against the Reich, you had to betray her. What's more, you had to feel proud about betraying her."*

"Thompson, the knife!"

Director Larry Lankford's high voice ripped Jody from her reflection. She pushed the dagger back into the sheath and hurried to the trailer door.

"Sorry!" she yelled. "I didn't know you were waiting!" She jumped down the steps, rushed past the guard, and ran around the trailer.

"You didn't know?" Lankford yelled. "We're waiting to the tune of two thousand dollars a minute!" The director's chin rose from his red ascot and he began clapping. "That's thirty-three dollars," he said with a clap, "sixty-six dollars, ninety-nine dollars—"

"I'm coming," Jody panted.

"—one hundred and thirty-two—"

Jody felt foolish for having believed Assistant Director Hollis Arlenna, who'd said that Lankford wouldn't be ready to shoot for another ten minutes. As a production assistant had warned her, Arlenna was a little man with a big ego, and he fed it by making other people feel small.

As Jody neared, the AD stepped between her and the director. Breathing heavily, Jody stopped and handed him the dagger. He avoided her eyes as he turned and jogged the short distance to the director.

"Thank you," Lankford said affably as the young man handed him the blade.

While the director showed his actor how to hand the dagger to his son, the assistant director backed away from them. He didn't look at Jody, and stopped well short of where she was standing.

Why am I not surprised? she thought.

After less than a week on location, Jody already knew how the film business worked. If you were smart and ambitious, people tried to make you look stupid and clumsy so you weren't a threat. And if you screwed up, people distanced themselves from you. It was probably that way in any business, though movie people seemed to have made a bitchy art form of it.

As Jody walked back to the prop trailer, she thought about how much she missed the support system she and her friends had had back at Hofstra. But that was college and this was the real world. She wanted to be a film director, and she was lucky to have landed this internship. She was determined to come through it stronger and wiser. And as pushy as the rest of them, if that was what it took to survive.

As Jody reached the trailer, the elderly German guard gave her a reassuring wink.

"These bullies can't yell at the stars, so they yell at you," he said. "I wouldn't worry about it."

"I won't, Mr. Buba," Jody lied, smiling. She picked up the clipboard hanging on the side of the trailer. Attached to it was a list of the scenes to be shot that day which detailed the props needed for every scene. "If that's the worst thing that happens while I'm here, I'll survive."

Mr. Buba smiled back at Jody as she climbed the steps. She would have killed right now for a smoke, but it wasn't permitted in the trailer and there wasn't time to stand around on the outside. She had to admit she'd have killed right now for even less. For instance, just to get Hollis out of her hair.

Upon reaching the doorway, Jody stopped suddenly and peered into the distance.

"Mr. Buba," she said, "I think I saw someone moving around in the woods."

The guard rose on the balls of his feet and looked over. "Where?"

"About a quarter of a mile away. They aren't in the shot yet, but I'd hate to be them if they ruin one of Lankford's takes."

"I agree," Buba said as he pulled the walkie-talkie from its belt-strap. "I don't know how they could have gotten through, but I'll have someone check on it."

As he radioed in the report, Jody returned to the trailer. She tried to forget about Lankford and his snit as she re-entered a darker world, a world where the tyrants carried weapons, not shooting scripts, and attacked nations instead of interns.

TWO

Thursday, 9:50 A.M., Hamburg, Germany

Paul Hood awoke with a start as the big jet thumped down on runway two at the Hamburg International Airport.

No—! yelled something deep inside of him.

His head resting against the sun-warmed shade, Hood kept his eyes shut and tried to hold onto the dream.

Just a moment longer.

But the engines screamed to slow the aircraft, and their roar blew the remnants of dream away. A moment later, Hood wasn't even sure what the dream had been, except that it had been deeply satisfying. With a silent oath, Hood opened his eyes, stretched his arms and legs, and surrendered to reality.

The lean, forty-three-year-old Director of Op-Center was stiff and sore after eight hours in the coach seat. At Op-Center, flights like these were called "shorts"—not because that was where they hurt, though they did, and not because the flights were short. They'd gotten the name because they fell short of the thirteen-hour barrier, the minimum flight-time requirement for a government official to buy a spacious business-class seat. Bob Herbert believed that Japan and the Middle East received so much attention from the U.S. government because trade negotiators and diplomats liked flying in style. He predicted that the day twenty-four-hour flights earned officials a first-class seat, Australia would become the next trade or political battleground.

But cramped as Hood had been, at least he felt rested. Bob Herbert was right. The secret to sleeping on airplanes had nothing to do with whether one reclined. He hadn't, yet he'd slept wonderfully. The key was silence, and the earplugs had worked perfectly.

Hood frowned as he sat up straight. *We've come to Germany at the invitation of Deputy Foreign Minister Hausen to look at millions of dollars of hi-tech equipment, and fifty cents worth of Brooklyn-made silicone makes me a happy man.* There had to be a moral in that.

Hood removed the plugs. As he poked them into their plastic container, he tried to capture at least the contentment he'd felt in his dream. But even that was gone. Hood raised the window shade and squinted into the hazy sunlight.

Dreams, youth, and passion, he thought. The most desirable things always fade. Could be that was why they were so desirable. In any case, he told himself, what the hell did he have to moan about? His wife and kids were happy and healthy and he loved them and his work. That was more than many people had.

Annoyed with himself, he leaned toward Matt Stoll. Op-Center's portly Operations Support Officer was sitting in the aisle seat to Hood's right. He was just removing his headphones.

''Good morning,'' Hood said.

''Good morning,'' Stoll said as he stuffed the headphones in the seat back. He looked at his watch, then turned his big, Kewpie-doll face toward Hood. ''We're twenty-five minutes early,'' he said in his precise, clipped tones. "I really wanted to hear *Rockin' '68* cycle through a ninth time."

"That's all you did for eight hours? Listened to music?"

"Had to," Stoll said. "At thirty-eight minutes in, you get Cream followed by the Cowsills and Steppenwolf. It's like Quasimodo's beautiful ugliness—'Indian Lake' sandwiched between 'Sunshine of Your Love' and 'Born to Be Wild.' "

Hood just smiled. He didn't want to admit that he'd liked the Cowsills when he was growing up.

"Anyway," Stoll said, "those earplugs Bob gave me melted right out of my head. You forget, we heavy people sweat more than you skinny people do."

Hood glanced past Stoll. Across the aisle, the gray-haired Intelligence Officer was still asleep.

Hood said, "Maybe it would've been better if I'd listened to music too. I was having this dream and then . . ."

"You lost it."

Hood nodded.

"I know the feeling," Stoll said. "It's like a power failure which takes your computer data with it. You know what I do when that happens?"

"Listen to music?" Hood guessed.

Stoll looked at him with surprise. "That's why you're the boss and I'm not. Yeah, I listen to music. Something I associate with good times. That takes me right to a better place."

From across the aisle, Bob Herbert said in his high Southern drawl, "Me? I rely on earplugs for peace of mind. They're worth stayin' skinny for. How'd they work for you, Chief?"

"Fantastic," said Hood. "I was asleep before we passed Halifax."

"Didn't I tell you?" Herbert asked. "You oughta try 'em in the office. Next time General Rodgers is in a funk or Martha goes into one of her bootlick rants, just slip 'em in and pretend to listen."

Stoll said, "Somehow, I don't think that'd work. Mike says more with silence than he does with words, and Martha's been E-mailing her screeds all around town."

"Gentlemen, cool it on Martha," Hood cautioned. "She's good at what she does—"

"Sure," Herbert said. "And she'll haul our asses into court for racial and sexual discrimination if we suggest otherwise."

Hood didn't bother to object. The first aspect of leadership he'd learned during his years as Mayor of Los Angeles was that you didn't change people's minds by arguing with them. You just shut up. That put you above the fray and gave you an aura of dignity. The only way your opponent could reach that high ground was by surrendering some of the low ground, which meant compromise. Sooner or later, they all came around to that. Even Bob, though it took him longer than most.

As the jet came to a stop and the passenger bridge was swung over, Herbert said, "Hell, it's a new world. I guess what we need are electronic earplugs. If we don't hear what we don't like, we don't run the risk of being politically incorrect."

"The information highway is supposed to *open* minds, not close them," Stoll said.

"Yeah, well, I'm from Philadelphia, Mississippi, and we didn't have highways back there. We had dirt roads that flooded in the spring, an' everyone pitched in to clean 'em up.''

The seatbelt sign was turned off and everyone rose except Herbert. As people collected their carry-on luggage, he leaned his head back, his eyes fixed on the overhead reading light. It had been fifteen years since he'd lost the use of his legs in the Beirut Embassy bombing, and Hood knew he was still self-conscious about not being able to walk. Though no one who worked with Herbert gave his handicap a thought, Herbert didn't like to make eye contact with strangers. Of all the things Herbert disliked, pity was at the head of the list.

''Y'know,'' Herbert said wistfully, ''back home, everyone started from the same end of the road and worked together. Differences of opinion were settled by trying it one way. If that didn't work you tried it another way and the job got done. Now,'' he said, ''you disagree with someone and you're accused of hating whatever minority they happen to belong to.''

Stoll said, ''Opportunism knocks. It's the new American dream.''

''Among some,'' Hood pointed out. ''Only among some.''

After the door was opened and the aisle had emptied, a German flight attendant came over with an airline wheelchair. Herbert's customized chair, with its cellular phone and built-in laptop, had been sent along as baggage.

The young attendant turned the chair around beside Herbert. She leaned across the chair and offered him a hand, which he declined.

''Not necessary,'' Herbert huffed. ''I've been doing this since you were in grade school.''

With his powerful arms, Herbert lifted himself over the armrest and dropped into the leather seat. As Hood and Stoll fell in behind, toting their carry-ons, he led the way through the cabin, wheeling himself.

The heat of the Hamburg summer permeated the passenger bridge, but it was mild compared to what they'd left behind in Washington, D.C. They entered the bustling, air-conditioned terminal, where the flight attendant turned them over to a government official Lang had sent to help them through customs.

As the attendant turned to go, Herbert grabbed her wrist.

"Sorry I snapped at you," he said. "But me and these"—he patted the armrest—"we're old friends."

"I understand," the young woman said. "And I'm sorry if I offended you."

"You didn't," Herbert said. "Not at all."

The woman took off with a smile as the government official introduced himself. He told them that a limousine was waiting to take them to the lakeside Alster-Hof Hotel once they were through customs. Then he pointed the way, standing well back as Herbert began wheeling through the terminal, past the window which looked onto busy Paul Baumer Platz.

"Well," Herbert said, "I think it's damned ironic."

"What is?" Hood asked.

"I can't find a square inch of common ground with my own people, yet I'm in an airport the Allies bombed to hell along with half of Hamburg. I'm here making nice with a flight attendant and getting ready to work on the same end of the road with guys who shot at my dad in the Ardennes. Takes some getting adjusted to."

"Like you said," Hood remarked, "it's a new world."

"Yeah," Herbert said. "New and darin' me to keep up with it. But I will, Paul. God in heaven help me, I will."

So saying, Herbert picked up the pace. He scooted around Americans, Europeans, and Japanese—all of whom, Hood was sure, were running the same race in their own way.

THREE

Thursday, 9:59 A.M., Garbsen, Germany

Werner Dagover's lip curled with disgust when he rounded the hill and saw the woman sitting behind the tree.

That was fine, fine work by the road team, he thought, *letting someone through.* There was a time in Germany when careers were destroyed by slipups like this.

As he approached, the barrel-chested sixty-two-year-old security guard vividly recalled being seven years old and having his Uncle Fritz come to live with them. The master saddler of an army riding school, Fritz Dagover had been the ranking official on duty when a drunken army sports instructor snuck a *Generalmajor*'s horse from the stable. He took it for a midnight ride and broke its leg. Though the instructor had committed the infraction without Fritz's knowledge, both men were court-martialed and dishonorably discharged. Despite the fact that civilian manpower was scarce during the war and Uncle Fritz was a trained leather-worker, he was unable to get work. He ended his life seven months later, swigging arsenic-laced ale from his canteen.

It's true, Werner reflected, *great evil was committed during the twelve-year Reich. But a high value was placed on personal responsibility. In purging everything from the past, we've also cast out discipline, the work ethic, and too many other virtues.*

Today, few guards were willing to risk their lives for an hourly wage. If their presence on a movie set, at a factory, or in a department store was not a deterrent, then it was too bad for the employer. The fact that they'd agreed to do a job didn't matter to most guards.

But it mattered to Werner Dagover of *Sichern*. The name of the Hamburg-based company meant "security." Whether it was a woman accidentally interrupting a shoot or a gang of thugs celebrating Hitler's birthday during this week's insidious Chaos Days, Werner would see to it that his beat was secure.

After notifying the dispatcher that there was a woman in the woods, apparently alone, Werner shut off his walkie-talkie. Drawing back his shoulders, he made sure his badge was on straight and pushed stray hairs under his hat. As he'd learned during his thirty-year tenure as a Hamburg police officer, one couldn't wield authority without looking authoritative.

As *Sichern*'s guard-at-large for this operation, Werner had been stationed in the command trailer on the main road of the small town. When the call came from Bernard Buba, he'd biked the quarter mile to the movie location and parked by the prop trailer. Then he'd made his way inconspicuously around the crew, past the hill, and headed into the twenty acres of forest. Beyond the woods was another road where *Sichern* guards were supposed to be watching for picnickers or birdwatchers or whatever this woman was.

As Werner neared the tree, his back to the sun, he stepped on a nutshell. The slender young woman rose with a start and turned. She was tall, with aristocratic cheekbones, a strong nose, and eyes that seemed like liquid gold in the direct sunlight. She was wearing a loose white blouse, jeans, and black boots.

"Hello!" she said breathlessly.

"Good morning," Werner replied.

The guard stopped two paces from the woman. He tipped his hat.

"Miss," Werner said, "a film is being shot just around the hill and we must keep the area clear." He extended his hand behind him. "If you'll come with me, I can escort you back to the main road."

"Of course," the woman said. "I'm sorry. I wondered what those men were doing on the road. I thought perhaps there had been an accident."

"You would have heard an ambulance," Werner noted.

"Yes, of course. " She reached behind the tree. "Let me just get my backpack."

Werner called his dispatcher on the walkie-talkie and explained that he was escorting a woman back to the main road.

"So—a movie," the woman said, slinging the backpack over her left shoulder. "Is anyone famous in it?"

Werner was about to tell her he didn't know much about movie actors when he heard leaves rustle above him. He looked up in time to see two men, dressed in green and wearing ski masks, jump from the lowest branch. The smaller man landed in front of him, holding a Walther P38. Werner couldn't see the larger man who dropped behind him.

"Don't speak," the gunman told Werner. "Just give us your uniform."

Werner's eyes shifted to the woman as she removed a folding-stock Uzi from the backpack. Her expression was cool now, impervious to the contemptuous look he gave her. She stopped beside the gunman, nudged him aside with her knee, and pressed the gun muzzle under Werner's chin. She glanced at the name tag on his breast pocket.

"Just so there's no misunderstanding, Herr Dagover," she said, "we kill heroes. I want the uniform *now*."

After hesitating a long moment, Werner reluctantly undid his belt buckle. He pressed down on the walkie-talkie to make sure it was snug in its loop, then laid the big leather belt on the ground.

As Werner began undoing the big brass buttons on his uniform, the woman crouched and scooped up the belt. Her eyes narrowed as she removed the walkie-talkie and turned it over.

The small red "transmit" light was glowing. Werner felt his throat go dry.

He knew it had been a risk to turn it on so the dispatcher could hear them. But sometimes the job required risks, and he didn't regret having done it.

The woman touched the "lock" button with her thumb, taking it off transmit. Then she looked from Werner to the man behind him. She nodded once.

Werner Dagover gasped as the man slipped two feet of copper wire around his throat and pulled tight. The last thing he felt was a ripping pain which girdled his neck and shot down his spine. . . .

Short, powerfully built Rolf Murnau of Dresden, in what was formerly East Berlin, stood at ease beside the oak. The nineteen-year-old was armed and attentive as he watched the hill that lay between them and the film set. He held the Walther P38 in one hand, but that was only his most obvious weapon. The ski mask tucked in his belt was lined with washers, making it a devastating and unexpected bludgeon in a fight. A sharpened hat pin hidden beneath the collar of his shirt was perfect for slitting throats. Stick in the point, drag it quickly to the side. And the crystal of his wristwatch made a surprisingly effective weapon when dragged across an opponent's eyes. The bracelet he wore on his right wrist could be slipped over his hand and used as brass knuckles in a fistfight.

Every now and then, Rolf turned to make sure no one approached from the road. No one did, of course. As planned, he and the other two members of *Feuer* had parked off the road and walked in when the guards were on their coffee break. The men were too busy chatting among themselves to notice.

Rolf's smoky eyes were alert, and his small, pale lips were pressed together. That, too, had been part of his training. He had worked hard to control his blinking. A warrior waited for an opponent to blink, then attacked. He had also learned to keep his mouth shut while drilling. A grunt told an opponent that a blow had worked or that you were struggling. And if your tongue were extended, a punch under the chin could make you bite it off.

Rolf felt strong and proud as he listened to the sluts and gays and moneymen beyond the hill on the movie set. All of whom would die in the flames of *Feuer*. Some would perish today, most of them later. But eventually, through people like Karin and the famous Herr Richter, the world vision of *Der Führer* would be realized.

The young man's head was covered with a black stubble which barely concealed the fire-red swastika cut into his scalp. Perspiration from a half hour in the mask gave the hair a bristly, boyish shine. It also dribbled into his eyes, but he ignored it. Karin was big on military formality, and she would not approve if he wiped his brow or scratched an itch. Only Manfred was permitted such liberties, though he rarely took them. Rolf enjoyed the discipline. Karin said that without it he and his comrades *"are like links which are not a chain."* She was right. In the past, in gangs of three or four or five, Rolf and his friends had attacked individual enemies but never an opposing *force*. Never the police or anti-terrorist squads. They didn't know how to channel their anger, their passion. Karin was going to change that.

To Rolf's right, behind the oak, Karin Doring finished removing Werner's uniform while the hulking Manfred Piper put it on. Once the corpse had been stripped to its underwear, the twenty-eight-year-old woman dragged it through the soft grasses toward a boulder. Rolf didn't offer to help. When they'd finally gotten a close look at the uniform, she'd told him to stand guard. And that was what he was going to do.

From the corner of his eye, Rolf saw Manfred squirm as he dressed. The plan required Karin and one of the men to get close to the movie set, which meant that one of them had to look like a *Sichern* guard. Because the guard had been so barrel-chested, the clothes would have looked ludicrous on Rolf. So although the sleeves were short and the collar was tight, Manfred got the job.

"I already miss my windbreaker," Manfred said as he struggled to button the jacket. "Did you watch as Herr Dagover came toward us?"

Rolf knew that Manfred wasn't addressing him, so he said nothing. Karin was busy hiding Werner's body in the tall grasses behind the boulder, so she also didn't answer.

"The way he adjusted his badge and hat," Manfred went on, "took pride in his uniform, walked erect. I could tell he was raised in the Reich. Very possibly as a Young Wolf. In his heart, I suspect he was still one of us.'' The co-founder of *Feuer* shook his large, bald head. He finished with the buttons and tugged the jacket sleeves as far as they would go. ''It's too bad that men of his pedigree get comfortable. With a little ambition and imagination, they could be of great use to the cause.''

Karin stood. She said nothing as she walked to the limb where she'd hung her weapon and backpack. She was not the talker that Manfred was.

Yet, thought Rolf, *Manfred is right.* Werner Dagover probably *was* like them. And when the firestorm finally came, they would find allies among people like him. Men and women who were not afraid to cleanse the earth of the physically and mentally deficient, of the foreign-colored, of ethnic and religious undesirables. But the guard had tried to signal his superiors, and Karin was not one to forgive opposition. She'd kill *him* if he questioned her authority, and she'd be right to. As she'd told Rolf when he dropped out of school to become a full-time soldier, if someone opposes you once, they'll do it again. And that, she'd said, was something no commander could risk.

Karin picked up her Uzi, slipped it in the backpack, and walked to where Manfred was standing. The thirty-four-year-old wasn't as driven or well read as his companion, but he was devoted to her. In the two years that Rolf had been with *Feuer,* he'd never seen them apart. He didn't know whether it was love, mutual protection, or both, but he envied them their bond.

When Karin was ready, she took a moment to slip back into the girl-on-a-lark persona she'd used on the guard. Then she looked toward the hill.

"Let's go," she said impatiently.

Putting his big hand around Karin's arm, Manfred led her toward the set. When they were gone, Rolf turned and jogged back toward the main road to wait for them.

FOUR

Thursday, 3:04 A.M., Washington, D.C.

As he looked at the short stack of comic books on his bed, General Mike Rodgers wondered what the hell had happened to innocence.

He knew the answer, of course. *Like all things, it dies,* he thought bitterly.

The forty-five-year-old deputy director of Op-Center had awakened at 2:00 and had been unable to get back to sleep. Since the death of Lieutenant Colonel W. Charles Squires on a mission with his Striker commandos, Rodgers had spent night after night replaying the Russian incursion in his mind. The Air Force was delighted with the maiden performance of their stealth "Mosquito" helicopter, and the pilots had been credited with doing everything possible to extract Squires from the burning train. Yet key phrases in the Striker debriefings kept coming back to him.

". . . we shouldn't have let the train get onto the bridge . . ."

". . . it was a matter of just two or three seconds . . ."

". . . the Lieutenant Colonel was only concerned with getting the prisoner off the engine. . . ."

Rodgers had done two tours of Vietnam, led a mechanized brigade in the Persian Gulf, and held a Ph.D. in world history. He understood only too well that "the essence of war is violence," as Lord Macaulay put it, and that people died in combat—sometimes by the thousands. But that didn't make the loss of each individual soldier any easier to endure. Especially when the soldier left behind a wife and young son. They were only beginning to enjoy the compassion, the humor, and—Rodgers smiled as he thought back on the too-short life—the unique savoir faire that was Charlie Squires.

Rather than lie in bed and mourn, Rodgers had driven from his modest ranch-style home to the local 7-Eleven. He would be going to see gangly Billy Squires in the morning and wanted to bring him something. Melissa Squires wasn't big on candy or video games for her son, so comic books seemed like a good bet. The kid liked superheroes.

Rodgers's light-brown eyes stared without seeing as he thought once more about his own superhero. Charlie had been a man who cherished life, yet he hadn't hesitated to give it up to save a wounded enemy. What he'd done enobled them all—not just the close-knit members of Striker and the seventy-eight employees of Op-Center, but each and every citizen of the nation Charlie loved. His sacrifice was a testament to the compassion that was a hallmark of that nation.

Rodgers's eyes fogged with tears, and he distracted himself by thumbing through the comic books again.

He had been shocked that comic books were twenty times more expensive than when he was reading them—$2.50 instead of twelve cents. He'd gone out with just a couple of bucks in his pocket and had to charge the damn things. But what bothered him more was that he couldn't tell the comic-book good guys from the bad guys. Superman had long hair and a mean temper, Batman was a borderline psychotic, Robin was no longer clean-cut Dick Grayson but some brat, and a cigarette-smoking sociopath named Wolverine got his jollies ripping people apart with his claws.

If Melissa doesn't approve of SweetTarts, these sure aren't going to go down real easy.

Rodgers dropped the stack of comic books on the floor, beside his slippers. He wouldn't give these to a kid.

Maybe I should wait and buy him a Hardy Boys book, he thought, though he wasn't entirely sure he wanted to see what had become of Frank and Joe. The brothers probably had lip rings, choppers, and attitude. Like Rodgers, their father Fenton was probably prematurely gray and dating a succession of marriage-minded women.

Hell, Rodgers decided. *I'll just stop at a toy store and pick up an action figure.* That, and maybe a chess set or some kind of educational videotape. Something for the hands and something for the mind.

Rodgers absently rubbed his high-ridged nose, then reached for the remote. He sat up on his pillows, punched on the TV, and surfed through vividly colored vacuous new movies and washed-out vacuous old sitcoms. He finally settled on an old-movie channel that was showing something with Lon Chaney, Jr., as the Wolfman. Chaney was pleading with a young man in a lab coat to cure him, to relieve his suffering.

"I know how you feel," Rodgers muttered.

Chaney was lucky, though. His pain was usually ended by a silver bullet. In Rodgers's case, as with most survivors of war, crime, or genocide, the suffering diminished but never died. It was especially painful now, in the small hours of the night, when the only distractions were the drone of the TV and the intrusion of headlights from passing cars. As Sir Fulke Greville once noted in an elegy, "Silence augmenteth grief."

Rodgers shut off the TV and switched off the light. He bunched his pillows under him and lay on his belly.

He knew he couldn't change the way he felt. But he also knew he couldn't afford to surrender to sorrow. There was a widow and her son to think about, plus the sad task of finding a new commander for Striker, and he had to run Op-Center for the rest of the week that Paul Hood would be in Europe. And today was going to be a low point on the job, what Op-Center's attorney Lowell Coffey II accurately described as "the welcoming of the Fox to the warren."

In the night, in that silence, it always seemed like too much to deal with. But then Rodgers thought about the people who didn't live long enough to become oppressed by life's burdens, and those burdens seemed less crushing.

Thinking that he *could* understand why a middle-aged Batman or anyone else might go a little nuts at times, Rodgers finally floated into a dreamless sleep. . . .

FIVE

Thursday, 10:04 A.M., Garbsen, Germany

Jody's mouth twisted as she entered the trailer and took a look at the prop list.

"Great," she said under her breath. "Just great."

The good-natured exasperation which had marked her conversation with Mr. Buba was tinged with genuine concern now. The item she needed was hanging in the tiny bathroom of the prop trailer. Getting to it around the clutter of tables and trunks would require delicate maneuvering. The way her luck was running today, Lankford would print the scene he was shooting after one take and move on to the next before she returned.

Placing the heavy clipboard on a table, Jody started out. Though it would have been faster to crawl under the tables, she was sure that if she did someone would see her. At graduation, when Professor Ruiz had informed her that she'd gotten this internship, he'd said that Hollywood might try to discourage her ideas, her creativity, and her enthusiasm. But he'd promised that they would heal and return. He'd warned her, however, never to sacrifice her dignity. Once surrendered, that could not be reacquired. So she walked rather than crawled, deftly edging, leaning, and twisting her way through the maze.

According to the prop list, she needed to get a reversible winter uniform which actually had been worn by a sailor on the *Tirpitz*. It was hanging in the bathroom because the closet was full of vintage firearms. The local authorities had ordered the guns locked up, and the closet was the only cubicle with a key.

Jody sidled the last few feet to the lavatory. There was a heavy trunk and a heavier table beside it, and she could only open the door partway. She managed to squeeze in, though the door shut behind her and she gagged. The camphor smell was overwhelming, worse than it had ever been at her grandmother's apartment in Brooklyn. Breathing through her mouth, she began flipping through the forty-odd garment bags, looking at the tags on each. She wished she could open the window, but a tic-tac-toe design of metal bars had been welded across it to deter thieves. Reaching the latch and lifting the window would be a pain.

She swore silently. *Could anything else possibly go wrong?* she asked herself. The tags were written in German.

There was a translation sheet on the clipboard and, with another quiet oath and a mounting sense of urgency, she cracked the door and squeezed back out. As she renegotiated the maze, Jody was suddenly aware of voices outside the trailer. They were coming closer.

Never mind the enthusiasm and creativity, Professor Ruiz, she thought. Jody could see her career ending in about twenty seconds.

The temptation to crawl was great, but Jody resisted. When she was near enough to the clipboard, she leaned over, hooked an index finger through the hole at the top, and pulled it toward her. Desperate, she began to hum, pretending that she was on the dance floor and moving like she hadn't moved since the freshman orientation dance. And soon she was back inside the lavatory, the door shut, the clipboard on the sink as she frantically compared the clothes tags to the computer printout attached to the scene list.

SIX

Thursday, 10:07 A.M., Garbsen, Germany

Mr. Buba turned as he heard the voices from behind the trailer.

"... I'm one of those people who never has any luck," a woman was saying. Her voice was raspy and she was speaking quickly. "If I go to a store, it's right *after* a movie star has been there. If I'm at a restaurant, it's the day before a celebrity dines there. In airports, I miss them by minutes."

Mr. Buba shook his head. *My, how this woman did go on. Poor Werner.*

"So here I am," she continued as they came around the corner. "I accidentally find myself on a movie set, just yards away from a star, and you won't even let me see one."

Mr. Buba watched as they approached. The woman was standing directly in front of Werner, whose hat was pulled low, his big shoulders hunched forward. She was waving her arms, practically dancing with frustration. Mr. Buba wanted to tell her that seeing a movie star was no big deal. That they were just like other people, if other people were pampered and obnoxious.

Still, he felt sorry for the young woman. Werner was a stickler for rules, but maybe they could bend them so the poor lady could see a movie star.

"Werner," said his colleague, "since this woman is already our guest, why don't we—"

Mr. Buba didn't get to finish his sentence. Stepping from behind the woman, Manfred swung Werner's billy club at the guard. The black wood crashed lengthwise against Mr. Buba's mouth, and the guard gagged on blood and teeth as he fell back against the prop trailer. Manfred hit him again, on the right temple, spinning Mr. Buba's head to the left. The guard stopped gagging. He slid to the ground and sat there, leaning against the trailer, blood pooling behind his neck and shoulders.

Manfred opened the door of the cab, threw Werner's bloody club in ahead of him, then climbed in. As he did, a man from the film crew shouted, "Jody!"

Karin faced away from the set. She knelt, pulled off her backpack, and slipped out her Uzi.

The short man shook his head and began walking toward the trailer.

"*Jody,* what the hell are you doing there, our soon-to-be *ex*-intern?"

Karin stood and turned.

The assistant director stopped. He was nearly fifty yards away.

"Hey!" he said. He squinted toward the trailer. "Who are you?" He raised an arm and pointed. "And is that one of our prop guns? You can't—"

A confident *pup-pup-pup* from the Uzi dropped Hollis Arlenna on his back, arms splayed, eyes staring.

The moment he hit the ground, people began screaming and running. At the prompting of a young actress, a young actor tried to make his way to the fallen assistant director. As he crawled toward Arlenna, toward Karin, a second burst from the Uzi slammed into the top of the actor's head. He crumpled in on himself. The young actress shrieked and continued shrieking as she watched from behind a camera.

The trailer's powerful engine growled to life. Manfred revved it, drowning out the cries from the set.

"Let's go," he yelled to Karin as he shut the door of the cab.

The young woman walked backward, behind her Uzi, toward the open door of the trailer itself. Expressionless, she jumped in, pulled up the collapsible stairs, and closed the door.

As Manfred roared off through the woods, Mr. Buba's dead body flopped lifelessly to the ground.

SEVEN

Thursday, 10:12 A.M., Hamburg, Germany

Jean-Michel thought it fitting that his meeting with the leader, the self-proclaimed New Führer, was taking place in the St. Pauli district of Hamburg.

In 1682, a church dedicated to St. Paul was erected here, on the hilly banks of the Elbe. In 1814, the French attacked and looted the quiet village and nothing was the same thereafter. Hostels, dance halls, and brothels were built to cater to the steamship sailors who came through, and by the middle of the century the St. Pauli region was known as a district of sin.

Today, at night, St. Pauli was still that. Gaudy neon signs and provocative marquees announced everything from jazz to bowling, live sex shows to tattooists, waxworks to gambling. Innocent-sounding questions like "Do you have the time?" or "Have you got a match?" brought visitors together with prostitutes, while drugs were offered by name in low, careful voices.

It was appropriate that the representative of the New Jacobins should meet Felix Richter here. The new French incursion, and the union of their movements, would change Germany again. This time, for the better.

The Frenchman had left his two traveling companions asleep in the room and caught a taxi outside his hotel

on An der Alster. The fifteen-minute ride to St. Pauli
ended at Grosse Freiheit, in the heart of the lurid entertainment district. The area was deserted, save for tourists
who wanted to see the sights without the enticements.

Jean-Michel pushed back his thick black hair and but-
toned his moss-green blazer. Tall and slightly over-
weight, the forty-three-year-old executive vice president
of *Demain* was looking forward to meeting Richter. The
few who knew him and the fewer who knew him well
agreed on two things. First, Richter was dedicated to his
cause. That was good. Monsieur Dominique and the rest
of the French team were dedicated people as well, and
M. Dominique loathed dealing with anyone who wasn't.

Second, people said that Richter was a man of wild,
sudden extremes. He could embrace you or decapitate
you, as whimsy dictated. In that respect, Richter appeared to have much in common with Jean-Michel's
own shadowy employer. M. Dominique was a man who
either hated or loved people, was generous or ruthless
as the moment dictated. Napoleon and Hitler were the
same way.

It is something in the makeup of leaders, Jean-Michel
told himself, *which does not permit them to be ambiv-
alent.* He was proud to know M. Dominique. He hoped
he would be proud to know Herr Richter.

Jean-Michel walked up to the black metal door at the
front of Richter's club, *Auswechseln.* There was nothing
on the door save for a fish-eye peephole and a buzzer
beneath it. To the left, on the jamb, was the marble head
of a goat. The Frenchman pressed the button and waited.

Auswechseln, or Substitute, was one of the most infamous, decadent, and successful nightspots in St. Pauli.
Men had to come with a date. Upon entering, the couple
was given one pink and one blue necklace with different

numbers; whoever had the matching number was their new date for the evening. Only well-dressed, attractive people were admitted.

A rough voice came from the open mouth of the goat.

"Who is it?"

"Jean-Michel Horne," the Frenchman said. He was about to add in German, *"I have an appointment with Herr Richter,"* but decided not to. If Richter's aides didn't know who was expected, then he was running a sloppy operation. One from which Jean-Michel and his associates would be wise to walk away.

A moment later the door opened and a bodybuilder over six and a half feet tall motioned Jean-Michel in. The big man shut and locked the door and put a massive hand on the Frenchman's shoulder. He moved Jean-Michel to a spot beside the register, patted him down thoroughly, then held him there for a moment.

Jean-Michel noticed the video camera on the wall and the tiny receiver in the big man's ear. Someone, somewhere, was comparing his image with the fax which had been sent from M. Dominique's office at *Demain*.

After a moment, the giant said, "Wait here." Then he turned and disappeared into the darkness.

Efficient, Jean-Michel thought as the big man's heavy footsteps thumped across the dance floor. But caution wasn't a bad thing. M. Dominique hadn't gotten where he was either by being careless.

Jean-Michel looked around. The only light came from four red neon rings around the bar to his right. They didn't tell him much about what the club looked like or whether the big man had even left the room. All that the Frenchman knew for certain was that despite the hum of the air vents the place smelled. It was a slightly nauseating blend of stale cigarette smoke, liquor, and lust.

After a minute or two, Jean-Michel heard fresh footsteps. They were considerably different from the first. They were confident but light and they tapped rather than scraped along the floor. A moment later, Felix Richter stepped into the red light of the bar.

Jean-Michel recognized the dapper thirty-two-year-old from the photographs he had seen. Not that the picture captured the dynamism of the man. Richter stood just under six feet tall, his blond hair short and carefully razor-cut. He was dressed in an impeccably tailored three-piece suit, highly polished shoes, and a black tie with red stripes. He wore no jewelry. Richter's people regarded that as effeminate, and there was no room in the party for that.

"Medals. That is all I allow our men to wear," Herr Richter had said once in an editorial in his newspaper, *Unser Kampf,* Our Struggle.

More impressive than Richter's attire, however, were his eyes. The photographs hadn't captured them at all. Even in the red light of the bar, they were riveting. And once they found their target they didn't move. Richter did not seem the kind of man to avert his eyes from anyone.

As the German neared, his right hand moved as if he were drawing a gun slowly. It slid up the leg and hip, then shot straight out. It was a curious but elegant move. The Frenchman shook the hand firmly, surprised by the strength of Richter's grip.

"It was good of you to come," Richter said. "Yet I thought that your employer would be visiting as well."

"As you know, M. Dominique prefers to conduct business from his factory," Jean-Michel said. "With the technology available to him, there's very little reason to leave."

"I understand," said Richter. "Never photographed, rarely seen, appropriately mysterious."

"M. Dominique is mysterious but not uninterested," Jean-Michel pointed out. "He has sent me to represent him in these discussions, and also to be his eyes and ears during Chaos Days."

Richter grinned. "And to make sure that the donation he generously gave to the celebration is being well spent."

Jean-Michel shook his head. "You're wrong, Herr Richter. M. Dominique is not like that. He invests in people he believes in."

The Frenchman released the German's hand and Richter fell in beside him. Richter took his guest's elbow and ushered him slowly through the darkness.

"Don't feel that you have to defend Dominique to me," Richter said. "It's good business to keep an eye on what your peers are up to."

Peers? Jean-Michel thought. M. Dominique owned a billion-dollar manufacturing company and controlled one of the most powerful right-wing groups in France . . . in the world. He recognized a very select few as his peers. Despite their parallel interests, Herr Richter was not among them.

Richter changed the subject. "The hotel room we booked for you," he said. "It's acceptable?"

"Extremely pleasant," Jean-Michel replied. He was still annoyed by Richter's arrogance.

"I'm glad," Richter said. "It's one of the few old hotels left in Hamburg. During the war, the Allies bombed most of the city to dust. Hamburg's misfortune for being a port. It's ironic, though, that so many of these old, wooden buildings survived." He swept his arm as if to embrace all of St. Pauli. "The Allies didn't attack prostitutes and drunks, only mothers and children. Yet they call *us* monsters for atrocities like the mythical Holocaust.''

Jean-Michel found himself responding to Richter's impromptu passion. Though it was illegal in Germany to deny the Holocaust, he knew that while Richter was in medical school he used to do so with regularity. Even having his full scholarship revoked for making anti-Semitic remarks did not stop him. Judicial officials were reluctant to prosecute agitators who were otherwise nonviolent, though they were finally forced to go after Richter when a foreign news crew videotaped his ''Jewish Lie'' speech at Auschwitz and aired it. He spent two years in prison, during which time his aides ran his young operation—making sure that Richter's personal legend grew.

Because of the man's courage and his devotion to the cause, Jean-Michel decided to forget their bad start. Besides, they had business to conduct.

They reached a table and Richter switched on a lamp in the center. Beneath the translucent shade was a small white Pan playing his pipes.

Jean-Michel sat down when Richter did. The light fell just short of the German's eyes, but Jean-Michel saw them anyway. They were almost as translucent as the shade. The man had made a fortune from this club and from a hostess service he operated in Berlin, Stuttgart, Frankfurt, and Hamburg. But the Frenchman was willing to bet that Richter had been a bastard even when he was poor.

The Frenchman looked up at the second floor. It was lined with doorways. Obviously, these were rooms for members who wanted to do more than dance.

"We understand you have an apartment here, Herr Richter."

"I do," Richter said, "though I only stay here one or two nights a week. I spend most of my time at the 21st Century National Socialist Party suites in Bergedorf, to the south. That's where the real work of the movement is done. Writing speeches, telephone solicitation, transmitting E-mail, radio broadcasts, publishing our newspaper—do you have this week's *Kampf*?"

Jean-Michel nodded.

"Excellent," Richter went on. "It's all very legitimate. Not like the early days, when the authorities hounded me for one alleged misdemeanor or another. So," he said, "you've come to honor Chaos Days. And to represent your employer in 'discussions,' as he called them in my one brief telephone connversation with him."

"Yes, Herr Richter." Jean-Michel leaned forward and folded his hands on the table. "I am here with a proposition."

Jean-Michel was disappointed. Richter didn't move.

"You have my attention," Richter said.

"It is not commonly known," said Jean-Michel, "but M. Dominique has been quietly underwriting neo-Nazi groups around the world. The Razorheads in England, the Soldiers of Poland, and the Whites Only Association in America. He's trying to build a worldwide network of organizations with a common goal of ethnic purity."

"Together with his New Jacobins," Richter said, "that would put his strength at some six thousand members."

"Close to that, yes," said Jean-Michel. "And when he goes on-line in America, those numbers are sure to increase."

"Almost certainly," said Richter. "I've seen copies of his games. They're most entertaining."

"What M. Dominique proposes, Herr Richter, is bringing your 21st Century organization into the fold. He will provide you with funds, access to *Demain* technology, and a role in shaping the future of the world."

"A role," said Richter. "As in a play."

"Not a play," Jean-Michel replied. "History."

Richter smiled coldly. "And why should I accept a part in Dominique's drama when I can direct my own play?"

Once again, Jean-Michel was shocked by the conceit of the man. "Because M. Dominique has resources the likes of which you can only dream of. And through his connections, he can offer you both political and personal protection."

"Protection from whom?" Richter asked. "The government won't touch me again. The two years I was in prison made me a martyr to the cause. And my people are devoted."

"There are other leaders," Jean-Michel said with a hint of menace. "Other potential New Führers."

"Are there?" Richter asked. "You're referring to someone in particular?"

The Frenchman had been anxious to use a little muscle on the man, and this seemed like the perfect opportunity.

"Frankly, Herr Richter," Jean-Michel said, "there has been talk that Karin Doring and *Feuer* are the rising stars of the movement."

"Has there been talk?" Richter said smoothly.

Jean-Michel nodded. The Frenchman knew that Felix Richter and Karin Doring had been outspoken adversaries two years before, when Karin came out of East Germany espousing terrorism while Richter, fresh from prison, was advocating political activism. The two criticized each other openly until members of *Feuer* ambushed and killed two members of Richter's group. The leaders finally held a summit in a Berlin hotel, where they agreed to pursue their own goals without criticizing the other. But there was still tension between the unvarnished East German guerrilla and the dapper West German physician.

"Karin is energetic, charismatic, bold," Jean-Michel said. "We have heard she planned and led the attack on the bank in Bremen, set the courtroom fire in Nuremberg—"

"She did that and more, yes," Richter said. "Karin is good at warfare. She's a cat who leads other cats, an alley fighter, a field commander. But what you and her followers fail to realize is that she isn't someone who can build or run a political party. She still insists on participating personally in every one of her missions, and one day the authorities or a mishandled bomb will get her."

"Perhaps," said Jean-Michel. "Meanwhile, in just two years, *Feuer* has acquired nearly thirteen hundred members with thirty full-time soldiers."

"That's correct," said Richter. "But they're mostly East Germans. Animals. In five years, I've acquired nearly five thousand members from *this* side of the old border. That, M. Horne, is the basis for a political movement. That," he said, "is the future."

"Each has its place," said Jean-Michel. "M. Dominique believes that either of you would make a potent ally, which is why he has instructed me to talk with her as well."

Those riveting eyes moved from the watch to Jean-

Michel. They were like little machines, precise and un-emotional. Jean-Michel watched them as Richter stood. The brief audience was obviously at an end. The French-man was openly surprised.

"I will come for you at your hotel at five-thirty to-night," the German said. "She and I will both be ap-pearing at tonight's rally in Hanover. Then you will see for yourself who leads and who follows. Until then, good morning."

As Richter turned and walked away, the big doorman appeared from the shadows behind Jean-Michel.

"Excuse me, Herr Richter," Jean-Michel said boldly.

Richter stopped.

Jean-Michel rose. "I have been instructed to report to M. Dominique this morning, not this evening," the Frenchman said. "What do I tell him about his offer?"

Richter turned. Even in the deep shadow, Jean-Michel could make out the nasty eyes.

"That I will consider his generous offer. In the mean-time, I desire his support and friendship," Richter said.

"Yet you dismiss me," Jean-Michel said.

"Dismiss you?" Richter said. His voice was soft, flat, and dark.

"I'm not a clerk or a bodyguard," the Frenchman said. "As a representative of M. Dominique, I expect courtesy."

Richter walked slowly toward Jean-Michel. "A rep-resentative of Dominique—"

"*Monsieur* Dominique," Jean-Michel said indig-nantly. "You at least owe him that respect. He wants to help you—"

"The French always support opposition leaders," Richter said. "You helped Dacko overthrow Bokassa in the Central African Republic in 1979, and you hosted the Ayatollah Khomeini while he was planning his return to Iran. The French hope for favors when these people come to power, though they rarely get them." He said icily, "I respect Dominique. But unlike you, M. Horne, I do not have to kowtow. He wants *my* help. I do not need his."

This man is preposterous, Jean-Michel thought. He had heard enough. "You will excuse me," he said.

"No," Richter said quietly. "I will not. You do not walk out when I am facing you."

The Frenchman glared at him for a moment, then turned anyway. He ran into the doorman. The big man grabbed Jean-Michel's neck and turned him around so he was facing Richter.

"Richter, are you *insane*?" Jean-Michel cried.

"Irrelevant," Richter replied. "I'm in command."

"Don't you know that M. Dominique will hear of this? Do you think he will approve? We—"

"We!" Richter interrupted. The German looked into Jean-Michel's eyes. "All of this *'We understand . . .'* and *'We have heard . . .'* " Richter raged. "*We,* monsieur? What are *you*?"

Richter's arm moved then, just as it did when they met. Only this time there was a knife in his hand. It stopped less than a quarter inch from Jean-Michel's left eye. Then he raised the knife so it was pointing straight toward the Frenchman's eyeball.

"I'll tell you what you are," Richter said. "You're a lapdog."

Despite his anger, the Frenchman felt his insides weaken and liquify. *This is madness,* he thought. He felt as if he were in a time warp. The Gestapo couldn't exist here, in an age of video cameras and immediate international outrage. But here it was, threatening him with torture.

Richter glared at him, his eyes all too clear, his voice level. "You speak to me as if you were my equal. What have you done in your life other than to ride a visionary's rocket?"

There was a lump of something in Jean-Michel's throat and he tried hard to swallow. He succeeded, but said nothing. Each time he blinked, the blade made a fine laceration in his eyelid. He tried not to moan but did, in spite of himself.

"I was wrong," Richter said. "You're not even a lapdog. You're the lamb the shepherd has sent in his stead. To make me an offer, but also to see what kind of teeth I have. And if I bite you?" he asked. "Then Dominique has learned something about me. He's learned that I am not awed by his functionaries. He's learned that in the future, he will have to treat me differently. As for you"—Richter gave a little shrug—"if I bite too hard, he simply replaces you."

"No!" Jean-Michel said. Indignation momentarily overcame his fear. "You don't understand."

"I do. I reviewed your credentials on my computer when you walked in the door. You joined Dominique's organization twenty-one years, eleven months ago and you rose because of your scientific knowledge. You received a patent for a four-bit video game chip which enabled *Demain* to sell highly advanced games at a time when other games were one or two bits. There was a *bit* of a row in the United States over that, because a California company said that your chip resembled one they were getting ready to market."

Jean-Michel shifted on his feet. Was Richter simply reciting the facts, or was he suggesting he knew something more about *Demain*'s origins.

"You have recently received a patent for a silicon chip which directly stimulates nerve cells, a chip which *Demain* will be using in its new computer software. But you were apolitical in school. When you were hired by *Demain,* you adopted Dominique's worldview. Only then did he bring you into the very special inner circle of his New Jacobins, to help him rid France of Algerians, Moroccans, Arabs, and our common enemy the Israelis. But the operative word is *help,* M. Horne. In the pecking order, ethnic wretches are dispensible. Devoted servants are higher, but they too are replaceable."

Jean-Michel did not speak.

"Then there's just one other matter we have to discuss," Richter said. "How deeply I bite the lamb."

Richter angled the knife so it was point-up. Jean-Michel tried to back away again, but the man behind him grabbed a fistful of hair and held him steady. Richter moved the blade higher until the tip was under the upper eyelid. He continued to move it up slowly, along the contour of the eye, as he spoke.

"Did you know that I studied medicine before I founded the 21st Century party?" Richter asked. "Answer."

"Yes." Hating himself for it, Jean-Michel added, "Please, Herr Richter. Please—"

"I was a doctor," Richter said, "and I would have made a good one had I decided to practice. But I elected not to, and do you know why? Because I realized I couldn't give care to genetic inferiors. I mention this because, as you can see, I found another use for my training. I use it to influence. To control the body and thus the mind. For example, if I continue to push the knife upwards, I know I'll encounter the lateral rectus muscle. If I cut that muscle, you will find it extremely difficult to look up or down. It will be necessary for you to wear an eyepatch after that, or you'll be disoriented as your eyes work independently, and''—he laughed— ''you will look rather freakish, with one eye staring straight ahead, the other one moving normally.''

Jean-Michel was panting, his legs wobbling violently. If the big man weren't holding him by the hair he'd have fallen. The knife was out of focus as the Frenchman looked at Richter's red-tinted face. He felt a prick above the eyeball.

''Please, no,'' he sobbed. ''*Mon Dieu,* Herr Richter—''

Tears smeared his vision, and the trembling of his jaw caused the eye to shake. Each move caused a fresh and painful nick.

Slowly, the German brought his left hand toward the knife. His fingers were facing down. He placed his palm against the bottom of the hilt, as though he were going to jam it up.

''Did you also know,'' Richter asked calmly, ''that what we're doing is part of the process of brainwashing? I've studied the techniques of the KGB, who worked miracles with them. What an individual is told in a state of pain and fear registers on the brain as truth. Of course, it has to be done over and over to be truly effective. Systematic and thorough.''

He pushed the knife gently upwards. The prick became a shooting pain that punched against the back of Jean-Michel's forehead.

Jean-Michel screamed and then began to whine. Despite the shame he felt, he couldn't stop himself.

''What do you think now about equality, my little lamb?'' Richter asked.

''I think,'' said Jean-Michel, swallowing hard again,

"that you have made your point."

"My *point*?" Richter said. "That's the first clever thing you've said, and I doubt it was intentional."

Richter twisted the knife again, drawing a scream from the Frenchman.

"My point, actually, is this. In the very near future, Dominique will need me far more than I need him. His New Jacobin soldiers are a small force, suited for local work. I, on the other hand, have the ability to become international. And I will. His new computer programs will be downloaded in American cities, but they can persuade only over time. I and my lieutenants can go to America, meet with and inspire American Nazis. We are people of the Fatherland, the home of the movement. You are a people who were conquered and learned to serve. The world will follow me and they will do so now, not five or ten or twenty years from now. Equally as important, they will give us money. And that, M. Horne, makes Dominique and myself more than just peers. It makes me his superior."

Richter smiled, and a moment later let the knife fall into his palm. He stepped back; as he did so, he slipped the knife back in its sheath under his sleeve.

Jean-Michel moaned, a combination of pain and relief.

"So," Richter said. "When you contact Dominique, tell him that I've given you a lesson in humility. I'm sure he will understand. You can also tell him that no one, not Karin Doring or anyone else, will ever lead the movement in Germany. That is *my* destiny. Have we any other business?"

The doorman relaxed his grip enough so that Jean-Michel could shake his head.

"Excellent," Richter said as he turned. "Ewald will

call you a taxi and give you a minute to collect yourself. I trust I will see you tonight. It will be an evening to remember.''

When Richter was gone, the big man released his captive. Jean-Michel crumpled to the floor, his entire body shaking as he rolled onto his side. His vision on the left side was blurry-red, as blood trickled from his upper lid and pooled on the lower.

Lying in a heap, his legs still limp, Jean-Michel pulled a handkerchief from his pocket. Where it touched his eye the cloth was stained pale-rose, blood diluted by tears. He suffered a stinging pain every time he blinked. Worse than the physical pain, however, was the spiritual pain. He felt like a coward for having fallen apart the way he did.

As Jean-Michel nursed his wound, he reminded himself that despite the abuse he'd taken, he'd done what M. Dominique had ordered. He'd made the offer and been rebuffed by a proudly unmanageable fop.

Richter did not suspect, however, the real reason that M. Dominique wanted and was determined to bring him into the fold. It was not to further the movement of ethnic purity, but to create a genuine concern for the German government. M. Dominique wanted to destabilize Germany just enough to make the rest of Europe wary of allowing the nation to dictate the future of the European Community. That role must fall to France, and France's mind would be made up by a handful of its billion-dollar business leaders. And where the European Community went, Asia and the rest of the world would follow.

And they will follow, he knew, especially with America in chaos. *And when that goal is achieved*, Jean-Michel thought, *M. Dominique would dispose of Richter*.

As the French had learned over a half century before, it was a bad idea to let German fascists become too powerful.

After several minutes, Jean-Michel managed to get to his knees. Then he pulled himself up on a chair and stood hunched over it. The wound was already beginning to scab and scratch the eye, and each blink renewed his hatred for the German.

But you have to put that away for now, he thought. As a scientist, Jean-Michel had learned to be patient. Besides, as M. Dominique had told him before he left, even a misstep teaches you something. And this one had taught them a great deal about the new Führer.

Finally putting away his handkerchief, the Frenchman made his way to the door. He did not look to Ewald for assistance. Opening it, he shielded his wounded eye from the harsh sunlight and walked slowly to the waiting cab.

EIGHT

Thursday, 11:05 A.M.,
Hamburg, Germany

The ride from the airport to the city center on the Autobahn took thirty-five minutes. As always when he traveled on business, Hood wished that he had time to stop and look at some of the buildings, monuments, and museums they passed. It was frustrating to catch just a glimpse, at ninety miles an hour, of churches which were old when the United States was young. But even if there had been time, Hood wasn't sure he'd be comfortable taking it. Wherever he went, he was adamant about doing the best he could on the business which brought him there. That didn't leave much time for sightseeing or play. His devotion to duty was one of the qualities which had earned him the sobriquet Pope Paul at Op-Center. He didn't know for sure, but he suspected that the nickname had been coined by Op-Center's Press Officer, Ann Farris.

Hood felt a curious sadness as he watched the modern skyscrapers flash by the darkened window. Sadness for himself and for Ann. The young divorcee barely concealed her affection for Paul, and when they worked alone together he felt dangerously close. There was something there, an intoxicating, seductive pull to which it would have been easy to succumb. But to what end?

He was married, with two young children, and he wasn't going to leave them. True, he didn't love making love to his wife any more. Sometimes, he hated to admit to himself, he'd just as soon skip it altogether. She wasn't the adoring, attentive, energetic Sharon Kent he had married. She was a mommy. She was a cable TV personality who had a life apart from the family and co-workers he knew only from Christmas parties. And she was older and more tired and not as hungry for him as she'd been.

While you, at least in your heart, he thought, *are still El Cid with his lance unsplintered and his stallion full of gallop.*

Of course, that was in his heart. He had to admit that in the flesh he wasn't the knight he'd once been either— except in Ann's eyes. Which was why he found himself getting drawn into them now and then.

Still, he and Sharon had built memories together, and a different kind of love than they'd once had. The thought of going home to his family after creating a pocket relationship at the office would have made him feel—well, he knew exactly how he'd feel. He'd thought about it enough on those long drives home from Andrews after long nights of reviewing press releases with Ann. He'd have felt like a goddamn earthworm, low and hiding from the light and wriggling through the dirt for what he needed to survive.

And even if he could've handled the guilt of it all, a relationship like that wouldn't be fair to Ann. She was a good woman with the heart of an angel. To lead her on, to give her hope where there was none, to become intimately involved with the lives of her and her son would have been wrong.

None of which stops you from wanting her, does it?

Hood asked himself. Maybe that was why he and Sharon both worked so hard. They were replacing the passion they'd once had with something they could still do enthusiastically, something that was fresh and different every day they did it.

But Lord God, Hood thought sadly, *what I wouldn't give for a night of what was.*

The Alster-Hof Hotel was situated between the city's two spectacular lakes, though Hood, Stoll, and Herbert barely had time to check in and wash up before heading back downstairs. Herbert glanced out the windows while Stoll did a quick electronic sweep to make sure the room hadn't been bugged.

"We've got a pretty nice view, huh?" Herbert said as they rode the elevator down. He was absently twirling an eighteen-inch-long section of broom handle he kept under the wheelchair's left armrest for protection. He also kept a two-inch Urban Skinner knife tucked under the right armrest. "Those lakes remind me of the Chesapeake, with all the boats."

"They're the Binnenalster and Aussenalster," a young German porter said helpfully. "The Inner Alster and Outer Alster."

"Makes sense," Herbert admitted. He replaced his stick in the hooks under the armrest. "Though I probably would have called them the Big Alster and Little Alster. The big lake's what—about ten times larger than the other?"

"Three hundred and ninety-five acres as compared with forty-five," the youth replied.

"I was in the ballpark," Herbert said as the elevator reached the lobby. "I still think my names are better. You can always tell big from little. But you may get 'em mixed up if you don't know which end of the city's in and which end's out.''

''Perhaps you should place a note in the suggestion box,'' the porter said, pointing. ''It's right over there, beside the letter box.''

Herbert looked at him. So did Hood, who couldn't tell whether the kid was being facetious or helpful. Germans weren't known for their sense of humor, though he'd heard that the new generation was learning a lot about sarcasm from American movies and TV.

''Maybe I'll do that,'' Herbert said as he rolled out. He looked over at Stoll, who was bent beneath the weight of his backpack. ''You've got the translator. What would those names be?''

Stoll punched the English words into his paperback-sized electronic translator. Almost at once, the German equivalent materialized in the liquid crystal display.

''Looks like they'd be called the *Grossalster* and the *Kleinalster*,'' Stoll informed him.

Hood said, ''Doesn't have a particularly elegant sound, does it?''

''No,'' Herbert agreed, ''but you know what? It beats hell out of what we have back in Philadephia, Mississippi. Dead Cat Pond, Mudworm Creek—''

''I kind of like those,'' Stoll said. ''They paint a picture.''

''Yeah, but not one you'd want on a postcard,'' Herbert said. ''Matter of fact, all we've got in our metal twirly thing at the general store are postcards of Main Street and the old schoolhouse and nothing else.''

''I'd rather have the pond and the creek,'' Stoll said.

As they made their way through the crowded lobby, Hood looked around for Martin Lang and Deputy Foreign Minister Richard Hausen. He had never met Hausen, but he was anxious to see the German electronics tycoon Lang again. They had spent some time together when Los Angeles hosted a dinner for international guests at a computer convention. Hood had been impressed with Lang's warmth, sincerity, and intelligence. He was a humanist who understood that without happy employees, he had no company. There were never any layoffs. Hard times were borne by the top levels of management, not the bottom.

When it came time to price the construction of the new brainchild of Mike Rodgers and Matt Stoll, the Regional Op-Center or ROC, Lang was the first person who came to mind for the computers they'd need. His company's patented photon-based technology *Leuchtturm,* Lighthouse, was adaptable, cutting edge, and expensive. As with most things in government, though, Hood knew that getting the ROC constructed at all would be a delicate balancing act. It would be difficult to get the half-billion-dollar budget for the ROC through Congress under any circumstances, more so if they bought foreign components. At the same time, Op-Center would have a rough time getting the ROC into foreign countries unless it contained hardware from those countries.

What it would ultimately come down to, Hood reflected, were two things. One, that Germany would soon be the leading country in the European Community. The ability to move a mobile spy center in and out with relative freedom would pre-position the U.S. to watch everything Europe did. Congress would like that. And two, Lang's company, *Hauptschlüssel,* Main Key, would have to agree to purchase many of the materials they needed for this and other projects from American companies. A good portion of the money would thus remain in the United States.

Hood felt confident that he could sell that to Lang. He and Matt were going to show him a new technology in which the Germans would surely want to become involved, something the small R&D division of Op-Center had stumbled upon while looking for a way to check the integrity of high-speed electrical circuitry. And though Lang was an honorable man, he was also a businessman and a patriot. Knowing all about the ROC's hardware and its capabilities, Lang could persuade his government to underwrite technological countermeasures for national security. Then Hood could go to Congress for the money to undermine *those,* money he would agree to spend with American companies.

He smiled. As strange as it seemed to Sharon, who loathed negotiating, and to Mike Rodgers, who was anything but diplomatic, Hood enjoyed this process. Getting things done in the international political arena was like a big, complex chess game. Though no player came through it unscathed, it was fun to see how many pieces you were able to retain.

They stopped near the house phones, away from the flow of guests. Hood took in the baroque decor of the lobby, as well as the thick, curious mix of smartly dressed businesspeople and casual tourists. Stepping out of the human traffic gave him the chance to appreciate the people, all of whom were focused on their own business, their own destinations, who they were with—

The golden hair flashed at him from the front door. It captured his eye not because of the movement itself but because of the *way* it moved. As the woman left the lobby, her head cocked right and the long blond hair snapped left, fast and confident.

Hood was transfixed. *Like a bird darting from a tree,* he thought.

As Hood watched, unable to move, the woman disappeared to the right. For a long instant he didn't blink, couldn't breathe. The noise in the lobby, so distinct a moment ago, became a distant drone.

"Chief?" Stoll asked. "You see 'em?"

Hood didn't answer. Forcing his legs to move, he bolted toward the door, maneuvering around the people and stacked luggage, shouldering his way around guests who were standing still, waiting and chattering.

A golden lady, he thought.

He reached the open door and rushed through. He looked to the right.

"Taxi?" asked the liveried doorman.

Hood didn't hear him. He looked toward the north, saw a cab moving toward the main thoroughfare. The bright sunlight made it impossible for him to see inside. He turned toward the doorman.

"Did a woman just get in that cab?" Hood asked.

"Ja," said the young man.

"Do you *know* her?" Hood demanded. Even as he said it, Hood realized he probably sounded a little scary. He took a long, deep breath. "I'm sorry," he said. "I didn't mean to yell like that. It's just—I think I know that woman. Is she a guest here?"

"Nein," said the doorman. "She dropped off a package and left."

Hood pointed a thumb to the lobby. "Dropped if off in there?"

"Not at the desk," said the doorman. "She gave it to someone."

An elderly English woman came over, needing a cab.

"Excuse me," the young man said to Hood.

While the doorman walked to the curb and blew his whistle, Hood looked down and tapped his foot impatiently. As he did, Stoll strolled up beside him, followed by Herbert.

"Hi," said Stoll.

Hood was staring at the curb, fighting a storm of emotions.

"You shoved off like a guy whose dog ran onto the highway," Stoll said. "You okay?"

Hood nodded.

"Yeah, I'm convinced," Herbert lied.

"No, really," Hood said distantly. "I, uh—never mind. It's a long story."

"So's *Dune*," Stoll said, "but I love it. Want to talk about it? You see somebody?"

Hood was silent for a moment, then said, "Yes."

"Who?" Herbert asked.

Hood answered almost reverently, "A golden lady."

Stoll clicked his tongue. "Ooookay," he said. "Sorry I asked." He glanced down at Herbert, who shrugged and gave him a don't-ask-me look.

When the doorman returned, Hood asked quietly, "Did you happen to see who she gave the package to?"

The doorman shook his head sadly. "I'm sorry. I was getting a cab for Herr Tsuburaya and didn't happen to notice."

"It's all right," Hood said. "I understand." He reached into his pocket and gave the doorman a ten-dollar bill. "If she happens to come back, would you try to find out who she is? Tell her that Paul . . ." He hesitated. "No. Don't tell her who wanted to know. Just try and find out, okay?"

"*Ja*," the doorman said appreciatively as he stepped to the curb to open the door of an arriving taxi.

Stoll nudged Hood with his hip. "Hey, for ten bucks I'll wait here too. Double coverage."

Hood ignored him. This was insane. He couldn't decide whether he'd walked into a dream or a nightmare.

As the men stood there, a black stretch limousine pulled up. The doorman dashed over and a stocky, silver-haired man emerged. He and Hood saw each other at the same time.

"Herr Hood!" Martin Lang said with a wave and a big, genuine smile. He came forward with short, quick strides, his hand extended. "It's wonderful to see you again. You look very, very well."

"Washington suits me better than Los Angeles," he said.

Though Hood was looking at Lang, he was still seeing the woman. The shift of the head, the blaze of hair—

Stop it, he yelled at himself. *You have a job to do. And you have a life.*

"Actually," Stoll muttered, "Paul looks good because he was able to sleep on the airplane. He'll be nudging Bob and me awake all day."

"I sincerely doubt that," said Lang. "You're not old like me. You have vitality."

As Hood introduced his associates, a tall, blond, distinguished-looking man in his middle forties emerged from the car. He walked over slowly.

"Herr Hood," said Lang, as the man arrived, "allow me to introduce Richard Hausen."

"Welcome to Hamburg," Hausen said. His voice was resonant and refined, his English impeccable. He greeted each man personally with a handshake and a little bow.

Hood was surprised that Hausen had arrived without a flock of assistants. American officials didn't go anywhere without at least two young, go-get-'em aides in tow.

Stoll had a different first impression. "He reminds me

of Dracula,'' the Operations Support Officer whispered.

Hood tended to ignore Stoll's frequent under-the-breath comments, though this one was near the mark. Hausen was dressed in a black suit. His face was pale but intense. And he exuded a distinctive Old World courtliness. But from what Hood had read before leaving, Dracula's nemesis Dr. Van Helsing would have been more accurate for this man. But instead of prowling for vampires, Richard Hausen hunted neo-Nazis. Op-Center's Staff Psychologist Liz Gordon had used the resources of the United Nations Gopher information site on the Internet to prepare a paper on Hausen. She described him as having a ''Captain Ahab-like hatred of right-wing radicals.'' Liz wrote that not only did Hausen see them as a threat to his nation's status as a member of the international community, but that ''he attacks them with a fervor which suggests personal animus, perhaps something in his past. It could well have been born and nurtured in the bullying he probably took as a child, something which happens to many farm boys who are sent to a larger city to go to school.''

Martha Mackall had suggested, in a footnote, that Hood should beware of one thing. Hausen might be seeking closer ties with the U.S. to infuriate nationals and actually draw attacks on himself. She wrote, ''That would give him a martyr image which is always good for politicians.''

Hood put that thought in the mental drawer marked ''maybe.'' For now, he took Hausen's presence at the meeting as an indication of just how much the German electronics industry wanted to do business with the U.S. government.

Lang led them to the limousine and what he promised would be the finest authentic German meal in Hamburg, as well as the best view of the Elbe. Hood didn't care what he ate or where. All he wanted was to quickly lose himself in work and conversation and get his feet back under him.

As it happened, Hood enjoyed the food enormously, though as the dessert plates were being cleared away, Stoll leaned over and confided that the eel soup and blackberries with sugar and cream just didn't satisify the same way as a nice, fat taco and strawberry shake.

The lunch was early by German standards, and the restaurant was empty. Conversation was characteristically political, sparked by discussion of the recent fiftieth anniversary commemoration of the Marshall Plan. In his nearly two decades of working with international executives, investors, and politicians, Hood found most Germans to be appreciative of the recovery program which had raised them from financial postwar ruin. He also found those same Germans to be staunch apologists for the actions of the Reich. Over the past few years, however, he'd also noticed that more and more Germans were also feeling proud about how they had accepted, fully, responsibility for their country's actions during World War II. Richard Hausen had taken an active hand in getting reparations for concentration camp victims.

Martin Lang was proud, but also bitter.

"The Japanese government didn't even use the word 'apology' until the fiftieth anniversary of the end of the war," Lang had said even before the appetizers were served. "And it took even longer for the French to acknowledge that the state had been an accomplice to the deportation of seventy-five thousand Jews. What Germany did was beyond imagining. But at least we, as a nation, are making an effort to comprehend what happened."

Lang had noted that a side effect of Germany's soul-searching was a measure of tension with Japan and France.

"It is as if by admitting our atrocities," he'd said, "we betrayed a criminal code of silence. We are regarded now as fainthearted, as not having had the strength of our convictions."

"Which is why," Herbert had muttered, "the Japanese had to be A-bombed to the peace table."

The other significant change Hood had noticed over the past few years was increasing resentment over the assimilation of the former East Germany. This was one of Hausen's personal *Zahnschmerzen* or "toothaches," as he politely described it.

"It's another country," he had said. "It would be as if the United States attempted to absorb Mexico. The East Germans are our brothers, but they adopted Soviet culture and Soviet ways. They are shiftless and believe that we owe them reparations for having abandoned them at the end of the war. They hold out their hands not for tools or diplomas, but for money. And when the young don't get it, they join gangs and become violent. The East is dragging our nation into a financial and spiritual abyss from which it will take decades to recover."

Hood had been surprised by the politician's open resentment. What had surprised him even more was their otherwise meticulous waiter openly grunting his approval as he filled their water glasses.

Hausen had pointed toward the waiter. "One-fifth of every mark he earns goes to the East," he'd said.

They did not discuss the ROC during the meal. That would take place later, in Hausen's Hamburg office. Germans believed in getting to know their partners before the seduction process began.

Toward the end of the meal, Hausen's cellular telephone chirped. He pulled it from his jacket pocket, excused himself, and half-turned to answer.

His bright eyes dulled and his thin lips turned down. He said very little.

When the call was finished, Hausen laid the phone on the table. "That was my assistant," he said. He looked from Lang to Hood. "There's been a terrorist attack on a movie location outside of Hanover. Four people are dead. An American girl is missing and there's reason to believe she has been kidnapped."

Lang grew ashen. "The movie—was it *Tirpitz*?"

Hausen nodded. The government official was obviously upset.

Herbert asked, "Do they know who did it?"

"No one has claimed credit," Hausen said. "But the shooting was done by a woman."

"Doring," Lang said. He looked from Hausen to Herbert. "This can only be Karin Doring, the leader of *Feuer*. They're one of the most violent neo-Nazi groups in Germany." His voice was a low, sad monotone. "It's as Richard was saying. She recruits young savages from the East and trains them herself."

"Wasn't there any security?" Herbert asked.

Hausen nodded. "One of the victims was a guard."

"Why attack a movie set?" Hood asked.

"It was an American and German production," Hausen said. "That's reason enough for Doring. She wants all foreigners out of Germany. But the terrorists also stole a trailer filled with Nazi memorabilia. Medals, weapons, uniforms, and the like.''

"Sentimental bastards," Herbert said.

"Perhaps," said Hausen. "Or they may want it for something else. You see, gentlemen, there is an abhorrent phenomenon, several years old, called Chaos Days."

"I've heard of that," Herbert said.

"Not through the media, I suspect," Hausen said. "Our reporters don't want to publicize the event."

"Sort of makes them accomplices to Nazi-style censorship, doesn't it?" Stoll wondered.

Herbert scowled at him. "Hell, no. I don't blame them. I've heard about Chaos Days from friends at Interpol. It really is a stinking business."

"It is that," Hausen agreed. He looked at Stoll, then at Hood. "Hate groups from all over Germany and even from other nations converge in Hanover, one hundred kilometers south of here. They have rallies and exchange their sick ideas and literature. Some, including Doring's group, have made it a tradition of attacking symbolic as well as strategic targets during this time."

"At least, intelligence leads us to believe that it's Doring's group," Lang put in. "She's quick and very, very careful."

Herbert said, "And the government doesn't crack down on Chaos Days for fear of creating martyrs."

"Many people in government are afraid of that, yes," Hausen said. "They are afraid of the increasingly open pride many otherwise right-thinking Germans have for what the nation, galvanized and mobilized under Hitler, was able to accomplish. These officials want to legislate radicalism out of existence without punishing the radicals themselves. During Chaos Days in particular, when so many antagonistic elements are out in force, the government treads carefully.''

''And how do you feel?'' Hood asked.

Hausen replied, ''I believe we should do both. Crush them where we see them, then use laws to fumigate those who crawl under rocks.''

''And you think this Karin Doring, or whoever, wanted the memorabilia for Chaos Days?'' Herbert asked.

''Passing out those mementoes would tie recipients directly to the Reich,'' Hausen said, thinking aloud. ''Imagine how that would motivate each and every one of them.''

''For what?'' Herbert asked. ''More attacks?''

''That,'' Hausen replied, ''or perhaps nothing more than a year of loyalty. With seventy or eighty groups vying for members, loyalty is important.''

Lang said, ''Or the theft might swell the hearts of those who read about it in the newspapers. Men and women who, as Richard says, still privately revere Hitler.''

Herbert asked, ''What's the scoop on the American girl?''

Hausen said, ''She's an intern on the film. She was last seen inside the trailer. The police believe she may have been abducted along with it.''

Herbert gave Hood a look. Hood thought for a moment, then nodded.

''Excuse me,'' Herbert said. He wheeled himself from the table and patted the telephone on his armrest. ''I'm going to find myself a nice, quiet corner and make some calls. Maybe we can add a little something to the intelligence pool.''

Lang rose and thanked him, then apologized again. Herbert assured him that there was nothing to apologize for.

"I lost my wife and my legs to terrorists in Beirut," he said. "Each time they show their sick faces, it gives me a chance to hunt more of 'em down." He looked at Hausen. "These bastards are *my* toothache, Herr Hausen, and I live to drill the bastards."

Herbert swung himself around and wheeled his way through the tables. With his departure, Hausen sat and tried to collect himself. Hood looked at him. Liz was right: something else was going on here.

"We've been fighting this battle for over fifty years," Hausen said gravely. "You can inoculate against disease and seek shelter from a storm. But how do you protect yourself from this? How do you fight hate? And it's a growth business, Herr Hood. Every year there are more groups with more members. God help us if they ever unite."

Hood said, "My deputy director at Op-Center once said you fight an idea with a better idea. I'd like to believe that's true. If not"—he cocked a thumb at Herbert, who was making his way onto a deck overlooking the river—"I'm with my intelligence chief over there. We hunt them down."

"They're very well hidden," Hausen said, "extremely well armed, and quite impossible to infiltrate because they accept only very young new members. We rarely know in advance what they are planning."

"Only for now," Matt told him.

Lang looked at him. "What do you mean, Herr Stoll?"

"You know that backpack I left in the car?"

Hausen and Lang both nodded.

Stoll smiled. ''Well, if we can all get together on this ROC thing, we're going to blow a lot of rotten slices right out of the bread box.''

NINE

Thursday, 11:42 A.M., Wunstorf, Germany

When Jody Thompson heard the shouts outside the trailer, she thought Hollis Arlenna was calling for her. Standing in the bathroom, she flipped even faster through the garments, cursing the prop people who had labeled them in German and Arlenna for being such a dork.

Then she heard the gunfire. She knew it wasn't a scene from the movie. She had all the guns in here, and Mr. Buba was the only one with a key. And then she heard the cries of pain and fear, and knew that something terrible was going on. She stopped checking the garment bags and leaned an ear close to the door.

When the trailer engine first roared, Jody thought that someone was trying to get it away from whatever was happening on the set. Then the door slammed and she heard someone moving around inside. The person didn't speak, which she knew was a bad sign. If it were a guard, he'd be on his walkie-talkie.

Suddenly, the bathroom seemed very warm and close. Noticing that the door wasn't locked, she gingerly lifted the bolt and threw it. Then she squatted between the garment bags, holding on to them so she didn't fall over.

She was going to stay put until someone came to get her.

She listened intently. Jody hadn't worn her watch, and her only sense of time passing was through sound. The intruder looking through the daggers on the far left table. Footsteps moving around the table filled with medals. Chests opening and closing.

Then, over the drone of the ceiling fan, Jody heard the intruder rattle the closet door on the other side of the trailer. A moment later there were four loud pops.

Jody squeezed the garment bags so tightly that her nails went through one of them. *What the hell was going on out there?* She backed against the wall, away from the door. Her heart was punching up against her jaw.

She heard the closet door bang open as the trailer turned a corner. A table leg scraped the floor as the person moved around it—not gingerly, as Jody had before, but roughly, impatiently.

The intruder was coming toward the bathroom door. Suddenly, it didn't seem like such a good idea to be in here.

Jody looked up, around, behind her. She saw the frosted glass of the window. But because of the metal bars, no one could get in. Or now, out.

Jody ducked down as the bathroom door handle jiggled. She hunkered down low behind the gently swaying clothes, then crept back beside the toilet. The tiny shower stall was to her rear and she leaned against the glass door. Her heart beat a heavy *crunch, crunch, crunch* in her ears. She started to whimper and bit the side of her thumb to keep from being heard.

A burst of gunfire drowned out the sound of her heart, of her whimpering. She screamed into her thumb as wood and plastic chips flew from the door, pelting the floor and garment bags. Then the door squeaked outward and a gun barrel pushed through the neat row of German uniforms. It pushed them to the side and a face peered down at her. A woman's face.

Jody looked from the compact machine-gun-like weapon to the coldness in the woman's liquid gold eyes. The girl was still biting on her thumb.

The woman motioned up with the gun and Jody stood. Her hands dropped to her sides and perspiration poured down her thighs.

The woman said something in German.

"I—don't understand," Jody said.

"I said pick up your hands and turn around," the woman barked in thickly accented English.

Jody raised her hands face-high, then hesitated. She had read, in one of her classes, about how hostages were often shot in the back of the head.

"Please," she said, "I'm an intern. I was assigned to this movie a few—"

"Turn!" the woman snapped.

"Please don't!" Jody said, even as she did what she was told.

When she was facing the window, Jody heard the uniforms being moved aside and felt the warm metal of the gun against the top of her neck.

"Please . . ." she sobbed.

Jody started as the woman patted her left side from breast to thigh, and then her right. The woman reached in front and felt along her waistband. Then she turned Jody around. The gun was pointing toward her mouth.

"I don't know what this is about," Jody said. She was crying now. "And I wouldn't tell anyone anything—"

"Quiet," the woman said.

Jody obeyed. She knew that she would do anything this woman told her. It was frightening to discover how completely her will could be suppressed by a gun and a person who was willing to use it.

The van stopped suddenly and Jody stumbled toward the sink. She hurried back to her feet, hands raised. The woman hadn't moved, didn't look as if her thoughts had been disturbed.

The trailer door opened and a young man walked over. He stood behind Karin and looked into the bathroom. He had a pale complexion and a swastika carved in his head.

Without taking her eyes off Jody, Karin turned slightly toward the young man and said, "Begin."

The man clicked the heels of his boots, turned, and started loading the relics into the trunks.

Karin continued to stare at Jody. "I don't like killing women," the woman said at last, "but I cannot take hostages. They slow me down."

That was it. Jody was going to die. She went numb. She began to sob. She had a flashback to being a little girl, to wetting her pants in first grade when the teacher had yelled at her, to crying and not being able to stop, to the other children laughing at her. Every scrap of confidence and accomplishment and dignity flooded away.

With the trickle of poise that remained to her, Jody fell to the floor. Facing the back of the bathroom, seeing the toilet and sink from the sides of her foggy eyes, she pleaded for her life.

But instead of shooting her, the woman ordered another man, an older man, to remove the uniforms. Then she closed the bathroom door. The girl waited, surprised, half-expecting gunfire to tear through the door. She stood sideways, on the toilet, to make as small and removed a target as possible.

But instead of gunfire, all she heard was a scraping sound followed by a loud *whump*.

Something had been pushed against the door.

She isn't going to kill me, Jody thought. *She's only going to lock me in here.*

Perspiration soaked her clothes as she waited. The three hijackers finished quickly in the trailer, and then were gone. She listened. Nothing.

Then one of the hijackers was outside the window. Jody leaned her ear to the wall, and listened. Something metal was turning, followed by clanking, and then the sound of metal being punctured once, twice, and then a third time. Then she heard fabric being ripped and she smelled gas.

The fuel tank, she thought with horror. They've opened it.

"No!" Jody screamed as she leapt off the toilet. She threw herself against the door. "You said you don't like killing women! *Please!"*

A moment later Jody smelled smoke, heard footsteps running from the van, and saw the orange of the flame reflected against the frosted glass of the window. They were going to burn the trailer with her in it.

The woman isn't killing me, Jody realized then. *She's just letting me die. . . .*

The girl threw herself against the door. It wouldn't budge. And as the orange grew brighter she stood in the middle of the small room screaming with fear and despair.

TEN

Thursday, 5:47 A.M., Washington, D.C.

Liz Gordon had just finished grinding up coffee beans and was lighting her first cigarette of the day when the phone rang.

"I wonder who that can be?" the thirty-two-year-old said to herself as she took a long pull on her cigarette. Ashes fell on her Mike Danger nightshirt and she brushed them off. Then she absently scratched her head through her curly brown hair as she listened to see where she'd left the cordless phone.

Since rising at five, Liz had been going over some of the things she might say when she visited the Striker team later this morning. At their third group session two days before, the elite but very young soldiers were still in shock as they mourned the loss of Charlie Squires. Rookie Sondra DeVonne was taking his death especially hard, sad for Charlie's family and also for herself. Through tears, the Private had said that she'd hoped to learn so much from him. Now all that wisdom and experience was gone. Not passed on.

Dead.

"Where *is* the freakin' phone?" Liz snarled as she kicked aside the newspapers by the kitchen table.

Not that she was afraid the caller would hang up. At

this hour it could only be Monica calling from Italy. And her roommate and best friend would not go away until she got her messages. After all, she'd been gone nearly an entire day.

And if Sinatra calls, thought Op-Center's Staff Psychologist, *you want to be able to get right back to him.*

For the three years they'd been living together, Liz's workaholic freelance musician friend had done all the nightclubs and weddings and Bar Mitzvahs she could get. She'd been working so hard, in fact, that Liz had not only ordered her to take a vacation, but had kicked in half the money to make sure she could go.

Liz finally found the phone sitting on one of the kitchen chairs. Before picking it up, Liz took a moment to change worlds. The dynamics between Liz and each of her patients were such that she created separate worlds in her mind for each of them, and inhabited those worlds fully in order to treat them. Otherwise, there would be spillover, lack of focus, distractions. Though Monica was her best friend, not a patient, it was difficult sometimes to make a clear distinction between the two.

As Liz slipped into her Monica world, she checked the message list from under the Chopin magnet on the refrigerator door. The only ones who had called were Monica's drummer, Angelo "Tim" Panni, and her mother, both of whom wanted to make sure she got to Rome okay.

"*Pronto,* Ms. Sheard!" she said as she clicked on the phone. A telephone hello was one of the two Italian words she knew.

The decidedly masculine voice on the other end said, "Sorry, Liz, it isn't Monica. It's Bob Herbert."

"Bob!" Liz said. "This is a surprise. What's happening in the land of Freud?"

"I thought Freud was Austrian," Herbert said.

"He was," Liz said, "but the Germans had him for a year. The Anschluss was in 1938. Freud died in 1939."

"That's almost not funny," Bob said. "It looks like the Fatherland may be flexing its muscles for a new era of empire-building."

She reached for her cigarette. "What do you mean?"

"Have you watched the news this morning?" Herbert asked.

"It doesn't come on till six," she said. "Bob, what the hell *happened*?"

"A bunch of neo-Nazis attacked a movie set," Herbert said. "They killed some of the crew, stole a trailer filled with Nazi memorabilia, and drove off. Although no one's heard from them, they appear to have taken an American girl hostage."

"Jesus," Liz said. She took several short puffs.

"It appears as if the group was led by a woman named Karin Doring. Heard of her?"

"The name is familiar," Liz said. She took the phone from the kitchen and began walking toward the study. "Give me a second and I'll see what we've got." She switched on the computer, sat down, and accessed the database in her office at Op-Center. In less than ten seconds, the file on Doring had been downloaded.

"Karin Doring," she said, "the Ghost from Halle."

"The Ghost from where?" Herbert asked.

"Halle," Liz said. She scanned the report. "That's her hometown in East Germany. They call her the Ghost because she's usually gone from the scene before anyone can catch her. She doesn't go in for ski masks and disguises, wants people to know who's behind things. And get this. In an interview last year with a newspaper called *Our Struggle,* she describes herself as a Nazi Robin Hood, striking a blow for the oppressed majority of Germany.''

''Sounds like a psycho,'' Herbert said.

''Actually, she doesn't,'' Liz said. ''That's the problem with people like this.'' Liz coughed, continued to draw on her cigarette, and spoke as she scanned the file. ''In high school, in the late 1970s, she was briefly a member of the Communist Party.''

''Spying on the enemy?''

''Probably not,'' Liz said.

''Okay,'' Herbert said, ''why don't I just shut up?''

''No, what you just said would be a logical assumption, though it's probably a wrong one. She was obviously looking for herself, ideologically speaking. The Communist left and the neo-Nazi right are very much alike in their rigidity of thought. All radicals are. These people can't sublimate their frustrations so they externalize them. They convince themselves, usually subconsciously, that others are causing their miseries—'others' meaning anyone who's different from them. In Hitler's Germany, they blamed unemployment on the Jews. Jews held a disproportionately high number of positions in banks, universities, medicine. They were visible, obviously prosperous, and very clearly different. They had different traditions, different sabbaths, different holidays. They were an easy target. The same was true of Jews in Communist Russia.''

''Gotcha,'' Herbert said. ''Have you got anything on this woman's contacts, hideouts, habits?''

Liz scanned the document. It was broken into sections labeled ''vital statistics,'' ''biography,'' and ''modus operandi.''

''She's a loner,'' Liz said, ''which in terrorist terms

means she always works with a small group. Three or four people, tops. And she never sends anyone on a mission she wouldn't undertake.''

''That's a match with today's attack,'' Herbert said. ''Any known hits?''

Liz said, ''They never claim credit—''

''Also a match with today.''

''—but witnesses have tied them to the firebombing of an Arab-owned shopping mall in Bonn and the delivery of a grenade-rigged liquor carton to the South African Embassy in Berlin, both last year.''

''Ruthless too,'' Herbert said.

''Yes,'' Liz said. ''That's part of her appeal to the hardcore neo-Nazis. Though it's strange. The store she attacked was a men's shop, and the liquor was delivered to a bachelor party.''

''Why is that strange? Maybe she hates men.''

''That doesn't fit in with Nazi ideology,'' Liz said.

''True,'' Herbert agreed. ''In war and genocide, they were equal-opportunity killers. This may be good news for the American kid, if she is a hostage. Maybe they won't kill her.''

''I wouldn't bet the ranch on that,'' Liz said. ''Sparing women isn't likely to be a commandment, just courtesy. It also says here that two of those witnesses who tried to I.D. her personally died within days of talking to the authorities. One in a car crash, one after a mugging. The crash victim was a woman. One woman who tried to quit her group *Feuer*—Fire—was also killed.''

''Watched and whacked,'' Herbert said. ''Just like the mob.''

''Not quite,'' Liz said. ''The retiree was drowned in a toilet after being beaten and slashed. This is one sick little *schatze*. Anyway, so much for sparing women.''

Liz scanned back to Karin's biography.

"Let's see if we can see where Ms. Doring is coming from," Liz said. She began reading, then said, "Here we are. Her mother died when she was six and she was raised by her father. Bet you dollars to pesos there was some nasty business going on there."

"Abuse."

"Yeah," Liz said. "Again, it's a classic pattern. As a girl, Karin was either beaten, sexually abused, or both. She sublimated like crazy as a kid, then looked for a place to put her anger. She tried Communism, didn't like it for whatever reason—"

"It was dying," Herbert contributed.

"Then she found the neo-Nazi movement and assumed the role of father figure, something her own father never did."

"Where is Papa Doring now?" Herbert asked.

"Dead," said Liz. "Cirrhosis of the liver. Died when Karin was fifteen, just about the time she became a political activist."

"Okay," said Herbert, "so we think we know who our enemy is. She's happy to kill men, willing to kill women. She assembles a terrorist group and roams the country attacking foreign interests. Why? To scare them off?"

"She knows she can't do that," Liz says. "Nations will still have embassies, and businesses will still come. More likely it's the equivalent of a recruitment poster. Something to rally other aggressive misfits around her. And by the way, Bob, it obviously works. As of four months ago, when this file was updated, *Feuer* had thirteen hundred members with an annual growth rate of nearly twenty percent. Of those members, twenty active, full-time soldiers move with her from camp to camp."

"Do we know where any of these camps are?"

"They keep changing," Liz said. "We've got three photographs in the file." She accessed them in turn and read each caption. "One was taken at a lake in Mecklenburg, the second was shot in a forest in Bavaria, and the third was in mountains somewhere along the Austrian border. We don't know how they travel, but it looks to me like they pitch tents whenever they get there."

"They probably move around in a bus or van," Herbert said. He sounded dejected. "Guerrilla groups that size used to travel in patterns to establish regular supply lines. But with cellular phones and overnight parcel delivery, they can arrange for pickups just about anywhere now. How many camps do we know about?"

"Just those three," Liz said.

The phone beeped. It had to be Monica calling for her messages. Her roommate would be frantic, but Liz wasn't going to answer.

"What about lieutenants?" Herbert asked. "Who does she rely on?"

"Her closest aide is Manfred Piper. He joined her after they graduated from high school. Apparently, she handles all the military matters and Piper does the fundraising, runs checks on aspiring members, that sort of thing."

Herbert was silent for a moment, then said, "We don't really have very much here, do we?"

"To understand her, yes," Liz said. "To catch her, I'm afraid not."

After a moment, Herbert said, "Liz, our German host thinks she may have pulled this heist off so she could pass out trinkets for Chaos Days, the little Mardi Gras of hate they have here. Considering her record of striking political targets, does that make sense?''

"I think you're looking at this the wrong way,'' Liz said. "What was the movie?''

Herbert said, "*Tirpitz.* About the battleship, I guess.''

Liz tapped into *Pictures in Motion,* a Web site listing movies in production around the world. After locating the film, she said, "The set *was* a political target, Bob. It was an American co-production.''

Herbert was silent for a moment. "So either the memorabilia was a bonus, or the American crew was.''

"You got it.''

"Look,'' Herbert said, "I'm going to have a chat with the authorities here, maybe pay a visit to one of these Chaos Days celebrations.''

"Watch it, Bob,'' Liz said. "Neo-Nazis don't hold doors for people in wheelchairs. Remember, you're different—''

"You bet I am,'' he said. "Meanwhile, give me a buzz on the cellular if you come up with anything else on this lady or her group.''

"Will do,'' Liz said. "Take care and *ciao,''* she added, using the other Italian word she knew.

ELEVEN

Thursday, 11:52 A.M., Toulouse, France

The wood-paneled room was large and dark. The only light came from a single lamp which stood beside the massive mahogany desk. The only items on the desk itself were a telephone, fax machine, and computer, all of them collected in a tight semicircle. The shelves behind the desk were barely visible in the shadows. On them were miniature guillotines. Some were working models, made of wood and iron. Others were made of glass or metal, and one was a plastic model sold in the United States.

Guillotines had been used for official executions in France until 1939, when murderer Eugen Weidmann was beheaded outside St. Peter's Prison in Versailles. But Dominique didn't like those later machines: the guillotines with the large, solid buckets to collect the heads, screens to protect the executioners from the spray of blood, shock absorbers to cushion the *thunk* of the blade. Dominique liked the originals.

Across from the desk, lost in the ghostly dark, was an eight-foot-tall guillotine which had been used during the French Revolution. This device was unrestored. The uprights were slightly rotted and the trestle was worn smooth from all the bodies that ''Madame La Guillotine'' had embraced. Drawn nearly to the cross-beam on top, the blade was rusty from rain and blood. And the wicker basket, also the original, was frayed. But Dominique had noticed particles of the bran which had been used to soak up blood, and there were still hairs in the basket. Hairs which had snagged the wicker when the heads tumbled in.

It all looked exactly as it did in 1796, the last time those leather straps were fastened under the armpits and over the legs of the doomed. When the lunette, the iron collar, had held the neck of its last victim—held it within a perfect circle so the victim couldn't move. However much fear possessed them, they couldn't squirm from the ram and its sharp blade. Once the executioner released the spring, nothing could stop the eighty-pound deathblow. The head dropped into its basket, the body was pushed sideways into its own leather-lined wicker basket, and the vertical plank was ready to receive the next victim. The process was so quick that some bodies were still sighing, the lungs emptying through the neck, as they were removed from the plank. It was said that for several seconds, the still-living brains in decapitated heads enabled the victims to see and hear the ghastly aftermath of their own execution.

At the height of the Reign of Terror, executioner Charles Henri-Sanson and his aides were able to decapitate nearly one victim every minute. They guillotined three hundred men and women in three days, thirteen hundred in six weeks, helping to bring the total to 2,831 between April 6, 1793, and July 29, 1795.

What did you think of that, Herr Hitler? Dominique wondered. The gas chambers at Treblinka were designed to kill two hundred people in fifteen minutes, the gas chambers at Auschwitz designed to kill two thousand.

Was the master killer impressed or did he scoff at the work of relative amateurs?

The guillotine was Dominique's prize. Behind it, on the wall, were period newspapers and etchings in ornate frames, as well as original documents signed by George Jacques Danton and other leaders of the French Revolution. But nothing stirred him like the guillotine. Even with the overhead lights off and the shades drawn he could feel it, the device which was a reminder that one had to be decisive to succeed. Children of nobles had lost their heads to that sinister blade, but such was the price of revolution.

The telephone beeped. It was the third line, a private line which the secretaries never answered. Only his partners and Horne had that number.

Dominique leaned forward in the fat leather chair. He was a lanky man with a large nose, high forehead, and strong chin. His hair was short and ink black, a dramatic contrast to the white turtleneck and trousers he was wearing.

He hit the speaker button. "Yes?" he said quietly.

"Good morning, M. Dominique," said the caller. "It's Jean-Michel."

Dominique glanced at his watch. "It's early."

"The meeting was brief, M. Dominique."

"Tell me about it," he said.

Jean-Michel obliged. He told him about the lecture he had been given under torture, and about how the German considered himself M. Dominique's equal. Jean-Michel also told him about what little he had picked up about Karin Doring.

Dominique listened to it all without comment. When Jean-Michel was finished, he asked, "How is your eye?"

"I think it will be all right," said Jean-Michel. "I've arranged to see a doctor this afternoon."

"Good," Dominique said. "You know you shouldn't have gone without Henri and Yves. That is why I sent them."

"I know, *monsieur,*" Jean-Michel replied, "and I'm sorry. I didn't want to intimidate Herr Richter."

"And you didn't," Dominique said. His voice was tranquil and his wide mouth was relaxed. But his dark eyes were heavy with rage as he asked, "Is Henri there?"

"Yes," Jean-Michel replied.

"Put him on," Dominique said. "And Jean-Michel? Be sure to take them with you tonight."

"I will, M. Dominique," Jean-Michel replied.

So the little Führer is on the march, thought Dominique, *bullying representatives.* He wasn't terribly surprised. Richter's vanity made him ideally suited to believe his own press. That, plus the fact that he was German. Those people did not comprehend the notion of humility.

Henri came on the line, and Dominique spoke with him for just a few seconds. When they were finished, Dominique punched off the speaker button and sat back.

Richter was as yet too weak to be a real force in Germany, but he would have to be put in his place before he became one. Firmly, and not necessarily gently. Richter was still Dominique's first choice, but if he couldn't have him he would have Karin Doring. She was also independent, but she also needed money. And after seeing what was going to happen to Richter, she would be reasonable.

The anger began to leave his eyes as he looked at the dark shape of the guillotine. Like Danton, who began his crusade against the monarchy as a moderate man, Dominique would become increasingly more severe. Otherwise, his allies and enemies both would perceive him as weak.

It would be a delicate thing, making sure that Richter was disciplined without driving him away. But as Danton had said in a speech to the Legislative Committee of General Defense in 1792, *"Boldness, and again boldness, and always boldness!"* The boldness of the guillotine, the boldness of conviction. Then as now, that was what people required to win a revolution.

And he would win this. Then he would settle an old debt. Not with Richter but with another German. One who had betrayed him on that long-ago night. The man who had put everything in motion.

He would destroy Richard Hausen.

TWELVE

Thursday, 11:55 A.M., Wunstorf, Germany

It was the bathroom fire alarm which stopped Jody from screaming.

Wisps of smoke seeping through the vent had triggered the alarm. The high whine pierced her panic and brought her back to the moment, to the situation at hand. She breathed in, calmed herself, then exhaled.

They're trying to blow the trailer up, she told herself.

As when she faced the gun, Jody knew that every second—any second—could be her last. Quickly, she went to the window and pushed her hand through the metal bars. She threw the latch with her fingertips, put her palms to the frosted glass, and pushed up. She pressed her face to the bars and watched the twisted length of cloth as it burned. It wasn't stuffed into the gas tank. It was just lying there, air flowing around it, providing the catalyst for the fire. She pushed her arm out the window, tried to reach the wick. She fell over a foot short.

"God, *no!*"

She threw herself back from the bars, pushed her hair from her eyes, and looked around. There had to be something she could use to reach it. Sink. Toilet. Nothing.

The sink—

She thought of dousing the fire, but there was nothing in the bathroom to use as a bucket or ladle.

"Think!" she screamed.

She turned around slowly. She saw the shower, but there were no bath towels. She tried to pull the towel bar off the back of the stall, couldn't, then noticed the showerhead. It was attached to a hose.

Quickly turning on the water, she yanked the head from the hook and pulled it toward the window. It didn't reach, short by inches.

The flame had nearly covered the mouth of the gas tank when, snarling with frustration, Jody dropped the showerhead and grabbed the hand towel. She pushed it in the toilet, then ran back to the window. Extending her hand, she swung the wet towel up and let it fall. She heard a hiss, then put her face to the window.

The upper portion of the flame had been extinguished. Part of the underside was still burning.

There was only the one towel, and it was gone now. Quickly pulling off her blouse, Jody plunged it into the toilet. This time, however, she slapped it as hard as she could against the side of the trailer. She didn't drop it, but let the water trickle down the wall. Then she pulled in the blouse, wet it again, and slammed it even harder against the trailer. The water ran down in a solid sheet, dousing the last of the flame and sending up a thin wall of smoke. It was the sweetest smell Jody had ever tasted.

"Screw you!" Jody shouted at the image of the woman in her mind. *"I don't like killing women,"* she said. "Well you didn't, *bitch*! You didn't get me!"

Jody pulled in her arm and put on the wet shirt. It was cold and felt good. She looked at the door.

"You're next," she said with fresh-earned confidence.

There was time, now, to work the towel bar from the shower stall. Putting her back against the front wall she kicked the bar free. Then she went to the bathroom door and put her shoulder to it. She opened it just enough to get the bar through, then used it as a lever. The door moved slowly, as Jody pulled against whatever had been pushed against it. After several minutes, she'd succeeded in opening a crack large enough for her to slip through.

She stepped over the upended table, ran to the door, and opened it.

"You didn't get me!" she said again, her jaw outthrust and her fists raised. She turned and looked at the trailer.

A shock sizzled down her back.

What if they're expecting to hear the explosion? she asked herself. And when they don't, will they come back?

Exhausted, Jody ran to the other side of the trailer. She used a twig to pull the smoldering cloth from the gas tank, then climbed back into the cab. She pushed in the cigarette lighter. While she waited for it to heat up, she tore strips of cloth from the inside lid of one of the trunks in the trailer itself. When the lighter was ready, she lit one of the pieces and walked toward the gas tank.

Jody used one strip to dry off the area, then laid another strip half in and half out of the tank. She used the burning strip to ignite the one in the tank, dropped it, and ran into the woods, away from the trailer. In all her years of movie watching, she'd seen a lot of cars and trucks blow up. But those were rigged to blow with carefully placed explosives, not a full tank of gasoline. She had no idea how big, how loud, or how destructive the blast would be.

It occurred to her to put her hands over her ears as she ran.

Only a minute or so passed when she heard the muffled timpani boom of the blast, followed by the louder rending of metal and the deafening explosion of the tires. A heartbeat later she was hit by the concussive heat wave which rolled from the blast. Jody felt the intense heat through her wet blouse and against her scalp. But she forgot about the heat as hot shards of metal rained down, along with particles of glass. She thought of the burning hail from *The Ten Commandments,* how when she saw the movie she remembered thinking there was no way to protect yourself from that. She dropped to the ground and covered her head with her arms, bent her chest to her knees. A large piece of fender tore through the canopy of trees and slammed to the earth just inches from her foot and she jumped.

She swung toward a tree and hugged it, kneeling, thinking that the branches might offer some protection against the larger chunks of the trailer. She held the tree tightly, sobbing again, as though all the courage had been drained out of her. She remained there even after the downpour had stopped. Her thighs were shaking wildly and she couldn't stand. After a moment, she couldn't even hold the tree anymore.

Letting go, Jody walked for a while. She was exhausted and lost and decided to rest. Though the soft, green grass looked inviting, she pulled herself up into a tree. Cradling herself in two closely spaced branches, she put her head on one of the branches and shut her eyes.

They left me to die, she thought. *They killed others. What gives them the right?*

The sobs came less frequently. The fear didn't go away. But along with a realization of how vulnerable she'd been was a sense of the strength she'd managed to find as well.

I didn't let them kill me, she told herself.

She saw Karin's face in her memory, vivid and cold. She hated it, hated how smug and confident the woman had been. Half of Jody wanted to let the monster know that they had nearly taken her life but not her spirit.

The other half of Jody wanted to sleep. Within a few minutes the sleep-half had won, though not without a struggle.

THIRTEEN

Thursday, 6:40 A.M., Quantico, Virginia

Mike Rodgers hadn't intended to visit Billy Squires until seven o'clock. But when he received a call from Melissa just after six, he pulled on his uniform, grabbed the comic books—he wanted to have something, and wouldn't have time to pick up anything else—and rushed over.

"It's nothing life-threatening," Melissa had said over the phone, "but could you come a little early? I want you to see something." Melissa had told him she couldn't elaborate since Billy was in the room. But when Rodgers got there, he'd see and understand.

The General hated mysteries, and during the forty-minute drive he'd tried to imagine everything it could be, from an infestation of ants or bats to something Billy might have done himself.

Nothing he considered even came close.

The Striker base was located at the FBI Academy in Quantico, Virginia. The team members were housed in apartments on the base; families had townhouses. Melissa and Billy lived in the largest of these, closest to the swimming pool. Regulations said that they would be allowed to stay in the commander's residence until a permanent new Striker leader was named. As far as Rodgers was concerned, they could live there as long as they liked and the new commander could stay somewhere else. There was no way he'd tear Billy from his friends until Melissa felt he was ready.

Besides, Rodgers thought as he showed his pass to the guard at the gate, *the way the search is going it'll be the millennium before we have a new commander.* The man he really wanted for the job, Colonel Brett August, had already turned him down twice. And he'd probably turn Rodgers down a third time when he called him again later. Meanwhile, Major Shooter, on loan from Andrews Air Force Base, was the temporary leader. Everyone liked him, and he was a masterful strategist. But he had no combat experience. There was no reason to assume he'd choke in the field, but no reason to assume he wouldn't. On the kinds of world-in-the-balance missions Striker had drawn in North Korea and Russia, it was a risk they couldn't afford.

Rodgers parked his brand-new, apple-red Blazer in the parking area and jogged toward the front door. Melissa opened it before he arrived. She looked okay, her posture relaxed, and Rodgers slowed down.

But then, the young woman had a habit of looking as if all was right with the world. Even when Charlie was alive, when he got riled up chicken-fighting in the pool or playing hockey in the rink or losing the spot for his seven-letter word in Scrabble, she was the portrait of composure. Now that her husband was gone, she did the picnics and outings with the rest of the Striker families, tried to keep life as normal as possible for her son. Rodgers could just imagine the tears she'd cried in the dark. But the operative word was "imagine." She rarely showed any of her sadness in public.

He hopped up the steps and they embraced warmly.

"Thanks for coming, Mike," she said.

"You smell nice," he smiled. "Apricot shampoo?"

She nodded.

"Never smelled that one before."

"I decided to change a few things." She looked down. "You know."

Rodgers kissed her on the forehead. "Of course."

He stepped past her, still smiling. It was strange coming here in the morning and not smelling the gourmet coffees that Charlie always drank.

"Where's Billy?" Rodgers asked.

"Taking a bath. He burns off energy playing in the tub, so he's calmer in school."

Rodgers heard the boy splashing now, upstairs. He looked back at Melissa. "Has he been acting up?"

"Only the last few days," Melissa said. "That's why I asked you to come here a little early."

Melissa crossed the small living room and motioned with a finger for Rodgers to follow. They entered the playroom, which was decorated with framed prints of warplanes. On top of the TV was a framed photo of Charlie with a black ribbon in the corner. Other photos of the family stood on the fireplace mantel and bookshelves.

Rodgers tried not to look at them as Melissa led him to the computer table. He set the comic books beside the printer as Melissa turned on the computer.

"I thought it would be a fun distraction to get Billy on the Internet," she said. "There's a gopher."

"Sorry?" Rodgers said.

"I take it you're not up on this?"

"No," Rodgers said. "You could say I'm a little down on high-tech inactivities, but that's another story."

Melissa nodded. "A gopher is a system of menus

which allows users relatively easy access to text archives on the Internet.''

''Like a Dewey Decimal card file,'' Rodgers said, ''in real libraries.''

''Like that.'' Melissa smiled. ''The point is, there are Web sites—forums—where kids who have lost a parent can talk to one another. It's all faceless and raceless. Billy got on-line and met some great kids there who had a lot to share with him. Then last night, one of them, a twelve-year-old named Jim Eagle, led Billy on a surfing expedition that took them to a locale called the Message Center.''

The computer whirred and Melissa leaned over the keyboard. She directed them to the Message Center, and as soon as they logged on Rodgers knew what the ''message'' was going to be.

The S's in the logo for the Message Center resembled the design of the Nazi SS. Melissa tapped into the FAQ list, the frequently asked questions listing, which was posted as a file for newcomers. Rodgers read it with increasing disgust.

The first question had to do with ''Netiquette'': the appropriate terms to call blacks, Jews, homosexuals, Mexicans, and other minorities. The second question listed the ten greatest figures in history and offered a short list of their accomplishments. Adolf Hitler was on top of the list, which also included murdered American Nazi leader George Lincoln Rockwell, Martin Luther King assassin James Earl Ray, Confederate cavalry General Nathan Bedford Forrest, and one fictional character: slave overseer Simon Legree from *Uncle Tom's Cabin*.

''Billy didn't understand what the FAQ list was all about, so he kind of blindly followed Jim Eagle into the conversation,'' Melissa said. ''This kid Jim—if he was a kid, which I doubt—is obviously someone who goes fishing among grieving, lonely kids and tries to hook them into the movement.''

''By giving them a new father or mother figure,'' Rodgers said.

''Exactly,'' Melissa replied as she brought Rodgers into the ongoing discussion.

There were short letters, full of misspellings, expressing hate of individual people and groups. There were others which provided new, hateful lyrics to old songs, and there was even a guide on how to kill and fillet a black woman.

''That's the one Billy saw,'' Melissa said quietly. She pointed to the printer. ''They even sent him the accompanying artwork. I left it there, tried not to make a big deal about it. I didn't want to scare him.''

Rodgers looked into the printer tray and saw the color printout. It was a photograph of side and overhead views, with arrows and instructions and a body from which the skeleton had been removed. Judging from the surroundings, it was taken in a morgue. Rodgers had been sickened by sights he'd seen on the battlefield, but that was always anonymous. This was personal and sadistic. It made him want to tear the First Amendment into tiny pieces, but he backed off when he realized that that would probably give him something in common with these bastards.

He picked up the paper and folded it into his pants pocket.

''I'll have Op-Center's tech people have a look at this,'' Rodgers said. ''We've got this Samson program we use to bring software down. Maybe we can stop them.''

''They'll only start up again,'' Melissa said. ''Besides, that's not the worst of it.''

The young woman leaned over the keyboard again. She went to a different Web site, where a short video-game sequence repeated every fifteen seconds.

The picture showed a man with a noose chasing a black man through the woods. The pursuer had to leap dead bodies and duck the feet of lynched black men in order to catch his quarry. The text above the scrolling artwork said, ''WE'VE GOT *NOOSE* FOR YOU! COMING IN JUST NINE HOURS AND TWENTY MINUTES: WHOA'S DOWNLOADABLE *HANGIN' WITH THE CROWD*. AND THERE'S MORE TO COME!''

Rodgers asked, ''You have any idea what WHOA is?''

''I do,'' said a voice from behind them. ''Jim told me.''

Rodgers and Melissa turned and saw Billy standing there. The young boy walked briskly toward them.

''Hey, Billy!'' Rodgers said.

He saluted the boy, who saluted back. Then he bent down and they hugged.

''Good morning, General Rodgers,'' Billy said. ''WHOA stands for Whites Only Association. Jim said they want to stop everyone else. 'Just say WHOA!' ''

''I see,'' Rodgers said. He continued to squat in front of the boy. ''How do you feel about that?''

He rolled a shoulder. ''I dunno.''

''You don't know?'' Melissa asked.

''Well,'' Billy said, ''last night, when I saw the photo I thought about my dad being killed. Then I was upset.''

''You understand,'' said Rodgers, ''that these people are really, really bad. And that most people don't believe the terrible things they believe in.''

"Jim said that people do but they just don't admit it."

"That isn't true," Rodgers said. "Everybody's got 'pet peeves,' little things that really annoy them like barking dogs or car alarms. And some people do hate one or two other people, like a boss or a neighbor or—"

"My dad hated people who drank instant coffee," Billy said. "He said they were Phyllis-somebodies."

"Philistines," Melissa said. She looked away quickly and rolled her lips together.

Rodgers smiled at the boy. "I'm sure your dad didn't really hate them. We use that word pretty freely when it's not exactly what we mean. The point is, Jim is wrong. I know a lot of folks, and I don't know anyone who hates whole bunches of people. Guys like Jim—it makes them feel good to put other people down. They have to hate, it's like a disease. A mental disease. If they didn't hate immigrants or people who followed a different religion, they'd hate people with different color hair, or people who were shorter, or people who liked hamburgers instead of hot dogs."

Billy chuckled.

"What I'm trying to say is, these people are evil and you shouldn't believe what they tell you. I've got books and videotapes about people like Winston Churchill and Frederick Douglass and Mohandas Gandhi."

"That's a funny name."

"It may sound a little strange to you," Rodgers said, "but his ideas are really good. All of these men have wonderful things to say, and I'll bring some of that stuff next time. We can read and listen to them together."

"Okay," Billy said.

Rodgers stood and cocked a thumb toward the printer stand. All of a sudden, a long-haired Superman didn't seem so bad.

"Meantime," Rodgers said, "I brought some comic books for you. Batman today, Gandhi next time."

"Thanks!" Billy said. He stole a look at his mother, who nodded once. Then he bolted over and grabbed the stack of magazines.

"You can read those after school," Melissa told her son as he flipped through them.

"Right," Rodgers said. "And if you finish getting ready, I'll give you a lift to school. We can stop at the diner for C-rations and maybe a video game, and you can be the first person to ride shotgun in my brand-new Blazer."

"A video game?" Billy said. "They have *Blazing Combattle* at the diner."

"Great," Rodgers said.

Billy threw the General a snappy salute, thanked him again for the comic books, and ran off.

As the boy thumped up the stairs, Melissa gently put her hand around Rodgers's wrist. "I owe you big time," she said. She kissed him on the cheek.

Rodgers was caught off guard and blushed. He looked away and Melissa released his arm. He started after Billy.

"Mike," Melissa said.

He stopped and looked back.

"It's okay," she said. "I feel very close to you too. What we've all been through—you can't help it."

The flushing around his collar intensified. He wanted to say something about how he loved them all, including Charlie, but he didn't. At that moment, he wasn't sure what he felt.

"Thanks," he said.

Rodgers smiled but said nothing more. Billy thundered back down the stairs and the General followed him, like straw caught in a whirlwind, as he raced across the living room, backpack in tow, carrying his young man's morning appetite into the parking lot.

"No sugar, General!" Melissa shouted as the screen door slammed behind them. "And don't let him get *too* excited on the video game!"

FOURTEEN

Thursday, 8:02 A.M., Washington, D.C.

Senator Barbara Fox and her two aides arrived at Andrews Air Force Base in the Senator's Mercedes. Senior aide Neil Lippes was sitting in the back, with the Senator. Junior aide Bobby Winter was driving, a briefcase on the seat beside him.

They were early for their 8:30 meeting, as the guard politely informed them before admitting the car.

"On the contrary," the white-haired Senator said through the window as they drove past. "We're about twenty-five million dollars too late."

The trio drove toward a nondescript, two-story building located near the Naval Reserve flight line at Andrews Air Force Base. During the Cold War, the ivory-colored building had been a ready room, a staging area for flight crews. In the event of a nuclear attack, it would have been their job to evacuate key officials from Washington, D.C.

Now, after a hundred-million-dollar facelift, the building was the headquarters of Op-Center, the seat of the National Crisis Management Center. The seventy-eight full-time employees who worked there were crack tacticians, logisticians, soldiers, diplomats, intelligence analysts, computer specialists, psychologists, reconnaissance experts, environmentalists, attorneys, and media liaisons. The NCMC shared another forty-two support personnel with the Department of Defense and the CIA, and commanded the Striker tactical strike team.

As her budget-conscious peers were quick to remind her, Senator Fox had been one of the authors of the NCMC charter. And there was a time when she supported its efforts. Originally, Op-Center had been designed to interface with and serve as backup for the Central Intelligence Agency, National Security Agency, White House, State Department, Department of Defense, Defense Intelligence Agency, National Reconnaissance Office, and the Intelligence and Threat Analysis Center. But after handling a hostage situation in Philadelphia which the Waco-shy FBI dropped in their lap, and uncovering and defusing a sabotage attempt against the space shuttle, Op-Center had earned parity with those agencies—and then some. What had been chartered as an information clearinghouse with SWAT capabilities now had the singular capacity to monitor, initiate, and/or manage operations worldwide.

And with those singular capacities came a new budget of sixty-one million dollars. That was forty-three percent higher than the second year, which had been only eight percent higher than the first. It was a budget the fifty-two-year-old four-term Senator from California was not about to accommodate. Not with an election coming up. Not with friends at the CIA and FBI demanding parity. Paul Hood was a longtime friend, and she'd used her influence with the President to help get him the job of Director. But he and his uppity second-in-command, Mike Rodgers, were going to have to scale their operations back. Scale them back more than they were going to like.

Winter parked the car behind a concrete flowerpot, which doubled as a barricade against potential terrorist car bombers. The three got out and crossed the slate walkway set in the close-cut grass. When they reached the glass door, a video camera took their picture. A moment later a woman's voice came from a loudspeaker beneath the camera, telling them to enter. There was a buzz and Winter pulled the door open.

Inside, they were greeted by two armed guards. One was standing in front of the security office, the other was behind the bulletproof glass. The guard on the outside checked their Congressional photo I.D.s, ran a portable metal detector over the briefcase, then sent them through the first-floor administration level. At the end of the hall was an elevator, where a third armed guard was standing.

"I see one place where we can prune the budget by about fifty thousand dollars," Barbara said to Neil as the elevator door closed.

The aides chortled as the silver-walled elevator shot downstairs, to the underground area where the real business of Op-Center was conducted.

Another armed guard was stationed outside the elevator—"Seventy-five thousand," Barbara said to her aides—and after they showed her their I.D.'s, the guard directed them to a waiting room.

Senator Fox glared at her. "We're here to see General Rodgers, not await his pleasure."

"I'm sorry, Senator. But he's not here."

"Not here?" The Senator looked at her watch. She exhaled through her nose. "My God, I thought that General Rodgers lived here." She looked at the guard again. "Has he a car phone?"

"Yes, ma'am."

"Call it, please."

"I'm sorry," she said, "but I don't have that number. Mr. Abram does."

"Then call *him*," the Senator said. "Tell Mr. Abram that we would like to see him. Tell him as well that we do not sit in waiting rooms."

The guard began to phone the Assistant Deputy Director. Although his shift officially ended at 6:00 A.M., he was empowered to act in the absence of a superior.

As she rang him, the elevator opened and Political and Economics Officer Martha Mackall stepped out. The handsome, forty-nine-year-old black woman was wearing her dour morning expression. It vanished when she saw the Senator.

"Senator Fox." She beamed. "How *are* you?"

"Ticked," the Senator replied.

The women shook hands.

Martha looked from the Senator to the young guard. "What's wrong?" she asked.

"I didn't think that Superman needed sleep," the Senator said.

"Superman?" Martha asked.

"General Rodgers."

"Oh." Martha laughed. "Gotcha. He said he was going to be stopping by the Squireses this morning."

"To look after the boy, I trust," the Senator said.

The guard looked away uncomfortably.

Martha extended her arm. "Why don't you wait in my office, Senator Fox? I'll have some coffee and croissants brought in."

"Croissants?" The Senator grinned. She turned to Neil and said, "Seventy-five thousand and a couple hundred."

The two men smiled, as did Martha. The Senator

knew that Martha had no idea what they were talking about. She smiled just to be make herself part of the group. There was nothing wrong with that, Senator Fox had to admit, except that while her smile showed a lot of teeth, it told the Senator nothing about the person behind them. The truth was, she didn't think Martha *had* a sense of humor.

As they walked down the carpeted corridor, Martha asked, "So how are things on the Congressional Intelligence Oversight Committee? I haven't heard of any serious repercussions about allowing Striker's Russian incursion."

"Considering that Striker prevented a coup, I'm not surprised," Senator Fox replied.

"Nor am I," said Martha.

"Last I heard, in fact," said the Senator, "President Zhanin told his aides at the Kremlin that he wanted to erect a plaque on the bridge, when it's rebuilt, honoring Lieutenant Colonel Squires."

"That would be wonderful," Martha smiled.

They had reached her office door, and Martha entered her code in the keypad on the jamb. The door clicked open and she allowed the Senator and her aides to enter first.

Even before Martha had shown the Senator to a chair, Bill Abram swung in.

"Morning, all," said the chipper, mustachioed officer. "Just wanted to let you know that General Rodgers phoned a minute ago from the car and said he'd be a little late."

Senator Fox's long face grew a little longer as her chin fell and her eyebrows rose. "Car trouble?" she asked.

Martha laughed.

Abram said, "He's caught in traffic. Says he didn't know it got so bad this late."

Senator Fox sat in a thickly cushioned armchair. Her aides stood behind her. "And did the General say *why* he was running late? He knew about our appointment."

"Yes, he remembered it," Abram said. His little mustache rose on one side. "But he, uh—he said to tell you he got caught up in a war simulation with Striker personnel."

Martha glared at Abram. "He didn't schedule any war simulations for this morning." The glare deepened. "It wasn't one of their chicken fights in the pool—"

"No," Abram assured her. He absently pulled at the ends of his bowtie. "This was something else. Something unplanned."

Senator Fox shook her head. "I'll wait," she said.

Bobby Winter still had the briefcase in his hand. When the Senator spoke he set it down, beside the chair.

"I'll wait," the Senator went on, "because what I have to say *can't* wait. But I promise you that when General Rodgers arrives, he's going to find an Op-Center vastly different from the one he left last night." Her small, ski-slope nose rose as she said, "Vastly and permanently different."

FIFTEEN

Thursday, 2:10 P.M., Hamburg, Germany

Paul Hood's party left the restaurant at 1:20. They dropped Bob Herbert at the hotel so he could continue making calls about the attack on the movie set. Then the group went on to Martin Lang's *Hauptschlüssel* facility, which was located a scenic thirty-minute drive northwest from Hamburg, in Gluckstadt.

Like Hamburg, the town was situated on the Elbe. Unlike Hamburg, it was quaint and Old World, the last place Hood would have expected to find a modern microchip factory. Not that the building looked like a factory. It resembled a truncated pyramid covered from top to bottom with dark mirrors.

"A stealth gumdrop," Stoll quipped as they approached.

"Not a bad description," Lang said. "It was designed to reflect the surroundings rather than intrude on them."

Hausen said, "After having a good look at how the Communists polluted the air, war, and beauty of East Germany, we began working harder to create buildings which not only complement the environment, but are also pleasing to the employees."

Hood had to admit that unlike American politicians, Hausen wasn't talking in neatly manicured sound bites.

Inside the three-story structure was a bright and uncluttered working environment. The main floor was divided into three sections. Just inside the door was a large, open space with cubicles in which people were working at computers. To the right were rows of offices. And in the far section, behind the cubicles, was a clean room. There, behind a glass partition, men and women in lab whites, masks, and caps were working on the complex photo-reduction process that turned full-size blueprints into micro-sized chips and printed circuits.

Still personable but subdued by the news of the attack on the film set, Lang said, "Employees work from eight to five with two half hour and one full hour breaks. We have a gymnasium and a pool in the basement, as well as small rooms with cots and showers for anyone who wants to rest or freshen up."

Stoll said, "I could just see cots and showers at the workplace in Washington. Nobody would ever get any work done."

After showing his guests around the smallish first floor, Lang took them to the more spacious second level. No sooner had they arrived than Hausen's cellular phone beeped.

"It may be news about the attack," Hausen said, walking toward a corner.

After Hausen left, Lang showed the Americans how the chips were mass-produced by quiet, automated machines. Stoll lingered behind the group, studying control panels and watching as cameras and stamping machines did work that used to be done by steady hands, soldering irons, and jigsaws. He set his backpack on a table and chatted with one of the technicians, an English-speaking woman who was using a microscope to spot-check finished chips. When Stoll asked if he could take a peek through the eyepieces, she looked at Lang, who nodded. Stoll had a quick look, and complimented the woman on her very fine-looking sound-digitizing processor chip.

After the second floor tour was finished, the group went to the elevator to wait for Hausen. He was hunched over his telephone, a finger in his ear, listening more than he was talking.

Meanwhile, Stoll peeked into his backpack. Then he scooped it up and rejoined the group. He smiled at Hood, who winked back.

"Alas," said Lang, "I won't be able to take you to the third-floor laboratories where research and development is being conducted. It's nothing personal, I assure you," he said, looking at Stoll. "But I fear our stockholders would revolt. You see, we're working on a new technology which will revolutionize the industry."

"I see," said Stoll. "And this new technology—it wouldn't happen to have anything to do with quantum bits and the superposition principle of quantum mechanics. Would it?"

For the second time that day, Lang paled. He seemed to want to speak but couldn't.

Stoll beamed. "Remember that rotten bread slice-thrower-outer I was telling you about?"

Lang nodded, still speechless.

Stoll patted the backpack he held in his tight fist. "Well, Herr Lang, I just gave you a little taste of what it can do."

In the corner of the laboratory, the world seemed to disappear for Richard Hausen. Even as he listened to a voice from the past, a nightmarish past, he couldn't believe it was real.

"Hello, *Haussier*," the voice greeted him in a thick

French accent. It had used the nickname Hausen had had as an economics student at the Sorbonne in Paris— *Haussier,* the financial bull. Very few people knew that.

"Hello," Hausen replied warily. "Who is this?"

The speaker said softly, "It's your friend and classmate. Gerard Dupre."

Hausen's face melted into pasty blankness. The voice was less angry, less animated than he remembered. But it *could* be Dupre, he thought. For a moment Hausen wasn't able to say anything else. His head filled with a nightmare collage of faces and images.

The caller intruded on the vision. "Yes, it's Dupre. The man you threatened. The man you warned not to come back. But now I have come back. As Gerard Dominique, revolutionary."

"I don't believe it's you," Hausen finally said.

"Shall I give you the name of the café? The name of the street?" The voice hardened. "The names of the girls?"

"No!" Hausen snapped. "That was your doing, not mine!"

"So you say."

"No! That's how it *was.*"

The voice repeated slowly, "So you say."

Hausen said, "How did you get this number?"

"There's nothing I cannot get," the caller said, "no one I cannot reach."

Hausen shook his head. "Why now?" he asked. "It's been fifteen years—"

"Only a moment of time in the eyes of the gods." The caller laughed. "The gods, by the way, who now want to judge you."

"Judge me?" Hausen said. "For what? Telling the truth about your crime? What I did was right—"

"Right?" the caller cut him off. "You ass. Loyalty, *Haussier*. That's the key to everything. Loyalty in bad times as well as in good. Loyalty in life and loyalty at the moment of death. That is one thing which separates the human from the subhuman. And in my desire to eliminate subhumans, I plan, *Haussier,* to begin with you."

"You are as monstrous now as you were then," Hausen declared. His hands were sweating. He had to grip the phone tightly to keep from dropping it.

"No," the caller said. "I am more monstrous. Very much more. Because not only do I have the desire to execute my will, but now I have established the means."

"You?" Hausen said. "Your father established those means—"

"I did!" the caller snapped. "Me. All me. Everything I have, I earned. Papa was lucky after the war. Anyone with a factory became rich then. No, he was as foolish as you are, *Haussier*. Though at least he had the good grace to die."

This is madness, Hausen thought. "Dupre," he said, "Or should I say Dominique. I don't know where you are or what you've become. But I, too, am more than I was. Very much more. I'm not the college boy you remember."

"Oh, I know." The caller laughed. "I've followed your moves. Every one of them. Your rise in the government, your campaign against hate groups, your marriage, the birth of your daughter, your divorce. A lovely girl, by the way, your daughter. How is she enjoying ballet?"

Hausen squeezed the phone tighter. "Harm her and I'll find you and kill you."

"Such rough words from so careful a politician," the

caller said. "But that's the beauty of parenthood, isn't it? When a child is threatened, nothing else matters. Not fortune nor health."

Hausen said, "If you have a fight, it's with me."

"I know that, *Haussier*," the caller said. "*Alors,* the truth is I've tried to stay clear of teenage girls. Such trouble. You understand."

Hausen was looking at the tile floor but was seeing the young Gerard Dupre. Angry, lashing out, hissing his hate. He couldn't succumb to fury himself. Not even in response to calculated threats against his girl.

"So you plan to judge me," Hausen said, forcing himself to calm down. "However far I fall, you'll fall farther."

"Oh, I don't think so," said the caller. "You see, unlike you, I've put layers upon layers of willing employees between myself and my activities. I've actually built an empire of constituents who feel the way I do. I even hired one who helped me follow the life and works of Richard Hausen. He is gone now, but he provided me with a great deal of information about you."

"There are still laws," Hausen said. "There are many ways in which one can be an accomplice."

"You would know, wouldn't you?" the caller pointed out. "In any case, on that Parisian matter time has run out. The law can't touch me or you. But think of what it would do to your image when people find out. When photographs from that night begin appearing."

Photographs? Hausen thought. The camera—could it have captured them?

"I just wanted you to know that I plan to bring you down," the voice said. "I wanted you to think about it. Wait for it."

"No," said Hausen. "I'll find a way to fight you."

"Perhaps," said the caller. "But then, there *is* that beautiful thirteen-year-old dancer to consider. Because while I have sworn off teenagers, there are members of my group who—"

Hausen punched the "talk" button to disconnect the caller. He shoved the phone back in his pocket, then turned. He put on a shaky smile and asked the nearest employee where the lavatory was. Then he motioned for Lang to take the others down without him. He was going to have to get away, think about what to do.

When he reached the bathroom, Hausen leaned over the sink. He cupped his hands, filled them with water, and put his face in it. He let the water dribble out slowly. When his hands were empty, he continued to hold them to his face.

Gerard Dupre.

It was a name he'd hoped he never hear again, a face he never wanted to see again, even in his mind's eye.

But he was back, and so was Hausen—back in Paris, back on the darkest night of his life, back in the shroud of fear and guilt it had taken him years to shake.

And with his face still in his hands he cried, tears of fear . . . and shame.

SIXTEEN

Thursday, 8:16 A.M., Washington, D.C.

After dropping Billy at school and giving himself a couple of minutes to shake off the adrenaline rush of two games of *Blazing Combattle,* Rodgers used his car phone to call Darrell McCaskey. Op-Center's FBI liaison had already left for work, and Rodgers caught him on his car phone. It would not have surprised the General if the two of them passed each other while talking. He was beginning to believe that modern technology was nothing more than some huckster's way of selling people two tin cans and a string for thousands of dollars. Of course, these tin cans were equipped with scramblers which switched high and low voice tones at one end and restored them at the other. Signals inadvertently picked up by another phone would be meaningless.

"Morning, Darrell," Rodgers said.

"Morning, General," McCaskey replied. He was his usual surly morning self as he said, "And don't ask me about last night's volleyball game. DOD nuked us bad."

"I won't ask about it," Rodgers said. "Listen, I've got something I need you to check on. A group named WHOA—Whites Only Association. Ever hear of them?"

"Yeah, I've heard of them. Don't tell me you got

wind of the Baltic Avenue. That was supposed to be a deep secret.''

"No," Rodgers said, "I didn't know about it."

A Baltic Avenue was the FBI's current code for an action being taken against a domestic adversary. They took the name from the game of *Monopoly*. Baltic Avenue was the first deed after passing "Go"—hence, the start of a mission. The codes changed weekly, and Rodgers always looked forward to Monday mornings when McCaskey shared the new ones with him. In recent months his favorite go-codes had been "Moses," which was inspired by "Let my people go," and "Peppermint Lounge," which came from the famous "go-go" discotheque of the 1960s.

"Is WHOA the subject of the Baltic Avenue?" Rodgers asked.

"No," McCaskey replied. "Not directly, anyway."

Rodgers knew better than to ask McCaskey more on this particular mission. Even though the line was scrambled, that was only effective against casual listeners. Calls could still be monitored and descrambled, and some of these white supremacist groups were pretty sophisticated.

"Tell me what you know about WHOA," Rodgers said.

"They're big time," said McCaskey. "They have a couple of paramilitary training camps in the Southeast, Southwest, and Northwest. They offer everything from make-your-own-bullet classes to afterschool activities for the tykes. They publish a slick magazine called *Pührer,* spelled like *Führer,* which actually has news bureaus and ad sales offices in New York, L.A., and Chicago, and they sponsor a successful rock band called AWED—All White Electric Dudes.''

"They're also on-line," Rodgers said.

"I know." McCaskey asked, "Since when do you surf the net?"

"I don't," Rodgers said, "but Charlie Squires' kid does. He picked up a hate game about blacks getting lynched."

"Shit."

"That's how I felt," Rodgers said. "Tell me what you know."

"Funny you should ask," said McCaskey. "I was just talking to a German friend in the Office for the Protection of the Constitution in Düsseldorf. They're all worried about Chaos Days, when all the neo-Nazis over there gather—the closeted ones in the open and the open ones in hiding, if you follow."

"I'm not sure I do."

McCaskey said, "Since neo-Nazism is illegal, admitted Hitlerites can't hold gatherings in public. They meet in barns or woods or old factories. The ones who pose as mere political activists, even though they're advocating Nazi-like doctrine, are able to meet in public."

"Got it," Rodgers said. "But why aren't the admitted Hitlerites under surveillance?"

"They are," said McCaskey, "when the government can find them. And even when they are found, some— there's this guy Richter, for example, who did jail time—go to court, claim harassment, and have to be left alone. Public sentiment against skinheads is high, but they feel that articulate, clean-cut jerks like Richter deserve to be left alone."

"The government can't afford to alienate too many voters."

"That," said McCaskey, "and make the neo-Nazis look like victims. Some of the Hitler wannabes have got sound bites and charisma that'd curl your toes. They play very well with the evening news crowd.''

Rodgers didn't like what he was hearing. This media-playing-into-the-hands-of-criminals thing was an old beef of his. Lee Harvey Oswald may have been the last killer to protest his innocence on TV and get blamed in the court of public opinion anyway—though even *that* jury didn't come back with a unanimous verdict. There was something about the hangdog face of a suspect and the determined face of a prosecutor that drove the underdog-loving public to the suspect.

''So what about this German friend of yours?'' Rodgers asked.

McCaskey said, ''The OPC is worried because in addition to Chaos Days, they've got this new phenomenon called the Thule Network. It's a collection of about a hundred mailboxes and bulletin boards which allow neo-Nazi groups and cells to communicate and form alliances. There's no way of tracking the correspondence to its source, so the authorities are helpless to stop it.''

''Who or what is Thule?'' Rodgers asked.

''It's a place. The legendary northern cradle of European civilization.'' McCaskey laughed. ''When I was a kid, I read a lot of fantasy novels, and a whole bunch of barbarian-type adventure stories were set there. *Ursus of Ultima Thule,* that sort of thing.''

''Manliness and European purity,'' Rodgers said. ''That's an irresistible symbol.''

''Yeah,'' said McCaskey, ''though I'd never have believed that a place which seemed so wondrous could come to stand for something so corrupt.''

Rodgers asked, ''I take it this Thule Network has made inroads to America?''

''Not per se,'' said McCaskey. ''We've got our own

homegrown demons. For about two years now, the Feds, the Southern Poverty Law Center in Alabama, and the Simon Wiesenthal Center have been closely monitoring the inroads hate groups have been making on the information highway. The problem is, like in Germany, the bad guys usually obey the law. Plus, they're fully protected by the First Amendment."

"The First Amendment doesn't give them the right to incite violence," Rodgers said.

"They don't. They may stink to the bone, but these people are careful."

"They'll slip up somewhere," Rodgers said confidently. "And when they do, I want to be there to nail them."

"So far, they haven't," McCaskey said, "and the FBI has been watching all the neo-Nazi Web sites—their five Internet playgrounds as well as the eight national computer bulletin boards. We've also got a reciprocal agreement with Germany to trade any information they pick up on-line."

"Only Germany?" Rodgers asked.

"Germany, England, Canada, and Israel," said McCaskey. "No one else wants to shake things up. So far, there's been nothing illegal."

"Only immoral," Rodgers said.

"Sure," said McCaskey, "but you know better than anyone that we've fought a whole lot of wars to give free speech to all Americans, including WHOA."

"We also fought a war to prove that Hitler was wrong," Rodgers said. "He was and he still is. As far as I'm concerned, we're still at war with these dirtbags."

"Speaking of war," McCaskey said, "I got a call from Bob Herbert before I left home. Coincidentally, he needs information on a German terrorist group named

Feuer. Did you hear about the attack this morning?''

Rodgers said that he hadn't watched the news, and McCaskey briefed him. The murders reminded him that neo-Nazis were as cold as the monsters who inspired them, from Hitler to Heydrich to Mengele. And he could not believe, *would* not believe, that people like these were on the minds of the Founding Fathers when they drafted the Constitution.

''Have we got anybody looking into what Bob needs?'' Rodgers asked.

''Liz has more info on *Feuer,*'' McCaskey said. ''I'm going to meet with her when I get to the office. I'll go over it and get the essentials right over to Bob, the CIA, and Interpol. They're looking for the perpetrators as well as the missing girl.''

''Okay,'' Rodgers said. ''When you're done with that, bring the data and let's you and Liz and me have a talk. I don't think my meeting with Senator Fox will last very long.''

''Ouch,'' said McCaskey. ''I've got to meet you *after* you see her?''

''I'll be okay,'' Rodgers said.

''If you say so,'' McCaskey said.

''You don't believe that.''

''Paul's a diplomat,'' McCaskey said. ''You're an ass-kicker. I've never seen a senator who responded to anything other than lips on their butts.''

''Paul and I talked about that,'' Rodgers said. ''He felt that since we've proven ourselves in Korea and Russia we should take a harder line with Congress. We feel that because of Striker's performance and sacrifices, Senator Fox will have a tougher time saying no to me on the budget increase we've requested.''

''An *increase*?'' McCaskey said. ''General, Deputy

Director Clayton at the Bureau tells me he's got to whack nine percent from his budget. And he got off lucky. Rumor is, Congress is talking a twelve-to-fifteen-percent cut for the CIA."

"The Senator and I will talk," Rodgers said. "We need more HUMINT out there. With all the changes going on in Europe and the Middle East and especially Turkey, we need more assets in the field. I think I can make her see that."

"General," McCaskey said, "I hope you're right. I don't think the lady has had a reasonable day since her daughter was murdered and her husband put a gun in his mouth."

"She's still on a committee whose job is to help safeguard the country," Rodgers said. "That has to come before anything."

"She also has taxpaying constituents to answer to," McCaskey said. "Anyway, I wish you luck."

"Thanks," Rodgers said. He did not actually feel as confident as he'd sounded, nor did he bother to tell McCaskey what A. E. Housman said about luck: "Luck's a chance, but trouble's sure." And whenever the thorny Fox was involved with a project, trouble *was* sure.

Two minutes later, Rodgers was off the expressway and headed toward the gate at Andrews AFB. As he drove the familiar roads, he phoned Hood on his cellular phone for the short morning check-in. He briefed him on what had happened with Billy, and told him that he was putting Darrell on the case to find out who was behind the game. Hood agreed completely.

After hanging up, Rodgers thought about the hate groups and wondered if they were more pervasive than ever, or if the instant media coverage simply made people more aware of them.

Or maybe it's both, he thought as he passed the sentry at the gate. The media coverage of these groups inspired like-minded racists to form their own groups, causing the media to report on the "phenomenon" of hate groups. *One dirty hand washes the other.*

Rodgers parked and walked briskly toward the front door. The meeting with Senator Fox was scheduled for 8:30. It was already 8:25. The Senator was usually early. She was also usually pissed if whoever she came to see wasn't early.

That will probably be strike one against me, Rodgers thought as he rode the elevator down. *Strike two if she's in an unusually bad mood.*

When the General exited in the lower level, the sympathetic look on the face of Anita Mui, the lower-level sentry, confirmed that the count was 0-and-2.

Well, he thought as he headed down the corridor, *I'll have to find a way to deal with that.* Commanders do, and Rodgers loved being a commander. He loved overseeing Striker and he loved running Op-Center when Hood was away. He loved the process of making things happen for America. Being even a small cog in that great machine filled him with indescribable pride.

And part of being that cog is dealing with other cogs, he told himself. Including politicians.

He stopped short as he passed Martha Mackall's office. The door was open and Senator Fox was sitting inside. He saw from the Senator's grim expression that he had struck out, even before he'd stepped to the plate.

He looked at his watch. It was 8:32. "Sorry," he said.

"Come in, General Rodgers," she said. Her voice was tight, clipped. "Ms. Mackall has been telling me about her father. My daughter was a tremendous fan of his music.''

Rodgers entered. ''We all liked Mack's stuff,'' he said as he shut the door. ''Back in 'Nam, we called him the Soul of Saigon.''

Martha was wearing her serious professional face. Rodgers knew it well. Martha had a habit of adopting the attitudes of people who could advance her career. And if Senator Fox was down on Rodgers, then Martha would be too. Even more so than usual.

Rodgers sat on the edge of Martha's desk. Since Senator Fox wanted the home court advantage, she was going to have to look up at him.

''Unfortunately,'' Senator Fox said, ''I didn't come here to discuss music, General Rodgers. I came to discuss your budget. I was disappointed when Director Hood's assistant telephoned yesterday to say that Mr. Hood had a more pressing engagement—spending money he won't have. But I decided to come here anyway.''

''Paul and I worked closely together preparing the budget,'' Rodgers said. ''I can answer any questions you have.''

''I have only one question,'' the Senator said. ''When did the Government Printing Office begin publishing fiction?''

Rodgers's stomach began to burn. McCaskey was right: Paul should have handled this.

Senator Fox placed the briefcase in her lap and popped the latches. ''You asked for an increase of eighteen percent at a time when government agencies are making across-the-board cuts.'' She handed Rodgers his own three-hundred-page document. ''This is the budget I will present to the finance committee. It contains my blue-pencil reductions totaling thirty-two percent.''

Rodgers's eyes snapped from the budget to the Senator. ''Reductions?''

''We can talk about how the remaining seventy percent is to be apportioned,'' Fox continued, ''but the cut will be made.''

Rodgers wanted to throw the budget back at the Senator. He waited a moment until the urge had passed. He turned and placed it on Martha's desk. ''You've got nerve, Senator.''

''So do you, General,'' Fox said, unfazed.

''I know,'' he replied. ''I've tested it against North Vietnamese, Iraqis, and North Koreans.''

''We've all of us seen your medals,'' she replied politely. ''This is not a mandate on courage.''

''No, it's not,'' Rodgers quietly agreed. ''It's a death sentence. We have a top-flight organization and we still lost Bass Moore in Korea and Charlie Squires in Russia. If you cut us back, I won't be able to give my people the support they need.''

''For what?'' the Senator said. ''More adventures overseas?''

''No,'' he said. ''Our government's entire intelligence focus has been on ELINT. Electronic intelligence. Spy satellites. Eavesdropping. Photo reconnaissance. Computers. These are tools but they aren't enough. Thirty, forty years ago we had a human presence around the world. HUMINT—human intelligence. People who infiltrated foreign governments and spy organizations and terrorist groups and used judgment, initiative, creativity, and courage to get us information. The best camera in the world can't pull blueprints from a drawer. Only a human operator can break into a computer which isn't on-line. A spy satellite can't look into a terrorist's eyes and tell you if he or she is really committed or if he can be turned. We need to rebuild those assets.''

''A pretty speech,'' said the Senator, ''but you do not have my support. We do not need this HUMINT to protect American interests. Striker stopped a Korean lunatic from bombing Tokyo. They saved the administration of a Russian President who has not yet proven that he is our ally. Why should American taxpayers underwrite an international police force?''

''Because they're the only ones who can,'' Rodgers said. ''We're fighting a cancer, Senator. You've got to treat it wherever it shows up.''

Martha said from behind him, ''I agree with Senator Fox. There are other forums in which the United States can address international concerns. The United Nations and the World Court are chartered and funded for that purpose. And there's NATO.''

Rodgers said without turning, ''So where were they, Martha?''

''Pardon me?''

''Where was the U.N. when that Nodong missile took off from North Korea? *We* were the surgeons who kept the Japanese from catching a fever of roughly eighteen million degrees Fahrenheit.''

''Again,'' said Senator Fox, ''that was a job well done. But it was a job you needn't have shouldered. The United States survived while the Soviet Union and Afghanistan battled one other, while Iran and Iraq were at war. We will survive other such conflicts.''

''Tell that to the American families of terrorist victims,'' Rodgers said. ''We're not asking for toys or luxuries here, Senator. I'm asking for security for American citizens.''

''In a perfect world we would be able to safeguard

every building, every airplane, every life,'' the Senator said. She closed the briefcase. ''But it is not a perfect world and the budget will be cut, as I've indicated. There will be no debate and no hearing.''

''Fine,'' Rodgers said. ''When Paul gets back, you can start by cutting my salary.''

Senator Fox shut her eyes. ''Please, General. We can do very nicely without the grandstanding.''

''I'm not trying to be dramatic,'' Rodgers said. He stood and tugged the hem of his jacket. ''I just don't believe in doing anything half-assed. You're an isolationist, Senator. You have been since the tragedy in France.''

''This has nothing to do with that—''

''Of course it does. And I understand how you feel. The French did not find your daughter's killer, didn't seem to care very much, so why help them? But you've let that get in the way of the larger picture, of our national interests.''

Martha said, ''General, I didn't lose anyone abroad and I agree with the Senator. Op-Center was created to help other agencies, not to help other nations. We've lost sight of that.''

Rodgers turned and looked down at Martha. ''Your father sang a song called 'The Boy Who Killed the Lights,' about a white kid who shut the lights in a club so a black singer could sing there—''

''Don't quote my dad to me,'' Martha snapped, ''and don't tell me that I'm lucky to be in this club, General. Nobody helped me get this gig—''

''If you'll let me finish,'' Rodgers said, ''that wasn't the point I was making.'' Rodgers remained calm. He didn't raise his voice to women. That wasn't how Mrs. Rodgers had raised her son. ''What I was trying to say before is that what Goschen called 'splendid isolation' simply doesn't exist anymore. Not in the music world and not in the political world. If Russia breaks down, it affects China, the Baltic republics, and Europe. If Japan suffers—''

"I learned all about the domino theory in elementary school," Martha said.

"Yes we all did, General Rodgers," Senator Fox said. "Do you really believe that General Michael Rodgers and Op-Center are the tent poles which hold the infrastructure up?''

"We do our part," Rodgers said. "We need to do more.''

"And I say we already do too much!" Senator Fox shot back. "When I was still new to the Senate, U.S. warplanes were not permitted to fly over France en route to bomb Tripoli and Benghazi. The French are supposed to be our allies! At the time, I said on the floor of the Senate that we bombed the wrong capital. I meant it. More recently, Russian terrorists blew up a tunnel in New York. Was the Russian Ministry of Security hot on the trail of these murderers? Did your new best friends at the Russian Op-Center warn us? Even today, are their operatives hunting for Russian gangsters on our shores? No, General, they are not.''

"Paul went to Russia to establish a relationship with their Op-Center," Rodgers said. "We believe we'll get their cooperation.''

"I know," the Senator said. "I read his report. And do you know when we'll get their cooperation? After we've spent tens of millions of dollars making the Russian Op-Center as sophisticated as our own. But that's when General Orlov will be retired, someone hostile to the U.S. will take his place, and we'll be left, again, with an enemy whom we've helped to make stronger.''

"American history is full of chances taken and losses incurred," Rodgers said. "But it's also full of relationships which have been built and sustained. We can't give up optimism and hope."

The Senator rose. She handed her briefcase to one of her aides and smoothed her black skirt.

"General," she said, "your penchant for dictums is well known, and I don't appreciate being lectured to. I am optimistic and I am hopeful that we can solve America's problems. But I will not support Op-Center as a base for international troubleshooters. A think tank, yes. An intelligence resource, yes. A domestic crisis management center, yes. A team of international Dudley Do-Rights, no. And for what I've just outlined, you will need only the budget I've given you."

The Senator nodded to Rodgers, offered her hand to Martha, then started to go.

"Senator?" Rodgers called after her.

The Senator stopped. She turned, and Rodgers took a few steps toward her. She was nearly as tall as Rodgers, and her clear blue-gray eyes held his.

"Darrell McCaskey and Liz Gordon are scheduled to work together on a project," Rodgers said. "I assume you've heard about the terrorist group that attacked the movie set in Germany?"

"No," Fox said. "There was nothing in this morning's *Post*."

"I know," Rodgers said. *The Washington Post* and CNN were how everyone in government got news. He was counting on the fact that she didn't know. "It happened about four hours ago. Several people were killed. Bob Herbert is over there on business and has asked for our assistance."

"And do you think that we should help German authorities investigate?" the woman asked. "What vital American interests are at stake? Is it cost effective? Which taxpayers will care?"

Rodgers weighed his words with care. He had laid the snare and Fox strode right in. This was going to hit the Senator hard.

"Only two taxpayers will care," Rodgers said. "The parents of a twenty-one-year-old American girl who may have been kidnapped by the terrorists."

The woman's strong blue-gray eyes melted. The Senator trembled slightly as she tried to remain erect. It was a moment before she could speak.

"You don't take prisoners, do you, General?"

"When the enemy surrenders I do, Senator."

She continued to look at him. All the sadness of the world seemed to be there in those eyes, and Rodgers felt like hell.

"What do you expect me to say?" the Senator asked. "Of course help them save the girl. She's an American."

"Thank you," Rodgers said, "and I'm very sorry. Sometimes American interests are hidden in the things we do."

Senator Fox looked at Rodgers a moment longer, then shifted her gaze to Martha. Bidding the woman a good morning, the Senator walked quickly from the office, her aides trailing close behind.

Rodgers didn't remember turning and picking up the budget, but it was in his hands as he started toward the door.

SEVENTEEN

Thursday, 2:30 P.M., Hamburg, Germany

Henri Toron and Yves Lambesc were not tired. Not any more. Jean-Michel's return had wakened the men, and the telephone call from M. Dominique had brought the two French bears to full attention.

Full, belated attention.

It was Jean-Michel's fault, of course. They'd been sent to be his bodyguards, but he had chosen to go by himself to the club in St. Pauli. The three had arrived in Germany at 1:00 A.M., and Henri and Yves had played blackjack until 2:30. If only Jean-Michel had wakened them, they'd have accompanied him—alert and ready to protect him from the Huns. But no. He'd let them sleep. What did he have to fear, after all?

"Why do you think M. Dominique sent us with you?" Henri had roared when he saw Jean-Michel. "To sleep or to protect you?"

"I didn't think I was in any danger," Jean-Michel had replied.

"When dealing with Germans," Henri had said gravely, "one is always in danger."

M. Dominique had called as Yves was putting ice cubes in a hand towel for Jean-Michel's eye. Henri took the call.

Their employer did not raise his voice. He never did. He simply gave them their instructions and sent them on their way. The two knew that they would be disciplined with a month of extra duty for having overslept. That was standard for a first infraction. Those who failed the cause twice were dismissed. The shame of letting him down was far more painful than the fingertip they were forced to leave in the basket of one of M. Dominique's little guillotines.

So they had cabbed to St. Pauli, and now they were leaning against a car parked down the street from *Auswechseln*. The streets were beginning to grow crowded with tourists, though the twenty-yard stretch between the Frenchmen and the club was relatively clear.

Barrel-chested, six-foot-four Henri was smoking a cigarette, and the inch-taller, broad-shouldered Yves was chewing homemade bubble gum. Yves had a Beretta 92F pistol in the pocket of his jacket. Henri was carrying a Belgian GP double-action pistol. Their job was simple: to go to the club and get Herr Richter on the phone by any means necessary.

For over two hours, Henri had watched the club door through the twisting smoke of cigarette after cigarette. When it finally opened, he tapped Yves on the arm and they hurried over.

A giant slab of a man was walking out. Henri and Yves acted as though they were going to walk past him, then turned suddenly. Before the big man was even out the door, Henri had pushed the gun in his gut and told him to get back in.

"Nein," he said.

Either the man was devoted to his boss or he was wearing a bullet-proof vest. Henri didn't bother to repeat the request. He simply drove his heel down hard on the man's instep and pushed him back inside. The big man fell moaning against the bar and Henri put the gun to his forehead. Yves also pulled his gun and disappeared into the darkness, to the right.

"Richter," Henri said to the man. *"Ou est-il?"*

The *Auswechseln* bouncer told him to go to hell in German. Henri knew what *Hölle* meant. The rest he figured out from the man's tone.

The Frenchman slid the gun down to the man's left eye. *"Le dernier temps,"* he said. *The last time.* "Richter! *Tout de suite!"*

A voice said in French from the darkness. "*No one* enters my club with a gun and makes demands. Let Ewald go."

Footsteps came toward them from the back of the club. Henri kept the gun pushed against the man's eye.

A shadowy figure appeared at the end of the bar and sat on a stool.

"I said let the man go," Richter repeated. "At once."

Yves approached him from the right. Richter did not look at him. Henri did not move.

"Herr Richter," Henri said, "my companion is going to punch in a number on the bar telephone and hand it to you."

"Not while you're holding my employee at gunpoint," Richter said firmly.

Yves reached Richter and stepped behind him. The German did not turn.

Henri looked at Richter in the darkness. The Frenchman had two options. One was to let this Ewald go. That would give Richter his way and set a bad precedent for the afternoon's proceedings. The other was to shoot Ewald. That might rattle Richter, but it might also bring the police. And it was no guarantee of getting Richter to do what he was told.

There was really only one thing to do. M. Dominique's instructions to them were to get Richter on the telephone and to do the other thing he had told them. They were not here to win a contest of wills.

Henri stepped back and released the bouncer. Ewald rose indignantly, snatched a quick, angry look at Henri, then walked protectively toward Richter.

"It's all right, Ewald," Richter said. "These men won't hurt me. They've come to deliver me unto Dominique, I think."

"Sir," the big man said, "I won't leave while they're here."

"Really, Ewald, I'm quite safe. These men may be French, but they aren't stupid. Now go. Your wife is waiting and I don't want her to worry."

The big German looked from his employer to Yves. He glowered at the Frenchman for a moment. "Yes, Herr Richter. Once again, good afternoon to you."

"Good afternoon," Richter said. "I'll see you again in the morning."

With a final sharp look at Yves, Ewald turned and strode from the club. He brushed roughly against Henri as he left.

The door clicked shut. Henri could hear his watch ticking in the silence. He cocked his head toward the black business phone sitting at the end of the bar.

"Now," Henri said to his partner. "Do it."

Yves lifted the receiver, punched in a number, and handed the phone to Richter.

The German sat with his hands in his lap. He didn't move.

"Put it on speaker," Henri scowled.

Yves punched the speaker button and hung up. The phone rang over a dozen times before anyone picked up.

"Felix?" said the voice on the other end.

"Yes, Dominique," said Richter. "I'm here."

"How are you?"

"I'm well," he said. He looked at Henri, who was lighting a new cigarette with the old. "Except for the presence of your two henchmen. Why do you insult me, *monsieur,* with the threat of force? Did you think I wouldn't take your call?"

"Not at all," Dominique said benignly. "That isn't the reason I sent them. To tell you the truth, Felix, they've come to close down your club."

Henri swore he could hear Richter's back straighten.

"Close down the club," Richter repeated. "For fleecing your lamb M. Horne?"

"No," said Dominique. "What happened was his fault for coming alone. My intent is to show you the futility of refusing my acquisition offer."

"By muscling me like a common mobster," Richter said. "I expected better from you."

"That, Herr Richter, is your problem. Unlike you, I have no pretensions. I believe in maintaining influence through any means at my disposal. Speaking of which, don't bother to call your escort service this afternoon to check on tonight's schedules. You'll find that the girls and boys have elected to join a rival service."

"My people won't stand for this," Richter said. "They won't be bludgeoned into submissiveness."

Henri noted a change in Richter's voice. He no longer sounded smug. And he could feel Richter's eyes on him as he put his old cigarette down on the guest register.

"No," Dominique agreed. "They won't be bullied. But they will follow you. And you will do as you're told, or you will lose more than just your livelihood.''

Within seconds, the register book began to smoke. Richter stood and took a step toward it. Henri raised the pistol. Richter stood still.

''This is spite, *monsieur,* not good sense,'' Richter said. ''Who benefits if we bloody each other? Only the opposition.''

''You drew first blood,'' Dominique said. ''Let's hope this is the last.''

A flame leapt from the page of the book and threw an orange light on Richter's face. His eyebrows were pulled in at the nose, his mouth turned down.

Dominique continued. ''You have enough insurance to start again. In the meantime, I will see to it that your group has the money to continue. The cause will not suffer. Only your pride is hurt. And over that, Herr Richter, I will lose no sleep.''

As the register pages curled into bouquets of black ash, Henri carried the book to the bar. He wadded cocktail napkins onto the flame, then made a trail of them to the CO_2 tank by the soda pump.

''Now I suggest you leave with my associates,'' Dominique said. ''This is not the kind of *feuer* with which you want to get involved. Good day, Felix.''

The phone clicked off, and a dial tone buzzed from the speaker.

Henri stepped toward the door. He motioned the other men over. ''There's only about two minutes of fuse,'' he said. ''We'd better go.''

Yves stepped from behind Richter. As he did, he took the gum from his mouth and stuck it under the bar.

Richter didn't move.

''Herr Richter,'' Henri said. ''So that you are not tempted to put out the fire, M. Dominique has instructed us to make sure that you leave—or make sure that you do not. Which will it be?''

Reflected flames burned in Richter's eyes as he glared at the men. Then his eyes snapped front and he walked briskly from the club. The men raced out behind him.

Richter didn't say a word as he walked down the street and hailed a cab. Henri and Yves set off in the other direction, hurrying toward the deep blue of the Elbe.

They didn't turn when they heard the explosion and the crash of debris and the screams of people who were hurt or frightened or calling for help. . . .

When the cab driver heard the blast, he pulled over. He looked back, swore, and jumped from the cab to see if he could help.

Felix Richter did not join him. He remained seated, staring ahead. Since he did not know what Dominique looked like, he didn't see a face. He saw only bright red hate. And there, in the close confines of the cab, he began to scream. He screamed from his abdomen until it was empty, screamed from his soul until it was drained, screamed until his throat and ears both ached. At breath's end, he filled his lungs and screamed again, pouring out hate and frustration through his voice.

When that breath was gone, he fell silent. Perspiration had formed on his forehead. It spilled into the corners of his eyes. He was breathing heavily, but he was calm and focused now. He stared ahead and saw the crowd which was gathering to watch the fire. Some of the people were staring at him and he glared back, unashamed and unafraid.

Looking at them, he thought, *The crowds. They were the Führer's people. They were blood his heart pumped throughout the land. The crowds.* . . .

There was no way, absolutely none, that he would join Dominique now. He refused to be the man's pawn or his trophy. And there was no way that he would allow Dominique to get away with this outrage.

But he cannot be destroyed, Richter thought. The Frenchman must be humbled. Caught off guard.

The crowds. The people. The lifeblood of a nation. They must respond to a strong heart. And the government, the body, must obey their wishes.

And as he glanced into the rearview mirror and watched the flames consume his club, Richter knew what he was going to do.

Leaving the cab, Richter walked two blocks—away, reluctantly, from the thickening mob. He caught another taxi, then headed to his apartment to make a phone call. A call he was sure would alter the course of German history . . . and that of the world.

EIGHTEEN

Thursday, 8:34 A.M., New York, New York

The three-story brownstone on Christopher Street in the West Village was built in 1844. The door, the windowsills, and the two-step stoop were the originals. Though the decades-old coat of brown paint was peeling, the appointments were handsome in their timeworn way. Because the building was so close to the shifting grounds by the Hudson River, floors had buckled slightly and many of the unpainted bricks had shifted. Their movement created gently waving, symmetrical lines across the building's facade. The mortar had been refilled where it had cracked and fallen out.

The building stood between a corner flower stand and a candy shop. Since coming to America in the early 1980s, the Dae-jungs, the young Korean couple who owned the flower stand, paid no attention to the men and women who came and went from the century-and-a-half-old building. Neither did Daniel Tetter and Matty Stevens, the middle-aged men who owned Voltaire's Candied Shop next door. Only a handful of times in the twenty-seven years that they'd been in business had Tetter and Stevens ever seen the off-premises owner from Pittsburgh.

Then three months ago, thirty-two-year-old Special

Agent in Charge Douglas diMonda of the New York bureau of the FBI and forty-three-year-old NYPD Division Chief Peter Arden visited the Dae-jungs and Tetter and Stevens at their homes. The shopkeepers were informed that four months earlier, a major case squad had been formed by the FBI and the NYPD, and that they were investigating the occupants of the brownstone. The florists and the candy-makers were told only that the lessee, Earl Gurney, was a white supremacist who was suspected of having masterminded violent anti-black and anti-gay activities in Detroit and Chicago.

What the merchants weren't told was that the paramilitary group to which Gurney belonged, Pure Nation, had been infiltrated by an FBI agent a year earlier. Writing in code to his ''mother'' in Grenda Hills, California, ''John Wooley'' reported on the Pure Nation training facility in the Mohawk Mountains of Arizona and their plans to hire themselves out as the military arm of other white supremacy organizations and militias. The agent knew that some enormous New York operation was being planned, something much larger than the ambushes that left three black men dead in Detroit and five lesbians raped in Chicago. Unfortunately, the agent was not sent to Manhattan with the strike force and did not know what Pure Nation was planning. Only Commander Gurney knew that.

After months of surveillance from the street and from parked cars, of taking fingerprints off bottles and cans in trash bags and running background checks, diMonda and Arden were sure they had a team of Pure Nation's most dangerous members in their midst. Six of the seven men and one of the two women living in the building had rap sheets, many involving violent crimes. However, the major case squad didn't know what Gurney might be planning. Phone taps picked up only conversations about the weather, jobs, and family, and there were no faxes. A search warrant to examine mail and parcels also turned up nothing. The occupants almost certainly assumed that they were being watched and listened to, a tacit indication that something was up.

Then, in the two weeks prior to approaching the Daejungs, Tetter, and Stevens, the stakeout team had seen something which made it imperative for them to begin moving in a force of their own. They noticed that the nine people who lived in the brownstone were bringing in more and more boxes, duffel bags, and suitcases. They would arrive in pairs, with one person always empty-handed, wearing a jacket and keeping both hands in pockets. The stakeout team did not doubt that there were guns in those pockets, as well as in the boxes, duffel bags, and suitcases. But diMonda and Arden didn't want to grab just a bag of guns. If there were a weapons cache upstairs, the major case squad wanted it all.

The idea of obtaining a search warrant to examine the premises was rejected. By the time a team reached the third floor—headquarters were usually located on the highest floors—any incriminating documents or computer diskettes would be destroyed. Besides, diMonda and Arden didn't want to play softball with these creatures. Bureau head Moe Gera agreed, and gave the go-ahead for a strike team to be put in place, quietly and unobtrusively.

The florists and confectioners gladly allowed their shops to be used as staging areas. They were frightened, not only of the assault but of possible repercussions. But they had all marched in the Village protest against skinhead attacks in the summer of 1995, and said they could not live with themselves if others died because of their

inactivity. DiMonda promised that the NYPD would provide protection for them both at home and on the job.

The positioning of the team was done over time. Ko-
rean-American FBI Agent Park was sent to work in the
Dae-jung shop. Tetter and Stevens hired Johns, a black
sales clerk who was a detective with the NYPD. Both
employees spent a lot of time outside the shops, smoking
cigarettes and being seen by the people who entered.
After two weeks, they brought in three more assistants
each, so there was a total of eight additional agents at
the site. All of them worked the day shift, which was
when the brownstone was most active. The legitimate
employees of both shops were paid to stay home.

Each new employee made sure that they were noticed
by the people coming and going at the brownstone. Noticed often, so that they would become invisible.

The cop on the beat was temporarily reassigned, replaced by Detective Arden. Concealing his bodybuilder
physique under loose-fitting clothes, diMonda worked
the street as a homeless man who occasionally slept on
their stoop and had to be shoved or kicked off. Gurney
himself actually complained to Arden to "keep that useless shit-stink" away from his home. Arden said that he
would do his best.

The FBI obtained a layout of the building from the
landlord, who thought he was showing the brownstone
to a prospective buyer. The blueprints were scanned into
a computer at the New York bureau. A three-
dimensional image of the interior was constructed from
it, and an assault plan was worked out. The day was
chosen, and an early-morning time was selected, when
the narrow, one-way street would be the least crowded.
People who were going to work would have already left,

and tourists would not yet have made their way to Greenwich Village.

Earlier on "M-morning," when it was still dark, undercover police officers made their way into the shops. Five officers were placed in each shop, and their job was to handle arrests once the vermin had been flushed out.

The primary squad in the two shops had been instructed to go into action when diMonda shouted, "Hey." Either it would come when someone pushed him, or when Arden tried to move him from the stoop. Once the primary squad moved, a twelve-person backup team would leave their van, which was parked around the corner on Bleecker Street. Six of them would go in only if they heard gunfire. When they went into action, police would seal off the street and make sure no one else left their apartments. If the neo-Nazis managed to get out of the building, the other six agents in the support group would be in position, in the street, to pick them up. An ambulance was also parked and waiting on Bleecker, in case it was needed.

It began at 8:34, with diMonda settling down on the stoop with a cup of coffee and a bagel. For the last few weeks, the first two people usually left the building between 10:00 and 10:30, took the PATH train to Thirty-third Street, and went to an office on Sixth Avenue. The office made no attempt to conceal what it was: a small editorial and advertising sales office for the racist magazine *Führer*. The visitors left the office with whatever they were supposed to bring back to the apartment. The FBI had examined cartons being shipped to the magazine and found no weapons of any kind; they could only assume that staffers were buying guns, ammunition, and knives on the street and storing them there for disbursement to Pure Nation or whoever else needed them.

The door to the brownstone opened at 8:44. When it did, diMonda threw his coffee cup to the right, in front of the candy shop, and fell back into the lobby. Arden, who had been waiting in the shop, made sure he stepped out when he saw the flying cup.

A young woman, dyed-blond and hard, stepped over diMonda.

"Officer!" she said. "Get this creature out of here!"

A tall, mustachioed man picked the much shorter diMonda up by the shirt and made ready to heave him to the sidewalk.

"Hey!" diMonda yelled.

An agent came from the flower shop and stood behind the woman. When she went to push diMonda, the agent jumped between them and pushed her back, toward the flower shop. She screamed at him as a second agent came out and told her she was under arrest. When she resisted, two officers cuffed her and hauled her into the back room.

Meanwhile, Arden had stepped into the lobby of the brownstone.

"What the hell are you doing?" the neo-Nazi yelled at Arden as his struggle with the scrappy diMonda moved onto the street. There, two agents were waiting to pull him into the candy shop.

"Don't worry, sir," Arden yelled. "I'll make sure this bum doesn't bother you again." That was for the benefit of anyone who might be listening from upstairs. Arden had already drawn his sleek 9-mm Sig Sauer P226 and was standing against the wall on the left side of the stairs.

DiMonda moved in on the right, holding his Colt .45 automatic. Then the eight remaining agents entered in pairs. The first two agents covered the first-floor room, just beyond the stairs. One crouched beside the door; the other remained near the stairs with a view of the first landing. The second two agents moved in between diMonda and Arden and took up positions on the first landing. They walked carefully up the stairs, staying to the middle of each step and climbing with their torsos straight. By centering their weight, they not only moved more efficiently, but caused less creaking on each of the old steps.

Then the next two agents went in, stopping halfway up the second flight of stairs. The fourth pair of agents went up and staked their claim on the second-floor landing. One agent covered the door, the other the stairs. The last pair of agents went halfway up the next flight. Then diMonda and Arden ascended to the last landing. DiMonda stood in front of the door while Arden took his position to the right of the door, beside the steps. His gun was pointing up, his eyes on his partner. He would be taking his cue from diMonda. If the FBI man went in, he'd follow. If he backed away, Arden would cover his retreat and follow.

DiMonda reached into the pocket of his tattered jacket and removed a small device which looked like a hypodermic syringe with a receptacle underneath that was roughly the size of three stacked dimes. He crouched, his gun in his right hand, and carefully inserted the thin tip of the device in the key slot. Then he put his eye to the back.

The FOALSAC—Fiber-Optic Available Light Scope and Camera—gave the user a fish-eye look into a room without generating any light or sound. The tiny receptacle underneath contained a cadmium battery and film to record whatever the camera saw. DiMonda carefully swept the device from the left to the right, tapping the bottom of the film cartridge each time he wanted to take a picture. When it came to trying these bastards, photographic evidence would be important. Especially since the FOALSAC revealed stacks of machine guns, a couple of M79 grenade launchers, and a small tepee consisting of FMK submachine guns. There were three people in the room. A man and woman were eating breakfast at a table in the right-hand corner, and the third person—Gurney—was sitting at a computer table, facing the door, working on a laptop computer. That meant the other four neo-Nazis were in the bedrooms downstairs.

DiMonda held up three fingers and pointed to the room. Arden looked back down the stairs. He held up three fingers and pointed to the room. Then he waited for the other agents to finish checking out their rooms.

Word came back that the other Pure Nation thugs were accounted for, two in each room. DiMonda gave the others a thumbs up, meaning that they were to proceed to the next step.

The men worked quickly, lest anyone inside decide to go for a newspaper or a walk.

DiMonda put away his FOALSAC. Because chances were good that the doors had been reinforced with metal bars, the agents would not attempt to kick them down. They attached plastique to the doors, to the left of the doorknobs. The charges would be powerful enough to blow the locks and jambs away. A small metal shield was placed over each plastique to direct the blast, and a magnetized, quarter-sized clock was attached to it. There was a plastic pull-strip in the top of the clock: when removed, it would start a ten-second countdown. At the end of the countdown, an electric charge would travel from the clock through the metal and trigger the plastique.

DiMonda cocked his head back. The man on the landing was watching him. When diMonda nodded, so did the other man. And so did the man on the steps below him. At the count of three, marked by diMonda nodding his head, all the agents pulled the plastic tab from their clocks.

As the silent countdown progressed, the agents on the landings moved quickly to the doors. During the planning of this assault, they'd considered every possible distribution of Pure Nationals. Now they were disbursing accordingly. For this configuration, agents Park and Johns went upstairs. Park stood behind diMonda and Johns was on the steps, beside Arden. The remaining two agents took up positions beside the first- and second-floor rooms.

DiMonda had moved to the left, lest he be struck by the doorknob when it blew off. He pointed to himself, then to Park and Johns in turn. Once inside, this was the order, from the left to the right, in which they would cover the Pure Nationals. Detective Arden would be their agent-at-large, assisting anyone who might need help.

The clock finished counting down and the plastique ignited. There was a boom, like a popping paper bag. As the brass knob blew out, the door swung in.

DiMonda went in first, followed by Park, Johns, and Arden. Smoke rolled in from the explosion and the men ran ahead of it, fanning out in a line. As they did, each man shouted "Don't move!" The cry came from the gut, loud and raw, designed to intimidate as much as possible.

Two of the white supremacists, a man and a woman,

rose at the blast but stood still. Gurney did not. He rose, threw the laptop at Park, and reached his right hand under the table.

Park lowered his gun and caught the computer. "Take him!" he shouted to Arden.

Arden was ahead of him. He swung his 9mm over as Gurney drew a Sokolovsky .45 automatic from a holster attached to the underside of the computer table. The .45 spat first, the first bullet catching the edge of Arden's Kevlar bulletproof vest. His left shoulder was shattered, but the impact threw him away from the fan of bullets. As they struck the wall behind him, Arden squeezed off rounds of his own. So did Park, who had crouched, set the computer down, and fired.

One of Arden's bullets caught the neo-Nazi in the left hip, the other in the right foot. Park put a hole in Gurney's right forearm.

Snarling viciously from the pain, Gurney dropped the .45 and fell to his left. Park hurried over and put his gun to the man's temple. During the four-second exchange, neither the woman nor the other man had moved.

There was no gunfire from the floors below, though the brief exchange on the third floor had brought the backup team racing into the building. They ran upstairs as Park was cuffing the bleeding gunman. DiMonda and Johns had put their own prisoners against the wall, face in, hands behind their backs. As they were handcuffed, the woman screamed that diMonda was a traitor to his race, and the man threatened retribution against his family. Both of them ignored Johns.

Three members of the backup team arrived and entered in two-one formation—two agents rushed in, fanning left and right, while the third dropped to her belly in the doorway, covering them. When they saw Arden and the white supremacist lying on the hardwood floor, and the other two neo-Nazis cuffed, they called for the ambulance.

As the backup team took charge of the prisoners, diMonda hurried to Arden's side.

"I can't believe this," Arden gasped.

"Don't talk," diMonda said. He knelt by his head. "If something's broken, you don't want to displace it even more."

"Of course something's broken," Arden wheezed. "My goddamn shoulder. Twenty years on the force and not one injury. Man, I had a no-hitter going till that prick tagged me. And it was a sucker punch. The old gun-under-the-table."

Despite his wounds, the gunman said, "You're going to die. You're all going to die."

diMonda looked over as he was loaded onto a stretcher. "Eventually, yeah," he said. "Till then, we're gonna keep beating the bush and flushing out snakes like you."

Gurney laughed. "You won't have to flush." He coughed, and said through his teeth, "We're coming to bite *you*."

NINETEEN

Thursday, 2:45 P.M., Hamburg, Germany

Hood and Martin Lang had both been startled when Hausen returned and announced that he had to leave.

"I'll see you later, in my office," he said as he shook Hood's hand. Then bowing slightly to Stoll and Lang, he left. Neither Hood nor Lang bothered to ask what was wrong. They simply watched in silence as Hausen walked briskly to the parking lot, where he'd parked his car earlier.

When he pulled away, Stoll said, "Is he Superman or something? This looks like a job for *Übermensch*'?"

"I've never seen him like that," Lang said. "He seemed very unsettled. And did you notice his eyes?"

"What do you mean?" Hood asked.

"They were bloodshot," Lang said. "He looked as if he'd been crying."

"Maybe there's been a death," Hood suggested.

"Perhaps. But he would have told us. He would have postponed our meeting." Lang shook his head slowly. "It's very strange."

Hood was concerned without knowing why. Though he barely knew Hausen, he had the impression that the Deputy Foreign Minister was a man of unusual strength and compassion. He was a politician who stood by what he believed because he felt it was best for his country. From the briefing paper Liz Gordon had prepared, Hood knew that Hausen had shouted down neo-Nazis at the first Chaos Days years before, and had written a series of unpopular newspaper editorials demanding the publication of the "Death Books from Auschwitz," the list the Gestapo kept of people who had died in the concentration camp. For Hausen to run from anything seemed out of character.

But the men still had work to do, and Lang tried to put a business-as-usual face on things as he led them to his office.

"What do you need for your presentation?" the industrialist asked Stoll.

"Just a flat surface," Stoll said. "A desk or floor'll do."

The windowless office was surprisingly small. It was lit by recessed fluorescent lights, and the only furniture was two white-leather sofas on opposite sides. Lang's desk was a long slab of glass resting on a pair of white marble columns. The walls were white and the floor was white tile.

"I take it you like white," Stoll said.

"It is said to have therapeutic psychological value," Lang said.

Stoll held up the backpack. "Where can I set this up?"

"On the desk is fine," Lang said. "It's quite sturdy and scratch resistant."

Stoll set the bag beside the white phone. "Therapeutic psychological value," he said. "You mean like, it's not as depressing as black or as sad as blue—that kind of thing?"

"Exactly," said Lang.

"I can just see me asking Senator Fox for the money to redo Op-Center entirely in white," Hood said.

"She'd see red," Stoll said, "and you'd never get the green."

Hood made a face and Lang watched intently as Stoll unpacked the bag.

The first object he removed was a silver box roughly the size of a shoebox. It had an iris-like shutter in the front, and an eyepiece in the back. "Solid-state laser with viewfinder," he said helpfully. The second object resembled a compact fax machine. "Imaging system with optical and electrical probes," he said. Then he removed a third object, which was a white plastic box with cables. It was slightly smaller than the first. "Power pack," Stoll said. "Never know when you're going to have to rev up in the wilderness." He grinned. "Or on a laboratory table."

"Rev up . . . what?" Lang asked as he watched attentively.

"In a peanut shell," Stoll said, "what we call our T-Bird. It directs a fast laser pulse at a solid-state device, generating laser pulses. These pulses only last—oh, about one hundred femtoseconds, which is a tenth of a trillionth of a second." He pressed a square, red button on the back of the power pack. "What you get are terahertz oscillations that wriggle around between the infrared and radio wave area of the spectrum. What *that* gives you is the ability to tell what's inside or behind something thin—paper, wood, plastic, almost anything. All you have to do is interpret the change in the waveforms to tell what's on the other side. And coupled with this baby"—he patted the imaging device—"you actually get to see what's inside."

"Like an X-ray," Lang said.

"Only without the X's," said Stoll. "You can also

use it to determine the chemical composition of objects—for example, the fat in a slice of ham. And it's much more portable.'' Stoll walked over to Lang and held out his hand. "Could I borrow your wallet?" he asked.

Lang reached into the breast pocket of his jacket and handed his wallet to the scientist. Stoll placed it on the opposite side of the desk. Then he went over and pressed a green button beside the white button.

The silver box hummed for a moment, and then the fax-like device began to scroll out a piece of paper.

"Pretty quiet," Stoll said. "I was able to do this in your lab without the technician next to me hearing it."

When the paper stopped moving, Stoll retrieved it and took a quick look at it. He handed it to Lang.

"Is that your wife and kids?" Stoll asked.

Lang looked down at the slightly fuzzy black-and-white image of his family. "Remarkable," he said. "This is quite amazing."

"Imagine what you'd get if you ran the picture through a computer," Stoll said. "Cleaned up the rough edges and brought out the details."

"When our lab first developed this technology," Hood said, "we were trying to find out how to tell what kinds of gases and liquids were inside bombs. That way, we could neutralize them without getting near them. The problem was, we had to have a receiver on the other side of the object to analyze the T-rays as they came out. Then our R&D team figured out how to analyze them at the source. That's what made the T-Bird work as a surveillance tool."

Lang said, "What's the effective range?"

"The moon," he said. "At least, that's as far as we've tested it. Looked inside the Apollo 11 lander. Armstrong and Aldrin were pretty tidy guys. Theoretically, it should work as far as the laser can travel.''

"My God," Lang said. "This is beautiful."

Hood had been standing off to a corner, and came closer now. "The T-Bird is going to be a vital component of the Regional Op-Center," said Hood. "But we need to make it more compact and also refine it to work with greater resolution so operatives can carry it in the field. We also need to be able to filter out extraneous images—for example, girders inside walls."

"That's where your smaller chips come in," said Stoll. "We want it so that a guy can stand outside an embassy and read the mail inside."

"It amounts to a technology swap," Hood continued. "You get what we have in that box . . . we get your chip."

Lang said, "It's amazing. Is there anything the T-Bird cannot see through?"

"Metal's the big thing," said Stoll, "but we're working on the problem."

"Amazing," Lang repeated as he continued to stare at the photograph.

"And the best thing?" Stoll said. "Until we iron out our problems, think of the money we can make selling foil-lined wallets."

TWENTY

Thursday, 8:47 A.M., Washington, D.C.

"You're a seriously flawed piece of work."

Martha Mackall's bitter pronouncement hung in the air for several seconds before Mike Rodgers responded. He stopped a few steps from the doorway. When he spoke, he was temperate. Much as he hated the fact, people couldn't respond to each other simply as people. Martha was more than his equal in an in-your-face confrontation. But a white male who went toe-to-toe with a black woman was begging for legal woes. That pendulum swing was the inevitable, even necessary, but infuriating legacy of creatures like WHOA.

"I'm very sorry you feel that way," Rodgers said. "And for what it's worth, I'm also sorry I upset the Senator."

"Frankly," Martha said, "it's not worth a whole hell of a lot. You used the death of her daughter to mess her up, and then you called her an enemy. Now you've got the chutzpah to say you're *very* sorry?"

"That's right," he said. "Only it's not chutzpah, Martha, it's regret. I'm sorry this had to be."

"Are you really?" she asked.

Rodgers started to go, but Martha jumped up. She stepped between him and the door, drew herself up, and came toward him until her face was less than a foot from his.

"Tell me, Mike," she said, "would you have pulled the same kind of stunt with Jack Chan or Jed Lee or any of the male senators we deal with? Would you have been that cold with them?"

The woman's tone made Rodgers feel as if he were on trial. He wanted to tell her where to go, but he settled for, "Probably not."

"You're damn right 'probably not,' " Martha said. "The old boys' club looks after its members."

"It isn't that," Rodgers said. "I would have treated Senators Chan and Lee differently because they wouldn't have tried to cut me off at the knees."

"Oh, then you think this was against *you*? The Senator's after our fat because she has it in for Mike Rodgers?"

"Partly," said Rodgers. "Not because of my gender or me personally, but because I believe that as the only remaining superpower the U.S. has a responsibility to intervene where and whenever necessary. And Op-Center is a crucial, quick-strike part of that. Martha, do you really think I was standing here promoting me?"

"Yeah," she said, "I do. That's sure what it sounded like."

"I wasn't," he said. "I was promoting us. You, me, Paul, Ann, Liz, the spirit of Charlie Squires. I was defending Op-Center and Striker. How much money, how many lives, would a new Korean war have cost? Or an arms race with a new Soviet Union? What we've done here has saved the nation billions of dollars."

While he spoke, he noticed Martha ease off slightly. Very slightly.

"So why didn't you talk to her like you're talking to me?" she asked.

"Because I was presented with a fait accompli," Rodgers said. "She'd've used my arguments for batting practice."

"I've seen you take worse from Paul," she said.

"I'm his subordinate."

"And isn't Op-Center subordinate to Senators Fox, Chan, Lee, and the other members of the Congressional Intelligence Oversight Committee?"

"To a degree," Rodgers admitted. "But the operative word there is *committee*. Senators Chan and Lee aren't uncompromising isolationists. They would've talked to Paul or me about the cuts, given us a chance to discuss them."

Martha raised a fist cheek-high and shook it. "Let's hear it for the smoke-filled rooms."

"Things got done in there."

"By men," Martha said. "God forbid a woman should make a decision and ask a man to implement it. If she does, you turn around and slug her."

"As hard as she slugged me," Rodgers said. "You think I'm a piece of work? Who's the one asking for equality *some* of the time?"

Martha said nothing.

Rodgers looked down. "I think this has gotten way out of hand. We have other problems. Some jerks are about to go on-line with video games about whites lynching blacks. I'm meeting with Darrell and Liz later to see if we can derail them. I'd like your input."

Martha nodded.

Rodgers looked at her. He felt like hell. "Listen," he said, "I don't like when anyone gets a bunker mentality. Especially me. I guess it comes with the territory. Army looks after Army, Marines after Marines—"

"Women after women," Martha said softly.

Rodgers smiled. "Touché. I guess, at heart, we're all still territorial carnivores."

"That's one way to spin-doctor it," she replied.

"Then here's another," Rodgers said, " 'I shall be an autocrat: that's my trade. And the good Lord will forgive me: that's his.' A woman said that. Catherine the Great. Well, Martha, sometimes I can be an autocrat. And when I am, I can only hope that you'll forgive me."

Martha's eyes narrowed. She looked as if she wanted to stay angry, but couldn't.

"Touché right back." She grinned.

Rodgers smiled again, then looked at his watch. "I've got to make a call. Why don't you check with Liz and Darrell to get up to speed, and I'll see you later."

Martha relaxed at the shoulders and stepped aside.

"Mike?" she said as he passed.

He stopped. "Yes?"

"That was still a pretty hard blow you gave the Senator," she said. "Do me a favor and call her later, just to make sure she's okay."

"I plan to," Rodgers said as he opened the door. "I, too, can be forgiving."

TWENTY-ONE

Thursday, 2:55 P.M., Hamburg, Germany

Bob Herbert spent a frustrating hour-plus on the phone.

Sitting in his wheelchair and using his private line, Herbert spent part of the time talking with his assistant at Op-Center, Alberto Grimotes. Alberto was fresh out of Johns Hopkins, a clever Ph.D. psychologist with good ideas. He was still very young and without a great deal of life experience, but he was a hard worker whom Herbert regarded as a kid brother.

Question one, Herbert said, was trying to figure out which of their intelligence allies they could tap for up-to-the-minute information about German terrorists. The men suspected that the Israelis, the British, and the Poles would be the only ones who followed those groups closely. No other nations had quite the same visceral, enduring fear of the Germans.

Herbert held on while Alberto checked their HU-MINT, Human Intelligence, database. This information from agents in the field was contained in what Herbert referred to as Op-Center's "pelt," the FUR file—Foreign Undercover Resources.

Herbert was always ashamed to go begging for intelligence scraps, but his own resources in Germany were slim. Before West and East Germany reunited, the U.S. was heavily involved with helping West Germany ferret out terrorist groups coming from the East. Since reunification, U.S. intelligence had virtually withdrawn from the country. The German groups were Europe's problem, not America's. With bone-deep budget cuts, the CIA, the National Reconnaissance Office, and other information-gatherers had their hands full trying to stay on top of China, Russia, and the Western Hemisphere.

So much for our crystal balls about the next big trouble spot, Herbert thought bitterly.

Of course, assuming that other governments did have German HUMINT, there was no guarantee that they would even be willing to share their information. Since the well-publicized U.S. intelligence security leaks in the 1980s, other nations were reluctant to tell too much of what they knew. They didn't want their own resources compromised.

"Hub and Shlomo have four and ten people in the field, respectively," Alberto said. He was referring to Commander Hubbard of British intelligence and Uri Shlomo Zohar of the Mossad.

Since this was an unsecured line, Herbert didn't ask for specifics. But he knew that most of Hubbard's agents in Germany were involved with stopping the flow of contraband arms from Russia, while the Israelis were watching the flow of arms to the Arabs.

"It looks like Bog's boys are still cleaning up the Russian mess," Alberto said. That was a reference to General Bogdan Lothe of Polish intelligence and the near-war with Russia. "You want a laugh?" Alberto asked.

"I could use one," Herbert said.

"Looking over this list, the only help I see us getting is from Bernard."

If the situation weren't so serious, Herbert would indeed have laughed. "Help from them?" he said. "It'll never happen. Never."

"It might," Alberto said. "Let me just read this report from Darrell."

Herbert tapped out "Alabamy Bound" on the armrest as he waited.

Bernard was Colonel Bernard Benjamin Ballon of France's Groupe d'Intervention de la Gendarmerie Nationale. Historically, that law-enforcement organization was deaf and blind when it came to hate crimes, especially those committed against Jews and immigrants. The Gendarmerie also had an understanding with the Germans. If French agents stayed out of Germany, Germany wouldn't reveal the names of the thousands upon thousands of collaborators who had helped the Nazis during the War. Some of those men and women were now business and political leaders, and they leaned on French intelligence offices to mind their own business.

In his forties, Ballon himself was one of the most rabid hit-injustice-in-the-balls kind of guys Herbert had ever met. And he was dragging the Gendarmerie, bucking and screaming, out of the muck of its own apathy.

Still, Ballon had a government to answer to. And that government was not fond of the United States. They were in the throes of intense, renewed nationalism, to the extent that they were tossing English words from their vocabulary, American foods off their menus, and Hollywood films off their movie screens. The idea that the French were in a position to help the U.S. was unsettling. The thought that he might have to go to those America-bashers was even more unnerving. The notion that they would even help the U.S. was positively absurd.

Alberto said, "Bernard's got a problem at home and has been looking into a possible connection between hostile elements in France and Germany. He contacted the Big I last month, and they contacted Darrell. Darrell helped Bernard get some information he needed."

"The Big I" was open-line slang for Interpol. Darrell was not only Op-Center's liaison with the FBI, but he interfaced with Interpol and other international anticrime organizations as well.

"What kind of information did Bernard want?" Herbert asked. He was still drumming on the armrest. He really, really didn't want to go to the French.

"That data is not in the file," Alberto said. "It's eyes only. I'll have to go to Darrell for it."

"Do," Herbert said, "and call me as soon as you have something."

"Okay," Alberto said. "Is there a secure line you can get to?"

"I won't have time for that," Herbert said. "You'll have to take a chance and call me on the chair. Also, brief General Rodgers."

"Of course. And since he's going to ask, where do I tell him you'll be?"

Herbert said, "Tell him I'm going to check out a few Chaos theories."

"Ah," said Alberto, "it's that time of the year, isn't it?"

"Right," Herbert said. "The annual diseased maniacs' convention. Which brings me to question number two. Have you got anything there on where the hub of these Chaos Days activities usually is?"

"Like a hospitality suite?" Alberto said.

"Not funny," Herbert said.

"Sorry," Alberto said. "Searching."

Herbert could hear the tap of the computer keys.

"Yes," Alberto said. "For the past two years, many conventioneers have kicked off events with a six P.M. toast at the Beer-Hall in Hanover."

"Why am I not surprised," Herbert said. Munich's infamous Beer-Hall Putsch of 1923 was when Hitler had made his first, failed attempt at seizing power in Germany. Only where Hitler failed, these men obviously intended to succeed.

The second half of Herbert's time on the telephone was spent tracking down an automobile with hand-operated gas and brake pedals. Several companies hired handicapped-accessible cars with drivers, but Herbert didn't want that. He intended to look for intelligence in the heart of the Chaos Days celebration, and didn't want to put a driver at risk.

He finally found a rental company which had a car, and even though it didn't have bulletproof glass and an ejection seat—he was just joking, he assured the humorless rental agent—they brought it to his hotel. Deciding to dress down, he took off his white shirt and tie and pulled on the *My Name is Herbert . . . Bob Herbert* sweatshirt his sister had given him. Then he donned his blazer and headed downstairs. With the help of the doorman, he put his wheelchair fully open in a special well in the seatless back. Then, with a map open on the passenger's seat, his detachable wheelchair phone beside it, and Matt Stoll's electronic translator beside that, Herbert took his new Mercedes on the road.

It was ironic, he thought—sad and ironic—that a man with restricted mobility represented the sum total of American HUMINT in Germany. On the other hand, he was a man with experience, desire, and a solid organization behind him. People had gone into the field with less than that. Much less. And though he didn't exactly expect to be inconspicuous, he subscribed to the intelligence dictum "Never underestimate what somebody might know; and never underestimate what someone might say if he's careless, stupid, or drunk." At the Beer-Hall he was likely to find a healthy dose of all of the above.

More than savoring the independence, he was thrilled to be back in action. Now he knew just how Mike Rodgers must have felt getting back in the saddle in Korea.

The drive from the hotel took under two hours. It was a straight ride down the north-south-running A1 Autobahn, where there was only a recommended speed limit, 100 to 130 km/h, though anyone going under 130 was considered a *grafin,* a countess—slow, stately, and matronly.

Herbert clipped along at nearly ninety miles an hour. He rolled down the front windows and felt the refreshing fury of the wind. Even at that speed, however, he missed none of the beautiful, green countryside of Lower Saxony. It was depressing to think that the intoxicating forests and centuries-old villages were the home of one of the most virulent hate movements in the history of civilization.

But that's Paradise for you, he knew. *Always a snake or two in every tree.*

He had felt differently about people and beauty when he first arrived in Lebanon with his wife. A gorgeous blue sky, ancient buildings ranging from the humble to the magnificent, devout Christians and Moslems. The French had withdrawn in 1946, and the religious "brothers" waged vicious war against one another. U.S. Marines helped put out the fire in 1958, but it erupted anew in 1970. Eventually, the U.S. returned. The skies were still blue and the buildings still awe-inspiring when a Moslem suicide-bomber attacked the American Embassy in Beirut in 1983. Fifty people died, and many more were injured. Since that time, beauty had never looked innocent or even especially appealing to Herbert. Even life itself, once so rich and full of promise, was more like marking time until he and his wife could be re-united.

Hanover was a remarkable contrast to the country-side—and to itself. Like Hamburg, it had been heavily damaged by bombing during World War II. Plunked be-tween the modern buildings and wide thoroughfares were pockets of sixteenth-century architecture, timbered homes beside narrow roads and old, Baroque gardens. It wasn't Herbert's cup of cocoa: he preferred the pure country in which he'd grown up. Ponds, gnats, frogs, and corner drugstores. But as he drove through the streets, he was surprised by these two strikingly different faces of Hanover.

Which is fitting, Herbert thought as he made his way to Rathenauplatz. *This city is a place with two very dif-ferent human faces as well.*

Ironically, the quaint section of the city was where most of the cafés and restaurants were located. The charm hid the vipers. He got there simply by noticing and following three skinheads on motorcycles. He didn't for a moment imagine that they were going to the Spren-gel Museum of modern art.

The drive took ten minutes. When he arrived, there was no mistaking the Beer-Hall. It was located in the middle of a row of coffeehouses and bars, most of which were closed. The tavern had a white brick facade and a simple sign with its name. The block letters were black and the background was red.

"Of course they are," Herbert muttered as he drove by. Those were the colors of Nazi Germany. Though displaying swastikas was illegal in Germany, these people had invoked the likeness without breaking the law. Indeed, as Hausen had mentioned during lunch, while neo-Nazism itself was illegal, these groups got around the ban by calling themselves every euphemism they could think of, from the Sons of the Wolf to the 21st Century National Socialists.

But if the Beer-Hall wasn't a surprise, the people gathered in front of it were.

The ten round picnic-style tables in front failed to contain the group, whose numbers grew even as Herbert watched. Nearly three hundred mostly young men were standing or sitting on the sidewalk, curb, or street, or were leaning against cars whose owners had failed to get them out in time and wouldn't be able to retrieve them until after these three days were over. The few pedestrians who were out moved quickly through the crowd. Ahead, four police officers were directing traffic. Cars maneuvered carefully around the crowds milling and drinking on the curb outside the Beer-Hall.

Herbert had expected an army of skinheads and brownshirts—shaved heads and tattoos, or crisply pressed pseudo-Nazi uniforms with armbands. There was a smattering of punks in pockets of ten here and half a dozen there. But most of the men and the few women he saw were dressed in casual designer clothes with fashionable if slightly conservative hairstyles. They were laughing and at ease, looking very much like young stockbrokers or attorneys who had come to Hanover for a convention. The scene was frightening in its ordinariness. This *could* be Herbert's beloved hometown.

With his trained eye, Herbert divided the tapestry into manageable fragments and then swallowed each image whole, rather than examining individuals. Later, if need be, he could pick out important details from memory.

As he inched by, Herbert also listened through the open window. He wasn't fluent in German, but he picked up enough to understand. These people were talking about politicians, computers, and *cooking,* for Chrissakes. It wasn't the way he'd imagined it would be, young men singing old German drinking songs. No wonder the authorities kept their distance from Chaos Days. If they cracked down here, they might have to lock up some of the nation's leading doctors, attorneys, stockbrokers, journalists, diplomats, or God knows who else. And God help them all if these people were ever motivated to move against the government. They weren't strong enough or united enough yet. But if they were, German rule could quickly unravel and be rewoven into a tapestry which the world would have every reason to fear.

His bowels tightened. Part of him screamed inside, *They have no right, the young bastards.* But another part of him knew that they had every right. Ironically, the defeat of Hitler had given them the right to say or do a great deal, as long as there was no racial or religious incitement or public denial of the Holocaust.

Toward the end of the street, there was a registration table with a half-dozen men and women behind it. The crowd waiting at the table was swelling, no one pushing, no one complaining, nothing to disrupt the general air of fellowship. Herbert slowed and watched as the organizers took money and passed out itineraries and sold black-and-red bumper stickers and lapel pins.

They've got a goddamn cottage industry going here, Herbert thought, amazed. All of it subtle, venomous, and legal. That was the problem, of course. Unlike the skinheads, who were considered low-caste neo-Nazis and spurned by people like these, the men and the few women here were smart enough to stay within the law. And when there was enough of them to field candidates and vote, Herbert had every confidence that they would change the law. Just as they'd done in March of 1933, when the Enabling Act gave Hitler dictatorial authority over the nation.

One of the hosts, a tall young man with sandy blond hair, stood stiffly behind the table. He shook the hand of each newcomer. He seemed less comfortable with the few grubbier skinheads than he did with the clean-cut men.

Even among the vermin there are castes, Herbert noted. He was intrigued as one of the scruffier new arrivals followed the handshake by throwing his arm in a traditional Nazi salute. It was an isolated, nostalgic gesture. The other men seemed uncomfortable with it. It was as though a drunk had come to the cash bar at a social function. They tolerated the salute but did not acknowledge it. Obviously there were schisms in the new Reich just as there had been in the old. Rifts which could be manipulated by outside forces.

Cars were piling up behind Herbert. Releasing the hand brake, he pressed his palm hard on the gas pedal and ripped down the street. He was angry: angry at these slick monsters, heirs to war and genocide, and angry at the system which allowed them to exist.

As Herbert rounded the corner, he saw that the side

streets were closed for parking. He was glad there was
no one here with a baton to direct traffic. That would
have been too much, like a goddamn country fair.

Turning down one of the streets, he found a place to
park. Then he pressed a button beside the radio. The left
back door opened and the well in which the wheelchair
sat slid to that side. The entire bucket emerged from the
car and deposited the wheelchair on the ground. Herbert
reached back and pulled it over. He also resolved to
make a deal with these people to get cars like this into
the U.S. They really made life a whole lot simpler.

Sliding into the wheelchair, he snuggled himself in
like a top-gunner. Then he pressed a button in the car
door to retract the bucket. When it was back inside, he
shut the car door and began rolling down the street, toward the Beer-Hall.

TWENTY-TWO

Thursday, 3:28 P.M., Toulouse, France

Dominique could feel victory. It had weight, it had presence, and it was near. Very near.

He felt it more strongly now that his New York attorney had phoned to say the NYPD and the FBI had taken the bait. They had arrested the Pure Nation team which Dominique had underwritten for these many, many months. Gurney and his people would bear their arrest and trial like true Nazis: proudly and unafraid. At the same time, they would send the FBI to arms caches and literature and would hand over the man who had raped the lesbians in Chicago. And the FBI would crow about its victories.

Its victories. Dominique grinned. *Their scavenger hunt.* A hunt which would eat up time and personnel and lead the crack law officers in the wrong direction.

It was astonishing to Dominique how easy it had been to dupe the FBI. They had sent an infiltrator. They always did. He was let in with other members. But because the agency infiltrator, John Wooley, was in his late twenties with no prior organization membership, two Pure Nation members had gone to California to visit the ''mother'' to whom he was writing. Although the FBI had rented a home for her and provided her with a cover, she made two or three calls a day from pay phones inside the local grocery store. Hidden video camera coverage of the phone numbers showed that the calls were made to the Phoenix bureau of the FBI. Pure Nation leader Ric Myers suspected that Mrs. Wooley was probably a veteran agent herself. The Pure Nationals let Wooley remain in the group so they could feed the FBI false information.

At this same time, Dominique had been looking for American neo-Nazis to carry out his work. Jean-Michel had found Pure Nation, and Wooley's presence fit in perfectly with Dominique's plans.

Mrs. Wooley and her "son" will be dealt with in time, Dominque reflected. In just a few weeks, when the United States was thrown into chaos, the Wooleys would become the first victims. The elderly woman would be raped and blinded in her rented home, and the infiltrator would be castrated and left alive, a deterrent to other would-be heroes.

Dominique stood looking through the one-way mirror in a conference room which adjoined his office, a room which looked down into his underground factory. Below him, in a facility which had been used to manufacture armor and weapons during the thirteenth-century Albigensian Crusade, workers were assembling video-game cartridges and pressing CD-ROM games. In a separate area, toward the well-insulated river side of the cellar, technicians were downloading samples of the games to outlets the world over. Consumers would be able to order the game in any format.

Most of the games he manufactured at *Demain* were mainstream entertainment. The graphics, sound, and gameplay were of such a high caliber that since 1980, when he made his first game, A Knight to Remember,

Demain had become one of the most successful software companies in the world.

The other games, however, were much, much closer to Dominique's heart. And they were the real future of his organization. Indeed, they were one of the keys to the future of the world.

My world, he thought. A world he would rule from the shadows.

Stripsy the Gypsy was the first of his important new games. It had been released nine months before and it was about a Gypsy woman of low morals. The object of gameplay was to beat information from villagers, locate the slut, then find articles of clothing she had scattered around the countryside. *Demain* had sold ten thousand copies worldwide. All of those sales came through mail order, from a Mexican address where authorities had been bribed and wouldn't touch his operation regardless of what kind of games he sold. It had been posted on the web and advertised in white supremacist magazines.

Stripsy the Gypsy was followed by the Ghetto Blasters, set in World War II Warsaw; Cripple Creek, a place to which the handicapped had to be led and drowned; Reorientation, a graphics game in which Asian faces had to be made Occidental; and Fruit Shoot, in which players were required to gun down gay men as they marched in a parade.

But his favorites were the newest ones. Concentration Camp and Hangin' with the Crowd were more sophisticated than the others. Concentration Camp was devilishly educational, and Hangin' with the Crowd allowed players to insert their own faces on the men and women who were hunting down blacks. Hangin' with the Crowd had already been previewed on-line in the United States, and record numbers of orders were being received for the game itself. Concentration Camp was about to be previewed in France, Poland, and Germany—at one very special place in Germany.

These games would help to spread the message of intolerance, but they were just the beginning. Four weeks after the release of these games, Dominique would undertake his most ambitious game project. It would be the culmination of his life's work and it would begin with a game sent free to on-line users. It would be called R.I.O.T.S.—Revenge Is Only The Start—and it would help to precipitate a crisis the likes of which America had anticipated only in its worst nightmares. And while America was distracted, and Germany wrestled with its own surging neo-Nazis, Dominique and his partners would expand their business empires.

Expand? he thought. *No. Seize what should always have been ours.*

In the 1980s, when President Mitterand needed to generate income for the government, many French businesses had been socialized. During the 1990s, those businesses began to collapse due to the costly burdens of health care, retirement packages, and catering to French citizens who were accustomed to being cared for from cradle to grave. The failing companies dragged numerous banks with them, all of which had helped to raise unemployment in France to a staggering 11.5 percent in 1995 and 15 percent now—twice that among well-educated professionals. And while that happened, the National Assembly did nothing. Nothing except to put its rubber stamp on whatever the President and his elite advisors wished.

Dominique would begin to change things by purchasing many of those companies and privatizing them.

Some employee benefits would be phased out, but the
unemployed would have jobs and the employed would
have security. He also planned to gain controlling interest in a French bank. *Demain* money would help prop
the bank up, and its international offices would enable
him to invest in countless operations abroad. Funds
could be moved around, taxes avoided, and currencies
traded favorably. He already had acquisition deals pend-
ing with a British movie studio, a Chinese cigarette
maker, a Canadian pharmaceuticals firm, and a German
insurance company. In foreign countries, having control
of important businesses was tantamount to having your
foot on the throat of the government.

Individuals and small corporations couldn't maneuver
like that, but international conglomerates could. As his
father once told him, *"Turning one hundred thousand
francs into a million francs isn't easy. But turning a
hundred million francs into two hundred million francs
is inevitable."*

What Japan had tried and failed to accomplish in the
1980s, to become the dominant world economy, France
would achieve in the twenty-first century. And Dominique would be the regent behind the throne.

"Germany," he muttered with contempt. They'd
started out in history as a conquered people, beaten by
Julius Caesar in 55 B.C. They'd had to be rescued by
Charlemagne, a Frank.

Dominique had already signed a French singer to record something he had written just a few weeks before,
"The Hitla Rap." With a goose-stepping tarantella beat,
it exposed the German people to be just what they were,
a nation of humorless boors. When he had achieved his
goals for France, Dominique had every intention of putting the Huns in their place—though he couldn't resist

the little head start he planned for Hausen.

Henri had phoned to report on his successful mission. The fire was all over the news there. Half an historic block had burned in St. Pauli before firefighters got it under control. That was good, though Dominique was curious what the lofty Herr Richter might do in response. Would he kill Jean-Michel en route to tonight's rally? Attack a *Demain* products distributor in Germany? He doubted it. That would raise the stakes to a dangerous height, nor would either act hurt Dominique very much at all. Would Richter capitulate and toe the line? He doubted that too. Richter was too proud to bend entirely. Might he tell the press about Dominique's secret activities? That was unlikely. Richter didn't know enough about them, and who would believe Richter in any event? He was a neo-Nazi purveyor of sex. In any case, nothing could be traced to Dominique.

But Richter *would* do something. He had to. Honor demanded it.

Turning from the window, Dominique made his way back to his office. Speculation was always fun, but ultimately it was pointless. There was only one thing Dominique knew for sure: he was glad to be in his position and not Richter's.

TWENTY-THREE

Thursday, 3:23 P.M., The Leine River, Germany

As she cleared a patch of trees and looked ahead, Karin Doring allowed herself a very rare smile.

The camp was one of the most beautiful sights she had ever seen. The spot on the Leine River had been bought by Manfred's family over a decade before. It was twenty acres of sweet-smelling woodland, with the river to the east and a high hill to the west, directly behind them. A deep gorge protected them to the north, and the trees provided cover from spying eyes in the air. The camp her followers had erected was a series of tents arranged in four rows of five, with two people in each tent. The tops were covered with foliage so they couldn't be seen from the air when the authorities went looking for the stolen movie prop van. The cars and vehicles which had brought them here were parked in rows to the south and were also camouflaged.

The nearest town of any size was Garbsen, which was nearly twenty miles to the south. The ground search for the terrorists who attacked the film set would start there and move toward Hanover, the seat of Chaos Days activities. That was well southeast of them. The authorities would not look for them here, in the middle of this Grimm Brothers fairyland. They couldn't spare the manpower. Not for three days, and by the end of Chaos Days Karin and her followers would be gone. Even if the police did conclude that the assault was her handiwork, and even if they did manage to find her camp, they would never take her and her followers. Sentries would warn her and attack dogs would delay the police while the mementoes were dropped into the lake or burned. A sad but necessary precaution, for there must be no evidence to tie them to the attack.

Let them try to catch us, she thought defiantly. And if it became necessary, they would fight to the last soldier. The German government could pass its apologetic laws, deny its past, kowtow to the United States and the rest of Europe. She and her followers would not bow. And in time, the rest of Germany would embrace the heritage she had helped to preserve.

The forty members of *Feuer* who had come here were among Karin's most devoted followers. Cheers rose from those nearest the perimeter as the van pulled up. By the time Rolf had parked beside the line of cars to the south, her *Feuermenschen,* her ''Firemen,'' as she called them, had arranged themselves in a semicircle before the van. They raised their right arms diagonally, held their fists thumbside up, and shouted over and over, *''Sieger Feuer!''* ''Conqueror Fire!''

Karin said nothing as she emerged. She walked to the back of the van, pulled open the door, and grabbed a steel helmet. There were hints of rust, and the black leather chinstrap was brittle and cracked. But the red, white and black, white shield on the right side and the silver-white *Werhrmachtadler,* an eagle and swastika on a black shield on the left, were vivid and clean.

Karin held the helmet in her open hands and stretched it before her, face high, as though she were crowning a king.

"Warriors of the cause," she said, "today we have enjoyed a great victory. These trappings of the Reich have been snatched from the curio-seekers and professors and resigned warriors. They are once again in the hands of fighters. They are once again in the hands of patriots."

The Firemen cried *"Sieger Feuer!"* in unison, and Karin handed the helmet to the young man nearest her. He kissed it, trembling, and held out his hand for more as Karin handed the relics to her followers. She kept an SA dagger for herself.

"Keep them safely," she said. "Tonight they will be reactivated. Tonight they will once again be the tools of war."

As she handed out the items, assisted by Rolf, Manfred walked from around the cab.

"There's a phone call for you," he said.

She looked at him as if to say, *"Who?"*

"Felix Richter," Manfred told her.

Karin's expression didn't change. It rarely did. But she was surprised. She didn't expect to speak with him tonight at the rally in Hanover, much less talk to him before then.

She handed Manfred the rifle she was holding. Without a word, she made her way to the driver's side of the van, climbed in, and shut the door. Manfred had left the phone on the seat. She picked it up and hesitated.

Karin disliked Richter. It wasn't just the old rivalry which made her feel that way—his political movement versus her military movement. Both were different means to the same goal, the realization of the dream that had been launched when Hitler was named Chancellor of Germany in 1933: the establishment of an Aryan world. Both knew that this could only come about through formidable nationalism followed by an economic blitzkrieg against foreign investments and culture. Both knew that these goals would take more organization and diversity than each now possessed.

What troubled her about Richter was that she had never been convinced of his devotion to Nazism. He seemed to be more interested in making Felix Richter a dictator of anything, it didn't matter what. Unlike Karin, who wanted Germany more than she wanted life itself, she always felt that he could be content ruling Myanmar or Uganda or Iraq.

She killed the mute button. "Good afternoon, Felix."

"Karin, good afternoon. Have you heard?"

"About what?"

"Then you haven't or you wouldn't ask. We've been attacked. Germany has. The movement."

"What are you talking about? By whom?"

"The French," said Richter.

The word alone was enough to blacken her day. Her grandfather had been an *Oberfeldarzt,* a lieutenant colonel in the medical troops in Occupied France. He was killed by a Frenchman while caring for German soldiers wounded during the fall of St. Sauveur. Growing up, she would lie in bed and listen as her parents and their friends swapped tales of French cowardice, disloyalty, and betrayal of their own country.

"Go on," Karin said.

"This morning," said Richter, "I met with Dominique's emissary to Chaos Days. He demanded that I fold my organization into his. When I refused, my club was destroyed. Burned."

Karin didn't care. The club was for degenerates, and she was happy to see it gone. "Where were you?" she asked.

"I was led out at gunpoint."

Karin watched the parade of her *Feuermenschen* as they made their way through the trees. Each soldier bore a symbol of the Reich. Not a one of them would have run from a Frenchman, gun or no gun.

"Where are you now?" she asked.

"I've just arrived at my apartment. Karin, these people intend to build a network of organizations to serve them. They imagine that we will be just another voice in their chorus."

"Let them imagine that," she said. "The Führer allowed other governments to imagine whatever they wished. Then he forced his will on them."

"How?" Richter asked.

"What do you mean?" she asked. "He did it through his will. Through his armies."

"No," Richter said. "He did it through the public. Don't you see? He tried to overthrow the Bavarian government in the Beer-Hall Putsch in 1923. He hadn't enough support and was arrested. In jail, he wrote *Mein Kampf* and set forth his plan for a new Germany. Within ten years he was in command of the nation. He was the same man saying the same things, but *My Struggle* helped him to win over the masses. Once he controlled them, he controlled the Fatherland. And once he did that, it didn't matter what other nations thought or did."

Karin was confused. "Felix, I don't need a history lesson."

"This is not history," he said, "this is the future. We must control the people and they're here, Karin, now. I have a plan for making tonight an evening history will remember.''

·The woman did not care for Richter. He was a conceited, self-serving fop who had the Führer's arrogance and some of his vision, but very little of his courage.

Or did he? she wondered. Could the fire have changed him?

''All right, Felix,'' she said, ''I'm listening. What do you propose?''

He told her. She listened carefully, her interest high and her respect for him rising slightly.

The glorification of Germany *and* Felix Richter permeated his every thought, his every word. But what he had to say made sense. And though Karin had undertaken every one of her thirty-nine missions with a plan, a result in mind, she had to admit that part of her responded to Richter's impulsive idea. It would be unexpected. Daring. Truly historic.

Karin looked out at the tents, at her warriors, at the artifacts they were carrying. This was what she loved, and it was all she needed. But what Richter had suggested gave her the opportunity to have that *and* strike at the French. The French . . . and the rest of the world.

''All right, Felix,'' she said. ''I agree that we should do this. Come to my camp before the rally and we'll arrange it. Tonight, the French will learn that they can't fight *Feuer* with fire.''

''I like that,'' Richter said. ''I like that very much. But one of them will learn it before then, Karin. Definitely before then.''

Richter hung up. Karin was sitting, listening to the dial tone, as Manfred wandered over. ''Is everything all right?''

"Is it ever?" she asked bitterly. She handed him the phone, which he placed in his windbreaker. Then she got out of the car and resumed the work she really enjoyed, putting arms into the hands of her followers, and fire in their hearts.

TWENTY-FOUR

Thursday, 3:45 P.M., Hamburg, Germany

Hood and Stoll had spent the early afternoon outlining their technical needs and financial parameters to Martin Lang. Later, Lang brought in several of his top technical advisors to find out how much of what Op-Center needed was doable. Hood was pleased, though not surprised, to discover that much of the technology they needed was already on the drawing board. Without an Apollo space program to underwrite research and development work and create the spinoffs, private industry had had to carry the load. These undertakings were costly, but success could mean billions of dollars in profits. The first companies to snare patents for important new technology and software would be the next Apple Computers or Microsoft.

The two sides had been closing in on costs for the Regional Op-Center technology when a loud gong resonated through the factory.

Hood and Stoll both jumped.

Lang placed a hand on Hood's wrist. "I'm sorry," he said, "I should have prepared you. That's our digital bell tower. It chimes at ten o'clock, twelve o'clock, and three o'clock and signals break time."

"Charming," said Hood, his heart racing.

"We feel it has a pleasant Old World feel," Lang said. "To create a sense of fraternity, the bell rings simultaneously in all of our satellite factories throughout Germany. They're linked fiber-optically."

"I see," Stoll said. "So that's your little Quasimodem, the bell-ringer."

Hood frowned deeply at that.

After the meeting and a half-hour ride back to Hamburg proper, Hood, Stoll, and Lang headed three miles northeast to the modern City Nord region. Within the nearly elliptical, encircling *Ubersee Ring* roadway were over twenty public and private administration buildings. These sleek structures housed everything from the Hamburg Electricity Works to international computer firms, as well as shops, restaurants, and a hotel. Every weekday, over twenty thousand people commuted to City Nord to work and to play.

When they arrived, Richard Hausen's neatly groomed young male assistant Reiner showed them right into the Deputy Foreign Minister's office. Stoll took a moment to stare at the framed stereogram hanging on the assistant's wall.

"Orchestra conductors," Stoll said. "Clever. I've never seen this one."

"It's my own design," Reiner said proudly.

Hausen's Hamburg office was located at the top of a complex in the southeastern sector, overlooking the 445-acre Stadtpark. When they entered, the Deputy Foreign Minister was on the phone. While Stoll sat down to have a look at Hausen's computer setup, Lang watching over his shoulder, Hood walked over to the large picture window. In the deep gold light of late afternoon, he could see a swimming pool, sporting areas, an open-air theater, and the famed ornithological facility.

As far as Hood could tell from looking at him, Hausen was once again his strong, outspoken self. Whatever had been bothering him earlier was either taken care of or somehow had been back-burnered.

Hood thought sadly, *If only I could do the same.* In the office, he was able to manage pain. He kept Charlie's death from getting to him because he had to be strong for his staff. He'd felt bad when Rodgers told him about the hate game in Billy Squires's computer, but there had been so much hate back in Los Angeles that it didn't shock him very much anymore.

All of that he could manage, yet the incident in the hotel lobby was still with him. All those fine thoughts about Sharon and Ann Farris and fidelity were just that: thoughts. Bullshit and words.

After just a few weeks, he had accepted Squires's death. Yet after more than twenty years *she* was still with him. He was surprised by the disorientation, the urgency, the near-panic he had felt speaking to the door-man.

God, he thought, how he wanted to despise her. But he couldn't. Now, as over the years, whenever he tried he ended up hating himself. Now as then, he felt that somehow he was the one who had screwed up.

Though you'll never know for sure, he told himself. And that was nearly as bad as what had happened. Not knowing *why* it had happened.

He absently ran his hand along the breast pocket of his sports jacket. The pocket with his wallet. The wallet with the tickets. The tickets with the memories.

As he looked out the window at the park, he asked himself, *And what would you have done if it had been her? Asked her, "So. How've you been? Are you happy? Oh, and by the way, hon—why didn't you put a bullet in my heart to finish the job?''*

"It's quite a view, is it not?" Hausen asked.

Hood was caught off guard. He came back to reality hard. "It is a magnificent view. Back home, I don't even have a window."

Hausen smiled. "The work we do is different, Herr Hood," he said. "I need to see the people I serve. I need to see young couples pushing baby carriages. I need to see elderly couples walking hand in hand. I need to see children playing."

"I envy you that," Hood said. "I spend my days looking at computer-generated maps and evaluating the merits of cluster bombs versus other weapon systems."

"Your job is to destroy corruption and tyranny. My arena is—" Hausen stopped, reached up as though plucking an apple from a tree, and pulled a word from the sky. "My arena is the antithesis of that. I try to nurture growth and cooperation."

"Together," Hood said, "we'd've made a helluva Biblical patriarch."

Hausen brightened. "You mean a judge."

Hood looked at him. "Sorry?"

"A judge," he repeated. "I'm sorry. I didn't mean to correct you. But the Bible is a hobby of mine. A passion, really, since I was in a Catholic boarding school. I'm particularly fond of the Old Testament. Are you familiar with the judges?"

Hood had to admit that he was not. He assumed they were like contemporary judges, though he didn't say so. When he was running L.A., he had a plaque on his wall which read, *When in doubt, shut up.* That policy had served him well throughout his career.

"The judges," Hausen said, "were men who rose

from the ranks of the Hebrew tribes to become heroes. They were what you might call spontaneous rulers because they had no ties to previous leaders. But once they took command, they were granted the moral authority to settle any and all disputes.''

Hausen looked out the window again. His mood darkened slightly. Hood found himself seriously intrigued by this man who hated neo-Nazis, knew Hebrew history, and appeared, as the old game-show host Garry Moore might've put it, ''to have a secret.''

''There was a time in my youth, Herr Hood, when I believed that the judge was the ultimate and correct form of leader. I even thought, *'Hitler understood that. He was a judge. Perhaps he had a mandate from God.'* ''

Hood looked at him. ''You felt that Hitler was doing God's work, killing people and waging war?''

''Judges killed many people and waged many wars. You must understand, Herr Hood, Hitler lifted us from defeat in a World War, helped to end a depression, took back lands to which many people felt we were entitled, and attacked peoples whom many Germans detested. Why do you think the neo-Nazi movement is so strong today? Because many Germans still believe that he was right.''

''But you fight these people now,'' Hood said. ''What made you realize that Hitler was wrong?''

Hausen spoke in hard, unhappy halftones. ''I don't wish to appear rude, Herr Hood, but that is something I have never discussed with anyone. Nor would I burden a new friend with it.''

''Why not?'' Hood asked. ''New friends bring new perspectives.''

''Not to this,'' Hausen said emphatically.

Hausen's lids lowered slightly and Hood could tell he

was no longer seeing the park or the people in it. He was somewhere else, somewhere depressing. Hood knew he was wrong. Together, they didn't make a patriarch or a judge. Together, they were a pair of guys haunted by things that had happened to them years before.

"But you are a compassionate man," Hausen said, "and I will share one thought with you."

From behind them, Stoll said, "Hold on, sports fans. What have we here?"

Hood looked back. Hausen put a hand on his shoulder to stop him from going to Stoll.

"It says in James 2:10, 'For whoever keeps the whole law but fails in one point has become guilty of all of it.' " Hausen removed his hand. "I believe in the Bible, but I believe in that above all."

"Gentlemen . . . *meine Herren,*" Stoll said. "Come hither, please."

Hood was more curious than ever about Hausen, but he recognized that familiar something's-wrong urgency in Stoll's voice. And he saw Lang with his hand over his mouth, as if he'd just witnessed a car crash.

Hood gave the stoic Hausen a reassuring pat on the back of the shoulder, then turned and hurried to the computer.

TWENTY-FIVE

Thursday, 9:50 A.M., Washington, D.C.

"I thank you, General. I thank you very sincerely. But the answer is no."

Sitting in his office, leaning back in his chair, Mike Rodgers knew very well that the voice on the other end of the secure telephone was sincere. He also knew that once the owner of that strong voice said something, he seldom retracted it. Brett August had been that way since he was six.

But Rodgers was also sincere—sincere in his desire to land the Colonel for Striker. And Rodgers was not a man who gave up on anything, especially when he knew the subject's weaknesses as well as his strong points.

A ten-year veteran of the Air Force's Special Operations Command, August was a childhood friend of Rodgers who loved airplanes even more than Rodgers loved action movies. On weekends, the two young boys used to bicycle five miles along Route 22 out to Bradley Field in Hartford, Connecticut. Then they'd just sit in an empty field and watch the planes take off and land. They were old enough to remember when prop planes gave way to the jet planes, and Rodgers vividly remembered getting juiced up whenever one of the new 707s would roar overhead. August used to go berserk.

After school each day, the boys would do their homework together, each taking alternate math problems or science questions so they could get done faster. Then they would build model airplanes, taking care that the paint jobs were accurate and that the decals were put in exactly the right place. In fact, the only fistfight they'd ever had was arguing about just where the white star went on the FH-1 Phantom. The box art had it right under the tail assembly, but Rodgers thought that was wrong. After the fight, they limped to the library to find out who was right. Rodgers was. It was halfway between the fin and the wing. August had manfully apologized.

August also idolized the astronauts and followed every glitch and triumph of the U.S. space program. Rodgers didn't think he ever saw August as happy as when Ham, the first U.S. monkey in space, came to Hartford on a public relations visit. As August gazed upon a real space traveler, he was euphoric. Not even when the young man told Rodgers that he'd finally coerced Barb Mathias into bed did he seem so utterly content.

When it came time to serve, Rodgers went into the Army and August went into the Air Force. Both men ended up in Vietnam. While Rodgers did his tours of duty on the ground, August flew reconnaissance missions over the north. On one such flight northwest of Hue, August's plane was shot down and he was taken prisoner. He spent over a year in a POW camp, finally escaping with another man in 1970. He spent three months making his way to the South, before finally being discovered by a Marine patrol.

August was unembittered by his experiences. To the contrary, he was heartened by the courage he had witnessed among American POWs. He returned to the U.S., regained his strength, and went back to Vietnam and organized a spy network searching for other U.S. POWs. He remained undercover for a year after the U.S. withdrawal, then spent three years in the Philippines helping President Ferdinand Marcos battle Moro secessionists. He worked as an Air Force liaison with NASA after that, helping to organize security for spy satellite missions, after which he joined the SOC as a specialist in counterterrorist activities.

Although Rodgers and August had seen one another only intermittently in the post-Vietnam years, each time they talked or got together it was as if no time had passed. One or the other of them would bring the model airplane, the other would bring the paint and glue, and together they would have the time of their lives.

So when Colonel August said he thanked his old friend sincerely, Rodgers believed it. What he didn't accept was the part that included "no."

"Brett," Rodgers said, "look at it this way. Over the past quarter century, you've been out of the country more than you've been in. 'Nam, the Philippines, Cape Canaveral—"

"That's funny, General."

"—now Italy. And at a nowhere-near-state-of-the-art NATO base."

"I'm moving onto the luxurious *Eisenhower* at sixteen hundred hours to parlay with some French and Italian hotdogs. You're lucky you caught me."

"Have I caught you?" Rodgers asked.

"You know what I mean," August replied. "General—"

"Mike, Brett."

"Mike," August said, "I like being over here. The Italians are good people."

"But think of the great times we'll have if you come

back home," Rodgers pressed. "Shit, I'll even tell you the surprise I was saving."

"Unless it's that Revell Messerschmitt Bf 109 model kit we were never able to find, there's nothing you can offer me that—"

"How about Barb Mathias."

There was an ocean-deep silence on the other end.

"I tracked her down," said Rodgers. "She's divorced, no kids, living in Enfield, Connecticut. She sells advertising space for a newspaper and says she'd love to see you again."

"You still know how to stack a deck, General."

"Hell, Brett, at least come back and let's have a face-to-face about this. Or do I have to get someone over there to *order* you to come back?"

"General," Brett said, "it'd be an honor to command a team like Striker. But I'd be landlocked at Quantico most of the time, and that'd drive me crazy. At least now I get to travel around Europe and put my two cents in on various projects."

"Two cents?" Rodgers said. "Brett, you've got a million goddamn bucks in your head and I want that working for me. How often does anyone there even listen to what you have to say?"

"Rarely," August admitted.

"Damn right. You've got a better mind for tactics and strategy than anyone in uniform. You *should* be listened to."

"Maybe," August admitted, "but that's the Air Force. Besides, I'm forty-five years old. I don't know if I can go running around the Diamond Mountains in North Korea shooting down Nodong missiles, or chasing a train through Siberia."

"Horseshit," Rodgers repeated. "I'll bet you can still

do those one-armed pushups you used to practice while we waited for planes at Bradley. Your own little astronaut training program.''

"I can still do 'em," August said, "though not as many as I used to."

"Maybe not, but they're a whole lot more than I can do," Rodgers said. "And they're probably a lot more than the kids of Striker can do." Rodgers leaned forward on his desk. "Brett, come back and let's talk. I need you here. Christ, we haven't worked together since the day we enlisted."

"We built that model of the F-14A Tomcat two years ago."

"You know what I mean. I wouldn't ask if I didn't think we'd be a good fit. Look, you've wanted to have time to write a book about Vietnam. I'll give you the time. You wanted to learn to play the piano. When are you going to do that?"

"Eventually. I'm only forty-five."

Rodgers frowned. "Funny how the age thing cuts both ways for you."

"Isn't it?"

Rodgers drummed his desktop. He only had one more card to play, and he intended to make this one work. "You're also homesick," he said. "You told me so the last time you were here. What if I promise that you won't be landlocked. I've been wanting to send Striker on maneuvers with other special forces teams around the world. Let's do it. We're also working on a Regional Op-Center facility. When that's up and running we'll move you and Striker around. You can spend a month in Italy with all your Italian pals, then in Germany, in Norway—"

"I'm doing that now."

"But for the wrong team," Rodgers said. "Just come back for a few days. Talk to me. Look over the team. You bring the glue, and I'll bring the airplane."

August was quiet.

"All right," he said after a long time, "I'll work out leave with General DiFate. But I'm only coming back to talk and build the kit. No promises."

"No promises," Rodgers agreed.

"And set up the dinner with Barb. You figure out how to get her to Washington."

"Done," said Rodgers.

August thanked him and hung up.

Rodgers sat back. He smiled a big, comfortable smile. After the run-in with Senator Fox and Martha, the General had felt like taking the Striker command job himself. Anything to get out of this building, away from the political bullshit, to do something more than just sit on his ass. The prospect of working with August lifted him up. Rodgers didn't know if he should be glad or ashamed at how easy it was to get in touch with the little boy in him.

The phone beeped.

He decided that as long as he was happy and doing his job, it didn't matter whether he felt five years old or forty-five. Because as he reached for the phone, Rodgers knew that the happiness wouldn't last.

TWENTY-SIX

Thursday, 3:51 P.M., Hanover, Germany

Bob Herbert huffed a little as he wheeled himself away from his car.

Herbert didn't have a motor on his wheelchair, and he never would. If he was ninety and frail, unable to wheel very far, he simply wouldn't go very far. He felt that being unable to walk didn't mean being incapacitated. While he was too old to try to do wheelies, like some of the kids in the rehabilitation center all those years ago, he didn't like the idea of puttering around when he could wheel himself. Liz Gordon once told him that he was using that to flagellate himself because he had lived while his wife had died. But Herbert didn't buy that. He liked moving under his own steam and he loved the endorphin rush he got from turning the millstone weight of the wheels. He had never been one to work out before the 1983 explosion, and this sure beat hell out of the biphetamines they used to take in Lebanon to stay awake in times of crisis. Which in Beirut was all the time.

As he guided himself up the slightly inclined street, Herbert decided against going to the registration desk and trying to sign up. He didn't know a helluva lot about German law, but he guessed he didn't have the right to

harass these people. He did, however, have the right to
go to a bar and order something to drink, which was
what he intended to do. That, plus find out what he could
about the whereabouts of Karin Doring. He didn't expect
to wrest information from anyone, but loose lips really
did sink ships. Outsiders were always amazed at how
much intelligence one picked up simply by eavesdropping.

Of course, he thought, *first you've got to get under
the eaves to catch the drops.* The crowd ahead might try
to stop him. Not because he was in a wheelchair: he
wasn't born that way, he'd earned his disability serving
his country. They'd try to stop him because he wasn't a
German and he wasn't a Nazi. But however much these
hotshots wished it weren't so, Germany was still a free
nation. They'd let him into the Beer-Hall or they'd have
an international incident.

The intelligence chief wheeled himself up the street
behind the Beer-Hall and came at it from the opposite
side. That way, he didn't even have to pass the registration area and see any more stiff-armed salutes.

Herbert turned the corner and rolled toward the Beer-
Hall, toward those two hundred or so men drinking and
singing out front. The men nearest him turned to look
at him. Nudges brought other heads around, a sea of
youthful devils with contemptuous eyes and hard laughs.

"Fellows, look who is here! It is Franklin Roosevelt
and he is searching for Yalta."

*So much for no one making a comment about my dis-
ability,* Herbert thought. Then again, there was always
one clown in every group. It puzzled him, though, that
the man had spoken in English. Then Herbert remembered what was written on his sweatshirt.

Another man raised his beer stein. "Herr Roosevelt,

you are just in time! The new war has begun!''

"Ja," said the first man. "Though this one will end differently.''

Herbert kept wheeling toward them. In order to reach the Beer-Hall, he was going to have to go through these natty Hitler Youths. Less than twenty yards separated him from the nearest men.

Herbert glanced to the left. The police officer was in the middle of the street, some two hundred yards past them. He was looking the other way, working hard to keep the traffic from stopping.

Did he hear what these cretins were saying, Herbert wondered, *or was he also working hard to stay the hell out of whatever happened?*

The men in front of him had been facing in various directions. When Herbert was just five yards away, they turned and faced him. He was two yards away. One yard. Some of them were already drunk, and their body language suggested that many were enjoying their pack mentality. Herbert guessed that only a quarter or so of the faces he saw had the intensity of people with convictions, warped as they were. The rest were the faces of followers. That was something a spy satellite couldn't tell you.

The neo-Nazis didn't move. Herbert rolled to within inches of their loafers and expensive running shoes, then stopped. In standoffs in Lebanon and other trouble spots, Herbert had always taken a low-keyed approach. There was an element of mutual assured destruction when standoffs ended prematurely: storm an airplane and you would get the hijackers but you might also lose some hostages. But no one could hold a hostage or stand in your way forever. If you waited long enough, a compromise could usually be reached.

"Excuse me," Herbert said.

One of the men glanced down at him. "No. This street is closed. It's a private party."

Herbert could smell the alcohol on his breath. He wasn't going to be able to reason with him. He looked at another man. "I've seen other people walking through. Will you excuse me?"

The first man said, "You are correct. You have seen other people walking through. But you are not walking so you may not pass."

Herbert fought the urge to run over this man's foot. All that would have done was bring a sea of steins and fists raining down on him.

"I don't want problems," Herbert said. "I'm just thirsty and I'd like to get a drink."

Several men laughed. Herbert felt like Deputy Chester Goode trying to enforce the law with Marshal Dillon out of town.

A man with a beer stein shouldered through the wall of men. He stood in front of them and held the beer straight out, over Herbert's head.

"You're thirsty?" the man said. "Would you like some of my beer?"

"Thanks," Herbert said, "but I don't drink alcoholic beverages."

"Then you are *not* a man!"

"Bravely spoken," Herbert said. He was listening to his own voice and was surprised at how calm it sounded. This guy was a chicken-shit with an army two or three hundred strong behind him. What Herbert really wanted to do was challenge him to a duel, like his daddy once did to someone who'd insulted him back in Mississippi.

The Germans were still looking down at him. The man with the stein was smiling but he wasn't happy.

Herbert could see it in his eyes.

That's because you just realized you don't gain much by pouring it on me, Herbert thought. *You've already said I'm not a man. Attacking me is beneath you.* On the other hand, this man had a beery brashness about him. He might just bring the heavy bottom of the stein down on his head. The Gestapo consider Jews to be subhuman. Yet they used to stop Jewish men on the street and pull out their beards with pliers.

After a moment, the man with the stein brought it to his lips. He took a sip and held it in his cheeks for a moment as though contemplating whether or not to spit. Then he swallowed.

The man stepped next to the wheelchair, on the right side. Then he leaned heavily with one hand on the telephone armrest.

"You were told that this is very private party," the youth said. "You are not invited."

Herbert had had it. He'd come here to reconnoiter, to gather intelligence, to do his job. But these guys had presented him with the "unexpected" which was very much a part of HUMINT operations. Now he had a choice. He could leave, in which case he wouldn't be able to do his job and he would lose all self-respect. Or he could stay, in which case he would probably get beaten all to hell. But he might—*might*—convince some of these punks that the forces which had defied them once were alive and well.

He chose to stay.

Herbert looked into the man's eyes. "Y'know, if I had been invited to your party," he said, "I wouldn't attend. I enjoy socializing with leaders, not followers."

The German continued to lean on the armrest with one hand, holding his stein in the other. But looking into

the German's blue-gray eyes, Herbert could see him de-
flating inside, his hubris leaking away like air hissing
from a balloon.

Herbert knew what was coming. He slipped his right
hand under the armrest.

The only weapon the German had left was his beer.
With a look of contempt, he tipped the stein over and
slowly poured the contents into Herbert's lap.

Herbert took the insult. It was important to show that
he could. When the neo-Nazi was finished and stood to
only scattered applause, Herbert yanked his sawed-off
broom handle from under the armrest. With a turn of
the wrist, he pointed the stick at the neo-Nazi and jabbed
him in the groin. The German cried out, doubled over,
and staggered back against his colleagues. He was still
holding the stein, clutching it reflexively, as though it
were a rabbit's foot.

The crowd yelled and surged forward, threatening to
become a mob. Herbert had seen that happen before,
outside of American embassies abroad, and it was a
frightening thing to behold. It was a microcosm of civilization unraveling, of humans regressing to territorial
carnivores. He began to wheel back. He wanted to get
to a wall, protect his flank, be able to bat at these Philistines like Samson with the jawbone of an ass.

But as he rolled away, he felt a tug on the back of
his wheelchair. He scooted back faster than he was
wheeling.

"Halt!" shouted a raspy voice from behind.

Herbert looked back. A skinny police officer, about
fifty years old, had stopped directing traffic and had run
over. He was standing behind him, holding the grips of
his chair, breathing heavily. His brown eyes were strong,
though the rest of him seemed a little shaky.

People began shouting things from the crowd. The police officer answered them. From the tone of their voices and the few words Herbert picked up, they were telling the officer what Herbert had done, and to mind his own business. And he was telling them that this *was* his business. Keeping the sidewalks orderly, as well as the streets.

He was hooted and threatened.

After the brief exchange, the officer said to Herbert in English, "Do you have an automobile?"

Herbert said that he did.

"Where is it parked?"

Herbert told him.

The police officer continued backing Herbert away. Herbert put his hands on the wheels to stop them from turning.

"Why do I have to leave?" Herbert asked. "I'm the wronged party!"

"Because my job is to maintain peace," the officer said, "and this is the only way I can do it. Our ranks are thin, spread out at rallies in Bonn, Berlin, Hamburg. I'm sorry, *mein Herr,* I don't have time to attend to the case of one man. I am going to take you to your automobile and so that you can leave this area of the city."

"But those bastards attacked *me,*" Herbert said. He realized he was still holding the stick, and replaced it before the police officer thought to take it away. "What if I want to press charges against them, expose the whole damn lot of them?"

"Then you will lose," said the officer. He turned Herbert around, away from the crowd. "They say that man was offering to help you into the Beer-Hall and you struck him—"

"Yeah, right."

"They say that you caused him to spill his beer. At the very least, they wanted you to pay for that."

"And you believe all this?"

"It doesn't matter what I believe," the police officer said. "When I turned, that man was hurt and you were holding a stick. That is what I saw, and that is what I would have put in my report."

"I see," Herbert said. "You saw one middle-aged man in a wheelchair facing two hundred healthy young Nazis and you concluded that I was the bad guy."

"As far as the law is concerned, that is correct," said the police officer.

Herbert heard the words and he understood their context. He heard it enough in the U.S. regarding other criminals, other punks, but they still amazed him. Both men knew that these bastards were lying, yet the group would get away with what they did here. And as long as no one in law enforcement or government wanted to put their own security in danger, they would continue to get away with it.

At least Herbert took some comfort in the fact that he would get away with it too. And giving that pig a poke was almost worth the beer bath he took.

As Herbert was wheeled away, car horns sounded in the traffic tie-up caused by the police officer's departure. They echoed the noise in his own soul, the noise of the anger and determination which filled him. He was leaving, but he resolved to get these goons. Not here and not now, but somewhere else and soon.

One of the men had separated from the crowd. He went into the Beer-Hall, strolled through the kitchen, exited by the back door, and used a trash can to climb the picket fence. He crossed through an alley and emerged on the same street as Herbert and the police officer.

They had already passed, headed toward the side street where Herbert had parked his car.

The young man followed them. As one of Karin Doring's personal lieutenants, he had been instructed to watch anyone who might be watching them. That was something those who were unaligned with any specific faction would not think to do.

He stayed well behind them, watching as the police officer helped Herbert into the car, as he placed the wheelchair in the back, as he stood there making sure that Herbert drove off.

The man pulled a pen and telephone from the inside pocket of his blazer. He described the license tag and the make of Herbert's rented car. When the police officer turned and walked briskly back toward his beat, the young man also turned and went back to the Beer-Hall.

A moment later, a van pulled out of a parking area located three blocks from Bob Herbert.

TWENTY-SEVEN

Thursday, 4:00 P.M., Hamburg, Germany

"What's the problem?" Hood asked as he reached Stoll's side.

Lang was looking pale and uncomfortable and Stoll was working the keys madly.

"Something really sick is going on," Stoll said. "I'll show you in a second—I was running a diagnostics program, trying to figure out how it got here."

Hausen stopped next to Hood. He asked, "How what got here?"

Stoll said, "You'll see. I'm not sure I want to try and describe it."

Hood was beginning to feel a lot like Alice after she went through the looking glass. Every time he turned around, people and events became more and more curious.

Stoll said, "I was checking out your cache memory capacities and I found a file that was put in at one-twelve P.M. today."

"One-twelve?" Hood said. "That's when we were having lunch."

"Right."

Hausen said, "But no one was here, Herr Stoll, except for Reiner."

"I know," Stoll said. "And by the way—he's gone now."

Hausen looked at Stoll strangely. "Gone?"

"Split," said Stoll. He pointed into the reception area. "Soon as I sat down here, he took his shoulder bag and Italian-cut jacket and vamoosed. Your computer's been answering the phones ever since."

Hausen's eyes went from Stoll to the computer. His voice was flat as he asked, "What have you found?"

"For one thing," Stoll said, "Reiner left you a little love letter, which I'll show you in a minute. First, though, I want you to see this."

Stoll's index fingers pecked out commands, and the seventeen-inch screen went from blue to black. White stripes slashed across the screen horizontally. They morphed into strands of barbed wire, then changed again to form the words CONCENTRATION CAMP. Finally, the letters turned red and pooled into blood which filled the screen.

Introductory screens followed. First, there was the principal gate at Auschwitz with the inscription *Arbeit macht frei.*

"Work liberates," Lang said from behind his hand.

Next came a succession of clear, detailed, computer-animated snippets. Crowds of men, women, and children walking through the gate. Men in striped camp uniforms facing a wall while guards whipped them with switches. Men being shorn of their hair. A wedding ring being handed to a member of the SS Death's Head Unit in exchange for shoes. Searchlights in towers piercing the early morning dark as an SS guard roared, *"Arbeitskommandos austreten."*

"Working parties fall out," Lang translated. His hand was trembling now.

Prisoners grabbing shovels and picks. Leaving the main gate and doffing their caps to honor the slogan. Being kicked and punched by the guards. Working on a section of road.

A large party of men threw down their shovels and ran into the darkness. And then the game began. A menu offered the player a selection of languages. Stoll selected English.

An SS guard appeared in close-up and spoke to the player. His face was an animated photograph of Hausen. Behind him was a pastoral setting of trees, rivers, and the corner of a red brick citadel.

"Twenty-five prisoners have escaped into the woods. Your job is to divide your force so that you can find them, at the same time maintaining the productivity of the camp and continuing the processing of the bodies of subhumans."

The game then jumped between vivid scenes of player-controlled guards and dogs hunting men in the forest, and bodies piling up in the crematoria. Stoll ordered the game to play itself, since he said he couldn't bring himself to put the bodies on the pallets for incineration.

"The letter," Hausen said as they watched the program. "What did Reiner's letter say?"

Stoll hit Ctrl/Alt/Delete and killed the game. Then he went back into the computer to retrieve Reiner's letter.

"The guy didn't talk much, did he?" Stoll asked as he jabbed the keys.

"No," said Hausen. "Why do you ask?"

Stoll said, "Because I have no idea what he wrote, but there sure wasn't much of it."

The letter came up and Lang leaned closer. He translated for the Americans.

" 'Herr Savior,' " he said, " 'I hope you enjoy this game, while it is still a game.' And it is signed, 'Reiner.' "

Hood was watching Hausen closely. His back straightened and his mouth turned down. He looked like he wanted to cry.

"Four years," Hausen said. "We were together four years. We fought for human rights in the newspapers, behind megaphones, on television."

"Looks like he was there just to spy on you," Hood said.

Hausen turned from the computer. "I can't believe it," he said sullenly. "I ate with his parents, at their home. He asked what I thought of his fiancée. It can't be."

"Those are exactly the kinds of things moles use to build trust," Hood said.

Hausen looked at him. "But four years!" he said. "Why wait until now?"

"Chaos Days," Lang offered. His hand fell limply to his side. "It was his perverted statement."

"I'd be surprised if that was the case," Hood said.

Lang looked at him. "What do you mean? Isn't it obvious?"

"No," said Hood. "This is a professional-quality game. My guess is that Reiner didn't produce it. He planted it for someone, someone who didn't need him here any longer."

The other three men were shocked as Hausen put his hands on his face and wailed.

"Christ, God," he moaned. His hands came down, became fists, shook tightly at his waist. "Reiner was part of the empire of constituents he was talking about."

Hood faced him. "That *who* was talking about?"

"Dominique," Hausen said. "Gerard Dominique."

"Who is Dominique?" Lang asked. "I don't know that name."

"You don't want to," Hausen said. He shook his head. "Dominique phoned to announce his return. Yet now I wonder if he was ever really gone. I wonder if he wasn't always there in the dark, his soul moldering as he waited."

"Richard, please tell me," Lang implored. "Who is this man?"

"He isn't a man," Hausen said, "he's Belial. The Devil." He shook his head as if to clear it. "Gentlemen, I'm sorry—I can't talk about this now."

"Then don't," Hood said, putting a hand on his shoulder. He looked at Stoll. "Matt, can you download that game to Op-Center?"

Stoll nodded.

"Good. Herr Hausen, do you recognize that photograph of yourself?"

"No, I'm sorry."

"It's okay," Hood said. "Matt, have you got anything in your arsenal to handle this?"

Stoll shook his head. "We need a program with a lot more muscle than my MatchBook. That diskette's only good for finding specific pictures. It's like a word-search."

"I see," Hood said.

"I'll have to run it through our photo file back home and see if we can find where it came from," Stoll told him.

"The scenery behind Herr Hausen is also a photograph," Hood said.

"A clear one too," Stoll said. "Probably not from a

magazine. I can have my office run the Geologue and see what it tells us.''

The Geologue was a detailed satellite relief study of the world. From it, computers could generate an acre-by-acre view of the planet from any angle. It would take a few days, but if the photograph hadn't been tinkered with, the Geologue would tell them where it was taken.

Hood told Stoll to proceed. The Operations Support Officer phoned his assistant, Eddie Medina, to let him know the images were coming.

Hood squeezed Hausen's shoulder. ''Let's go for a walk.''

''Thank you, no,'' Hausen replied.

''*I* need it,'' Hood said. ''This has been a strange morning for me too.''

Hausen managed a small smile. ''All right,'' he said.

''Good. Matt—call me on the cellular if you get something.''

''So let it be written, so let it be done,'' said the unflappable techno-whiz.

''Herr Lang,'' said Hood, ''Matt may need some help with the language.''

''I understand,'' Lang said. ''I'll stay here with him.''

Hood smiled graciously. ''Thanks. We won't be long.''

With his hand still on Hausen's shoulder, Hood and the German walked through the reception area to the elevator.

Hausen was lying, of course. Hood had encountered his kind before. He wanted very much to talk about whatever was bothering him, but his pride and dignity wouldn't allow it.

Hood would wear him down. It was more than a coincidence that what had just happened in the office was similar to what had happened this morning on Billy Squires's computer. And if this was happening simultaneously on two continents, then Op-Center needed to know why.

Fast.

TWENTY-EIGHT

Thursday, 10:02 A.M., Washington, D.C.

After his encouraging chat with Brett August, the morning sped by for Mike Rodgers. Matt Stoll's assistant Eddie briefed him on what was happening in Germany, and told him he'd put in a call for assistance to Bernard Ballon of the *Gendarmarie Nationale*. Ballon was on a mission against terrorists, the New Jacobins, and had not returned the call.

Rodgers was more concerned about Herbert going to check on Chaos activities by himself. Rodgers wasn't worried because Herbert was in a wheelchair. The man was not defenseless. He was worried because Herbert could be like a dog with a bone. He didn't like letting go of things, especially unsolved cases. And there was only so much Op-Center could do to help him. Unlike the U.S., where they could listen in on telecommunications through local FBI, CIA, or police offices, it was difficult to mount broad surveillance immediately overseas. Satellites could focus on individual cellular telephones or even small regions, but they also picked up a lot of garbage. That was what he'd been trying to tell Senator Fox earlier. Without people on the scene, surgical operations were difficult.

Herbert was a good person to have on the scene. Part

of Rodgers worried about what Herbert would do without a moderating force like Paul Hood—though another part of him was excited by the prospect of Bob Herbert unleashed. If anyone could make the case for putting money into a crippled HUMINT program, it was Herbert.

Liz Gordon arrived shortly after Eddie's call. She updated the General on the mental state of the Striker team. Major Shooter had brought his 89th MAU charm—"more accurately," she said, "his lack thereof"—to Quantico and was drilling the squad by the book.

"But this is a good thing," she said. "Lieutenant Colonel Squires tended to mix things up a lot. Shooter's regimentation will help them to accept that things are different now. They're hurting real bad and many of them are punishing themselves by drilling hard."

"Punishing themselves for thinking they failed Charlie?" Rodgers asked.

"That, plus guilt. The Survivor's Syndrome. They're alive, he isn't."

"How do you convince them they did their best?" Rodgers asked.

"You can't. They need time and perspective. It's common in situations like these."

"Common," Rodgers said sadly, "but brand-new to the people who are having to deal with it."

"That too," Liz agreed.

"Practical question," Rodgers said. "Are they fit for service if we need them?"

Liz thought for a moment. "I watched them work out a little this morning. No one's mind wandered, and except for a lot of angry energy they seemed fine. But I have to qualify that. What they were doing this morning were rote, repetitive exercises. I can't guarantee how they'll react under fire.''

"Liz," Rodgers said, slightly annoyed, "those are exactly the guarantees I need.''

"Sorry," she said. "The irony is, I'm not concerned that the Strikers would be afraid to act. To the contrary. I'm worried that they would overact, a classic Guilt Counterreaction Syndrome. They would put themselves at risk to make certain that someone else isn't hurt, to ensure that what happened in Russia doesn't happen again.''

"Is there anyone you're particularly worried about?" Rodgers asked.

Liz said, "Sondra DeVonne and Walter Pupshaw are the shakiest, I think."

Rodgers tapped a finger on the desk. "We've got mission plans for bare-bones, seven-person teams. Do I have seven people, Liz?''

"Probably," Liz said. "You probably have at least that."

"That still doesn't help me.''

"I know," she said, "but right now I just can't give you any assurances. I'm going back this afternoon for individual sessions with several of the Strikers. I'll be able to tell you more then."

Darrell McCaskey knocked and was told to come in. He sat down and opened his power book.

"All right," Rodgers told Liz. "If you're unsure about anyone, give them leave. I'll call Shooter and have him second four or five backup members from Andrews. He can bring them up to speed in several key positions and move them in if he has to."

Liz said, "I wouldn't have him bring them to the base just yet. You don't want to demoralize the people who are struggling to overcome guilt and grief.''

Rodgers loved and respected his Strikers, but he wasn't sure that Liz's way was the best way. Back in the sixties, when he was in Vietnam, no one gave half a damn about sadness and syndromes and God knows what else. Your buddy died in an ambush, you made sure you got your platoon the hell out of there, had a meal, a sleep, and a cry, and were back on patrol the next morning. You might still be weeping, and you were sure as shit a bit more careful or a little angrier or burning to inflict some collateral damage, but you were still out there with your M16, ready to work.

"Fine," Rodgers said sharply. "The backup personnel can drill at Quantico."

"One thing more," Liz said. "It might not be a good idea for me to give anyone leave. A report ascribing AWL to even low-level bereavement like this can be pretty stigmatizing. It would be better," she went on, "if I got Dr. Masur to find something physically wrong with them. Something they can't check themselves, like anemia. Or maybe a bug some of them picked up in Russia."

"Jesus," Rodgers said, "what am I running here, a kindergarten?"

"In a way, that's exactly what you're doing," Liz said testily. "I don't want to get too heavy, but we relate a great deal in our adult lives to losses or hurts we suffered in our childhood. And that's what comes out in times of stress or suffering, the lonely kid in us. Would you send a five-year-old into Russia, Mike? Or Korea?"

Rodgers wiped his eyes with the heels of his hands. First it was coddling, now he was lying and playing games with his own people. But she was the psychologist, not him. And Rodgers wanted to do what was best for his team, not what was best for Mike Rodgers. Frankly, though, if it were up to him he'd spank a five-year-old who didn't do what he was told, and they'd be better for it. But then, that kind of fathering went out with the sixties too.

"Whatever you say, Liz," Rodgers said. He looked at McCaskey. "Tell me something healing, Darrell."

McCaskey said, "Well, the FBI's pretty happy."

"The Baltic Avenue?" Rodgers asked.

McCaskey nodded. "It went off perfectly. They got the Pure Nation group *and* their computer. It's got names, addresses, couple of bank accounts, right-wing subscription lists, weapons caches, and more."

"Like what?" Rodgers asked.

"The big catch was their plans to attack a Chaka Zulu Society meeting in Harlem next week. Ten men were going to take hostages and demand a separate state for black Americans."

Liz snorted.

"What's wrong?" Rodgers asked.

"I don't believe it. Groups like Pure Nation aren't political activists. They're rabid racists. They don't demand states for minorities. They erase them."

McCaskey said, "The FBI is aware of that, and they think that Pure Nation is trying to moderate their image to gain acceptance among whites."

"By taking hostages?"

"There was a draft of a press release in the computer," McCaskey said. He accessed a file in the power book and read from the screen. "Part of it said, " 'Seventy-eight percent of white America does not want blacks living among them. Rather than disrupt the white world with dead on both sides, we appeal to that great majority to petition Washington, to echo our demand for a new Africa. A place where white citizens will not be subjected to rap noise, unintelligible language, clown clothes, and sacrilegious portraits of black Jesuses.' " McCaskey looked at Liz. "That still seems pretty rabid to me."

Liz crossed her legs and shook her foot. "I don't know," she said. "There's something not right about it."

"What do you mean?" Rodgers asked.

Liz said, "Hate, by its very nature, is extreme. It's intolerance pushed as far as it can go. It doesn't seek an accommodation with the object of its loathing. Hate seeks its destruction. That press release is just too— fair."

"You call exiling a race of people *fair*?" McCaskey asked.

"No, I don't," she said. "But by the standards of Pure Nation, that's downright decent. That's why I'm not buying it."

"But Liz," said McCaskey, "groups can and do change. Leadership changes, goals change."

She shook her head. "Only the public face changes, and that's a cosmetic alteration. It's so right-thinking people give them a little rope so they can hang the objects of their hate."

"Liz, I agree. But some Pure Nationals do want black people dead. Others simply don't want them around."

"This particular group is thought to have raped and lynched a black girl in 1994. I would say that they more than don't want blacks around."

McCaskey said. "But even in hate groups, policies have to evolve. Or maybe there's been a schism. Groups like these always suffer rifts and breakaway factions.

We're not exactly dealing with the most stable people on the planet."

"You're wrong about that," Liz said. "Some of these people are so stable it's scary."

Rodgers said, "Explain."

"They can stalk a person or a group for months or more with a single-mindedness of purpose that'd shock you. When I was in school, we had a case of a neo-Nazi custodian in a Connecticut public school. He lined all the corridors, both sides, with plastique. Put it in behind the molding while pretending to scrape gum off the floor. He was found out two days before blowing up the school, and later confessed that he had snuck the plastique in a foot a day."

"How many feet were there?" Rodgers asked.

Liz said, "Eight hundred and seventy-two."

Rodgers had not taken sides during the debate, but he had always believed in overestimating an enemy's strength. And whether she was right or not he liked the hard line Liz Gordon was taking against these monsters.

"Assuming you're right, Liz," Rodgers said. "What's behind it? Why would Pure Nation write a press release like that?"

"To jerk us around," she said. "At least, that's what my gut tells me."

"Follow the thread," Rodgers urged.

"Okay. They set up a shop on Christopher Street, which is populated heavily by gay establishments. They targeted a black group for hostage-taking. The FBI busts them up, there's a public trial, and gays and blacks are openly outraged."

"And attention gets focused on hate groups," McCaskey said. "Why on earth would they want that?"

Liz said, "Attention gets focused on *that* hate group."

McCaskey shook his head. "You know the media. You uncover one snake, they'll want to do a white paper on the nest. You find one nest, and they'll go after other nests."

"Okay," Liz said, "you're right about that. So the media shows us other nests. Pure Nation, Whites Only Association, the American Aryan Fraternity. We see a parade of psychos. What happens then?"

"Then," said McCaskey, "the average American gets outraged and the government cracks down on hate groups. End of story."

Liz shook her head. "No, not the end. See, the crackdown doesn't end the groups. They survive, go back underground. What's more, there's backlash. Historically, oppression breeds resistance forces. The aftermath of this aborted Pure Nation attack—if there were, in fact, really going to be one, which we can't be sure of—will be a rise in black militancy, gay militancy, Jewish militancy. Remember the Jewish Defense League's 'Never Again' slogan from the 1960s? Every group will adopt some form of that. And when this widespread polarization threatens the infrastructure, threatens the community, the average white American will get scared. And ironically, the government won't be able to help because they can't crack down on minorities. They come down on blacks, then blacks cry foul. Come down on gays, Jews, the same thing. Come down on *all* of them, and you've got a goddamn war on your hands."

Rodgers said, "So the average American, normally a good and fair person, gets drawn toward the radicals. Pure Nation and WHOA and the rest of them start to look like society's salvation."

"Exactly," said Liz. "What was it that Michigan militia leader said a few years ago? Something like, 'The natural dynamic of revenge and retribution will take its course.' When word gets out about Pure Nation, and what they were planning, that's what's going to happen here.''

"So Pure Nation takes the fall," said Rodgers. "They get hunted, arrested, disbanded, and outlawed. They're the martyrs to the white cause."

"And loving it," Liz said.

McCaskey made a face. "This is like a surreal 'House that Jack Built.' '' He said in a singsong voice, "These are the white supremacists who sent out a group of their own to be caught and sacrificed, to breed minority backlash, which scares the whites, who create a groundswell of support for others in the white supremacist movement." He shook his head vigorously. "I think you're both attributing way too much forethought to these degenerates. They had a plan and it got busted up. End of story."

Rodgers's phone beeped. "I'm not sure I buy all of what Liz is suggesting either," he said to McCaskey, "but it's worth considering."

"Think of the damage Pure Nation could do as decoys," Liz said.

Rodgers felt a chill. They could, in fact, lead the proud, victorious FBI every which way but right. With the media following their every step, the FBI could never even admit that they'd been duped.

He picked up the phone. "Yes?"

Bob Herbert was on the other end.

"Bob," said Rodgers. "Alberto briefed me a few minutes ago. Where are you?"

From the other end of the phone, Herbert said calmly,

"I'm on a road in the middle of the boonies in Germany, and I need something."

"What?"

Herbert replied, "Either a lot of help fast, or a real short prayer."

TWENTY-NINE

Thursday, 4:11 P.M., Hamburg, Germany

Hamburg has a distinctive, very seductive radiance in the late afternoon.

The setting sun sprinkles light across the surface of the two lakes, raising a glow like a thousand phantoms. To Paul Hood, it looked as if someone had turned a bright light on beneath the city. Ahead, the trees in the park and the buildings to the sides were positively iridescent against the deepening blue of the sky.

The air in Hamburg is also different from other cities. It's a curious mix of nature and industry. There's the taste of salt, which is carried from the North Sea by the Elbe; of the fuel and smoke of the countless ships which travel the river; and the countless plants and trees which thrive in the city. It isn't noxious, Hood thought, as in some cities. But it is distinctive.

Hood's reflection on the environment was brief. No sooner had they left the building and began walking toward the park than Hausen began talking.

"What has made this day so strange for you?" Hausen asked.

Hood didn't *really* want to talk about himself. But he hoped that by doing so he could loosen Hausen's tongue a little. Give and take, take and give. It was a waltz familiar to anyone who had lived and worked in Washington. This just happened to be a little more personal and important than most of those other dances.

Hood said, "While Matt, Bob, and I were waiting for you in the hotel lobby, I thought I saw—no, I could have *sworn* I saw a woman I once knew. I ran after her like I was possessed."

"And was it she?" Hausen asked.

"I don't know," Hood said. Just thinking about what had happened made him exasperated all over again. Exasperated that he'd never know if it were Nancy, and exasperated because that woman still had a hold on him. "She got into a cab before I could reach her. But the way she held her head, the way her hair looked and moved—if it wasn't Nancy, it was her daughter."

"Has she one?"

Hood shrugged but said nothing. Whenever he thought about Nancy Jo, he was upset by the thought that she could very well have a child or a husband, could actually have a life away from him.

So why the hell are you dwelling on it again? he asked himself. *Because,* he thought, *you want to get Hausen to talk.*

Hood took a healthy breath and blew it out. His hands were deep in his pockets. His eyes were on the grass. Reluctantly, his mind went back to Los Angeles, nearly twenty years ago.

"I was in love with this girl. Her name was Nancy Jo Bosworth. We'd met in a computer class at USC in our last year of graduate school. She was this delicate and vivacious angel, with hair that was like layers of golden wings." He grinned, flushed. "It's corny, I know, but I don't know how else to describe it. Her hair was soft and full and ethereal and her eyes were life itself. I called her my little golden lady and she called me her big silver knight. Man, was I smitten.''

''Obviously,'' Hausen said

The German smiled for the first time. Hood was glad he was getting through; this was killing him.

''We got engaged after we got out of school,'' Hood continued. ''I gave her an emerald ring that we picked out together. I landed a position as an assistant to the Mayor of Los Angeles and Nancy went to work for a video game company designing software. She actually flew north, to Sunnyvale, twice a week just so we wouldn't have to be away from each other. And then one night, in April of 1979—April 21st, to be exact, a date which I tore out of my datebooks for the next few years—I was waiting for her outside a movie theater and she failed to show. I called her apartment, no one was there, so I rushed over. I drove like a crazy person, in fact. Then I used my key, went in, and found a note.''

Hood's pace slowed. He could still smell the apartment. He could still feel the tears and the thickness that filled his throat. He remembered the song that was playing in the apartment next door, ''The Worst That Could Happen'' by the Brooklyn Bridge.

''The note was handwritten, quickly. Not Nancy's usual careful penmanship. It said that she had to go away, she wouldn't be coming back, and I shouldn't look for her. She took some clothes, but everything else was still there: her records, her books, her plants, her photo albums, her diploma. Everything. Oh, and she took the engagement ring I gave her. Either that or she threw it away.''

''No one else had any idea where she was?'' Hausen asked, surprised.

''No one. Not even the FBI, which came and asked

me about her the next morning without telling me what she had done. I couldn't tell them much, but I hoped they *would* find her. Whatever she had done, I wanted to help. I spent the next few days and nights looking for her. I visited professors we'd had, friends, talked to her coworkers, who were all very concerned. I called her father. They weren't close, and I wasn't surprised that he hadn't heard from her. I finally decided that I must have done something wrong. Either that, or I figured she'd been seeing someone else and eloped.''

"Gott," Hausen said. "And you never heard from her after that?''

Hood shook his head slowly. "I never heard *of* her either,'' he said. "I wanted to, out of curiosity. I didn't try anymore, though, because it would've been excruciating. I have to thank her for one thing, though. I lost myself in work, made a lot of great contacts—we didn't call it networking back then.'' He smiled. "And eventually I ran for and won the office of Mayor. I was the youngest in the history of Los Angeles.''

Hausen looked at Hood's wedding band. "You also married.''

"Yes,'' said Hood. He glanced at the gold ring. "I married. I have a wonderful family, a good life.'' He lowered his hand, rubbed the pocket with his wallet in it. He thought of the tickets which even his wife didn't know about. "But I still think of Nancy now and then, and it's probably a good thing it wasn't her at the hotel.''

"You don't know that it wasn't her,'' Hausen pointed out.

"No, I don't,'' Hood agreed.

"But even if it was,'' said Hausen, "your Nancy belonged to another time. A different Paul Hood. If you saw her again, you would be able to deal with it, I think.''

''Perhaps,'' said Hood, ''though I'm not so sure this Paul Hood is all that different. Nancy was in love with the boy in me, the kid who was adventurous in life and love. Becoming a father and a mayor and a Washingtonian didn't change that. Inside, I'm still a kid who likes to play Risk and gets a kick out of Godzilla movies and who still thinks that Adam West is the only Batman and George Reeves is the only Superman. Somewhere inside, I'm still the young man who saw himself as a knight and Nancy as a lady. I honestly don't know how I'd react if I saw her face-to-face.''

Hood put his hands back in his pockets. He felt the wallet again. And he asked himself, *Who do you think you're fooling?* He knew damn well that if he saw Nancy face-to-face he'd fall for her all over again.

''So that's my story,'' Hood said. He was facing ahead, but his eyes shifted to the left, toward Hausen. ''Now it's your turn,'' he urged. ''Did that phone call back in your office have anything to do with a lost love or mysterious disappearances?''

Hausen walked in dignified silence for a short while, then said solemnly, ''Mysterious disappearances, yes. Love, no. Not at all.'' He stopped and faced Hood. A gentle wind was blowing, stirring the German's hair, lifting the end of his coat. ''Herr Hood, I trust you. The honesty of your pain, your feelings—you are a compassionate man and a truthful one. So I will be honest with you.'' Hausen looked to the left and right, then down. ''I'm probably mad to be telling you this. I've never told anyone. Not even my sister, and not my friends.''

''Do politicians have any friends?'' Hood asked.

Hausen smiled. ''Some do. *I* do. But I wouldn't burden them with this matter. Yet someone has to know now that he has returned. They have to know in the event that anything happens to me.''

Hausen looked at Hood. The agony that came into his eyes was like nothing Hood had ever seen. It shocked him, and his own pain evaporated as his curiosity intensified.

''Twenty-five years ago,'' said Hausen, ''I was a political science student at the Sorbonne in Paris. My best friend was a fellow named Gerard Dupre. Gerard's father was a wealthy industrialist, and Gerard was a radical. I don't know whether it was the immigrants who took jobs from French workers, or simply his own black nature. But Dupre hated Americans and Asians, and he especially hated Jews, blacks, and Catholics. Dear God, he was consumed by hate.'' Hausen licked his lips. He looked down again.

It was clear to Hood that this taciturn man was struggling as much with the process of confession as he was with the memory of whatever it was he had done.

Hausen swallowed and went on. ''We were dining at a café one night—at *L'Exchange* on the Rue Mouffetard on the Left Bank, a short walk from the university. The café was inexpensive, popular with students, and the air there was always heavy with the smell of strong coffee and loud disagreements. It was just after our junior year had begun, and that night everything was annoying Gerard. The waiter was slow, the liquor was warm, the night was chilly, and the collected speeches of Trotsky were only those he gave in Russia. Nothing from Mexico, which Gerard thought was an abominable omission. After paying the bill—he always paid, for he was the only one with money—we went for a walk along the Seine.

"It was dark and we encountered a pair of American students who had just arrived in Paris," Hausen continued with effort. "They had gone to take some pictures by a remote section of riverbank, under a bridge. The sun had set and they couldn't find their way back to the dormitory, so I started to give them directions. But Gerard interrupted and said that he thought Americans knew everything. He was yelling, very angry at the two of them. He said that they came to a country and took over, so how could these two not know where they were going?"

Hood felt his insides tighten. He had a feeling where this was headed.

"The girls thought he was joking," Hausen continued, "and one of them put her hand on Gerard's arm to say something—I don't recall what. But Gerard said how dare she talk down to him and he pushed her away. She stumbled back over her own foot, into the river. The water wasn't deep there, but of course the poor girl didn't know that. She screamed. God, how she screamed. Her friend dropped her camera and ran to help, but Gerard grabbed her. He held her with the inside of his elbow around her neck. She was gasping, the girl in the water was screaming, and I was paralyzed. Nothing like this had ever happened to me before. Finally, I ran to help the girl in the river. She had swallowed water and was coughing. I struggled to get her to stand still, let alone pull her out. Gerard was angry that I tried to help, and while he yelled at me he held the girl very hard. . . ."

Hausen stopped. The anguish in his eyes had spread. His brow was pale now, and his mouth was slack. His hands were trembling. He balled them to make them stop.

Hood took a step toward him. "You don't have to continue—"

"I do," Hausen insisted. "Now that Gerard is back, the story must be told. I may fall, but he must be brought down as well." Hausen rolled his lips together and took a moment to compose himself. "Gerard dropped the girl to the ground," he continued. "She was unconscious. Then he ran to the river, jumped in, and pushed the other girl down. I tried to stop him, but I lost my footing and went under. Gerard held her there"—Hausen was pushing down with his hands—"yelling things about American girls being whores. By the time I got up it was too late. The girl was bobbing in the river, her brown hair floating behind her. Gerard left her, pulled himself from the water, and dragged the other girl in. Then he told me to come away with him. I was in a daze. I fumbled in the dark, picking my things up, and went with him. God help me, without even knowing if the girl he'd choked was dead I left with him."

"And no one saw you?" Hood asked. "No one heard and came to see what was happening?"

"Perhaps they heard, but no one cared. Students were always shouting about something, or screaming because of the rats by the river. Perhaps they thought the girls were making love by the river. The shrieks—it could have been that."

"What did you do after you left?" Hood asked.

"We went to Gerard's father's estate in the south of France and remained there for several weeks. Gerard asked me to stay, to go into business with them. He really did like me. We were of different social backgrounds, yet he respected my views. I was the only one who told him that he was a hypocrite, living in luxury and enjoying his family's money while admiring Trotsky and Marx. He liked the way I challenged him. But I couldn't do it. I couldn't stay with him. So I returned to Germany. But I found no peace there, and so . . .''

He stopped, looked down at his fists. They were shaking and he relaxed them.

''So I went to the French Embassy in Germany,'' Hausen said, ''and I told them what had happened. I told them everything. They said they would question Gerard, and I told them where they could find me. I was willing to go to jail, just to appease my guilt.''

''And what happened?''

''The French police,'' Hausen said bitterly, ''are different from other police forces. They look to settle cases, not solve them, particularly when they involve foreigners. To them, these were unsolved murders and they would remain unsolved.''

''Did they even question Gerard?''

''I don't know,'' Hausen said. ''But even if they did, think of it. A word of a French billionaire's son against that of a poor German boy.''

''But he had to have explained why he left school suddenly—''

Hausen said, ''Herr Hood, Gerard was the kind of man who could convince you, who could *really* convince you, that he left school because Trotsky's Mexican speeches were omitted from a text.''

''What about the parents of the girls? I can't believe they let it go at that.''

''What could they do?'' Hausen asked. ''They came to France and they demanded justice. They petitioned the French Embassy in Washington and the American Embassy in Paris. They offered rewards. But the girls' bodies were returned to America, the French turned their backs on the families, and that was that, more or less.''

"More or less?"

There were tears in Hausen's eyes. "Gerard wrote to me several weeks later. He said he would return some day, to teach me a lesson about cowardice and betrayal."

"Other than that, you didn't hear from him?"

"Not until today when he phoned me. I went back to school, here in Germany, ashamed and consumed with guilt."

"But you hadn't done anything," Hood said. "You tried to stop Gerard."

"My crime was remaining silent immediately afterwards," Hausen said. "Like the many who smelled the fires at Auschwitz, I said nothing."

"There's a matter of degree, don't you think?"

Hausen shook his head. "Silence is silence is silence," he said. "A killer is at large because of my silence. He now calls himself Gerard Dominique. And he has threatened me and my thirteen-year-old daughter."

"I didn't realize you had children," Hood said. "Where is she?"

"She lives with her mother in Berlin," Hausen said. "I'll have her watched, but Gerard is elusive as well as powerful. He can bribe his way to people who disapprove of my work." He shook his head. "Had I yelled for the police that night, held Gerard, done something, I might have known peace over the years. But I didn't. And there was no way I could atone other than to fight the hatred that had driven Gerard to kill those girls."

Hood said, "You had no contact with Gerard, but did you hear anything about him over the years?"

"No," said Hausen. "He vanished, just like your Nancy. There were rumors that he had gone into business with his father, but when the old man died Gerard closed down the airbus parts factory that had been so profitable for so many years. He was rumored to have become the power behind many executive boards without ever being on any, but I don't know that for a fact.''

Hood had other questions for the man, questions about the elder Dupre's business, about the identities of the girls, and about what Op-Center could do to help Hausen with what was shaping up as a serious case of blackmail. But his attention was snatched away by a soft voice that called him from behind.

''Paul!''

Hood turned, and the glow of Hamburg seemed to dim. Hausen and the trees and the city and the years themselves disappeared as the tall, slender, graceful angel walked toward him. As he found himself once again standing in front of a movie theater, waiting for Nancy.

Waiting for the girl who finally had arrived.

THIRTY

Thursday, 4:22 P.M., Hanover, Germany

Bob Herbert had not phoned Mike Rodgers when he first saw the white van.

It had appeared in his rearview mirror while he drove around the city, trying to figure out what to do. He'd paid little attention to the vehicle as he tried to come up with some way of getting information about the kidnapped girl. Though the straightforward approach had failed, he'd been thinking that bribery might work.

When Herbert turned off Herrenhauser Strasse onto a side street and the van turned as well, he gave it a second look. In the front and back of the van were faces wearing ski masks. Glancing at the map and speeding up, Herbert took a few sharp turns just to make sure the van was following him. It was. Someone must have watched him go and sent the goon platoon after him. As the city of Hanover darkened with the fast-falling night, Herbert phoned Op-Center. Alberto put him through to Mike Rodgers.

That was when Herbert asked for fast help or a short prayer.

"What's wrong?" Rodgers asked.

"I had a run-in with some neo-Nazi back at a beer house," Herbert said. "Now they're after my ass."

"Where are you?"

"I'm not sure," Herbert said. He looked around. "I see lime trees, a lot of gardens, a lake." A large sign flashed by. "Thank you, God. I'm at a place called Welfengarten."

"Bob," said Rodgers, "Darrell's here. He's got the phone number of the local police. Can you write it down and call?"

Herbert reached into his shirt pocket for a pen. He doodled on the dashboard to get the ink flowing. "Shoot," he said.

But before he could write it down, the van rammed his fender. As the car bolted forward, the shoulder strap of the seatbelt tore into his chest. Herbert swerved to avoid a car in front of him.

"Shit!" he yelled. He drove around the car and sped up. "Listen, General, I've got troubles."

"What?"

"These guys are ramming me. I'm going to pull over before I cream a pedestrian. Tell the *Landespolizei* I'm in a white Mercedes."

"No, Bob, don't stop!" Rodgers yelled. "If they get you into the van, we're screwed!"

"They're not trying to kidnap me!" Herbert shouted back. "They're trying to kill me!"

The van smashed into him again on the left rear side. The right side of the car hopped onto the sidewalk, where Herbert nearly clipped a man walking his terrier. Herbert managed to swerve back onto the road, though his right front fender clipped a parked car. The collision tore the fender down and caused it to scrape noisily against the asphalt.

He stopped. Afraid the chrome might rend his tire, Herbert threw the car into reverse to try to rip the fender free. It came loose with a slow groan and a loud squeal, then clattered to the street.

Herbert looked in his side mirror to make sure he could pull away again. The scene was surreal. Pedestrians were running and cars were now racing past. And before he could safely return to the now-disordered flow of traffic, the van pulled up beside him, on the left. The figure in the passenger's seat faced him. He stuck a submachine gun from the open window and trained it on the car.

He fired.

THIRTY-ONE

Thursday, 4:33 P.M., Hamburg, Germany

Dressed in a short black skirt and jacket, with a white blouse and pearls, Nancy looked as if she were walking from a mirage. Hazy, slow, rippling.

Or maybe she looked that way because of the tears in Hood's eyes.

He winced, shook his head, made fists, felt a thousand different emotions with every step she took.

It is *you*. That was the first.

It was followed by, *Why did you do it, damn you?*

Then, *You're more breathtaking than I remembered. . . .*

And, *What about Sharon? I should leave, but I can't.*

Finally, *Go away. I don't* need *this. . . .*

But he did need it. And as she drifted toward him, he filled his eyes with her. He allowed his heart to fill with the old love, his loins to fill with the old lust, his mind to fill with the precious memories.

Hausen said, ''Herr Hood?''

Hausen's voice seemed muffled and soft, as though it were coming from a hole far, far below him.

''Are you all right?''

''I'm not sure,'' Hood replied. His own voice seemed to be coming from that hole.

Hood didn't take his eyes off Nancy. She didn't wave, she didn't speak. She didn't look away and she didn't break her poised, sensual stride.

"It's Nancy," Hood finally told his companion.

"How did she find you here?" Hausen wondered aloud.

The woman arrived. Hood couldn't even imagine what he looked like to her. He was shocked, open-mouthed, teary, his head moving slowly from side to side. Hood was no silver knight, he was sure of that.

There was a vague look of amusement on Nancy's face—the right side of her mouth was pulled up slightly—but it changed quickly to that wide, knee-weakening smile he knew so well.

"Hello," she said quietly.

The voice had matured, along with the face. There were lines to the sides of the blue eyes, on her once-smooth forehead, along the upper lip—that beautifully curved upper lip, which rested on a slightly bee-stung lower lip. But they were not detracting, those lines. To the contrary. Hood found them almost unbearably sexy. They said that she had lived, loved, fought, survived, and was still vital and unbowed and alive.

She also looked fitter than she had ever been. Her five-foot-six-inch body looked sculpted, and Hood could imagine her having gotten into aerobics or jogging or swimming. Gotten into it and throttled it, made it do exactly what she wanted to her body. She had that kind of discipline, that kind of will.

Obviously, he thought with a flash of bitterness. *She was able to walk out on me.*

Nancy was no longer wearing the cherry-red lipstick he remembered so well. She had on a calmer watermelon color. She was also wearing a hint of sky-blue eye shadow—that was new—and small diamond earrings. He fought a nearly losing battle to put his arms around her, to crush her to him from cheek to thighs.

He settled for: "Hello, Nancy." It seemed an inadequate thing to say after all this time, though it beat the epithets and accusations which came to mind. And as one who had been martyred by love, he found the saintly minimalism of it appealing.

Nancy's eyes shifted to Hood's right. She offered Hausen her hand.

"Nancy Jo Bosworth," she said to Hausen.

"Richard Hausen," he said.

"I know," she replied. "I recognized you."

Hood didn't hear the rest of the exchange. *Nancy Jo Bosworth,* he repeated. Nancy was the kind of woman who would have hyphenated her name. *So she isn't married.* Hood felt his soul begin to glow with joy, then burn with guilt. He told himself, *But you are.*

Hood jerked his head toward Hausen. He was conscious of moving it like that, of jerking it. Otherwise, it wouldn't have budged. Facing Hausen, Hood saw a look of compassion bordering on sadness in the man's eyes. Not for himself but for Hood. And he appreciated the empathy. If Hood weren't careful here, he was going to ruin a lot of lives.

Hood said to Hausen, "I wonder if you would give me just a minute."

"Certainly," Hausen said. "I'll see you back in my office."

Hood nodded. "What you were saying a moment ago," he said. "We'll talk more. I can help with that."

"Thank you," the German said. After snapping a polite bow at the woman, he walked away.

Hood looked from Hausen to Nancy. He didn't know

what she saw in his eyes, but what he saw in hers was deadly. The softness and desire were still there, still an electric combination, still damn near irresistible.

"I'm sorry," she said.

"It's all right," Hood said. "He and I were nearly finished."

The woman smiled. "Not about this."

Hood's neck and cheeks went red. He felt like an ass.

Nancy touched his face. "There was a reason I left the way I did," she said.

"I'm sure there was," Hood said, recovering slightly. "You always had reasons for everything you did." He put his hand on hers and moved it back to her side. "How did you find me?"

"I had to return papers to the hotel," she said. "The doorman told me a 'Paul' had been looking for me, and that he was with Deputy Foreign Minister Hausen. I called Hausen's office and came right over."

"Why?" Hood asked.

She laughed. "God, Paul, there are a dozen good reasons. To see you, to apologize, to explain—but mostly to see you. I missed you terribly. I followed your career in Los Angeles as best I could. I was very proud of what you'd done."

"I was driven," he said.

"I could see that, which is funny. I never thought of you as ambitious that way."

"I wasn't driven by ambition," he said, "but by despair. I kept busy so that I wouldn't become Heathcliff, sitting up at Wuthering Heights waiting to die. That's what you did to me, Nancy. You left me sick and so confused that all I wanted to do was find you, make whatever was wrong right again. I wanted you so badly that if you'd run off with another man I would have envied him, not hated him.''

''It wasn't another man,'' she said.

''It doesn't matter. Can you begin to understand that level of frustration?''

Now Nancy blushed slightly. ''Yes,'' she said, ''because I felt it too. But I was in terrible trouble. If I'd stayed, or if I told you where I'd gone . . .''

''What?'' Hood demanded. ''What would have happened? How could anything have been worse than what *did* happen?'' His voice cracked and he had to fight back sobs. He half-turned from her.

''I'm sorry,'' Nancy said more emphatically.

She came closer and stroked his cheek again. This time he didn't remove her hand.

''Paul, I stole the blueprints for a new chip my company was going to make and sold them to an overseas firm. In exchange for the blueprints, I got a ton of money. We would have been married, we would have been rich, and you would have been a deadly-great politician.''

''Is that what you think I wanted?'' Hood asked. ''To be successful on someone else's efforts?''

Nancy shook her head. ''You never would have known. I wanted you to be able to run for office without worrying about money. I felt that you could do great things, Paul, if you didn't have to worry about special interest groups and campaign contributions. I mean, you could get away with that sort of thing then.''

''I can't believe you did that.''

''I know. That's why I didn't tell you. And after everything fell apart, that's one reason I still couldn't tell you. On top of losing you, I didn't want your scorn.'' She said, ''You could be pretty judgmental about things illegal in those days. Even little things. Remember how upset you were when I got that parking ticket outside the Cinerama Dome when we saw *Rollerball*? The ticket you'd warned me I'd get?''

''I remember,'' Hood said. *Of course I remember, Nancy. I remember everything we did. . . .*

She lowered her hand, turned away. ''Anyway, I did get found out somehow. A friend—you remember Jessica.''

Hood nodded. He could still see those pearls she was always wearing, smell her Chanel, as if she were standing right beside him.

''Jess was working late,'' Nancy said, ''and as I was getting ready to meet you at the movies she phoned to tell me two FBI agents had been there. She said the men were on their way to question me. I only had time to gather up my passport, some clothes, and my Bank-Americard, write you that short note, and get the hell out of my apartment.'' She looked down. ''Out of the country.''

''Out of my life,'' Hood said. He pressed his lips together tightly. He wasn't sure he wanted Nancy to continue. Each word made him suffer, tortured him with the blighted hopes of a twenty-year-old man in love.

''I said there was another reason I didn't contact you,'' Nancy said. She looked up again. ''I assumed you would be questioned or watched, or your phone would be tapped. If I had called or written, the FBI would have found me.''

''That's true,'' Hood said. ''The FBI did come to my apartment. They questioned me, without telling me what you'd done, and I agreed to let them know if I heard from you.''

''You did?'' she seemed surprised. ''You'd have turned me in?''

"Yes," he said. "Only I never would have abandoned you."

"You'd have had no choice," she said. "There would have been a trial, I'd have gone to prison—"

"That's true. But I'd have waited."

"Twenty years?"

"If that's how long it took," Hood said. "But it wouldn't have. Industrial espionage committed by a young woman in love—you'd have been able to plea-bargain and been free in five years."

"Five years," she said. "And then you'd have married a criminal?"

"No. You."

"Okay, an ex-con. No one would've trusted me—or you—around any kind of a secret. Your dreams of a life in politics would have ended."

"So *what*?" he said. "Instead, I felt as though my life had ended."

Nancy stopped speaking. She smiled again. "Poor Paul," she said. "That's all very romantic and just a little theatrical, which is one of the things I loved about you. But the truth is, your life *didn't* end when I left. You met someone else, someone quite lovely. You married. You had the children you wanted. You settled down."

I settled, he thought before he could stop himself. He hated himself for thinking it and apologized silently to Sharon.

"What did you do after you left?" Hood asked, wanting to talk instead of think.

"I moved to Paris," Nancy said, "and I tried to get a job designing computer software. But there wasn't a lot for me to do there. There wasn't much of a market yet and there was a real protectionist thing going, keeping Americans from taking French jobs. So after burning through the blood money I'd been paid—it's expensive to live in Paris, especially when you have to bribe officials because you can't get a visa and have your name show up at the American Embassy—I moved to Toulouse and began working for the company.''

"The company?''

"The one I sold the secrets to,'' she said. "I don't want to tell you the name, because I don't want you doing anything out of your famous white-knight spite. Because you know you would.''

Nancy was right. He'd have gone back to Washington and found a dozen different ways for the U.S. government to lean on them.

Nancy said, "The not-so-funny thing was, I always suspected that the guy I sold those plans to was the one who turned me in, to force me to come over and work for him. Not because I was so brilliant, mind you—I stole my best idea, right?—but because he felt that if I depended on him I could never turn on him. I hadn't wanted to go to him because I was ashamed of what I'd done, but I needed to work.'' She smiled unhappily. "To top it all off, I failed at love repeatedly because I compared everyone to you.''

"Gee,'' he said, "I can't tell you how much better that makes me feel.''

"Don't,'' Nancy said. "Don't be like that. I still loved you. I bought the *Los Angeles Times* at an international newsstand just to keep up on your activities. And there were times, so very many times, that I wanted to write or phone. But I thought it was best not to.''

"Then why did you decide to see me now?'' Hood asked. He was in pain again, rocking between that and sadness. "Did you think it would hurt any less today?''

"I couldn't help myself," she admitted. "When I heard that you were in Hamburg, I had to see you. And I think that you wanted to see me."

"Yes," he said, "I ran after you in the hotel lobby. I wanted to see you. I needed to see you." He shook his head. "Jesus, Nancy. I still can't believe it's you."

"It is," she said.

Hood looked into those eyes with which he had spent so many days and nights. The pull was both extraordinary and awful, a dream and a nightmare. His strength to resist them just wasn't in the same class.

The cool twilight breeze chilled the perspiration along Hood's legs and back. He wanted to hate her. Wanted to walk away from her. But what he wanted most of all was to go back in time and stop her from leaving.

Her eyes held him as she slipped her hands around his. Her touch jolted him, then settled into an electric tingle that raced from his chest to his toes. And he knew he had to get away from her.

Hood stepped back. The electric connection broke. "I can't do this," he said.

Nancy said, "You can't do what? Be honest?" She added a little jab, the kind she had always been so good at. "What did politics do to you?"

"You know what I mean, Nancy. I can't stay here with you."

"Not even for an hour? For coffee, to catch up?"

"No," Hood said firmly. "This is my closure."

She grinned. "This is not closure, Paul. This is anything but that."

She was right. Her eyes, her wit, her walk, her presence, her everything had breathed new life into something that had never quite died. Hood wanted to scream.

He stepped up beside her, looking north while she looked south. "Jesus, Nancy, I'm not going to feel guilty about this. *You* ran away from *me*. You left without an explanation and I met someone else. Someone who threw in her lot with me, who trusted me with her life and heart. I won't do anything to cheapen that."

"I didn't ask you to," Nancy said. "Coffee isn't betrayal."

"It is the way we used to drink it," Hood said.

Nancy smiled. She looked down. "I understand. I'm sorry—for everything—sorrier than I can say, and I'm sad. But I do understand." She faced him. "I'm staying at the Ambassador and I'll be here until this evening. If you change your mind, leave a message."

"I won't change my mind," Hood said. He looked at her. "As much as I'd like to."

Nancy squeezed his hand. He felt the charge again.

"So politics didn't corrupt you," she said. "I'm not surprised. Just a little disappointed."

"You'll get over it," Hood said. "After all, you got over me."

Nancy's expression changed. For the first time Hood saw the sadness that had been hidden beneath her smile and the longing in her eyes.

"Do you believe that?" she asked.

"Yes. Otherwise, you couldn't have stayed away."

She said, "Men really don't understand love, do they? Not on my best day, with the closest pretender to the Paul Hood throne, did I ever meet anyone as bright or as compassionate or as gentle as you." She leaned over and kissed him on the shoulder. "I'm sorry I disturbed you by coming back into your life, but I wanted you to know that I never got over you, Paul, and I never will."

Nancy didn't look at him as she walked back toward the edge of the park. But he looked at her. And once again Paul Hood was standing alone, two movie tickets in his wallet, suffering the absence of a woman he loved.

THIRTY-TWO

Thursday, 4:35 P.M.,
Hanover, Germany

As soon as he saw the gun, Bob Herbert threw his car into reverse and crushed the hand-controlled gas pedal down. The sudden backward acceleration threw him hard against his shoulder harness, and he cried out as it snapped tight against his chest. But the bullets from the van missed the driver's seat, pelting the hood and the front fender as the car rocketed away. Herbert continued moving away, even after his vehicle's right rear side struck a street light and caromed off, skidding onto the road. Oncoming cars braked fast or swerved to avoid him. The drivers shouted and blasted their horns.

Herbert ignored them. He looked ahead and saw the front-seat passenger of the van lean out the window. The man trained the gun on Herbert.

"Sons of bitches don't give up!" Herbert yelled. Slowed because he had to do everything by hand, Herbert slammed the gas pedal down and spun the steering wheel to the left. Then he braced himself against the wheel with his left arm. Racing ahead, he quickly covered the fifteen feet which separated him from the van. He rammed the van's left rear fender. Metal twisted and screamed as they collided, the van was thrown forward, and Herbert swung his Mercedes into the street. Still pressing hard on the gas, he raced past the driver's side and sped ahead.

Traffic had now stopped well behind them and pedestrians were running away in all directions.

Then Herbert remembered the cellular phone. He scooped it up. ''Mike, are you still there?''

''Christ, didn't you hear me shouting?''

''No. Jesus, now I got two continents mad at me!''

''Bob, what's—''

Herbert didn't hear the rest. He dropped the phone in his lap and swore as a tram turned onto the street in front of him. Speeding up, he swept around it, putting the tram between him and the van. He hoped the gunman didn't shoot the tram out of frustration and sheer cussedness.

Herbert retrieved the phone. ''Sorry, General, I didn't hear that.''

''I said what's going on?''

''Mike, I've got these lunatics with guns who decided we had to have our own private Grand Prix in Hanover!''

''Do you know where you are?'' Rodgers asked.

Herbert glanced in his rearview mirror as the van screeched around the tram. ''Hold on,'' he said to Rodgers.

He set the phone down on the passenger's seat and put both hands on the wheel as the van shot onto the road. As it raced after him, Herbert looked forward. Hanover was a blur as he raced onto Lange Laube, made a few quick turns, and was on Goethe Strasse. Fortunately, he realized, traffic was lighter than it might have been at this hour because people had stayed out of town during Chaos Days.

Herbert heard Mike Rodgers's voice coming from far

away. "Shit!" he said, snatching up the phone as he sped ahead. "Sorry, Mike. I'm here."

"Where exactly are you?" Rodgers asked.

"I've got no idea."

"Can you see any signs?" Rodgers interrupted.

"No," he said. "Wait, yes." His eyes fixed on a street sign as it whipped past. "Goethe Strasse. I'm on Goethe Strasse."

"Hold on," Rodgers said. "We're bringing a map up on the computer."

"I'll hold on," Herbert said. "Man, I've got nowhere to go."

The van spun onto Goethe Strasse, clipped a car as it did, then accelerated. Herbert didn't know whether these jerks had some kind of legal immunity, zero brains, or just a lot of mad, because they obviously weren't giving up. He figured they were pissed because he was an American *and* a handicapped man, and he'd stood up to them. That kind of behavior simply could not be tolerated.

And of course, he thought, *there isn't a policeman in sight.* But as the officer back at the Beer-Hall had said, most of the *Landespolizei* were tied up watching other meeting places and events. Besides, no one expected a car chase in the middle of the city itself.

Rodgers came back on. "Bob—you're okay there. Get onto Goethe Strasse and continue east if you can. It's a straight run to Rathenau Strasse, which runs south. We'll try to get help to you over there—"

"Shit!" Herbert cried again, and dropped the phone.

As the van got closer, the gunman leaned from the window and began firing low, at the tires. Herbert had no choice but to drive into the less-crowded oncoming lane, the lane heading into town. He quickly put himself out of range.

Cars swung out of his way as he raced ahead. Suddenly, his flight was halted and his orientation rattled as he thumped hard into a pothole. Pinwheeling a half-turn toward the oncoming van, Herbert tapped the brake and took command of the spin. The van shot past him as he stopped facing west, facing the way he'd come.

The van screamed to a stop some fifty yards behind him.

Herbert was back within range. He grabbed the phone and hit the gas.

"Mike," he said, "we're goin' the other way now. Back along Goethe to Lange Laube."

"Understood," Rodgers said. "Darrell's on the phone too. Stay cool and we'll try to get you some help."

"I'm cool," Herbert said as he glanced back at the roaring van. "Just make sure I don't end up *cold*," he said.

He looked in his rearview mirror and saw the gunman reloading his weapon. They weren't going to give up, and sooner or later his luck would run out. As he looked in the mirror, he saw the wheelchair and decided to get in front of the van, press the button to activate the bucket, and dump his wheelchair under their wheels. It might not stop them, but it would certainly cause some damage. And if he lived, he'd have fun filling out the requisition form for a new one.

Reason for Loss. He thought of the only essay section of form L-5. *"Dropped it from a speeding car to foil neo-Nazi assassins."*

Herbert slowed, let the van come closer, then pressed the button on the dash.

The rear door remained closed as a singsongy female

voice informed him, *"I'm sorry. This device will not operate while the car is in motion."*

Herbert slammed his palm on the gas pedal and sped up. He watched the van closely in his rearview mirror, staying dead-center in front of them as much as possible so the gunman wouldn't have much of a shot from the side window.

Then he saw the gunman put his foot to the windshield and push it out. The glass flew up and away in a fluid sheet, then shattered into countless, jagged pellets as it hit the road.

The man poked the gun out and sighted on the car. He fought to steady his weapon in the whipping wind. It was a nightmarish sight, a thug riding shotgun in a van.

Herbert only had a moment to act. He smashed his hand down on the brake, the Mercedes stopped suddenly, and the van rear-ended him hard. His trunk folded up and in like a ribbon. But above it, he saw the gunman tossed forward. The man was thrown at the waist across the lower portion of the window frame. The gun flew from his hands, onto the hood of the van, and slid over the side. The driver was also thrown ahead, his chest colliding hard with the steering wheel. He lost control of the van, though the vehicle stopped as his foot slipped from the gas.

Herbert's only wound was another unpleasant scrape across his chest, inflicted by the shoulder strap.

There was a moment of clear silence, broken by cars honking from far off, and people approaching cautiously, yelling to other people to get help.

Not sure that he had put the car or its occupants out of commission, Herbert pressed down on the gas to get away. The car didn't move. He could feel his tires racing, but he could also feel the tug of the two fenders locked together.

He sat still for a moment, realizing for the first time how his heart was racing as he wondered if he could get himself and the wheelchair out.

Suddenly, the van bellowed back to life. Herbert felt a rough tug and looked in the rearview mirror. A new driver had taken the place of the old one and had shifted into reverse. Now he moved ahead, then shifted back, then jerked ahead.

Trying to shake me loose, Herbert thought, even as the vehicles unhooked. Without stopping, the van continued to back up. It sped off, then turned a corner and vanished.

The intelligence officer sat gripping the steering wheel, trying to decide what to do. In the distance, he heard the siren which had sent the neo-Nazis on their way. One of those loud ones which made the Opel police cars sound like Buicks. People began coming up to the window and speaking to Herbert softly, in German.

"*Danke,*" he said. "Thanks. I'm all right. *Gesund.* Healthy."

Healthy? he thought. He thought of the police coming to question him. German police were not famed for their friendliness. At best, he would be treated objectively. At worst . . .

At worst, he thought, *the police station has a couple of neo-Nazi sympathizers. At worst, they put me in prison. At worst, somebody gets to me in the middle of the night with a knife or a length of steel wire.*

"Screw that," he said. Thanking the onlookers again and politely urging them to get out of the way, Herbert quickly shifted gears, picked up the phone, and set off after the van.

THIRTY-THREE

Thursday, 11:00 A.M., Washington, D.C.

It was nicknamed the Kraken, after the fabled, many-tentacled sea monster. And it was set up by Matt Stoll when he was hired as one of Op-Center's first employees.

The Kraken was a powerful computer system which was linked to databases worldwide. The resources and information ranged from photo libraries to FBI fingerprint files, from books in the Library of Congress to newspaper morgues in every major city of the United States, from stock prices to air and rail schedules, from telephone directories around the world to troop and police strength and deployment in most cities at home and abroad.

But Stoll and his small staff had designed a system which not only accessed data, it analyzed it. An ID program written by Stoll allowed researchers to circle a nose or an eye or mouth on a terrorist's face and find it anywhere it appeared in international police or newspaper files. Landscapes could likewise be compared by highlighting the contour of a mountain, horizon, or shore. Two full-time day and night operators were stationed at the Archive, which could handle over thirty separate operations at once.

It took the Kraken less than fifteen minutes to find the photograph of Deputy Foreign Minister Hausen. It had been snapped by a Reuters photographer and published in a Berlin newspaper five months before, when Hausen had arrived to give a speech at a dinner of Holocaust survivors. When he received the information, Eddie couldn't help but resent the cruelty of the juxtaposition of this particular image in the game.

The landscape behind Hausen took a little longer to identify, though here the programmers got lucky. Instead of asking for a worldwide check, Deirdre Donahue and Natt Mendelsohn started with Germany, then moved to Austria, Poland, and France. After forty-seven minutes, the computer found the spot. It was located in the south of France. Deirdre located a history of the view, wrote a complete summary, and added it to the file.

Eddie faxed the information to Matt. Then the long, powerful tentacles of the Kraken rested as the monster went back to watching, silently, from its secret lair.

THIRTY-FOUR

Thursday, 5:02 P.M., Hamburg, Germany

As he walked back to the office building, Paul Hood was showered with memories. Crisp, detailed memories of the buried but unforgotten things he and Nancy Jo had done and said to each other nearly twenty years ago.

He remembered sitting in a Mexican restaurant in Studio City, discussing whether or not they would eventually want kids. He thought they would; she definitely did not. They ate tacos and drank bitter coffee and debated the pros and cons of parenthood into the small hours of the morning.

He remembered waiting for a Paul Newman movie to start in a Westwood theater while he and Nancy discussed the House Judiciary Committee's debate on whether President Nixon should be impeached. He could still smell the popcorn she had, taste the Milk Duds he ate.

He remembered talking through the night about the future of technology after playing the black-and-white video game Pong for the first time. He should have known, by the way she whipped his butt, that that was the field she was destined to conquer.

He hadn't thought of these things in years, yet he could recall so many of the exact words, the smells and sights, Nancy Jo's expressions and what she was wearing. It was all so vivid. So was her energy. He had been smitten with that, even a little intimidated. She was the kind of woman who looked under every rock, explored each new world, looked into every fresh field. And when that lovely dervish wasn't working, she was playing with Hood in discos and in bed, yelling herself hoarse at Lakers or Rams or Kings games, shouting with frustration or delight from behind a Scrabble rack or video-game joystick, biking through Griffith Park and hiking in Bronson Caverns while she tried to find the spot where *Robot Monster* was filmed. Nancy could barely sit through a movie without pulling out a pad and making notes. Notes she couldn't read later because they'd been scribbled in the dark, yet that didn't matter. It was the process of thinking, of creating, of doing which had always fascinated Nancy. And it was her energy and enthusiasm and creativity and magnetism which had always fascinated him. She was like a Greek muse, like Terpsichore, her mind and body dancing here and there as Hood followed, entranced.

And goddamn you, he thought, *you still are entranced.*

Hood didn't want to feel the things he was feeling again. The longing. The desire to wrap his arms around that whirlwind and rush madly into the future with her. Hold on desperately to make up for all the time they had lost. He didn't want to feel it, but a big part of him did.

Christ, he yelled at himself, *grow up!*

But it wasn't that simple, was it? Being an adult, being sensible, would only tell him how things happened, not what to do about them.

How *did* they happen? And how did Nancy manage to overwhelm the two decades of rage he felt and the new life he had built?

He could follow, as if it were a staircase, each step that had brought him to where he was now. Nancy disappeared. He slipped into despair. He met Sharon in a framing store. She was there to get her cooking school diploma framed while he was selecting a matte for his signed photo from the Governor. They talked. They exchanged numbers. He called. She was attractive, intelligent, *stable*. She wasn't creative outside the kitchen she loved, and she didn't glow in that same supernatural way that Nancy did. If there were such a thing as past lives, Hood could imagine a dozen or more souls flowing through Nancy's veins. You couldn't see anyone in Sharon but Sharon.

But that was good, he told himself. You want to settle down and raise children with someone who *can* settle down. And that wasn't Nancy. Life wasn't perfect now, but if he wasn't in heaven with Sharon all the time, he was happy to be in Washington with a wife and family who loved him and respected him and weren't going to run off. Did Nancy ever really respect him? What *had* she seen in him? During the months following her departure, when he'd done the forensics on their relationship and his love had turned to ash, he'd never really understood what he'd brought to the party.

Hood reached the building lobby. He entered the elevator, and as the speed lift reached Hausen's floor Hood began to feel manipulated. Nancy had left, shown up a score of years later, and presented herself to him. *Offered* herself to him. Why? Guilt? Not Nancy. She had the conscience of a circus clown. A pie in the face, seltzer down the waistband, *oops!* A big laugh and all was forgotten, at least by her. And people accepted it because she was selfish but endearing, not malicious. Loneliness? She was never lonely. Even when she was alone she was with someone who could keep her amused. A challenge? Maybe. He could picture her asking herself, *Have you still got it, Nancy old girl?*

Not that it really mattered. He was back in the present, back in the real world where he was in his forties, not twenties, living with his precious little planets instead of a wild, soaring comet. Nancy had come and she had gone, and at least he knew what had happened to her.

And maybe, he thought suddenly and surprisingly, *you can stop blaming Sharon because she isn't Nancy.* Did some deep, regretful part of him feel that? he wondered. God, it scared him, the cobwebbed corridors to which that staircase of his had taken him.

To complete his emotional buffet, Hood felt guilty for having left poor Hausen standing there, his soul exposed, a black part of his history on his lips. He'd left him without a shoulder or the help of the man to whom he'd just confessed.

Hood would make his apologies and Hausen, gentleman that he was, would probably accept them. Besides, Hood had bared his own soul and men understood men that way. Where tragedies of the heart or mistakes of youth were concerned, men freely gave one another absolution.

Hausen was standing beside Stoll in the main office. Lang was still at Stoll's right.

Hausen met Hood with concerned eyes. "Did you get what you needed?" he asked.

"Pretty much," Hood said. He smiled reassuringly. "Yes, thank you. Everything okay here?"

Hausen said, "I'm glad we spoke." He managed to smile as well.

Stoll was busy typing in commands. "Chief, Herr Hausen wasn't forthcoming about where you'd gone," he said without looking up, ''but *I* find it strange that Paul Hood and Superman are never around at the same time.''

''Cool it,'' Hood warned.

''At once, Boss,'' Stoll replied. ''Sorry.''

Now Hood felt guilty for having jumped on *him*. ''Never mind,'' he said in a gentler tone. ''It's been a wicked afternoon. What have you found out?''

Stoll brought the game's title screen back on the monitor. ''Well,'' he said, ''as I was just telling Herrs Hausen and Lang, this game was installed with a time-release command by the Deputy Foreign Minister's assistant, Hans—''

''Who seems to have vanished,'' Lang contributed. ''We tried him at home and at his health club, and there's no answer.''

''And his E-mail address at home isn't receiving,'' Stoll said. ''So he's definitely on the lam. Anyway, the photo of Herr Hausen is from coverage of a speech he gave to Holocaust survivors, while this landscape is from here.''

Stoll hit the recycle command, dumped the title screen, and brought up the photo downloaded from Op-Center's Kraken.

Hood leaned forward and read the caption. '' 'The Tarn at Montauban, le Vieux Pont.' '' He straightened. ''France or Canada?'' he asked.

''The south of France,'' Stoll said. ''When you arrived, I was just about to bring up Deirdre's report on the place.'' He used the keyboard to bring up the file. Then he read, ''It says, 'The *route nationale,* blah-blah, goes north and northwest with the River Garonne to meet the Tarn at Montauban, population 51,000. Town consists of such-and-such' ''—he skimmed the demographic makeup while scrolling the screen—"and—ah. Here. 'The building is a stronghold built in 1144 and has historically been associated with regionalism in the south. As a fortress, it helped fight off attacks by Catholics during the Religious Wars, and has remained a symbol of defiance to the locals.' " Stoll continued to scroll the screen.

Hood said, "Does it say anything about who owns the place?"

"I'm a-checkin'," said Stoll. He typed in the word "owner" and ordered a word search. The screen jumped several paragraphs and a name was highlighted. Stoll read, " 'Sold last year for the manufacture of software, with provisions that the owner not make alterations in— yadda, yadda. Here," he said, "owner. A privately held French company named *Demain*, which was incorporated in the city of Toulouse in May of 1979."

Hood shot Stoll a look, then ducked toward the screen. "Hold on," he said. He read the date. "Tell Deirdre or Nat to get me more information on that company. Quickly."

Stoll nodded, cleared the screen, and rang up "The Keepers of the Kraken," as he called them. He E-mailed for more information on *Demain*, then sat back, folded his arms, and waited.

The wait was not a long one. Deirdre sent over a short article from the June 1980 issue of a magazine called *Videogaming Illustrated*. It read:

GAMES OF TOMORROW

Are you Asteroid-ed out?
Have you been Space Invader-ed to death?

Even if you still love yesterday's hits, a new star in the video-game firmament, the French company *Demain*, which means "tomorrow," has developed a different kind of cartridge to play on your Atari, Intellivision, and Odyssey home systems. Their first cartridge, the quest game A Knight to Remember, will be in stores this month. It is the first game which will be made available for the three leading video-game systems.

In a press release, company research and development head Jean-Michel Horne says, "Thanks to a revolutionary and powerful new chip we have developed, graphics and gameplay will be more detailed and exciting than in any previous game."

A Knight to Remember will sell for $34.00 and will be packaged with a discount coupon for the company's next release, the superhero game Ooberman.

Hood took a moment to contemplate the article and weigh the implications. It helped to put together some pieces.

Nancy stole plans for a new chip and sold them to a company, possibly—no, probably—this *Demain*. Gerard, a racist, makes a fortune manufacturing video games. On the sly, he puts money into hate games.

But why? As a hobby? Certainly not. Little doses of hate like that would be too small and unsatisfying for a man like the one Richard Hausen described.

Assume he did make hate games, though, Hood thought. Charlie Squires's kid surfed into one. What if that were Dominique's? Could Gerard be using the Internet to send them around the world?

Again, Hood thought, *assume yes.* Why do that? Not just to make money. From what Hausen said, Dominique has enough of that.

He would have to have something bigger in mind, Hood thought. Hate games appearing on the Internet. Confident threats to Hausen. Were they timed to coincide with Chaos Days?

It all seemed to be going nowhere. Too many pieces were missing, and there was one person who might be able—but willing?—to tell him what that could be.

"Herr Hausen," Hood said, "would you mind if I borrowed your driver for a short while?"

"Not at all," Hausen said. "Do you need anything else?"

"Not at the moment, thanks," Hood replied. "Matt, please send this article to General Rodgers. Tell him that this Dominique may be our hate-game peddler. If there's any more background to be had—"

"We'll get it," Stoll said. "Your wish is my command."

"I appreciate it," Hood said, patting Stoll on the back and already headed toward the door.

As he watched Hood move through the reception area, Matt Stoll folded his arms again. "There's no doubt about it. My boss *is* Superman."

THIRTY-FIVE

Thursday, 5:17 P.M., Hanover, Germany

"Bob," said the caller, "I've got good news."

Herbert was glad to hear that his assistant Alberto had good news. Not only did he ache where the seatbelt had pulled at his chest, but the thought that his attackers would escape left him seething. Herbert had been unable to find the van, so he'd pulled over on a side street and used his cellular phone to call Op-Center. He'd told Alberto what had happened and asked him to have the National Reconnaissance Office try to find the van for him. When they did, Herbert intended to go to the site. The German police were spread so thin he knew he couldn't count on them. Herbert had to rely on himself to bring these people to justice.

Herbert was surprised when the phone beeped just six minutes after he'd called. It took five times longer than that to move a satellite eye from where it was to someplace else.

Alberto said, "You're in luck. The NRO was already watching your area for Larry, who's looking into the kidnapping of the film intern. He wants to beat Griff on this one. And it's a good thing too. All our other satellites have been pressed into service watching a developing situation in the southern Balkans."

Larry was CIA Director Larry Rachlin. Griff was FBI Director Griff Egenes. Their rivalry was old and relentless. Like Op-Center, both organizations had access to NRO data. However, Egenes hoarded information like squirrels hoarded nuts.

"What's the NRO got?" Herbert asked. He was uncomfortable talking to Alberto on an unsecure line, but there wasn't any choice. He just hoped no one was listening.

"For Larry, nothing. No sign of the van, no sign of the girl. Darrell says Griff hasn't got anything either, though. None of his regular police sources seem to be around."

"I'm not surprised," Herbert said. "They're all in the field riding herd on neo-Nazis."

"Better that than riding with them," Alberto observed.

"True," said Herbert. "Now what about the van, Alberto? You stalling or something?"

"As a matter of fact, I am," he said. "Boss, you're just one man with zero backup. You shouldn't be going—"

"Where is it?" Herbert demanded.

Alberto sighed. "Stephen found it, and it's a definite match. It's banged up just where you said it'd be. It's headed west on one of the *Autobahnen*—though from just the photo, I can't tell you which one."

"That's okay," said Herbert. "I'll find it on the map."

"I know it's a waste of breath to try and talk you out of it—"

"You got that right, son."

"—so I'll just tell General R. what you're doing. Is there anything else you need?"

"Yes," Herbert said. "If the van gets off the auto-bahn, give me a jingle."

"Of course," said Alberto. "Stephen knows you, Bob. He said he'll have his people keep an eye on it."

"Thank him," Herbert said, "and tell him he gets my vote for this year's Conrad. On second thought, don't. That'll get his hopes up."

"Aren't his hopes always up?" Alberto asked as he signed off.

Herbert hung up and grinned; after what he'd just been through, it felt good to smile. As he checked his map to find the roads to the east-west running Autobahn, he thought about the Conrads and his smile broadened. They were a fun, unofficial award given at a very private dinner each year by America's leading intelligence figures. The dagger-like trophy honored the government's top intelligence figure and was named in honor of Joseph Conrad. The author's 1907 novel, *The Secret Agent,* was one of the first great espionage tales, about an agent-provocateur who worked the back streets of London. The dinner was just five weeks away, and it was always a blast—thanks in no small part to poor Stephen Viens.

Herbert noted the route he needed to take, then urged his wounded mechanical steed ahead. It went, albeit with some clanks and whines which weren't there before.

Viens had been Matt Stoll's best friend in college, and he was as serious as his classmate was flip. Since his appointment as assistant director and then director of the NRO, Viens's amazing technical talents had been largely responsible for the facility's increasing effectiveness and importance. During the past four years, the one hundred satellites under his command had provided detailed, black-and-white photographs of the earth at whatever magnification was required. Viens was fond of saying,

"I can give you a picture covering several city blocks or the letters on a children's block."

And because he was so serious, Viens took the Conrads so seriously. He really did want one, everyone knew it, and for that reason the voting committee colluded to keep it from him by one vote, year after year. Herbert always felt bad about the deception, but as CIA Chief and Conrad Chairman Rachlin said, "Hell, we *are* covert operatives, after all."

Actually, Herbert intended to lie to Larry and then vote for Viens this year. Not because of his body of work but for his integrity. Since the increase of terrorist activity in the U.S., the Pentagon had launched four hundred-million-dollar-apiece satellites code-named *Ricochet*. They were positioned a mean 22,000 miles over North America and were designed to spy on our own country. If they knew about it, everyone from the far left to the extreme right would have a problem with Big Brother's eyes in the skies. But because those eyes were under Viens's command, no one who *did* know feared that they would be misused for personal or political gain.

Herbert got back on the Autobahn, though the Mercedes didn't race as smoothly as it had before. He could only manage fifty miles an hour—"slower than mud," as his Grandmother Shel used to say back in Mississippi.

And then the phone beeped. Coming so soon after Alberto called, Herbert guessed that this would be Paul Hood ordering him back. But Herbert had already decided he wouldn't return. Not without somebody's pelt being in somebody's canoe.

Herbert answered the phone. "Yes?"

"Bob, it's Alberto. I just got a new photograph, a 2MD of the entire region."

A 2MD was a two-mile-diameter view with the van

at the center. The satellites were pre-programmed to move in or out at quarter-mile intervals with simple commands. Different incremental views required a different, more complex set of commands.

Alberto continued, "Your party has gotten off the Autobahn."

"Where?" Herbert said. "Give me a landmark."

"There's only one landmark, Bob. A small, wooded area with a two-lane road leading northwest."

Herbert glanced along the horizon. "There are a lot of trees and woods out here, Alberto. Is there anything *else*?"

"One thing," said Alberto. "Police. About a dozen of them surrounding what's left of a blown-out vehicle."

Herbert's eyes fixed on a point ahead, but he didn't see it. He was only thinking of one thing. "The movie trailer?" he asked.

"Hold on," Alberto said. "Stephen's downloading another photo."

Herbert clapped his lips together. Op-Center's link with the NRO allowed Alberto to see the photograph at the same time as Viens's people did. The CIA had the same capacity, though without operatives in the field here they wouldn't be able to get anyone over, either officially or undercover.

"I've got a quarter-mile view," Alberto said. There was chatter behind him. "I've also got Levy and Warren looking over my shoulder."

"I hear them." Marsha Levy and Jim Warren were Op-Center's photo reconnaissance analysts. They were a perfect team. Levy had an eye like a microscope, while Warren's talent was the ability to see how details fit in the overall picture. Together, they could look at a photograph and not only tell you what was in it, but what might be under it or out of sight, and how everything got there.

Alberto said, "They tell me there are the remains of wooden furniture in there, which the movie trailer had. Computer magnification of the wood, Marsha says the grain looks like larch."

"That would make sense," Herbert said. "Cheap and durable for getting banged around the countryside."

"Right," Alberto said. "Jimmy thinks the fire started on the right rear at what looks like the gas tank."

"A fuse," Herbert said. "Give them time to run."

"That's what Jimmy says," said Alberto. "Hold on—we've got another one coming in."

Herbert looked ahead, watching for an exit. The van hadn't had that much of a head start. It would have to be coming up soon. He wondered if it were by design or coincidence that the van had come this way.

"Bob," Alberto said excitedly, "we just got a quarter-mile view to the east of the wreck. Marsha says she sees part of a rough dirt road and what could be a person in one of the trees."

"Could be?"

Marsha came on. Herbert could picture the tough little brunette wresting the phone from Alberto.

"Yes, Bob, it could be. There's a dark shape under the leaves. It's not a branch and it's too big to be a hive or bird's nest."

"A scared kid might hide in a tree," Herbert said.

"Or a cautious one," Marsha said.

"Good point. Where's the white van now?" Herbert asked.

"It was in the picture with the trailer," said Marsha. "None of the police are looking over."

That'd be a kick in the head, thought Herbert. The

local police in cahoots with the local neo-Nazi militia.

There was an exit coming up on the right. Beyond it, Herbert saw a wooded area, the beginning of a magnificent sprawl of countryside.

"I think I'm where I need to be," Herbert said. "Is there any way to get to that tree without being seen by the police?"

There was a muted conference on the other end of the line.

Alberto came on. "Bob, yes. You can exit, pull to the right off the road, and take that dirt road."

"I can't," Herbert said. "If the kidnappers headed into the woods instead of out, I don't want to run into them. Or them into me."

"All right," said Alberto. "Then you can circumvent them by going—let's see, southeast . . . uh, roughly one third of a mile to a stream. Cross to the east, to about a quarter of a mile to . . . shit, there's no landmark there."

"I'll find it."

"Boss—"

"I'll *find* it. What's next?"

Alberto said, "Then you go northeast about seventy-five yards to a gnarly old whatever-it-is. Marsha says it's an oak. But that's pretty rough terrain."

"I once climbed the steps of the Washington Monument. I went up backwards, on my ass, and came down frontwards."

"I know. But that was eleven years ago, and it was here at home."

"I'll be fine," Herbert said. "You take a paycheck, you gotta do the shit work as well as the easy stuff."

"This isn't 'shit work,' Boss. This is a man in a wheelchair trying to climb ledges and cross streams."

Herbert felt a flash of doubt, but he flushed it away.

He wanted to do this. No, he *needed* to do this. And in his heart, he knew he could.

"Listen," Herbert said. "We can't call the police because we don't know if some of them are in with these gorillas. And how long will it be before the girl decides to turn herself in because she's hungry or tired? We don't have any other options."

"We do have one," Alberto said. "Larry's people are probably drawing the same conclusions from these photos that we are. Let me call over and see what they want to do."

"Nix," said Herbert. "I'm not gonna cool my seat while someone's life is in danger."

"But you'll *both* be in danger—"

"Kid, I've been in danger just sitting in my damn car today," Herbert said as he exited the Autobahn. "I'll be careful and I'll get to her, I promise. I'll also be taking the phone. The vibrating ringer will be on, but I won't be opening my yap if I'm worried that someone'll overhear."

"Of course," Alberto said. "I'm still against this," he added, "but good luck, Boss."

"Thanks," Herbert said as he pulled off the two-lane roadway. There was a rest station with gas, food, and rooms: no vacancies, the sign said, which told Herbert that they were either full of visiting neo-Nazis or that the owners didn't want them around. He swung into the lot and parked behind the modern, one-story building, then crossed his fingers as he pressed the button to release his chair. He feared his bumper-car chase might have affected the mechanics of the Mercedes. But it didn't, and five minutes later he was rolling up a gentle slope in the blue-orange light of approaching dusk.

THIRTY-SIX

Thursday, 5:30 P.M., Hamburg, Germany

The stretch limousine arrived at Jean-Michel's hotel promptly on the half hour.

The afternoon news had been full of the St. Pauli fire along with condemnation for the club's owner. Feminists were glad and Communists were glad and the press behaved as though they had been vindicated. It seemed to Jean-Michel that Richter was as widely castigated for his career in the escort and social club trade as he was for his political beliefs. Old tape was run of Richter defending himself, claiming that he was in the "peace of mind" business. The company of females put men at ease so that they could meet great challenges. His businesses made this possible.

And Richter is no fool, Jean-Michel had thought as he watched the broadcasts. Condemnation by feminists, Communists, and the press—none of whom were much liked by the average German—only served to drive those men closer to Richter's 21st National Socialist Party.

Jean-Michel had gone outside the hotel at 5:25. Waiting under the awning, he had not been sure that Richter would come. Or if he did show up, that he wouldn't arrive with a truck filled with militiamen to exact vengeance for the fire.

But that wasn't Richter's style. From what they'd heard, it was Karin Doring's. Richter had pride, and after the limousine stopped and the doorman opened the door, Jean-Michel looked to his left. He nodded. M. Dominique had insisted that Henri and Yves go with him, and they climbed in with Jean-Michel between them. They faced the rear of the car with their backs to the partition that separated them from the driver. Yves shut the door. Each man was an unhealthy gray in the dim light which passed through the dark-tinted windows.

Jean-Michel was not surprised to find Richter considerably more subdued than before. The German was sitting alone in the backseat, across from them. He sat quite still, looking at them but not speaking. Even when Jean-Michel greeted him, Richter nodded once but said nothing. Once they were under way, the German didn't take his eyes off Jean-Michel and his bodyguards. He watched them from the shadows, his hands in the lap of his fawn-colored suit pants, his shoulders erect.

Jean-Michel didn't expect him to be talkative. However, as Don Quixote had said, it was the responsibility of the victor to minister to the wounds of the vanquished. And there were things which needed to be said.

"Herr Richter," he said softly, "it was not M. Dominique's wish for things to escalate as they did."

Richter's eyes had been on Henri. They shifted to Jean-Michel, moving like tiny gears.

"Is that an apology?" the German asked.

Jean-Michel shook his head. "Consider it an olive branch," he said. "One which I hope you'll accept."

Richter replied unemotionally, "I spit on it and you."

Jean-Michel seemed slightly taken aback. Henri grumbled restlessly.

"Herr Richter," said Jean-Michel, "you must realize that you cannot beat us."

Richter smiled. "Those are the same words Hauptmann Rosenlocher of the Hamburg police has used for years. Yet I'm still here. And thank you for the fire, by the way. The Hauptmann is so busy trying to figure out who wanted me dead that he and his overworked staff of uncorruptibles have allowed me to slip away."

Jean-Michel said, "M. Dominique is not a policeman. He has been a very generous benefactor. Your political offices were untouched and M. Dominique has made money available to you so that you can reestablish yourself professionally."

"At what price?" Richter asked.

"Mutual respect."

"Respect?" Richter snapped. "It's subservience! If I do what Dominique wishes he'll allow me to survive."

"You don't understand," Jean-Michel insisted.

"Don't I?" Richter replied.

The German reached into his jacket pocket, and both Henri and Yves started forward. Richter ignored them. He withdrew a cigarette case, put a cigarette in his mouth, and replaced the case. He froze, looking at Jean-Michel.

"I understand you very well," Richter said. "I've been thinking all afternoon, trying to understand why it was so important to keep me down."

He withdrew his hand, and before Jean-Michel saw that he was not holding a cigarette lighter, it was too late. The compact FN Model Baby Browning pistol spit twice, once to the left of Jean-Michel, once to the right. The bang was loud, drowning out the distinctive *thunk* as the bullet passed through the forehead of each bodyguard.

As the car turned left, both bodies slumped toward the driver's side. His ears buzzing, Jean-Michel made a long, frightened face as Henri flopped against him. Brownish-red blood pooled in the small, neat wound and spilled over. It streamed down the bridge of the dead man's nose. Half-screaming, half-moaning, Jean-Michel used a shoulder to nudge the body against the door. Then he looked at the dead Yves, whose bloody trickle had broken into spidery red lines on his face. Finally, Jean-Michel turned terror-wide eyes on Richter.

"I'll have them buried in the woods when we arrive," said Richter. He spat the cigarette to the floor. "By the way, I don't smoke."

Still holding the gun, the German leaned forward. He removed the pistols in Yves's and Henri's shoulder holsters and placed one of the guns on the seat to his right. He examined the other.

"An F1 Target Pistol," Richter said. "Army issue. Were these former army men?"

Jean-Michel nodded.

"That would explain their incredibly poor reflexes," Richter said. "The French military never did know how to train soldiers to fight. Not like the German military."

He set the guns down, patted Jean-Michel's chest and pockets to make sure he had no weapons, then sat back. He crossed his legs and put his hands on his knee.

"Details," Ricther said. "If you see them, smell them, hear them, remember them, then at worst you will survive and at best you will succeed. And trust," he said darkly, "is something you should never give. I made the mistake of being honest with you, and I paid for it."

"You tortured me!" Jean-Michel practically

screamed. Jean-Michel was unnerved by the presence of the dead men, but he was rattled even more by the cavalier way with which Richter had dispatched them. The Frenchman fought the impulse to throw himself from the door of the limousine. He was M. Dominique's representative. He must try to maintain his composure, his dignity.

"Do you really think that's why Dominique attacked me?" Richter asked. He smiled for the first time, seemed almost paternal now. "Be wise. Dominique attacked me to put me in my place. And he has. He reminded me that I belong on top of the ladder, not in the middle."

"On top?" Jean-Michel said. The man's gall was astounding. Indignation helped Jean-Michel forget his fear, his vulnerability. "You are on top of nothing but two corpses"—he shook his hands toward either side—"for which you will be made to account."

"You are wrong," the German replied evenly. "I still have my fortune, and I'm on top of the largest group of neo-Nazis on earth."

"That's a lie. Your group is not—"

"What it was," Richter interrupted. He smiled mysteriously.

Jean-Michel was confused. Confused and still very frightened.

Richter settled back into the thick leather seat. "This afternoon was quite an epiphany, M. Horne. You see, we all get caught up in business and objects and trappings. And we lose sight of our own strengths. Stripped of my livelihood, I was forced to ask myself, 'What *are* my strengths? What are my goals?' I realized I was losing sight of those. I did not spend the remainder of the afternoon mourning what happened today. I telephoned my supporters and asked them to come to Hanover this evening at eight o'clock. I told them I'll have an announcement to make. One that will change the tenor of politics in Germany—in all of Europe.''

Jean-Michel watched him, waiting.

Richter went on. ''Two hours ago, Karin and I agreed to merge *Feuer* and the 21st Century National Socialists. We will announce the union in Hanover tonight.''

Jean-Michel sat forward abruptly. ''The two of you? But this morning you said she wasn't a leader, she—''

''I said she wasn't a visionary,'' Richter pointed out. ''That's why I will lead the new union and she'll be my field commander. Our party will be known as *Das National Feuer*—The National Fire. Karin and I will be meeting at her camp. We'll lead her people to Hanover and there, with my followers, as well as the thousand or so believers who are already present, nearly three thousand of us will create an impromptu march the likes of which Germany hasn't seen for years. And the authorities will do nothing to stop us. Even if they suspect Karin of today's attack on the movie set, they won't have the courage to arrest her. Tonight, M. Horne—tonight you will see the birth of a new force in Germany, led by the man you sought to humble this afternoon.''

As Jean-Michel listened, he was struck with the numbing realization of what he had wrought, how he had let M. Dominique down. For a moment, the Frenchman forgot his fear.

Jean-Michel said quietly, ''Herr Richter. M. Dominique has plans of his own. Grand plans, better financed and farther along than yours. If he can throw the United States into turmoil—and he can, and will—he can certainly fight you.''

''I expect him to try,'' said Richter. ''But he won't take Germany from me. What will he use? Money?

Some Germans can be bought, but not all. We are not French. Force? If he attacks me, he creates a hero. If he kills me he has to deal with Karin Doring, who will find him, I promise you. Do you remember how effective the Algerians were paralyzing Paris in 1995, bombing the subways and threatening the Eiffel Tower? If Dominique moves against us, the National Fire will move against France. Dominique's organization is large, a very easy target. Our operation is smaller and more mobile. He can destroy a business today or an office tomorrow, and I'll simply relocate. And each time, I'll exact a greater price from his big elephant's hide."

The limousine had been driving south from Hamburg, and day was fast becoming night. The world outside the darkened windows reflected the blackening feeling in Jean-Michel's soul.

Richter took a long breath, then said barely above a whisper, "In just a few years this country will be mine. Mine to restore, just as Hitler built the Reich on the wreckage of the Weimar Republic. And the irony is that you, M. Horne, were the architect. You showed me that I was facing an enemy I didn't anticipate."

Jean-Michel said, "Herr Richter, you mustn't regard M. Dominique as an enemy. He can help you, still."

Richter sneered, "You are the perfect diplomat, M. Horne. A man burns down my business. Then you not only tell me but actually *believe* he is my ally. No," said Richter. "I think it's fair to say that my goals are different from those of Dominique."

"You're wrong, Herr Richter," Jean-Michel said. He found courage in his desire not to disappoint M. Dominique. "Your dream is to restore German pride. M. Dominique supports that goal. A stronger Germany strengthens all of Europe. The enemies are not here but in Asia and across the Atlantic. This alliance means a great deal to him. You know his love of history, of re-establishing old bonds—''

"Stop." Richter held up his hand. "I saw, this afternoon, what our alliance means. It means that he commands and I serve."

"Only because he has a master plan!"

Fury seemed to envelope Richter. He exploded from his seat. "Master plan!" he roared. "While I was sitting in my office, shaking with anger and calling my supporters and trying to resurrect my dignity, I asked myself, 'If Dominique is not the supporter of my cause, as he represented himself to be, then what *is* he?' And I realized that he is a beekeeper. He is raising us here in Germany and America and Britain to buzz through the corridors of power to sting, to distract, to disorient. Why? So that the backbone of each nation, its business and industry, invests its capital and future in the only stable site in the west: France." Richter calmed, but his eyes remained fierce. "I believe that Dominique wants to create an industrial oligarchy with himself at its head."

Jean-Michel said, "M. Dominique wants to expand his industrial power base, yes. But he doesn't want it for himself or even for France. He wants it for Europe."

Richter snickered. *"Lass mich in Ruhe,"* he said dismissively. He sat back with the guns close by. Then he reached over to the bar between the seats, drank from a bottle of sparkling water, and shut his eyes.

Leave him alone, Jean-Michel thought. This was insane. *Richter* was insane. There were two bodies in the car, the world was about to be disordered and reconfigured, and this madman was taking a nap.

"Herr Richter," Jean-Michel implored, "I urge you

to cooperate with M. Dominique. He can and he *will* help you, I promise.''

Without opening his eyes, the German said, ''M. Horne, I don't care to listen to anymore. It's been a long and stressful day and it will be two hours, at least, before we reach our destination. Some of the country roads are a bit shabby. You might want to close your eyes as well. You look a little peaked.''

''Herr Richter, please,'' Jean-Michel persisted. ''If you'd only listen.''

Richter shook his head. ''No. We'll be silent now, and later, *you* will listen. And then you will report to Dominique. Or perhaps you will elect to remain here. Because you will see why I am confident that Felix Richter and not Gerard Dominique will be the next Führer of Europe.''

THIRTY-SEVEN

Thursday, 5:47 P.M., Hamburg, Germany

The Ambassador Hotel was located on Heidenkamp-sweg, on the other side of Hamburg. Hood was barely aware of being driven through the crowded streets or over the crisscrossing beauty of the narrow canals and basins. When the car pulled up, Hood bolted out and ran to the house telephones. He asked the operator for Ms. Bosworth. An awful silence followed, as he waited to be told that she had checked out or that she had lied to him about where she was staying and there was no one here by that name.

"Hold on, please," the operator said in English, "and I will ring that room for you."

Hood thanked the man, then held on. His heart was thumping out of control. His mind was everywhere yet nowhere. He would think about Gerard Dominique and the hate games, but he always ended up back on Nancy. What they'd had. What she'd done. What they'd lost. And then he would get angry with himself because his heart was out of control that way too. He was consumed, again, with Nancy Jo. Even though his hunger could go, *would* go nowhere.

"Hello?"

Hood leaned on his forearm, against the wall. "Hi," he said.

"Paul? Is that you?" Nancy sounded genuinely surprised, and pleased.

"Yes, Nancy. I'm in the lobby. Can we talk?"

"Of course! Come up."

He said, "It might be better if you came down."

"Why? Are you afraid I'll attack you the way I used to?"

"No," Hood said, uncomfortable with his thoughts. He wasn't afraid at all, damn him.

"Then come on up and help me pack," she insisted. "Fifth floor, turn right, last door on the left."

She hung up and Hood stood there for a moment, listening to the dial tone. At least it drowned out his heart.

What are you doing, asshole? he asked himself. After a moment of self-pity, he answered, *You're going to find out information about Gerard Dominique. About hate games. About what might be going on in Toulouse. And then you're going to go back to Hausen's office to report on what you've found.*

Replacing the phone in its cradle, Hood turned toward the elevators and rode to the fifth floor.

Nancy answered the door wearing tight jeans and a pink polo shirt. The shirt was tucked in, emphasizing her delicate shoulders. The raised collar showed off her long neck. She had pulled her hair into a ponytail like the one she'd used to wear when they went bike riding.

She smiled her perfect smile, then turned and walked back to the bed. There was an open suitcase on the cover. As she packed the last of her toiletries, Hood walked over.

"I'm pretty surprised to see you," Nancy said. "I

thought when we said good-bye, that was it.''

"Which time?" Hood asked.

Nancy looked up. Hood stood at the foot of the bed and watched her.

"Touché," Nancy said with a little smile. She finished packing, closed the suitcase, and set it on the floor. Then she sat down slowly, gracefully, like a lady riding sidesaddle. "So what is it, Paul?" she asked, the smile fading, softening. "Why did you come?"

Hood said, "Truthfully? To ask you a couple of questions about your work."

Nancy stared at him. "Are you serious?"

He shut his eyes and nodded.

"I think I'd rather have heard something untruthful," she said. She rose and turned away. "You haven't changed, have you Paul? Romantic as Scaramouche in the bedroom, celibate as St. Francis on the job."

"That's not true," he said. "This is a bedroom, and I'm being celibate."

Nancy looked at Paul and he smiled. She started to laugh. "That's two for you, St. Paul," she said.

"It's Pope Paul now," he corrected her. "At least, that's what they call me in Washington."

"I'm not surprised," Nancy said. She walked toward him. "Coined, I'm willing to bet, by a frustrated female admirer."

"As a matter of fact, it was," Hood said. He blushed.

Nancy walked up to him, and he began to turn away from her. She put her hands on his waist, hooked fingers into his belt loops, and stopped him. She looked up into his eyes.

"All right, Pope Paul," she said. "What did you want to ask me about my work?"

Hood looked down at her. He didn't know what to do

with his arms and put them behind him, his left forearm in his right hand. One of her knees was beside his, inside his leg.

Well what the hell did you think was going to happen? he asked himself. *You knew this wasn't going to be easy.* What bothered him more, though, was that this was exactly what a big part of him had wanted. God help him, but it did.

"This is silly," he said. "How am I supposed to talk to you like this?"

"You just did," she pointed out softly. "Now do it again."

Hood's forehead was hot, his heart was on overdrive, and blood was racing everywhere. He smelled the apricot shampoo in her hair, felt her warmth, saw those eyes he had looked down into so often in the dark—

"Nancy, no," he said firmly. He took her wrists and held them as he stepped back. "We can't do this. We can't."

She looked down as her magnificent, sensual posture deflated.

"Your work," Hood said, breathing deeply. "I need you to tell me—I mean," he said, calming, "I'd like you to tell me what you're working on."

She shot him a disgusted look. "You're out of your mind, you know that?" she asked. She crossed her arms and half-turned.

"Nancy—"

"You reject me and you still want me to help you. I've got a teensy-weensy problem with that, Paul."

"Like I said before," Hood told her, "I didn't reject you. I didn't reject you at all."

"Then why am I here and you over there?"

Hood reached into his jacket pocket and withdrew his

wallet. "Because you rejected me."

He took out the two movie tickets and let them flutter to the bed. Nancy looked at them.

"You rejected me," he said, "and I made myself another life. I won't jeopardize that. I can't."

Nancy picked up the tickets, ran them gently between her thumb and forefinger, then suddenly tore them in half. She gave one set of stubs to Hood and put the other in her jeans pocket.

"I didn't reject you," she said quietly. "Not a day has crept by that I didn't wish I'd grabbed you and taken you with me. Because I saw this in you as well, the conviction of a goddamn knight. You were the only person I ever knew who didn't need New Year's Eve to make resolutions. You always did what you thought was right and then stuck to your decisions."

Hood put the stubs in his wallet. "If it's any consolation, I wish to hell you had grabbed me and taken me with you." He grinned. "Though I'm not sure how I would've taken to being Paul and Nancy, the jet-setting Bonnie and Clyde."

"Shittily," she said. "You'd probably have made me turn myself in."

Hood embraced her, pulled her head to his chest. She held onto him tightly, then tighter still. But it was innocent this time. And a part of him was very, very sad.

"Nance?" he said.

"I know," she replied, still snuggled in his arms. "You want to know about my work."

"Something rotten's happening on-line," he said.

"But something nice is happening here," she said. "I feel safe. Can't I enjoy it a little bit longer?"

Hood stood there listening to his watch tick, looking at the sky darkening outside the window, concentrating on anything but the dream that was in his arms and in his memory. He stood there thinking, *Checkout is in the early afternoon. She stayed to see me, hasn't checked out because she's anticipating more.*

But that wasn't why he was here. An end had to be made.

"Nancy," he said into her ear, "I have to ask you a question."

"Yes?" she said expectantly.

"Have you ever heard of a man named Gerard Dominique?"

Nancy stiffened in his arms, then pushed off against his chest. "Could you possibly be *more* romantic?"

His face turned as if he'd been slapped by the rebuke. "I'm sorry," he said quietly. "You know—" he started, stopped, looked into her eyes. "You know I *can* be. You should know that I want to be. But I didn't come here for romance, Nancy."

Her own eyes pained, she looked at her watch. "There's a plane I can still catch and I think I'll go catch it." She looked from her watch to the bed to her suitcase. "I don't need a ride, thanks. You can go."

Hood didn't move. It was as if two decades had evaporated and he was standing in her apartment, caught in one of those arguments that had started as a flake and had suddenly become a blizzard. It was funny how memory diminished those, but there *had* been a lot of them.

"Nancy," Hood said, "we think that Gerard Dominique may be behind the hate video games which have begun showing up in America. A game like that just showed up on Hausen's computer, with Hausen in it."

"Video games are easy to make," Nancy said. She went to the closet, got her stylish off-white jacket, and pulled it over her shoulders. "Scanning someone's picture in is also easy. Any well-equipped teenager could do it.''

"But earlier today, Dominique phoned and threatened Hausen.''

"Government officials are threatened all the time,'' Nancy said. "And maybe he deserved it. Hausen gets on a lot of people's nerves.''

"Does his thirteen-year-old daughter get on people's nerves too?''

Nancy's lips came together slowly. "I'm sorry,'' she said.

"Of course you are,'' Hood said. "The question is, can you help me? Do you work for this man?''

Nancy turned away. "You think that because I betrayed an employer years ago I'll do it again.''

"This isn't the same thing, is it?'' Hood asked.

Nancy sighed. Her shoulders rolled forward. Hood could feel the storm die aborning.

"Actually,'' she said, "it's exactly the same thing. Paul Hood needs something and once again I'm ready to flush my life down the toilet so he can have it.''

"You're wrong,'' he said. "I didn't ask for the first one. That was your doing.''

"Let me bask in the waves of compassion,'' she said.

"I'm sorry. I feel bad for that headstrong girl, but what you did affected a lot of lives. Yours, mine, my wife's, whoever you were with, whoever we might have touched together—''

"Your kids,'' she said bitterly, "our kids. The kids we never had.''

Nancy stepped forward and put her arms around Hood. She began to cry. Paul held her closer, felt her shoulder blades heaving against his open hands. *What a waste,* he thought. *What a tragic goddamned waste this all was. . . .*

"You don't know how many nights I lay in bed alone," Nancy said, "cursing myself for what I did. I wanted you so bad I was going to go back and turn myself in. But when I called Jessica to see how you were, she told me you had a new girlfriend. So what was the point?"

"I wish you had come back," he said. "And I wish I'd known all of this then."

Nancy nodded. "I was stupid. Insecure. Scared. Angry at you for filling my place. I was a lot of things. I guess I still am. In many ways, time stopped for me twenty years ago and started up again this afternoon." She stepped back and pulled a tissue from the nightstand. She blew her nose and wiped her eyes. "So here we are, full of regrets and one of us at least feeling that you can't go back. And that one isn't me."

"I'm sorry," Hood said.

"Me too," she said back. "Me too." Nancy took a deep breath, stood tall, and looked into his eyes. "Yes," she said, "I work for Gerard Dominique. But I'm not privy to his politics or personal life, so I don't think I can help you there."

"Is there anything you can tell me? What are you working on?"

"Maps," she said. "Of American cities."

"You mean like regular road maps?" Hood asked.

She shook her head. "They're what we call point-of-view maps. A traveler inputs the street coordinates and what appears on the computer screen is exactly what you're looking at. Then you input where you want to go, or ask what's around the next corner, or where the nearest subway or bus stop is, and the computer shows you. Again, from your point of view. You can also get a printout of an overhead map if you want. It helps people plan what they're going to see and how they're going to get around in a particular city.''

''Has Dominique ever done travel guides before?''

''Not to my knowledge,'' Nancy said. ''This'll be a first.''

Hood thought for a moment. ''Have you seen any marketing plans?''

''No,'' Nancy said, ''but that doesn't surprise me. That's not my area. Though one thing which did surprise me is that we haven't done any press releases on these programs. Usually, the publicists come and ask me questions like what's unique about this program or why do people have to have it. That actually happens pretty early in the process so the sales people can solicit orders at the consumer electronics shows. But on this, nada.''

Hood said, ''Nancy—I have to ask this, and I'm sorry. It won't go any farther than myself and my closest associates.''

''You can take out an ad in *Newsweek*,'' she said. ''I can't resist you when you're so damn doing-your-job earnest.''

''Nancy, there may be lives at risk.''

''You don't have to explain,'' she said. ''It's one of the things I loved about you, Sir Knight.''

Hood flushed. ''Thank you,'' he said, and tried to concentrate on what he was doing. ''Just tell me, is *Demain* working on any kind of new technology? Something that ordinary video-gamers would find compelling?''

''Constantly,'' she said. ''But the one we're closest to marketing is a silicon chip which stimulates nerve cells. It was developed for amputees to be able to operate prosthetic limbs or for the augmentation of diminished spinal cord function.'' She grinned. ''I'm not sure whether we actually developed that one, or if it came to *Demain* the same way my old chip did. In any case, we've changed it quite a bit. When it's placed inside a joystick, the chip generates gentle pulses to make a player feel a kind of subtle contentment or harsher pulses to suggest danger. I've tried it. It's all pretty subliminal, something you might not even be aware of. Like nicotine.''

Hood was feeling slightly overwhelmed. A feel-good, feel-bad chip marketed by a bigot. Hate games on-line in the U.S. It seemed like it should be science fiction, but he knew that the technology was out there. Along with the venom to use it.

''Could the two of them be combined?'' he asked. ''Hate games and a chip that affects emotions.''

''Sure,'' Nancy said. ''Why not?''

''Do you think Dominique would?''

''Like I said,'' Nancy told him, ''I'm not part of his inner circle. I just don't know. I didn't even realize he could be churning out hate games.''

''You say that as though it would surprise you,'' Hood observed.

''It would,'' Nancy said. ''You work with someone and you form certain ideas about them. Dominique is a patriot, but a radical?''

Hood had given Hausen his word that he wouldn't say anything about Dominique's past. He doubted that Nancy would believe him in any case.

''Did you ever do anything with images from Toulouse?'' Hood asked.

Nancy said, ''Sure. We used our delicious little fortress as the background for some kind of promotional download.''

''Did you ever see the finished product?''

Nancy shook her head.

''I think I did,'' Hood said. ''It was in the game in Hausen's computer. Nancy, one more thing. Is it possible that those maps you created could be used in games?''

''Of course,'' she said.

''With figures superimposed?'' Hood asked.

''Yes. You could integrate photographs or computer-generated images. Just like in motion pictures.''

Hood was beginning to get a picture he didn't like. He walked slowly toward the phone, sat down on the bed, and picked up the receiver.

''I'm going to call my office,'' he said. ''There's something happening that I'm starting to get real worried about.''

Nancy nodded. ''Since the world's hanging in the balance, you don't have to reverse the charges.''

Hood looked at Nancy. She was smiling. *God bless her,* he thought. She was as prone to psychotic mood swings as ever.

''Actually,'' Hood said as he punched in Mike Rodgers's number, ''the world, or a good part of it, may very well be hanging in the balance. And you may be the only one who can save it.''

THIRTY-EIGHT

Thursday, 12:02 P.M., Washington, D.C.

After noting the information Hood needed, Rodgers farmed it out to Ann, Liz, and Darrell. Ordinarily, information requests went directly to the divisions responsible for surveillance, personal dossiers, code-breaking, and the like. But Hood needed a lot of different information, and asking Rodgers for it was both convenient and an expedient way of bringing his number two up to date.

Rodgers told Hood he'd get back to him as soon as possible.

Moments later, Alberto phoned to tell Mike Rodgers what Bob Herbert was up to. Rodgers thanked him and told him that he didn't want to bother Herbert with a return call. Even if the ringer were off, the vibration might distract him. Besides, the intelligence chief knew that his colleague would be behind him. As the only battle-tested warriors among the Op-Center elite, they enjoyed a very special bond.

Rodgers hung up, feeling an equal measure of pride and concern for Herbert. His instinct was to call for an extraction team to be flown in from one of the American bases in Germany. But during Chaos Days a stand down order had been issued to all American troops stationed in Germany, and all leaves cancelled. The last thing the governments of Germany and America wanted was an incident involving the military that might galvanize the neo-Nazis. It was best, under the circumstances, to let Herbert go in alone.

Rodgers was reflecting on Herbert's chances for success when Darrell McCaskey arrived. He was wearing one of his pained looks and carrying a short stack of distinctive white FBI folders with the Bureau's seal on front and "Eyes Only" stamped beneath.

"That was quick," Rodgers said.

McCaskey sat heavily in an armchair. "That's because we've got what Larry Rachlin would call *bupkis* on this Dominique character. Man, has he lived a careful life. I've got some other stuff for you too, but that was the big nothing."

"Let's have it anyway," Rodgers said.

McCaskey opened the top file. "His name was originally Gerard Dupre. His father ran a successful Airbus spare parts manufacturing plant in Toulouse. When the French economy imploded in the 1980s, Gerard had already moved the family business into video games and computers. His company, *Demain,* is privately held and worth an estimated $1 billion."

"*That* kind of money is not—what'd you call it?"

"*Bupkis,*" McCaskey said, "and no, it isn't. But he looks clean as Lady Godiva's horse. The only blot seems to be some money-laundering scheme he worked through the Nauru Phosphate Investment Trust Fund, and he got wrist-slapped for that."

"Tell me about it," Rodgers said. Nauru sounded familiar, though he couldn't figure out why.

McCaskey looked at the file. "In 1992, Dominique and some other French businessmen reportedly gave money to a nonexistent bank there, while the money actually went through a series of banks to Switzerland.''

''And then where?''

McCaskey said, ''It was disbursed to fifty-nine different accounts throughout Europe.''

''So funds could have gone from any of those fifty-nine accounts to anywhere else.''

''Exactly,'' said McCaskey. ''Dominique was fined for not paying French taxes on the money, but he paid up and that was that. Since a couple of the intermediary banks were in the U.S., the FBI started keeping a file on him.''

Rodgers said, ''Nauru's in the Pacific, isn't it?''

McCaskey read from the file. ''It's north of the Solomon Islands, about eight square miles big. It's got a president, no taxes, the highest per capita income in the world, and one business. Phosphate mining. Used for fertilizer.''

That was where he'd heard of it, Rodgers thought. He'd slumped down while thinking about Herbert, but was now sitting tall. ''Yes, Nauru,'' Rodgers said. ''The Japanese occupied it during World War II and enslaved the natives. And the Germans had it for some time before that.''

''I'll have to take your word for it,'' McCaskey said.

''What about Dominique's name?'' Rodgers asked. ''He changed it from Dupre. Was he ashamed of his family?''

''Liz was working with me and wondered the same thing as the data came through,'' McCaskey said. ''But there's no evidence of that. He was raised a strict Roman Catholic, and what Liz thinks is that he may have taken the name from St. Dominic. The FBI's file says that he gives a lot of money to Dominican charities and to a school named after the most famous Dominican, St. Thomas Aquinas. Liz thinks that being one of the so-called *Domini canes,* the dogs of the Lord, would have appealed to Dupre's sense of orthodoxy and empire-building.''

"As I recall," Rodgers said, "Dominic also had a reputation as being something of an inquisitor. Some historians regard him as the brains behind the bloody massacre of the Albigenses of Languedoc."

"Again, I'm out of my element," McCaskey said. "But now that you mention it, there is an interesting possible connection here," he said. He looked in the second dossier, which was marked *Hate Groups*. "Have you ever heard of the Jacobins?"

Rodgers nodded. "They were thirteenth-century French Dominican friars. Because they set up headquarters in the Rue St. Jacques, they were called Jacobins. During the French Revolution, anti-monarchists who met in a former Jacobin convent were called Jacobins. They were a violent, very radical factor in the Revolution. Robespierre, Danton, and Marat were all Jacobins."

McCaskey frowned. "I don't know why I bother to try and tell you anything related to history. Okay. Now have you heard of the New Jacobins?"

"Ironically, I have," Rodgers said. "Just today, in fact. Alberto said something that a Colonel in the Gendarmarie Nationale was going after them."

"That would be Colonel Ballon," McCaskey said. "He's an odd duck, but they're his pet cause. For seventeen years, the New Jacobins have targeted foreigners in France, mostly Algerian and Moroccan immigrants. They're the exact opposite of the glory hounds who call and claim credit for every kidnapping and hijacking. They strike hard and fast and then vanish."

"Seventeen years," Rodgers said thoughtfully. "When did Dominique change his name?"

McCaskey smiled. "Bingo."

Rodgers stared ahead as he followed the thread. "So Gerard Dominique may be involved with, possibly even head a group of French terrorists. Then if we know that, so must the French.''

"We'll have to wait and see what Ballon says," McCaskey said. "I'm told he's on a stakeout now and is in no mood to take calls."

"It's going that well?"

"Apparently," said McCaskey. "Dominique is as reclusive as billionaires come."

Rodgers said, "But being reclusive doesn't make him untouchable. If you can't take him by a frontal assault, there's always a flanking maneuver. What about the money Dominique sent through Nauru? We might be able to get to him through that. It could be just one branch of a big damn tree."

"Undoubtedly," said McCaskey. "A man like Dominique could be using hundreds if not thousands of banks to finance groups like that the world over."

"Okay, but why?" Rodgers asked. "He's created a front that's worldwide and there has to be a weak spot. Is he power hungry? Doesn't sound like it. He's a French patriot. So why would he care what happens in England or South Africa or anywhere else? Why would he spread himself out like that?"

"Because he's also an international businessman," McCaskey said. "One of the first things lost in terrorist confrontations is confidence in the system. If it's an airplane hijacking, we lose faith in airport security. Air travel drops for a while. If it's a tunnel bombing, people take bridges or stay at home."

"But the infrastructure recovers."

"That's been true so far," McCaskey pointed out. "But what if several systems were to be weakened at once? Or the same system is hit repeatedly? Look at Italy. The Red Brigade kidnapped Prime Minister Aldo

Moro and shook them up for months in 1978. Cut to 1991, when Albanian refugees began flooding Italy because of political turmoil at home. Terrorists hit Italy again. Thirteen years had passed, almost to the week, yet the international business community started having flashbacks. To them, Italy was out of control again. There was no confidence in the government. Foreign investments began to drop almost at once. What would have happened if the terrorism had kept up or spread? The financial damage would have been immeasurable. Look at Hollywood.''

"What about it?''

McCaskey said, "You think the studios began opening soundstages in Florida because it was sunnier there, or real estate was cheaper? No. They were afraid that earthquakes and racial unrest could destroy the film industry.''

Rodgers was trying to digest everything McCaskey had thrown at him. From McCaskey's own expression, so, obviously, was he.

"Darrell,'' Rodgers said thoughtfully, "how many white supremacist groups would you estimate there are in the United States?''

"I don't have to estimate,'' he said. He flipped through several pages in the second file in his lap, the file marked *Hate Groups*. "According to the FBI's latest white paper, there are seventy-seven different white supremacist-neo-Nazi-skinhead groups, with a total membership of some thirty-seven thousand people. Of those, nearly six thousand people belong to armed militias.''

"What's the disbursement?''

"Nationally?'' McCaskey asked. "Basically, they're in every state of the union and in every major city of each state, including Hawaii. Some target blacks, some

Asians, some Jews, some Mexicans, some all of the above. But they're everywhere."

"That doesn't surprise me," Rodgers said. He was angry, but he refused to be daunted. He recalled, from his extensive readings in history, how the Founding Fathers themselves were bitterly disappointed that independence didn't mean an end to inequality and hate. Rodgers remembered one quote from a letter Thomas Jefferson wrote to John Adams. To attain that goal, Jefferson had written, *"Rivers of blood must yet flow, and years of desolation pass over; yet the object is worth rivers of blood, and years of desolation."* Rodgers would not permit himself or anyone serving beside him to buckle under the load.

"What are you thinking?" McCaskey asked.

"How I want to kick a bunch of damn-fool ass for Thomas Jefferson." Rodgers ignored McCaskey's confused stare. He cleared his throat. "Did anything else turn up on the Pure Nation computer?"

McCaskey went to the third and final folder. "No," he said, "and we're all kind of surprised how little new information there is."

"Bad luck or did they manage to erase it?"

"I'm not sure," McCaskey said. "Everyone at the Bureau is afraid to look this gift horse in the mouth. It looks like it's going to be great PR, especially among blacks. No one was hurt and we've got some bad guys behind bars."

"But it was a little too easy," Rodgers said for him.

"Yeah," McCaskey replied, "I think so. And I think the Bureau thinks so too. The biggest question is why an outside group was sent in to attack the Chaka Zulu people. One of the most virulent hate groups in the nation, the Koalition, is based in Queens. That's right over the East River, closer than Pure Nation was even in New York. Yet there appears to have been no contact between the two.''

Rodgers said, ''I wonder if this is similar to what the Axis used to do.''

''What, disinformation?''

Rodgers nodded. ''Bob and I have a file on it. If you have time look it up—*Das Bait*. The essence of it is, if you want to mislead a foe, let them capture a unit loaded with misinformed soldiers. If the enemy buys into what they say, ten or twelve men can effectively tie up a division or even a whole army waiting for an invasion that never comes or hunkering down in the wrong place. The Allies refused to do this because of the harsh treatment accorded prisoners of war. But the Germans and Japanese did it regularly. And if the captured soldiers didn't *know* they were lying, there was no way the information could be drugged out of them. You had to put your people in the field and investigate. How many people did the FBI have on the case?''

''Roughly thirty.''

''And now?'' Rodgers asked. ''How many people are checking down leads or investigating Pure Nation?''

''About seventy or eighty nationwide.''

''And those are the top experts in white supremacist groups,'' Rodgers said. ''So a handful of Pure Nationals gets taken and what happens? The FBI loses the guts of its anti-white-supremacist force.''

McCaskey thought for a moment, then shook his head. ''That makes sense as a tactic, but it doesn't sound macho enough for the Pure Nationals. They believe in force of arms, not sleight of hand. They'd rather go down fighting.''

''Then why didn't they?'' Rodgers asked.

"Oh, the bastards fought," McCaskey said. "They tried to kill our guys—"

"But they didn't," Rodgers said. "And they still let themselves get taken."

"They were outgunned. The FBI can still fight," McCaskey added defensively.

"I know," said Rodgers. "But if Pure Nation's so macho, why did they surrender? Wouldn't it have helped their cause if they became martyrs and made the FBI look like ruffians?"

"They aren't Kamikazes," McCaskey said. "They're brash and ruthless but they want to live."

"Live," Rodgers said. "These people are barely going to suffer. What's the worst charge these people are facing? They fired at federal agents. They plotted. They stockpiled arms. If they plea-bargain, they're looking at seven to ten years each in prison. Seven to ten years of cable TV and gyms. Out by the time they're thirty-five, forty years old. They're hailed as heroes by their people. That would appeal to any attention-craving sicko."

"Possibly," McCaskey said, "but it doesn't fit in with any of the profiles we've ever seen. Surrender to misinform, then sit in jail? No," McCaskey said, "I still say that isn't enough to satisfy these people."

"And I say we may be looking at a new breed of white supremacist. One who may be adept at playing games."

McCaskey looked at him. He started to say something, then stopped.

Rodgers said, "I know what you're thinking. You still feel we're giving them the benefit of too much forethought."

"Of *any* forethought," McCaskey said. "I don't want to underestimate the enemy, but these are people governed by a bunker mentality and blind rage. Any variation would be an aberration.''

"They're also trained followers,'' Rodgers said. "If you dangle the right prize you can get them to do your bidding. Think about that. What kind of a prize *would* get white supremacists to do what they're told?''

"Freedom,'' McCaskey said. "The freedom to attack what they detest.''

"I'll buy that,'' Rodgers said. "And what gives any person a moral right to attack?''

McCaskey said, "If they're attacked first.''

"Okay,'' Rodgers said. He was getting wound up. McCaskey might not agree, but he felt that there was something here. "Assume you want to make a group attack you. You antagonize them. You make them feel threatened—''

The phone beeped.

"The hate games,'' McCaskey said.

"That's not enough,'' Rodgers said.

There was sudden fear and understanding in McCaskey's eyes. "That, plus letting them know you intend to attack them. You let a black group know they're a target and that galvanizes *all* blacks. Christ, Mike,'' McCaskey said. "There's the impetus for Pure Nation to let itself get arrested. To let Chaka Zulu know that they were a target, even if they weren't. Before you know it, all blacks are behind the militant Zulu group— and a lot of whites have no choice but to stand against them.''

Rodgers nodded vigorously as the phone beeped again. He glanced at it. Ann Farris's calling code was on the LED display at the base.

"That's exactly what happened in the 1960s,'' McCaskey said, "when the Black Panthers became the militant allies of a number of civil rights groups.''

Rodgers said, ''If all of this really does fit together—Dominique, his money, hate groups, and the destabilization of Europe and the U.S.—we'd have one serious worldwide disaster.'' Rodgers put the phone on speaker. ''Sorry to keep you waiting, Ann.''

''Mike, Darrell told me you needed a check on press releases from *Demain*,'' she said. ''I called D'Alton and D'Alton, their New York press people, and got the latest stuff faxed over.''

''And?''

''It's all run-of-the-mill tub-thumping about games,'' Ann said, ''except for one. It's about a new joystick.''

''What's it say?''

''That with the new Enjoystick, you don't just play the game—you feel it.''

Rodgers sat up taller. ''Go on.'' This was a perfect match with the hate games. He felt a chill in the small of his back.

Ann said, ''It's FCC-approved and it's a new technology which stimulates nerve cells through a patented fingerprint-operated biolink. I guess that's to make sure you only use the link on your hands and not on other parts of the body. It says here that with an Enjoystick, you'll feel all the thrills and excitement that your video-game character experiences on-screen.''

Rodgers said, ''Along with the hate and love and all stops in between.''

''It doesn't say anything about that,'' Ann told him, ''but I can't believe something like this exists. I feel like I'm in a science fiction movie.''

''You're not,'' Rodgers said. ''A lot of people still don't understand the power of this technology, but it's there just the same. Thanks, Ann. This was a big help.''

"Any time, Mike," she said.

Rodgers hung up. Despite—*or because of?* he asked himself—the pressure of piecing together the Pure Nation puzzle, he was gratified by the short, pleasant exchange. He and Ann had never been charter members of each other's fan clubs. She made no secret of her infatuation with and unqualified defense of Paul Hood. That had often put her at odds with Rodgers, whose approach to crisis management was less diplomatic than Hood's. But Rodgers was working on that, and Ann was trying hard to accept that there was more than Hood's way of doing things.

There's probably a lesson for all of civilization in that, Rodgers thought. Unfortunately, this wasn't the time to don his purple robes and go proselytizing.

Rodgers looked at McCaskey, who was making shorthand notes on the cover of one file at his rapid 140-word-per-minute speed.

"It's all here, Mike," McCaskey said excitedly. "Dammit, it's all friggin' here."

"Let's have it."

McCaskey finished and looked up. "Let's say that Dominique uses bank setups like the one in Nauru to filter money to white supremacist movements. He throws us off the trail by giving us Pure Nation as busywork while at the same time he's quietly greasing the wheels of other groups. He's also getting ready to download hate games, games which can be played with the Enjoysticks. People feel good going after minorities." He looked at Rodgers. "I agree with Ann—that's a little bit too *Amazing Stories* for me—but let's put it in the mix for now. It's really not *that* crucial."

"Agreed," said Rodgers.

"Blacks are outraged by the games. Newspapers are

outraged. Right-thinking citizens everywhere are outraged,'' McCaskey said. ''Meanwhile, Pure Nation
doesn't cop a plea, like you said. Uh-uh. They go to trial
because a public forum is exactly what they want. And
the trial happens soon because the evidence is compelling, the FBI pressures the courts to make room, and
Pure Nation won't object to any jurors the prosecution
wants. Their macho needs are satisfied by being the sac-
rificial lambs. They present their case articulately, and if
they're good—and many of these people are—they actually sound *rational*.''

''I'll buy that,'' Rodgers said. ''A core of whites will
secretly buy into a lot of what they say. Whites who
blame high taxes on welfare and unemployment, and
blame welfare and unemployment on blacks.''

''Exactly. Black activists become more outraged as
the trial progresses, and someone on either side, it
doesn't matter which, does something to provoke an incident. The bottom line is rioting. Dominique's operatives make sure it spreads, that there are major
explosions in New York and Los Angeles, Chicago and
Philadelphia, Detroit and Dallas, and pretty soon the
U.S. is on fire.''

''Not just the U.S.,'' Rodgers said. ''Bob Herbert's
up against the same problem in Germany.''

''There you are,'' said McCaskey. ''Dominique raises
hell everywhere in the world—except France. That's
why the New Jacobins operate silently, efficiently, without publicity.'' McCaskey opened Dominique's file, rif-
fled through the pages. ''These guys are unique among
terrorists because they truly do terrorize. There are very
few reported incidents, but most of the time they
threaten people with violence. And then they give specific orders: this group of people leave such-and-such

town or when they return they'll make good their threat. It isn't something big, like get the British out of Ireland. They always order something manageable.''

"Surgical strikes which don't get much press," Rodgers said.

"Try *no* press," said McCaskey. "The French don't give a shit. So with everything else going on, France seems relatively stable. And with Dominique wooing banks and industry and investors, he becomes a serious world player. Maybe the most serious player.''

"While anyone who tries to tie him to terrorism can't," said Rodgers.

"Or they get a nighttime visit from the New Jacobins for even trying," said McCaskey, reviewing the file. "These guys have all the earmarks of the old Mafia. Strongarm tactics, hits, executions, the works.''

Rodgers sat back. "Paul should be back at Richard Hausen's office in Hamburg by now." He looked at a notepad on his desk. "It's RH3-star on the autodial. Bring him up to date and tell him I'm going to try and get through to Colonel Ballon. Unless we've taken a few too many leaps of faith, Dominique is someone we need to get to. And Ballon sounds like the only man who can do that.''

"Good luck," said McCaskey. "He's pretty thorny.''

"I'll wear gloves," said Rodgers. "If I can swing it, and I think I can, I intend to offer him something he won't be able to find in France.''

McCaskey stood. "What's that?" he asked as he straightened a bad back slowly.

Rodgers replied, "Help."

THIRTY-NINE

Thursday, 6:25 P.M., Wunstorf, Germany

Physically, this had been the most demanding, frustrating, and rewarding hour of Bob Herbert's life.

The terrain he'd had to cross was covered with sticks, rotting leaves and tree trunks, rocks, and thick patches of mud. There was one small stream, less than a foot deep, which slowed him further, and at times the ground sloped upward so steeply that Herbert had to get out of his wheelchair and drag it behind him as he worked his way up the incline. At several minutes past six it had begun to get dark in the heavy, unshadowed way that thick woods do. Though his chair was equipped with a powerful flashlight beside each footrest, Herbert was unable to see farther ahead than the diameter of each wheel. That slowed him as well, since he didn't want to go rolling into a gorge and end up like that five-thousand year-old hunter who was found frozen face-down on a mountaintop somewhere.

God only knows what they'd make of me in five thousand years, Herbert thought. Though now that he considered it, he had to admit he relished the idea of a cadre of stuffy academics puzzling over his remains in A. D. 7000. He tried to imagine how they'd interpret the Mighty Mouse tattoo on his left bicep.

And he hurt. From the twigs that stuck him and the muscles that pained him and the chest that still hurt from where the seatbelt had pulled during the chase through Hanover.

Herbert picked his way through the woods, guided by the thirty-year-old Boy Scout pocket compass which had been around the world with him. As he did, he kept track of the distance he covered by counting the turns of his wheel. Each complete revolution was four yards. While he made his way, he also tried to make sense of the neo-Nazis' trip out here. They couldn't have radioed a police ally for assistance, since other officers would have heard. This was the only way to do it. But *why* did they need help? The only thing he could think of was that they needed someone to find him. That sounded grandiose, he knew, but it made sense. The neo-Nazis had fled at the siren, feared he might be able to I.D. them, and wanted to get to him if he went to the station to file a report. A police officer would know who he was and where he was staying.

Herbert shook his head. It would be ironic if he found the girl here. He'd gone to Hanover to try to get information, and these jerks might have led him right to her without even knowing it.

He smiled. Who would have thought that a day which began in a coach-class airplane seat would grow old with him trudging through the wilds, hunting a lost girl, pursued by neo-Nazis?

After a few minutes more, Herbert arrived at the tree where Alberto thought the girl might be. It was unmistakable: tall, twisted, and dark. The tree was three hundred years old at least, and Herbert couldn't help but think about the tyrants it had seen come and go. He felt a flash of shame as he thought how foolish their antics must seem to this stately life.

Reaching down, Herbert removed the flashlight from the footrest. He shined it into the tree.

"Jody," he said, "are you up there?"

Herbert felt a little foolish calling up a tree for a young woman. But he looked up into the leaves and listened. He heard nothing.

"Jody," he said, "my name is Bob Herbert. I'm an American. If you're up there, please come down. I want to help you."

Herbert waited. Again, there was no sound. After a minute, he decided to go around the tree and have a look up the other side. But before he could move, he heard a branch snap behind him. Herbert looked back, thinking it was Jody. He was startled to see a large figure standing in the shadows beside a tree.

"Jody?" he asked, though he could see from the hulking shape it wasn't her.

"Mein Herr," said a deep, masculine voice, "please raise your hands."

Herbert obeyed. He lifted them slowly, face-high. As he did so, the man walked toward him through the darkness. As he approached the wheelchair, fell within the glow of the flashlights, Herbert could see that the man was a police officer. But he wasn't dressed like any of the officers at the van. This man was wearing what looked like a police-issue blue overcoat and a cap.

And then it hit him. The siren. The sudden termination of the chase. The drive out here. The whole thing had been a setup.

"Nice," Herbert said.

The police officer stopped a few feet away—too far to reach even if Herbert could snatch his stick from under the armrest. The man stood with his legs shoulder-width, his expression hidden in the shadows under the brim of his cap. Through the open front of his coat, Herbert saw a cellular phone hooked to his black leather belt.

The intelligence chief just looked up at him and said, "They called you from the van when they were still in the city, didn't they? They pretended to run from your siren, knew I'd follow them, and then you followed me."

The officer did not appear to understand. Not that it mattered. Herbert was disgusted with himself. It would have been easy for the police to find out who had rented the car. He'd made it even worse for himself by using his corporate damn charge card. National Crisis Management Center, U.S.A., the official name of Op-Center. That, coupled with his dramatic appearance in Hanover, told them he was probably looking for something. After calling Jody's name, they knew exactly what. The only way he could have made this any easier for them was by handing out copies of the NRO photographs.

He was glad, at least, that that hadn't been Jody the satellite saw in the tree. If she'd been here, she'd be seconds from death, along with him.

Herbert wasn't going to ask the man for his life. He didn't want to die, but he couldn't live with himself knowing he'd asked a dirtbag like this for anything. He'd gotten sloppy, and this was the price. At least, he told himself, he wouldn't have to schlep all the way back to the car.

I wonder if I'll hear the crack of the gun before the bullet hits, he thought. He was near enough. It would be close.

"Auf Wiedersehen," the German said to him.

FORTY

Thursday, 6:26 P.M., Toulouse, France

Located just a short ride from the popular Place du Capitole and the Garonne River, the Rue St. Rome is one of the shopping streets in old Toulouse. Many of the two- and three-story medieval structures there sag or slant with age. The floors are buckled due to their proximity to the river. But these buildings do not fall. It's as if they're telling the brash, new, out-of-place signs for Seiko watches or mopeds, the once-new TV aerials and still-new satellite dishes, *"No. We won't surrender this street to you."* And so, after centuries of watching ramparts come and go, of bearing silent witness to countless lives and dreams, the facades still look out on the crooked network of narrow roads and hurrying masses.

Situated in a third-floor room of one of those structures, a dilapidated old store called *Magasin Vert* which he had rented, Colonel Bernard Ballon of the Gendarmerie Nationale was watching the live pictures being broadcast from outside the *Demain* factory to four small TV monitors. The plant was located some thirty kilometers north of the city center. But for all the intelligence he was collecting, the plant might just as well have been situated thirty kilometers north of the earth's center.

Ballon's men had placed hidden cameras at all four sides of the ancient edifice in the ancient town of Montauban. They videotaped every truck and employee that entered or left. All they needed to see was one known member of the New Jacobins. Once one of the terrorists had been spotted, Ballon and his elite tactical squad would be inside within twenty minutes. The cars were parked nearby, the men were sitting around audio equipment and other video monitors, and the weapons were in duffel bags in the corner. The search warrants, too, were in order provided they had what the courts called *"raison de suspicion."* Reason for suspicion. Reasons which would survive a defense assault in court.

But however close Dominique's "big push" might be, the reclusive tycoon wasn't getting careless. And Ballon suspected that the push was close indeed. After seventeen long and frustrating years of following the elusive billionaire; after seventeen years of tracking, arresting, and trying to break members of the New Jacobin terrorist organization; after seventeen years of watching his own interest become an obsession, Ballon was certain that Dominique was ready to make something happen. And not just the heralded launch of his new video games. He had launched new games before and they had never required this level of manpower.

Or this level of commitment from Dominique, Ballon thought.

Dominique was staying at the factory more and more at night instead of going home to his red-brick estate in the countryside outside of Mountauban. Employees were working longer shifts. Not just the company's video-game programmers but also the technicians who worked on Internet projects and hardware. He watched their comings and goings on the monitors.

Jean Goddard . . . Marie Page . . . Emile Tourneur.

The Frenchman knew them all by sight. He knew their backgrounds. He knew the names of family members and friends. He'd looked under every rock he could find to learn more about Dominique and his operation. Because he was convinced that twenty-five years ago, when he was a rookie police officer in Paris, this man had gotten away with murder.

The forty-four-year-old officer shifted stiffly in the folding wooden chair. He stretched his short legs and looked distractedly around the makeshift command center. His brown eyes were bloodshot, his weathered jaw was covered with stubble, and his small mouth was slack. Like the seven other men in the room, he was dressed in jeans and a flannel workshirt. They were workers, after all, in Toulouse to restore the building they'd rented. Downstairs, three other men were busy sawing wood they'd never be using.

It had been extremely difficult to convince his superiors to let him undertake this month-long stakeout. The Gendarmerie Nationale was supposed to be an entirely independent caste-blind national police force. But they were very much aware of the legal forces and deadly publicity Dominique could muster against them.

"And for what?" Commander Caton had asked him. *"Because you suspect him of a crime that is more than two decades old? We can't even prosecute him!"*

That was true. Too much time had passed. But did that make the crime or the person who committed it any less monstrous? Upon investigating the crime scene that night, Ballon had learned that wealthy Gerard Dupre had been seen in the area with another man. He'd discovered that they had left Paris for Toulouse after the murders. And the police hadn't wished to pursue them. *Hadn't wished to pursue Dupre,* Ballon thought bitterly, *the upper-class pig.* As a result, he had quite possibly gotten away with murder.

Ballon had resigned from the police force in utter disgust. Then he'd joined the Gendarmerie and studied the Dupre family. Over the years his hobby became a passion. He learned from sealed files in the government archives in Toulouse about how the elder Dupre had been a collaborator during World War II. How he'd infiltrated the Resistance and informed on many of its members. At least thirty deaths over four years were attributed to that *batard.* After the war, Dupre founded a successful business manufacturing spare parts for the Aerospatiale Airbus. He established his company using money from the United States. Money which had been earmarked for the rebuilding of Europe.

Gerard, meanwhile, appeared to resent everything about his father. *Père* Dupre had sold information to the Germans to survive the War. So Gerard surrounded himself with young German students who needed his money to get by. *Père* Dupre had stolen money from the Americans after the War. So Gerard designed software to appeal to Americans, to have them give him their money. *Père* Dupre hated the Communists. Which is why, as a student, Gerard was drawn to them. Everything he did was an act of defiance against his father.

But then something happened to the younger Dupre. After leaving the Sorbonne, he began collecting historical documents. Ballon had talked to some of the autograph dealers from whom Dupre had made purchases. It seemed to amaze Dupre that he could own important letters written by the great figures of the past.

One dealer had told the Gendarmerie officer, *"Gerard seemed to feel as if he were looking over the shoulders of great men. Watching history unfold brought fire to his eyes."* Dupre bought documents from the French Revolution, as well as actual costumes and weapons and memorabilia. He purchased religious letters that were even older. He even bought guillotines.

A psychiatrist who worked for the Gendarmerie said, *"It is not uncommon for people disappointed with the real world to cocoon themselves, to create a safe reality with letters or mementos."*

"And might he then wish to expand that?" Ballon had asked.

"Very possibly," he'd been told. *"Enlarge the haven, as it were."*

When Dupre changed his name to Dominique, there was no longer any question in Ballon's mind that he had begun to see himself as a modern-day saint. The patron saint of France. Or else he had gone mad, or perhaps both. And when the New Jacobins began terrorizing foreigners at the same time, Ballon had little doubt that they were the soldiers guarding Dominique's spiritual fortress—a France that was pure, as chaste as the original Jacobins had envisioned.

The Gendarmerie had refused to launch an official investigation into Dominique. It wasn't just because he was a powerful man. As Ballon quickly discovered, the Gendarmerie was only slightly less xenophobic than Dominique. The only reason he didn't resign was so that he could keep the idea alive that the law was supposed to serve the public—*all* of it. Regardless of national origin or religion. The son of a Belgian Jewish mother who had been disinherited when she married his poor, French Catholic father, Ballon understood what hate could do.

If he quit the force, the bigots would win.

However, as Ballon watched the video of the factory, he wasn't certain that they hadn't already won.

Ballon pushed his strong fingers along his cheek. He savored the sandpaper roughness of his face. It was manliness that he felt nowhere else in his life. How *could* he feel manly as he sat inactive in this stuffy old room? As they reviewed procedure over and over in case they ever got inside. Code words. "Blue" for attack. "Red" for stay where you were. "Yellow" for retreat. "White" for civilians in danger. Light pulses via the radio in case audio would give someone away. One tone to close in. Two to stay where they were. Three to retreat. Emergency contingencies. He was beginning to wonder if Dominque knew about the investigation and was intentionally doing nothing in order to embarrass Ballon and put a stake in the heart of his investigation.

Or are you just being paranoid?

After this long at any task, Ballon had heard that paranoia was an inevitability. He had once had one of Dominique's men tailed, a longtime employee named Jean-Michel Horne. Horne had gone to a meeting whistling and Ballon's first thought was that he was whistling to annoy Ballon.

He rubbed his face harder. *It's working,* he thought as he exploded from the chair with disgust. He checked the urge to kick it through a ten-pane window that was older than he was.

The other men in the room jumped.

"Tell me, Sergeant!" Ballon demanded. "Tell me why we should not simply storm the place? Shoot Dominique and be done with it!"

"I honestly don't know," replied Sergeant Maurice Ste. Marie, who had been sitting beside him. "I'd rather die in action than die of boredom.''

"I *want* him,'' Ballon said, ignoring his subordinate. His hand became a fist and he rattled it at the TV monitor. He put his entire body into the shaking of the fist. ''He is a corrupt, twisted maniac who wants to corrupt and twist the world.''

''Unlike us,'' said Sergeant Ste. Marie.

Ballon fired him a look. ''Yes, unlike us! What do you mean?''

''We are obsessed men who want to keep the world free so that it can continue to breed lunatics like Dominique. Either way, it seems a hopeless tangle.''

''Only if you give up hope,'' said Ballon. He retrieved his chair, slammed it back into place, and sat down heavily. ''I lose sight of that sometimes, but it's still out there. My mother always hoped her family would forgive her for marrying my father. That hope was in every birthday card she ever sent them.''

''Did they ever forgive her?'' asked Sergeant Ste. Marie.

Ballon looked at him. ''No. But hope kept my mother from becoming deeply depressed about it. Hope, plus the love she had for my father and me, filled that emptiness.'' He turned back to the screen. ''Hope and the hate I have for Dominique keeps me from becoming too depressed. I *will* get him,'' he said as the telephone rang.

One of the young officers answered the phone. There was a scrambler attached to the mouthpiece, one which mixed high and low voice tones at one end and descrambled them at the other.

''Sir, it's another call being routed from America.''

Ballon screamed, ''I *told* them before not to put anyone through. It's either a bloody opportunist trying to ride our efforts across the finish line, or a saboteur trying to hold us back. Whichever it is, tell them to go to hell!''

"Yes, sir.''

"Now they want to help me. *Now!*'' Ballon muttered. "Where have they been for seventeen years?''

Sergeant Ste. Marie said warily, "Perhaps this is not what you think.''

"What are the chances of that?'' Ballon asked. "Dominique has employees the world over. It's better if we stay insulated, uncontaminated.''

"Inbred,'' Ste. Marie added.

The Colonel looked at the crisp color video picture of leaves moving slowly beside the wall of the ancient fortress which was now a factory. Ste. Marie had a point. These four days here had been totally unproductive.

"Wait!'' Ballon barked.

The soldier repeated the command into the telephone. His face was expressionless as he watched the commander.

Ballon rubbed his face. He wouldn't know the answer to that unless he took the call. *And what was more important?* he asked himself. *Pride or getting Dominique?*

"I'll take it,'' he said.

He walked briskly toward the phone, arm extended as Sergeant Ste. Marie watched with delight.

"Don't look so pleased,'' Ballon said to him as he passed. "It was my own decision. You had nothing to do with it.''

"No, sir,'' Ste. Marie replied as he continued to look very pleased.

Ballon took the phone. "This is Ballon. What is it?''

"Colonel,'' said the dispatcher, "I have a phone call from General Michael Rodgers of the National Crisis Management—''

"Colonel Ballon,'' Rodgers cut in, "forgive the interruption but I need to talk to you.''

"C'est evidement."

"Do you speak English?" Rodgers asked. "If not, give me a minute to get a translator—"

"I speak English," Ballon said reluctantly. "What is it, General Rodgers?"

"I understand you're trying to close in on a mutual enemy."

"Trying, yes."

"We believe," Rodgers said, "that he's planning to download computer software which will help to cause rioting in cities around the world. We believe he intends to use those riots to throw the economies of major American and European nations into chaos."

Ballon's mouth began to go dry. This man was either a godsend or the pawn of Satan himself. "How do you know this?"

Rodgers said, "If we didn't, the government would take away all the money they give our team."

Ballon liked that too. "What about his terrorist squads? What do you know about those?" he asked, hoping for some new information. *Any* new information.

"Nothing," Rodgers admitted. "But we suspect he's working closely with several neo-Nazi groups in America and abroad."

Ballon was silent for a moment. He still didn't trust this man entirely. "Your information is interesting but not very useful," he said. "I need evidence. I need to find out what's going on inside his fortress."

Rodgers said eagerly, "If that's the problem, I can *help.* I was calling, Colonel Ballon, to offer you the assistance of a NATO commander in Italy. His name is Colonel Brett August, and his speciality is—"

"I have read white papers by Colonel August," said

Ballon. "He is a brilliant counterterrorist operative."

"And a lifelong friend of mine," said Rodgers. "He'll assist you if I ask him. But I also have equipment in Germany which I'll lend to you."

"What kind of equipment?" Ballon asked. He was getting suspicious again. This man seemed like too much of a good thing. A good thing he wouldn't be able to resist. A good thing who might be taking his marching orders from Dominique. A good thing which might end in an ambush.

"It's a new kind of X-ray device," Rodgers said. "One with which my operator can probably work some near-miracles."

"A new kind of X-ray," Ballon said dubiously. "That isn't going to help. I don't need to know where people are—"

"It might be able to read papers for you," Rodgers said. "Or lips."

Ballon was attentive but still wary. "General Michael Rodgers," he said. "How do I know you're not working with Dominique?"

Rodgers said, "Because we also know about a pair of murders he committed twenty-five years ago. We know about them because we know the person who was with him at the time. I can tell you nothing more—except that I want Dominique brought to justice."

Ballon looked at his men, who were all looking at him. "Watch the monitors!" he yelled.

They did. Ballon was dying to get out of there and into action.

"All right," said the Colonel. "How do I get in touch with this miracle worker of yours?"

Rodgers said, "Stay where you are. I'll have him phone you there."

Ballon agreed and hung up. Then he told Ste. Marie to take three men outside and watch the building. If it looked as though anyone was staking them out or closing in on them, they were to radio him at once.

But Ballon had a feeling in his gut that General Rodgers was one of the good men, just as he'd had a feeling in his gut about Dominique being one of the bad men.

I only hope my gut is not getting soft, he said as Ste. Marie and the men left and he continued to stand by the telephone.

FORTY-ONE

Thursday, 9:34 A.M., Studio City, California

He called himself Streetcorna, and he sold audio tapes from a panther-skin backpack. Every day for more than a year, around seven in the morning, the young man would leave his battered old Volkswagen in the parking lot behind the strip of stores off Laurel Canyon in Studio City, and walk toward Ventura Boulevard. As he walked, his black leather sandals dragged unhurriedly along the sidewalk, propelled by long, lean legs which were visible beneath the dried leaves of his Sudanese *pagne*. The skirt was held up by a shoulder strap made of leopard skin. Beneath the straps was a sweat-stained black T-shirt with white lettering which read "STREET-CORNA RAP." His hair was shaved around the sides, leaving only a large clump in the center which was woven with wood into a latticed cone. His eyes were invisible behind his wraparound shades. The tiny diamond studs in his nostrils and tongue shined with perspiration and saliva.

Streetcorna always took his time as he walked to his spot. Heading out, he would smile as he drew on a joint to get ready for the day's huckstering and performing. As the smoke loosened him up, he would move his spindly arms and bony hands with the rhythm in his head.

His thighs began to move to the beat and he shut his eyes and clapped his hands slowly as he walked.

Each day, he had a new lyric. Today it was, *"IgotIgot Igot I got I got what I need if I got my weed. Smokin' gives me creed 'gainst the slick man's greed. Ana greed like his seed 'severywhere while I bleed. I'm not freed no indeed brother heed foll' my lead."*

Streetcorna stopped walking at the corner, though he kept on moving. He doffed his backpack without losing the beat, unzipped it to reveal the prerecorded cassettes inside, switched on a small tape recorder, then continued his performance. He usually sold five or six tapes a day on the honor system. Since he was too busy to stop, a small, handwritten sign on a cardboard instructed potential customers to deposit what they wanted. Most left five dollars, a few one or two, some ten. He averaged thirty dollars a day, enough for smoke, gas, and food.

"AllIallI allI all I need. . . ."

His biggest score was the day he was brought to the studios across the street on Radford Avenue. He appeared on an evening sitcom, in a street scene, and earned enough money to prerecord some music. Before that, everything was recorded live, in the street, as he sang it. Everyone who bought a Streetcorna tape had an original. Now, they had a choice.

Streetcorna usually wrapped his day at eight or nine in the evening, after the video store down the street had rented most of what it was going to rent and the drugstore and bookstore closed and the traffic slowed. Then he returned to his car, drove to a side street or a grocery store parking lot, and read in his car by streetlight or candlelight.

On the last day of his life, Streetcorna arrived at his post at 7:10 in the morning. He sold one tape for ten dollars during the next two hours, lit a joint at 9:15, and went into his rap, *"I'm a dissin' the Districk, the ho's in Deecee."*

As he rapped with his eyes shut, two young men crossed Laurel Canyon. They were blond, tall, and walking slowly as they ate pita sandwiches. They were wearing tennis whites and carrying gym bags. When they neared Streetcorna, one man stopped slightly behind him on his right, the other slightly behind him on his left. As pedestrians rushed by, trying to make the Walk signal on the light, the men calmly took tire irons from their bags and slammed them into the front of the man's knees.

Streetcorna fell with a howl, his sunglasses shattering as his face hit the pavement. People began to slow and watch as the young man screamed again and curled painfully into a fetal position. Before he could turn and look at his attackers, however, the men raised the irons and brought them down viciously on the side of his head. His skull broke on the first strike, splashing the concrete with blood, but the men delivered two more blows apiece. Streetcorna jerked with each of the blows, then died.

"Jesus!" a young woman screamed as the horrible reality of what had happened made its way through the crowd, like a serpent. "Jesus!" she screamed again, her face entirely white. *"What have you done?"*

As one of the young men stood, the other patted their victim down.

"Silenced his crap," said the man who had risen.

An old black woman leaning on a well-worn cane yelled, "Someone call the police! Someone help!"

The youth looked at her, then walked to where she was standing, by the drugstore. People moved out of his way. The old woman leaned her body away from him but her expression remained defiant.

"Hey!" a middle-aged white man yelled, inserting himself between them. "Back off—"

The attacker drove his right heel down hard on the man's left instep. The middle-aged man crumpled in pain. The black woman backed against the window of the drugstore.

The savage youth put his face in hers and said, "You shut your stinking hole."

"Not as long as I'm breathing American air," she replied.

With a sneer, the youth drove the front of the iron into her mouth. She doubled over and he pushed her down easily.

The young white man lurched forward and threw himself over her.

"Got them," said the other young man as he pulled the keys from Streetcorna's pocket. He rose.

The assailant withdrew casually, as though he were returning to his corner to serve again after hitting a net ball. The two men stood side-by-side as a crowd gathered and formed a loose, threatening circle around them.

"They can't get us all!" someone yelled.

The man with the keys reached into his bag and withdrew a .45. "Like hell we can't," he said.

The crowd didn't so much part as come apart. The men walked through, up Laurel Canyon, ignoring the glares of the pedestrians and the shouts of those in the back. They found Streetcorna's car and got in. They knew it from days of having watched the rapper. Turning onto Laurel Canyon, they headed up into the Hollywood Hills. Unpursued, they were quickly swallowed in the traffic headed toward Hollywood.

Police arrived nearly seven minutes later, and a helicopter search was ordered. The chopper spotted the car parked near the intersection of Coldwater Canyon and Mulholland Drive. It was abandoned and clean. Employees at the fire station on top of the hill remembered seeing a car idling on the side of the road, but no one could remember what kind it was or what the driver looked like. No one saw the Volkswagen arrive or the waiting car leave.

When the police confiscated Streetcorna's bag, there were no tapes, just four hundred dollars and change.

FORTY-TWO

Thursday, 6:41 P.M., Hamburg, Germany

Paul Hood arrived at Hausen's office with Nancy walking a few paces behind him. She entered tentatively, as though she weren't sure whether she'd find friends or enemies here. What she found, at the moment, were people completely wrapped up in their own concerns.

Hausen was talking on a cellular phone in the reception area. He had obviously determined that the security of his office phones had probably been compromised. The cellular phone wasn't secure, but at least he wouldn't have to worry that the enemy was listening to everything he said.

Lang was sitting on the edge of the desk, lips pressed tightly together as he looked down at Hausen. Matt Stoll was still sitting at Hausen's computer in the main office.

Hausen was speaking forcefully in German with someone named Erwin. German always seemed harsh to Hood, but this conversation seemed especially so. And Hausen did not look pleased.

Lang walked over to them. Hood introduced him to Nancy. "This is Nancy Jo Bosworth. She's an employee of *Demain*." Even as he said it, he couldn't believe the words were coming from his mouth. He had to have been insane to have gone back to get her. Completely and utterly insane.

"I see," Lang said with a polite, pursed smile.

"I'm not a friend of Dominique's," she added. "I don't know him."

"It appears that few do," Lang said, still smiling tightly.

Hood excused himself to introduce Nancy to Stoll. Then he left them together and returned to the outer office.

"What is Herr Hausen doing?" he asked Lang.

"He's talking with the French Ambassador in Berlin, trying to arrange an immediate trip to France to investigate the matter of this game and its maker. Herr Hausen wants to confront this man Dominique in the presence of French authorities." Lang leaned closer. "He tried calling Dominique directly but was unable to get through. He seems unusually agitated by all of this. He takes hate crimes so very personally."

Hood asked, "How is it going with the Ambassador?"

"It isn't going well at all," Lang said. "Dominique apparently has a great deal of influence over there. He controls banks and several industries and a horrifying number of politicians."

Hood gave Hausen a short, sympathetic look, then stepped into the main office. He knew how difficult it was dealing with the system in Washington. He couldn't begin to imagine the red tape which had to exist between nations. Especially nations with a longstanding hate-hate relationship such as these two.

He stood beside Nancy as she watched Stoll guide fluidly animated dogs running through a swamp. He found it difficult to concentrate on the game.

"How're you doing, Matt?" Hood asked.

Stoll hit "P" to pause. He turned around, his eyebrows arched. "This is one nasty game, Chief. What the characters do to people with ropes, knives, and dogs is not to be believed. You'll be able to see for yourself later," he said. "I've hooked up the VCR and I'm playing through. I'll watch the tape later in slow motion to see if there are subliminal messages or other clues or anything I've missed."

Nancy said, "I take it this is the game Herr Hausen received."

"Yup," Stoll said, unpausing the game. Almost immediately, one of the dogs he was controlling fell into quicksand and began sinking.

"Shit!" he yelled. "Y'know, I was doing okay when I was alone—"

"Deal with it," Nancy said. She leaned over him and pushed the "down" arrow on the keyboard.

"Hey, what are you doing?" Stoll demanded. "Don't mess with my game—"

"You missed something," Nancy said.

"I *what?*"

As she held the button down, the dog drifted through the quicksand and emerged in an underground cavern. She switched between the left and right arrows, collecting Nazi memorabilia and racking up points.

Hood walked over. "How did you know that was there?"

"This is an adapatation of a game I designed called The Bog Beast," Nancy replied. "Same game screens—background, foreground elements, traps. Different characters and scenario, though. I had a swamp monster running from its creator and angry villagers. This is obviously very much different."

"But it's definitely your game," Hood said.

"Absolutely." She turned the controls back to Stoll. "Exit by crawling into the storm drain on the left," she said.

"Thanks," he huffed as he continued playing.

Hood stepped away. He resisted the urge to take Nancy's hand and pull her along. But he'd noticed Stoll's eyes dart toward them while they stepped toward the corner. For all its quality and top-level security clearances, Op-Center was no different from other offices. It talked. His people could keep state secrets, but the phrase "personal secrets" was almost an oxymoron.

Nancy came of her own accord. Hood could see the concern, love, and lingering disappointment in her eyes.

"Paul," she said softly, "I know I screwed up in the past, but this isn't my doing. Any number of people could have made these changes."

"You mean people in the inner circle of Dominique's."

Nancy nodded.

"I believe you," Hood said. "The question is, what are we going to do about it?"

Hood's cellular phone beeped and he excused himself. "Hello?"

"Paul," said the caller, "it's Darrell. Can you talk?"

Hood said that he could.

McCaskey said, "I've met with Liz and Mike, and it looks to us like this fellow you were asking about is Mr. Hate himself. And powerful enough to avoid arrest."

"Explain."

"He appears to use a network of banks to launder money and finance hate groups worldwide. The law sniffs around him but never bites. Meanwhile, it looks like he's getting set to introduce a new joystick which helps players feel as if whatever they're seeing on the screen is very real."

"I assume this joystick is compatible with the hate games."

"Sure is," said McCaskey. "But our immediate problem isn't any of that. The Pure Nation team that got picked up this morning may have been a plant. It looks like they and the hate games could be part of a larger plan to turn U.S. cities into racial war zones. Again," he said, "we have no hard evidence. Only some tenuous links and gut feelings."

"Our gut feelings are usually on the money," Hood said. "Does it look like there's any kind of timetable?"

"Tough to say. The media are all over Pure Nation, and we think they're going to milk that forum."

"Of course they will," said Hood.

"The games are also ready to launch," McCaskey said. "If this is a coordinated effort, the coordinator isn't going to let the fear grow cold. A couple of strikes against blacks and communities won't just ignite, they'll explode. I've just been talking with my associates at the Bureau. We agree that in a worst-case scenario, incidents could begin erupting within days, if not hours."

Hood didn't bother to ask how a single foreign businessman had been able to put so much of what Rodgers called "bad news" in position without being discovered. He knew the answer. Dominique had money, autonomy, and patience. With money and patience alone, the Japanese Aum Shinrikyo cult had been able to operate from a Manhattan office from 1987 to 1995, buying everything from a computer equipment to a laser system capable of measuring plutonium to several tons of steel for the manufacture of knives. All of this was going to be used to help begin a war between Japan and the United

States. Though it was unlikely the war would have occurred, the nuclear destruction of a U.S. city might well have been achieved if investigators of the Senate Permanent Investigations Committee, working with the CIA and the FBI, had not been able to penetrate and arrest the members of the doomsday cult.

Hood asked, "What are the chances of stopping this from your end?"

"Obviously," said McCaskey, "until we know the scope of the man's ambitions or even specific targets, I can't say."

"But you think—you feel—that all of this is being generated by one man?"

McCaskey said, "That's how it looks from here."

"So if we were to get to the one man," Hood said, "we could put the brakes on everything."

"Conceivably," McCaskey said. "At least, that's the way it looks to me."

"Let's work on that," Hood said. "Meanwhile, has anybody heard anything from Bob?"

McCaskey said, "Actually . . . yes."

Hood didn't like the way that sounded. "What's he doing?"

McCaskey explained and Hood listened, feeling guilty as all hell for having let Herbert go off on his own. Chasing around the woods, a man in a wheelchair against a van-load of neo-Nazis. It was absurd. Then he got angry. Op-Center had lost Private Bass Moore in Korea and Lieutenant Colonel Charlie Squires in Russia. Herbert should have realized that if anything happened to him, Congress would chain the entire operation to a desk. Herbert had no right to jeopardize the entire organization. Finally, Hood felt a rush of pride. Herbert was doing something which distinguished Americans from most other nationalities. He was fighting injustice, regardless of who it was being directed against.

But righteous or not, Herbert was a semi-loose cannon, a U.S. government operative hunting neo-Nazis in Germany. If he broke the law or even if he were found out, the neo-Nazis would spin it as if they were being persecuted, ganged up on. It would send a firestorm of criticism sweeping over Op-Center, Washington, and Hausen.

Then, of course, there was always the danger that the neo-Nazis would rather eliminate Herbert. The men in the van might not have known who he was. But even knowing, not all radicals wanted publicity. Some of them just wanted their enemies dead.

If he thought Herbert would listen, Hood would have ordered him back to the hotel. And if it weren't for two big "ifs," Hood would have gone so far as to ask Hausen to send some people to collect him: *if* he trusted Hausen's security, which he no longer did; and *if* he weren't afraid they'd blunder into an otherwise quiet stakeout and thus *create* a situation.

"Is Viens watching Herbert?" Hood asked.

"Unfortunately, no," McCaskey told him. "Steve's only got one eye in the region and he couldn't keep it tied up. As it was, he had to put Larry off to get Bob some of what he needed."

"Thank him for me," Hood said sincerely, even as he was swearing inside. That was it, then. Hood was just going to have to let this play out, hope that Herbert remained anonymous and safe.

"Paul," McCaskey said then, "hold on a moment. I've got a priority call coming in."

Hood waited. CNN was running on the hold line. There was something about a celebrity's death in Atlanta. Hood only got to hear a few words about it before McCaskey was back.

"Paul," McCaskey said, "Mike's on the line as well. We may have a situation."

"What is it?" Hood asked.

"I just heard from my contact Don Worby at the FBI," McCaskey said. "They've just been notified about five white-on-black killings at the same time in five different cities. New York, Los Angeles, New Orleans, Baltimore, and Atlanta. In each case, two-to-four young white males ambushed a black rap singer. In Atlanta, they got Sweet T, the number-one female rapper, as she was leaving her apartment—"

"That must have been what I just heard," Hood said.

"Where?" McCaskey asked.

"On CNN."

"Those bastards," McCaskey said. "Maybe we ought to hire HUMINT resources from them."

Rodgers came on the line and said somberly, "Do you realize what we've just had here? Those attacks were a modern-day *Kristallnacht*."

The connection hadn't occurred to Hood, but Rodgers was right. The assaults were similar to Crystal Night, when the Gestapo orchestrated acts of vandalism against Jewish houses of worship, cemeteries, hospitals, schools, homes, and businesses throughout Germany. Thirty thousand Jews were also arrested, beginning the Jewish incarceration in concentration camps like Dachau, Sachsenhausen, and Buchenwald.

The attacks were similar, he thought, *yet there was something different—*

"No," Hood said suddenly with alarm. "This was not another Crystal Night. It was only a prelude."

"How so?" Rodgers asked.

Hood said, "Neo-Nazis killed rappers. That'll enrage the so-called gangstas and their hard-core audience. They turn on whites, many of whom don't approve of rap to begin with, and you end up with more racial incidents, riots, and American cities on fire. *That's* when the neo-Nazis return. When white America is tired of rioters being contained rather than attacked. When too few arrests are made. When the media shows black radicals demanding white blood. That's when the new Crystal Night, the coordinated, armed attacks, begins."

"But how do the neo-Nazis benefit?" Rodgers asked. "They can't break the law and then run for office."

"The prettified ones can," said Hood. "The ones who distance themselves from the lawbreakers but not from the intolerance which motivates them."

The plan made sense, and the more Hood thought about it, the more brilliant it seemed in its simplicity. He thought of his own daughter, Harleigh, whose musical mix included rap. Hood was in favor of free expression, but he insisted on hearing any album with a parent's advisory sticker—not to censor but to discuss. Some of the lyrics were pretty brutal, and in his soul he had to admit that he wouldn't mind if some of the rappers went into another line of work. And he was a one-time liberal politician. From talks with other parents at the school and at church, he knew that they felt much more strongly. If blacks started avenging dead rappers, he suspected that white, middle-class sympathies would be with the murderous whites, who would probably claim they'd been making pre-emptive strikes. And retaliatory attacks by blacks would only legitimize those claims. Riots might ensue, the police would be forced to hold back to some degree, and the neo-Nazis would become the violent angels of whites. Not to mention potential winners in future elections.

Less than fifty-five years after Hitler's death, the monsters could actually become a political force in the U.S., Hood thought.

"Broken dreams of harmony instead of broken windows," Hood said. "It's a nightmare."

Rodgers said, "Paul, we can still stop this thing. If we can expose Dominique's operation to the people, they'll see how they were manipulated."

"If you can tell me how to get to him," Hood said, "I'll be happy to do it."

"There may be a way," Rodgers said. "I've just spoken with Colonel Bernard Ballon of France's Groupe d'Intervention de la Gendarmerie Nationale. He's in Toulouse and he's after the same quarry as we are, albeit for different reasons."

"Different how?" Hood asked as Hausen entered the inner office. The German looked distraught.

Rodgers said, "Ballon believes that Gerard Dominique is the head of a group of French terrorists known as the New Jacobins. Their activities against immigrants certainly fit what we know about Dominique."

"And what does the Colonel plan to do with Dominique?" Hood asked.

Hood saw Hausen's eyes sweep past Nancy and lock on him when he mentioned the name.

"We didn't discuss that," Rodgers said. "Officially, I gather he's supposed to arrest him and his bunch. But with Dominique's money and influence, Ballon is obviously worried he'll get off."

"Not necessarily," Hood said. He was still looking at Hausen and thinking about the murder of the two girls. "What about unofficially?"

Rodgers said, "From my talk with Ballon, he sounds

like the kind of guy who'd love to see him accidentally-on-purpose fall down a flight of concrete steps."

Hood said, "I take it, Mike, you've got some way we can work together."

"Just one," said Rodgers. "He needs accurate information and satellite surveillance just isn't cutting it."

"Say no more," said Hood. He glanced over at Matt Stoll's innocent-looking backpack. "How do I contact Colonel Ballon?"

As Hood wrote down the telephone number, he watched Hausen. He had seen the German get agitated before, but now his face revealed something more. It was as though the veneer of two and a half decades had suddenly flaked away leaving only hate, naked and unashamed. Hood told Rodgers he'd let him know what was happening, and reminded McCaskey to keep him briefed on what Herbert was doing. Then he hung up and looked at Hausen.

"How did you make out?" Hood asked.

"Poorly," said Hausen. "The French Ambassador will 'let me know' if we can come in. Which in diplomatese means to go to hell." The eyes dug into him. "What is all this about Dominique?"

Hood said, "There's a Gendarmerie Nationale officer who is in Toulouse and is eager to hand M. Dominique his head." He looked at Nancy. "Sorry, but that's how it is."

Her mouth scrunched unhappily. "I understand," she said, "but I think I'd better be going."

She turned to go. Hood stepped toward her and grabbed her hand.

"Nancy, don't go back there."

"Why?" she asked. "You think I need someone's protection to survive a shitstorm?"

Hausen turned toward Stoll and Lang and busied himself with learning about the game.

Hood led her a few steps away, toward the back of the office. "*This* shitstorm, yes," he said. "If Ballon gets in, everyone at *Demain* will be investigated, and as far back as possible."

"There are statutes of limitations."

"That's true," Hood said. "There won't be legal ramifications. But think about blacklists. What company will hire someone who has committed industrial espionage or embezzled or was involved in insider trading?"

"A company just like *Demain*," she answered.

Hood took a step toward her. He was still holding her hand, and his grip softened. He was now holding the hand of a woman, not a captive. "There aren't very many companies like *Demain*," he said, "and thank God for that. What they're doing is wrong. And whatever happens, you mustn't go back there."

"Every large corporation has a few demons."

"Not like these," said Hood. "If this Pandora's box is opened, hundreds, perhaps thousands of people will die. The world will change, and not for the better."

Though her eyes were at once defiant and sad, her touch was willing. Hood wanted to kiss her, shelter her, love her. And then he asked himself, *Who am I to talk about immorality?*

"So," she said, "you don't want me going back. And you also want my help bringing Dominique to justice."

Holding her hand, looking into her eyes, he said quietly, "I do."

The wistful, tender way he'd spoken hit her almost as hard as the words he'd selected. She squeezed his hand. He squeezed back.

"Even if you get him, Dominique will get rich man's

justice,'' Nancy said. ''The kind the French government loves to dispense because it buys summer homes for officials.''

''Dominique won't be able to buy his way out of everything he's done,'' Hood promised.

''And what about me?'' she asked. ''Where does a whistle-blower go?''

''I'll help you when this is all over,'' Hood said. ''I'll see to it that you have work.''

''Well, golly gee and thanks,'' Nancy said. ''Haven't you figured out yet that that's *not* what I need from you, Paul?''

She half-turned, looked down, and ran her tongue across her upper lip. Hood continued to hold her hand. There was nothing he could say, nothing which wouldn't give her false hope.

After a moment, she faced him again. ''Of course I'll help,'' she said. ''Whatever you need I'll do.''

''Thanks,'' Hood said.

''Don't mention it. What are ex-fiancées for?''

Hood touched her cheek, then turned to the pad on which he'd written Ballon's number. He didn't look back at Nancy as he placed the call. The yearning in his eyes would have given her the answer, and it wasn't an answer that would do either of them any good.

FORTY-THREE

Thursday, 6:44 P.M., Wunstorf, Germany

The crack Bob Herbert heard was not the report of the gun. He knew that because the bullet would have struck his brain and shut it down before the sound of the gunshot reached him.

Also, he realized that the sound had come from above.

The branch fell heavily through the trees. Though the police officer hopped aside, out of the way, he couldn't avoid the young woman who dropped from the tree a moment later. She crashed down on him, spilling them both to the ground. But she had landed on top and got off first. Because he had managed to hold onto the gun, she rose, stepped on his wrist, and wrested it away.

"Here!" she said, pushing the weapon into Herbert's hands.

He aimed it at the police officer's head. When the man didn't stir, Herbert looked at the young woman. She was standing unsteadily to Herbert's left, obviously shaken by her plunge.

"Jody Thompson?" Herbert asked.

She nodded twice. She was nearly gasping. Her heart was probably racing from fear, poor thing.

"My name's Herbert. Bob Herbert. I work for the

U.S. government. I want to thank you for what you did.''

She said in breathless chunks, "It's not . . . the first time . . . I've fallen for a guy."

He smiled. She was pumped up by fear and maybe a little excitement. "I assume you didn't just fall from the tree—''

"No," she said. "I'd been walking and got lost. I fell asleep up there. I woke when I heard you and saw what he was going to do."

"I'm glad you're a light sleeper," Herbert said. "Now I think we'd better make sure our playmate is—''

Jody screamed, *"Look out!"*

Herbert hadn't turned his back on the police officer, but he'd made the mistake of looking at the girl. The German had pushed off from the ground before the American could fire. He dove for the gun. The wheelchair spilled over backward with the two men on it and four hands scrapped for the weapon.

Herbert lost the gun in the struggle, and decided not to try and find it. Lying on his back with the police officer on top of him, he reached under the right armrest and slipped the Urban Skinner from its sheath. Jody jumped toward the police officer, pulling at his coat. As she did, Herbert closed his fingers around the knife's palm-fitted hilt. The two-inch blade was sticking up from his right-hand fist, between his second and third fingers.

The police officer was fumbling around the wheelchair, around Herbert, his fingers digging and probing. As Jody screamed and tore at the German, Herbert's left hand shot up. He grabbed a handful of black hair to hold the German's head in place. Then he drove the knife up hard, into the soft flesh under his chin. He cut to the heart side, slicing both the internal and external jugular veins. The trapezius muscle, on the outside of the neck, stopped the knife from exiting.

The German stopped looking for the gun though he didn't stop moving. He tried to push the knife from his throat, but the combination of Herbert pulling down on his head and pressing up with the blade made that impossible. Herbert didn't want him to open his mouth, to scream. He also didn't want Jody, who was still on top of him, to see his face or the wound.

Within a few seconds the police officer was finding it difficult to breathe. He tried to roll off Herbert as blood filled his mouth and dribbled from between his lips. But Herbert held him in the deathlock.

The German glared down with pain and shock as the soil beneath them turned muddy with blood. He made weak, babylike attempts to beat at Herbert, then spat blood and dropped limp on Herbert's chest.

This time, Herbert knew, he wouldn't be getting up. When the German finally fell still, Herbert told Jody to back off and turn around.

"Are you sure?" she asked.

"I'm sure," he replied.

She rose weakly, and as soon as she'd walked off several yards Herbert pushed the German off. The intelligence chief wriggled to the side, out of his chair and away from the body. Then he cleaned his knife on the police officer's coat and slipped it back in its sheath.

"Are you all right, Jody?"

She nodded. "Is he dead?"

"Yes," Herbert said. "I'm sorry."

She nodded again briskly.

He waited a moment, then said, "If you help me back

into my chair, we can get out of here.''

Jody did. As she struggled to help him up, she said, ''Mr. Herbert—''

''Bob,'' he said.

''Bob,'' Jody said, ''what do you know about the people who tried to kill me?''

Herbert thought back to the satellite view of the area. ''I believe they're at a lake north of here.''

''How far north?''

''A few miles,'' Herbert said. He picked up his phone. ''I'm going to let my superiors know I've found you, get you to Hamburg, and fly you home from there.''

''I don't want to go yet,'' she said.

''Why?'' he asked. ''Are you tired—hurt? Hungry? I don't have any food—''

''No, none of that,'' Jody said. ''While I was up in the tree, I was thinking how much I hate them.''

''Me too,'' Herbert said. ''People like them took away my legs and my wife for reasons that don't even matter any more.''

''And I was thinking,'' Jody went on, ''that maybe I survived for a reason.''

''You did,'' Herbert said. ''To go home to your folks.''

''If that's true,'' she said, ''then I'll get home to them. Only a little later. I want to do something about what's going on here.''

''Good,'' Herbert said. ''When you get back to the States, sell the movie rights to your story. I'm serious. Let people know what's happening in the real world. Just make sure Tom Selleck plays me, okay? And that you hold on to creative control. Otherwise, it'll get all crapped up.''

"I studied film," Jody said, "and right now we haven't got a climax."

Herbert made a face. "Bull," he said, and spread his fingers headline-size. He swept them to the side. "Long Island girl helps government agent kill German neo-Nazi police officer," he said. "Seems like a helluva climax to me."

"It isn't," she replied. "A better one would be: American girl makes grandfather proud by fighting his old enemies. More substance, less sensation."

"You're loco," Herbert said as he began punching in a number. "As we used to say in Beirut, 'Gutsy but nutsy.'"

"Sometimes you just have to do what you have to do." Jody walked over to the police officer. She picked up his gun and brushed off the dirt by wiping it on her jeans.

"Put that down," Herbert said. "We don't need it going off by accident and bringing reinforcements."

Jody examined the weapon. "We were using a P38 like this in the movie," she said. "The prop man showed me how to work it."

"Hooray for him. Did you fire it?"

She nodded. "I hit a log from about ten yards away."

"Nice," Herbert said. "But there are two things you need to know. First, that's a P5, not a P1—which is the official name of the Walther P38 you used. They're both 9-×-19mm, and you'll find them remarkably similar. As for the second thing, logs don't shoot real well. People do a lot better."

Herbert finished inputting the telephone number and waited. Jody pressed her lips together and stalked over. She touched the disconnect button.

"Hey!" he said. "Get that finger out of here."

"Thanks for your help, Mr. Herbert—Bob—but I'm going."

"No you're not. There are probably hundreds of psycho-militants out there and you don't know what they're like."

"I think I do."

"You *don't!*" he yelled. "That woman who captured you was Karin Doring. Do you know why she didn't kill you? Woman-to-woman courtesy."

"I know," Jody said. "She told me."

"She won't make that mistake twice," Herbert said. "And the bottom-feeders who work for her won't make that mistake once. Shit, you probably won't even get past the sentries."

"I'll find a way. I can be sneaky."

"Even assuming you are, or assuming the sentries are green or they choke or both, what'll you do if you get there? Kill Karin?"

"No," Jody said. "I don't want to be like her. I just want her to see me. I want her to see that I'm alive and unafraid. She left me without anything in the trailer. No hope, no pride, zero. I've got to get that back."

"But you *have!*"

"What you're seeing now?" Jody asked. "This isn't pride, it's shame. The fear of shame. The fear that I'm too afraid to face her. I need to bite the ear of my torturer."

Herbert was totally confused. "Excuse me?"

"It's something my grandfather once did. If I don't do that I'll never be able to walk into a dark room or down a lonely street without being afraid. My grandfather also said that Hitler controlled people through fear. I want these people to know that they didn't scare me. I can't do that from anywhere but the camp."

Herbert wheeled a half-turn closer to her. "There's some truth to what you're saying, but going back there isn't the way to accomplish anything. You'll have about ten seconds of glory before they cut you down."

"Not if you help me," Jody said. She leaned toward him. "I just want to show my face. That's all. If I don't run from this, I'll never run from anything. But if I do run, then that witch will have succeeded. She'll have killed an important part of me."

Herbert couldn't argue the point. If he was Jody, he'd want to do just what she was suggesting and then some. But that didn't mean he was going to go along with her.

Herbert said, "And how am I supposed to live with *my*self if anything happens to you? Besides, think about it. You stayed calm. You fought back. You saved my life. You don't have anything to prove."

"No," Jody said. "My demon is still out there. I *am* going and you can't stop me. I can outrun you."

"Don't be fooled by the wheelchair, Jody Joyner-Kersee," Herbert said. "When I want to, I can fly." He removed her finger and began redialing. "Besides, I can't let you die. We're going to need you at a trial. I was with a German government official this morning, Deputy Foreign Minister Richard Hausen. He's devoted to their destruction. Get your vengeance that way."

"He's devoted to their destruction," Jody repeated. "And they're probably devoted to his. Hundreds against one. Who do you think is going to win?"

"That depends who the 'one' is."

She replied, "Exactly."

Herbert looked at her. "Touché," he said, "but you're still not going."

Jody's mouth twisted. She rose and started walking away. "Bullshit. *Bullshit!*"

"Jody, quiet down!" Herbert hissed. "Jody—come back."

She shook her head and kept walking. Swearing, Herbert hung up and started after her. As he rolled up the slight dirt incline in a small thicket of trees, twigs cracked behind him. He stopped, listened, swore again.

Someone was coming. Either they'd heard them or had come to check on the police officer. Not that it mattered. Jody was about twenty yards off and still moving away. He couldn't call to her lest he give himself away. There was only one thing to do.

It was charcoal-gray dark beneath the leaves. Slowly, quietly, Herbert rolled behind one of the trees. He listened.

There were two sets of footsteps. They stopped moving just about where the body would be. The question was, would they continue or retreat?

After a moment the footsteps continued in their direction. Herbert slid his stick from beneath the armrest and waited. Jody's footsteps retreated to the right. He was frustrated at not being able to call to her and tell her to stop.

He let his breathing fall to his abdomen to relax him. "Buddah Belly" they had called it when he was in rehabilitation. When he was taught that a man wasn't measured by whether he could walk but whether he could act . . .

Two men walked past. He thought he recognized them from the van. Herbert waited until they had walked by. Then he quickly wheeled behind the second man, swung his stick sideways, and clubbed him hard in the thigh. The man doubled over. When his friend turned around, his submachine gun at his side, Herbert brought the stick swinging back into his left kneecap. The man dropped face-forward, toward Herbert. Herbert struck him hard on the head. As the first man groaned and struggled to get back to his feet, Herbert hit him on the back of the neck. He flopped down, unconscious. Herbert sneered as he looked down at the two men.

I ought to kill them, he thought, his hand reaching for the Urban Skinner. But that would make him as vile as they were, and he knew it. Instead, he returned his stick to the armrest. Picking up the compact submachine gun, a Czech Skorpion, he set it in his lap and wheeled after Jody.

Even though he rolled as quickly as possible through the blue-black darkness of the woods, he knew that she had probably gone too far to catch. He thought about calling Hausen for help, but who could Hausen trust? According to Paul, the politician didn't even know that his own personal assistant was a neo-Nazi. Herbert couldn't call the police. He'd killed a man and would probably be hauled off before Jody could be extricated. And even if they were working on the side of the law, what understaffed group of peacekeepers would march into a remote camp of militant radicals at the height of Chaos Days? Especially radicals who had calmly decimated the crew of a movie set.

As he had been trained from his earliest days in intelligence work, Herbert took stock of the things he knew for certain. First, in this situation he could only rely on himself. Second, if Jody reached the camp before him she would be killed. And third, she was probably going to reach the camp before him.

Gritting his teeth against the pain of his bruises, he gripped his wheels and hurried after her.

FORTY-FOUR

Thursday, 6:53 P.M.,
Toulouse, France

As Colonel Ballon sat watching the video monitor he thought, like most Frenchmen, how little he cared for Americans. Ballon had two younger sisters who lived in Quebec, both of whom were full of stories about how Americans were imperious and cocky and crude and just too damn *near*. His own experiences with tourists in Paris, where he was based, indicated to him quite clearly what the problem was. Americans wanted to be French. They drank, they smoked, and they dressed like the French did. They affected artistry and insouciance like the French did. Only they refused to speak like the French did. Even in France, they expected everyone to speak English.

Then there was the military. Because of Napoleon's disastrous Russian campaign and World War II, they assumed that members of the French armed forces were vastly inferior to American soldiers and deserved only the bones they deigned to throw them.

But Bonaparte and the Maginot Line were aberrations in an otherwise proud military history, he told himself. Indeed, without the French military helping George Washington there would not be a United States. Not that the Americans would ever acknowledge that. Any more than they would allow that the Lumiere brothers, not Edison, invented motion pictures. Or that the Montgolfier brothers, not the Wright brothers, were the ones who enabled people to fly. The only good thing about Americans was that they gave him someone other than Germans to hate.

His phone beeped and he regarded it for a moment. That would be him. Paul Hood. Ballon didn't really want to talk to this Mr. Hood, but he didn't want to let Dominique get away even more. Thus resolved—quickly, as with all things—he snatched up the phone.

"Oui?"

"Colonel Ballon?"

"Oui."

The caller said without missing a beat, *"Je suis Paul Hood. Vous avez besoin d'assistance?"*

Ballon was caught off guard by that. *"Oui,"* he replied. *"Eh . . . vous parlez la langue?"* he asked.

"Je parle un peu," Hood said.

He spoke a little French. "Then we'll speak English," replied Ballon. "I don't want to hear you murder my tongue. I'm particular about that."

"I understand," said Hood. "Six years of French in high school and college didn't exactly make me a linguist."

"School does not make us anything," Ballon said. "Life makes us what we are. But talk is not life, and sitting in this room is not life. Mr. Hood, I want Dominique. I've been told you have equipment which will help me get him."

"I do," Hood said.

"Where are you?"

"Hamburg," said Hood.

"Very good. You can fly here on one of the airbuses

which made Dominique's father a fortune. If you hurry, you can be here in about two hours.''

''We'll be there,'' said Hood.

''We?'' Ballon felt his passion leak away. ''Who else is there?''

Hood said, ''Deputy Foreign Minister Richard Hausen and the two other persons in my party.''

Ballon had been glowering. Now he was sulking. *It had to be a German,* he thought. *And* that *German in particular. God does not love me as He promised He would.*

''Colonel Ballon,'' Hood said, ''are you there?''

''Yes,'' he said glumly. ''So now I don't have to just sit here for two hours. I can fight with my government to get an attention-hungry German government official into France on an unofficial visit.''

''I take a different view of him,'' Hood said. ''Attention can be selfless if it's for a worthy cause.''

''Don't lecture me about selflessness. He's a general. I fight in the trenches. But,'' Ballon added quickly, ''this is pointless. I need you, you want him, so that is that. I'll make a few calls and I will meet you at the Aerodrome de Lasbordes at eight o'clock.''

''Hold on,'' Hood said. ''You've asked your questions now I want to ask mine.''

''Go ahead.''

''We think Dominique's preparing to launch an on-line campaign designed to spread hate, inspire riots, and destabilize governments.''

''Your associate General Rodgers told me all about this chaos project.''

''Good,'' said Hood. ''Did he also tell you we want him stopped, not threatened.''

''Not in so many words,'' Ballon said. ''But I believe

that Dominique is a terrorist. If you can help me prove that, I will go into his factory and stop him.''

"I'm told he's avoided arrest in the past.''

"He has,'' Ballon said. "But I intend to do more than arrest him. Let me give you an overview which I hope will answer all of your questions. We French are very solidly behind our entrepreneurs. They've prospered in the winter of our economy. They've thrived despite government manacles. And I admit, with some shame, that a great many Frenchmen approve of the work of the New Jacobins. No one likes immigrants here, and the New Jacobins attack them like pack dogs. If people knew that Dominique was behind those attacks, he would be an even greater hero.''

Ballon's eyes burned through the image on the TV. He saw, in his mind, Dominique sitting smug and comfortable in his office.

"But while we French are an emotional people, most of us also believe in concord. In healing wounds. In harmony. You Americans see that as waving a white flag, but I see it as civilized. Dominique is not civilized. He violates the laws of France and God. Like his father, he has a conscience made of diamond. Nothing scratches it. It is my intention to make him answer for his crimes.''

Hood said, "I believe in moral crusades and I'll back yours with the full resources of my organization. But you still haven't told me where this crusade is headed.''

Ballon replied, "To Paris.''

"I'm listening,'' said Hood.

"I intend to arrest Dominique, confiscate his papers and software, and then resign from the Gendarmarie. Dominique's attorneys will see to it that he never goes to trial. But while that process is under way, I'll go to the press with a catalogue of his crimes. Murders and rapes he has committed or ordered, taxes he hasn't paid, businesses and properties he misappropriated, and more that I couldn't reveal as a government employee.''

''A dramatic gesture,'' Hood said. ''But if French law is anything like American law, you'll be sued, drawn, and quartered.''

''That is correct,'' replied Ballon. ''But my trial will be Dominique's trial. And when it's over he'll be disgraced. Finished.''

''So will you.''

''Only this career,'' Ballon said. ''I'll find other honorable work.''

''Do your teammates feel the same way you do?''

''Not all,'' he admitted. ''They're committed only to—what's the word? The limitations? Boundaries?''

''Parameters,'' said Hood.

''Yes.'' Ballon snapped his fingers. ''They're committed to the parameters of the mission. That's all I ask of you as well. If you help me prove what *Demain* is doing, if you give me a reason to go inside, we can bring Dominique down. Today.''

Hood said, ''Fair enough. One way or another, we'll get there.'' He added, *''Et merci.''*

Ballon replied with a gruff thank you of his own, then sat holding the handset. He dropped his finger on the plunger.

''Good news?'' asked Sergeant Ste. Marie.

''Very good news,'' Ballon replied without enthusiasm. ''We have help. Unfortunately, it's an American *and* a German. Richard Hausen.''

Ste. Marie moaned. ''We can all go home. The Hun will take Dominique singlehandedly.''

''We'll see,'' said Ballon. ''We'll see what his pluck is like when there are no reporters present to admire it.''

With a short aftershock of outrage—"Americans *and* a German," he declared—Ballon called the office of an old friend in the CDT, the *Comite Departemental de Tourisme,* to see if they could simply look the other way when the plane arrived, or if he'd have to tangle with the territorial carnivores in Paris. . . .

FORTY-FIVE

Thursday, 6:59 P.M., Hamburg, Germany

Martin Lang was on his cellular phone as Hood helped Matt Stoll gather together his equipment. Lang was phoning the airport outside of Hamburg, ordering the corporate jet to be readied. Stoll was zipping up his backpack and looking anxious.

"Maybe I missed something when you were explaining it to Herr Lang," Stoll said, "but tell me again why I'm going to France."

Hood said, "You're going to T-Ray the *Demain* factory in Toulouse."

"That part I got," said Stoll. "But someone else is going to go inside, right? Professionals?"

Hood looked from Stoll to Hausen. The German was standing in the doorway between the two offices, phoning to arrange for clearances for Lang's Learjet 36A. The aircraft held two crew members and six passengers and had a range of 3,151 miles. At an average speed of four hundred miles an hour, they should arrive right on schedule.

"Done," said Lang, hanging up. He checked his watch. "The plane will be waiting at seven-thirty."

Hood was still watching Hausen as a thought occurred to him. One which chilled and then annoyed him. Hausen's aide had turned on him. What if the office was bugged?

Hood pulled Stoll aside. "Matt, I'm getting sloppy. That kid who worked for Hausen, Reiner. He could have left a bug here."

Stoll nodded. "You mean, like this one?" He reached into his shirt pocket and withdrew a folded-over piece of cellophane tape. Inside was a gumdrop-shaped object slightly larger than a pinhead. "I did a sweep of the room while you were away. I forgot to tell you in the heat of the hate game showing up and all that."

Hood sighed and squeezed Stoll's shoulders. "Bless you, Matt."

"Does that mean I get to stay here?" he asked.

Hood shook his head.

"Just thought I'd ask," Stoll said disconsolately.

As he walked away, Hood was angry with himself for having overlooked that. He turned to Nancy, who had walked over. They were going into a potentially dangerous situation where a screwup could cost them the mission, a career, or a life.

You've got to focus on the job, he remonstrated himself. *You can't be distracted by Nancy and all the might-have-been scenarios.*

"Anything wrong?" Nancy asked.

"No," he said.

"Just standing around, beating yourself up." She smiled. "I remember the look."

Hood flushed. He glanced up to make sure that Stoll wasn't watching.

"It's okay," Nancy said.

"What is?" he asked impatiently. He wanted to get out of here, break the tempting closeness.

"Being human. Making a mistake now and then or

wanting something that isn't yours. Or even wanting something that was yours.''

Hood turned toward Hausen so as not to make it seem as if he were turning away from Nancy. But he was. And she obviously knew it because she stepped between the men.

''God, Paul, why do you put this burden on yourself? This burden to be so *perfect*?''

''Nancy, this isn't the time or place—''

''Why?'' she asked. ''You think we'll have another?''

He said bluntly, ''No. No, we probably won't.''

''Forget me for a moment. Think about you. When we were younger, you worked hard so you could get ahead. Now you *are* ahead and you're still pushing. Who's it for? Are you trying to set an example for your kids or your subordinates?''

''Neither,'' he said with an edge. Why was everyone always on his back about his ethics, work and otherwise? ''I'm only trying to do what's right. Personally, professionally, just what's *right*. If that's too simple or too vague for everybody, it isn't my problem.''

''We can leave,'' Hausen said. He put the phone in his jacket pocket and walked briskly toward Hood. He was obviously pleased, and unaware that he was interrupting anything. ''The government has given clearance for us to leave at once.'' He turned to Lang. ''Is everything set, Martin?''

''The jet is yours,'' Lang said. ''I won't be joining you. I'd only be in the way.''

''I understand,'' Hausen said. ''The rest of us had better be going.''

Stoll struggled into the backpack with the T-ray imaging unit. ''You betcha,'' he said glumly. ''Why go to the hotel where I can have room service and a hot bath, when I can go to France and fight terrorists?''

Hausen extended an arm toward the door. He had the eager, impatient manner of someone hurrying dinner guests out into the night. Hood hadn't seem him so animated all day. Was this, as he suspected, Ahab finally closing in on the White Whale—or was it, as Ballon believed, a politician about to score an unprecedented public relations coup?

Hood took Nancy's hand and started toward the door. She resisted. He stopped and turned back. She was no longer the confident woman who strode toward him in the park. Nancy was a sad and lonely figure, seductive in her need.

He knew what she was thinking. That she should be opposing them, not helping them destroy what was left of her life. As he watched her stand there, he flirted with the idea of telling her what she wanted to hear, of lying to her and saying that they could try again. His job was to protect the nation and he needed her help for that.

And once you tell that lie, he thought, *you can lie to Mike and your staff, to Congress, even to Sharon.*

''Nancy, you'll have work,'' Hood told her. ''I said I'd help you and I will.'' He was going to remind her again who walked out on whom, but what was the point? Women weren't consistent or fair.

''But that's my problem, not yours,'' Nancy said. It was as if she'd read his mind and was determined to prove him wrong. ''You say you need my help if you get inside. Fine. I won't walk out on you a second time.''

Snapping her head the way she did in the hotel lobby, she walked toward Hausen. The long, blond hair swept to the side, as if it were brushing away doubt and anger.

Hausen thanked her, thanked them all, as the five of

them entered the elevator for the quick ride to the lobby.

Hood stood beside Nancy. He wanted to thank her, but just saying it didn't seem to be enough. Without looking at her, he squeezed her hand and quickly released it. From the corner of his eye he saw Nancy blink several times, the only break in her otherwise stoic expression.

He couldn't remember when he felt both this close and this far from a person. It was frustrating being unable to move in one direction or the other, and he could only imagine how much worse it felt for Nancy.

And then she let him know by reaching over and squeezing his hand and not releasing it as tears crept from her eyes. The *ping* of the elevator as they reached the lobby broke their touch but not the spell as she released him and they walked, eyes ahead, toward the waiting car.

FORTY-SIX

Thursday, 1:40 P.M., Washington, D.C.

When he was a kid growing up in Houston, Darrell McCaskey carved his own Smith & Wesson automatic made out of balsa wood and kept it tucked in his belt at all times, the way he'd read the real FBI agents did. He screwed an eye-hook to the front of the weapon and attached a rubber band to the "gun sight." When the rubber band was hooked to the hammer and released, he could fire small cardboard squares like bullets. Mc-Caskey kept the squares in his shirt pocket where they were accessible and safe.

Darrell wore the gun starting in sixth grade. He kept it hidden under his button-down shirt. It gave him a John Wayne-rigid walk that the other kids teased him about, but Darrell didn't care. They didn't understand that keeping the law was everyone's responsibility as well as a full-time job. And he was a short kid. With hippies and yippies popping up and demonstrations and sit-ins happening everywhere, he felt better with a beltful of protection.

McCaskey shot the first teacher who tried to take the gun from him. After writing an essay in which he carefully researched the Constitution and the right to bear arms, he was permitted to keep the weapon. Provided he didn't use it other than for self-defense against radicals.

As a rookie FBI agent, McCaskey loved stakeouts and investigations. He loved it even more when he was an Assistant Special Agent in Charge and had more autonomy. When he became a Special Agent in Charge and then a Supervisory Special Agent, he was frustrated because there were fewer opportunities to spend time in the street.

When McCaskey was offered the position of Unit Chief in Dallas, he took the promotion largely because of his wife and three kids. The pay was better and the job was safer and his family got to see him more. But as he sat behind a desk coordinating the actions of others, he realized just how much he missed stakeouts and investigations. Within two years, joint activity with Mexican authorities gave him the idea to form official alliances with foreign police forces. The FBI Director approved his plan to draft and spearhead FIAT—the Federal International Alliance Treaty. Quickly approved by Congress and eleven foreign governments, FIAT enabled McCaskey to work on cases in Mexico City, London, Tel Aviv, and other world capitals. He moved his family to Washington, quickly rose to Deputy Assistant Director, and was the only man Paul Hood asked to become Op-Center's interagency liaison. McCaskey had been promised and given relative autonomy, and got to work closely with the CIA, the Secret Service, his old friends at the FBI, and more foreign intelligence and police groups than before.

But he was still deskbound. And thanks to fiber optics and computers, he didn't leave his office the way he did when he was revving up FIAT. Because of diskettes and E-mail, he didn't even have to walk over to the Xerox machine or even lean over to the out box. He wished he could have lived in the time of his childhood heroes, G-man Melvin Purvis and Treasury Man Eliot Ness. He could almost taste the exhilaration of chasing Machine Gun Kelly through the Midwest, or Al Capone's thugs up rickety stairways and across dark rooftops in Chicago.

He frowned as he pushed buttons on his phone. *Instead, I'm entering a three-digit code to call the NRO.* He knew there was no shame in that, though he didn't see himself inspiring kids to make their own balsa-wood telephones.

He was put right through to Stephen Viens. The NRO had been downloading satellite views of the *Demain* plant in Toulouse, but they weren't enough. Mike Rodgers had told him that if Ballon and his people had to go in, he didn't want them going in blind. And despite what Rodgers had told Ballon, none of Matt Stoll's technical team knew to what degree the T-Rays would be able to penetrate the facility, or how much it would tell them about the layout or distribution of forces.

Viens had been using the NRO's Earth Audio Receiver Satellite to eavesdrop on the *Demain* site. The satellite used a laser beam to read the walls of a building the way a compact disc player read a CD. However, instead data pits in the surface of a disc, the EARS read vibrations in the walls of buildings. Clarity depended upon the composition and thickness of the walls. With favorable materials such as metals, which vibrated with greater fidelity and resonance than porous brick, computer enhancement could recreate conversations which were taking place within the buildings. These triple-paned windows were no good: they didn't vibrate sufficiently to be read.

"The structure is red brick," Viens said thickly.

McCaskey's head dropped.

"I was just about to call and tell you, but I wanted to make sure we couldn't get anything," Viens continued. "There are newer materials inside, probably Sheet rock and aluminum, but the brick is soaking up whatever's coming off them."

"What about cars?" McCaskey asked.

"We don't have a clear enough shot at them," said Viens. "Too many trees, hills, and overpasses."

"So we're screwed."

"Basically," said Viens.

McCaskey felt as if he were in command of the world's most sophisticated battleship in dry dock. He and Rodgers and Herbert had always bemoaned the lack of on-site human intelligence, and this was a perfect example of why it was needed. *"Billions for modern hardware but none for Mata Hari,"* as Herbert had once put it.

McCaskey thanked Viens and hung up. How he yearned to be a man in the field on this one, to be the intelligence linchpin of a major operation with everything depending on him. He envied Matt Stoll, in whose hands the intelligence gathering rested. It was too bad that Stoll probably didn't want the job. The computer jockey was a genius but he didn't function well under pressure.

McCaskey went back to his computer, sent the photographs right to memory, then booted the Pentagon SITSIM, situation simulation, for an ELTS: European Landmark Tactical Strike. The residual political fallout of destroying national treasures was extremely high. So it was the policy of the United States military not to damage historical structures, even if it meant taking casualties. In the case of the *Demain* factory, acceptable "injury" as they called it—as though the structures were living things—would be "single-round defacement of stone or discoloration capable of complete restoration." In other words, if you stitched a wall with bullets you were in deep trouble. And if you stained it with blood, you'd better be packing a bucket and mop.

Dipping into the French architectural database, he brought up a layout of the fortress they had to enter. The diagram was useless: it showed the way the place had looked in 1777 when the adjacent Vieux Pont bridge was constructed. Dominique had made some changes since then. If he had obtained permits, none of them were filed anywhere. If he had submitted blueprints, none of those were on hand either. It had been easier getting plans of the Hermitage out of St. Petersburg for the Striker incursion. This Dominique had obviously been greasing a lot of palms over many, many years.

McCaskey returned to the NRO photographs, which still showed him nothing. He envied Stoll, but he had to admit that the man would have something to be nervous about. Even with Ballon's help, they would be seriously outgunned if the situation degenerated to that. They would also be too restrained. The file on the New Jacobins was skimpy, but the information it contained had chilled him, details of methods they used to ambush or kill victims and tortures they devised to intimidate or extract information. He would have to forward that data to Hood if they went in. And he would point out that even Melvin Purvis and Eliot Ness would have thought this one over before going in.

There's no time to get Striker into position, McCaskey thought, *and the only tactician we have close to the site, Bob Herbert, is incommunicado.*

He punched in Mike Rodgers's number to tell him the bad news about the fortress . . . and to try to figure out if there were anything they could do to keep their bold but inexperienced field force from being butchered.

FORTY-SEVEN

Thursday, 8:17 P.M.,
Wunstorf, Germany

Bob Herbert had gone through two emotional phases during his rehabilitation.

The first was that his injury wasn't going to beat him. He was going to shock the experts and walk again. The second—which he entered when he got out of the hospital and his therapy became full-time—was that he was never going to be able to do a damn thing.

When he started working on strengthening his arms, his lower back, and his abdomen, they hurt like the Devil's own pitchfork digging into his sinew. He wanted to give up, let the government pay him disability, and watch TV and not move from his house. But a pair of saintly nurses alternately prodded and pushed him through rehabilitation. One of them, in a less saintly moment, showed him that he could still have a gratifying sex life. And after that, Herbert never wanted to give up on anything again.

Until now.

Because he didn't want anyone in the camp to know he was coming, he wasn't able to use the small, powerful headlights Op-Center's Chief Electrician Einar Kinlock had built into his wheelchair. The ground was uneven and rough. Sometimes it sloped sharply, other times it ended in sheer drops. In the dark, the chair was constantly getting caught in the undergrowth. Herbert had to push hard to escape, and twice he ended up on the ground. Righting the chair and climbing back in were the toughest things he'd ever had to do, and getting up the second time left him drained. As he settled into the leather seat, his shirt was wet with cold perspiration and he was so tired he was shaking.

He wanted to stop and call for help. But he reminded himself that he couldn't be sure of anyone. That fear was more like the old Nazi Germany than anything he had encountered.

He continually checked the phosphorescent pocket compass he carried. But after more than an hour of pushing himself, he saw headlights about an eighth of a mile to the southwest. He stopped and watched carefully where the vehicle went. It was moving slowly along the rough road Alberto had told him about, and he waited as it passed. Though the brake lights were dim, he saw them flash in the distance. The interior lights went on, dark figures moved away from him, and then there was blackness again, and silence.

Obviously, that was where he needed to be.

Herbert moved over the lumpy ground toward the car. He avoided the road in case anyone else was coming, his arms nearly numb with the effort of crossing this last stretch of woods. He only hoped that Jody didn't take him for a neo-Nazi and drop from a tree.

Upon reaching the car, a limousine, he edged forward. The Skorpion was still in his lap, so he tucked it under his leg where it wouldn't be seen. He could still grab it quickly if he had to. As he neared, he saw the tops of tents with smoke from campfires rising beyond them. He saw young men standing between the tents, looking toward the fires. And then he saw at least two or three hundred people facing a clear spot by the lake, a spot where a man and a woman stood alone.

The man was speaking. Herbert wheeled himself behind a tree and listened, able to understand most of the German.

". . . that this day ends an era of struggling at cross purposes. From tonight forward, our two groups will work together, united by a common goal and a single name: *Das National Feuer.*"

The man shouted the name not just for effect but to be heard. Herbert felt his strength return as well as his anger rise as the crowd cheered. They whooped and raised both arms high as if their team had just won the World Cup. Herbert wasn't surprised that these people eschewed the Nazi salute and cries of *Sieg Heil!* Though they surely wished for salvation and victory, and though they had ruffians and killers among them, they were not the Nazis of Adolf Hitler. They were far more dangerous: they had the advantage of having learned from his mistakes. However, almost everyone was holding something aloft, either a dagger or a medal or even a pair of boots. They were probably the artifacts stolen from the movie trailer. So Hitler wasn't entirely unrepresented in this new Nuremberg rally.

Herbert turned from the fires so his eyes would again adjust to the darkness, and peered around for Jody.

When the cheering died, he heard a voice whisper behind him, "I waited for you."

Herbert turned and saw Jody. She looked nervous.

"You should've waited for me back there," Herbert whispered, pointing the way he'd come. "I could've used some help." He took her hand. "Jody, let's go back. Please. This is insane."

She gently tugged her hand away. "I'm scared, but now more than ever I have to fight it."

"You're scared," Herbert whispered, "and you're also obsessing. You're fixated on a goal which has taken on a life of its own. Believe me, Jody, going over to them isn't as big as you're making it."

Herbert's voice was drowned out as the speaker continued. Herbert wished he didn't have to hear him, his voice carrying clearly, forcefully, without a megaphone. Herbert tugged at Jody. She refused to budge.

The German said, "The woman beside me, my co-leader Karin Doring . . ."

Applause rolled from the mob spontaneously, and the man waited. The woman bowed her head but didn't speak.

"Karin has sent emissaries to Hanover," the man shouted as the applause quieted. "In just a few minutes we will all go to the city, to the Beer-Hall, to announce our new union to the world. We will invite our brothers there to join the movement and together we will show civilization its future. A future where sweat and industry will be rewarded . . ."

There was more applause and cheering.

". . . where perverse cultures and faiths and peoples will be segregated from the heart's blood of society . . ."

The applause and cheering built. It remained strong.

". . . where spotlights will play across our symbols, our accomplishments."

The applause grew to a torrent and Herbert used the cover of the din to yell at Jody.

"Come *on,*" he said, pulling at her hand again. "These people will fall on you like dingoes."

Jody looked out at them. Herbert couldn't make out her expression in the dark. He had the urge to shoot *her* in the foot, throw her across his lap, and start wheeling back.

The speaker yelled, "And if the authorities in Hanover turn on us, let them! *Let them!* For over a year I have been personally harassed by Hauptmann Rosenlocher of the Hamburg police. If I drive too quickly he is there. If I play music too loudly he is there. If I meet with my colleagues, he is there. But he will not beat me. *Let them target us individually or together!* They'll see that our movement is organized, that our will is strong."

Jody stared out at the rally. "I don't want to die. But I don't want to live pathetically."

"Jody, you won't—"

She wrenched her hand from Herbert. He didn't try to get it back. He wheeled after her, cursing the stubbornness which had stopped him from getting a goddamned motor. Then he cursed this kid who he understood and had to respect even though she didn't listen to reason. Any more than he did.

As the applause died, Jody's footsteps seemed quite loud to Herbert. Also, apparently, to the sentry nearest them, who turned. He saw them in the light of the fires and shouted to the young men and women who were standing nearest to him. A moment later the sentry was moving forward and the others were forming a line behind him with the clear intention of letting Jody and Herbert nowhere near the front of the crowd or Karin Doring or Jody's goal.

Herbert stopped. Jody did not. With a snort of disgust, Herbert wheeled after her.

FORTY-EIGHT

Thursday, 8:36 P.M., Southwest of Vichy, France

"There was never any question that I would know how to fly."

Paul Hood stood behind Richard Hausen as he piloted the Learjet through the skies over France. He was speaking loudly to be heard over the two powerful turbofan engines. Lang's full-time pilot, Elisabeth Stroh, sat beside him. She was a handsome young brunette about twenty-seven, whose French and English were impeccable. Lang's instructions to her had been to fly in with them, wait with the jet, and fly out with them again. Her conversation had been limited to communication with the tower in Hamburg and now in Toulouse, and remarks to the passengers about their flight plan. If she was interested in what Hausen was saying, she didn't show it.

Hood had been sitting in the cabin with Stoll and Nancy. After nearly ninety minutes in the air, he needed to get away from them both: Stoll because he hadn't stopped talking, and Nancy because she didn't want to start.

Seated in one of the plush sofas which lined the walls of the cabin, Stoll had been saying that he never thought of himself as a team player. He went to work for Op-

Center because he *was* a loner, because they needed a self-starter who liked to sit at a desk and write software and troubleshoot hardware. He pointed out that he wasn't a Striker and was not obligated to go into the field. He was doing this out of respect for Hood, not courage. The rest of the time he spent complaining about possible glitches in the T-Ray. He said he wasn't offering any guarantees. Hood told him he understood.

Nancy, on the other hand, sat looking out the window for most of the time. Hood asked what she was thinking about, but she wouldn't say. He could guess, of course. He wished that he could comfort her.

Nancy did offer some information about the layout of the *Demain* facility. Stoll dutifully morphed her descriptions with the floor plan. It had been sent from Op-Center via a remote-access software package designed by Stoll. Thanks to the Ultrapipeline capacity of the NRO's Hermit satellite, mainframes at Op-Center were able to communicate wirelessly with computers in the field. Stoll's patented software boosted the data transfer capacity of the Hermitlink from two- to five-kilobyte blocks using elements of Z-modem file transfer protocol and spread-spectrum radio transmission in the 2.4- to 2.483-gigahertz range.

Not that the link helped. There wasn't much Nancy could tell them. She knew the setup of the manufacturing and programing areas, but knew nothing of the executive suites or of Dominique's private quarters.

Hood left Nancy with her thoughts and Stoll in the relative comfort of a multiuser Dungeon computer game which he used to relax. Venturing into the cockpit, Hood listened while the eager, almost buoyant Hausen told him about his youth.

Hausen's father Maximillian had been a pilot with the

Luftwaffe. He'd specialized in night fighting, and had flown the first operational sortie of the Heinkel He 219 when it shot down five Lancasters. Like many Germans, Hausen did not speak apologetically of his father's wartime exploits. Military service could not be avoided, and it didn't diminish Hausen's love or respect for Maximillian. Still, as the German spoke about his father's activities, Hood found it difficult not to think of the families of the young crew members of those downed Lancasters.

Perhaps sensing Hood's discomfort, Hausen asked, "Did your father serve?"

Hood said, "My father was a medic. He was stationed at Fort McClellan in Alabama setting broken bones and treating cases of"—he looked at Elisabeth—"various diseases."

"I understand," Hausen said.

"So do I," Elisabeth put in.

The woman gave him a half-smile. Hood returned it. He felt as if he was back in Op-Center trying to walk the tightrope between political correctness and sexual discrimination.

"And you never wanted to be a doctor?" Hausen asked.

"No," Hood said. "I wanted to help people and I felt that politics was the best way. Some people of my generation thought revolution was the answer. But I decided to work with the so-called establishment."

"You were wise," Hausen said. "Revolution is rarely the answer."

"What about you?" Hood asked. "Did you always want to be in politics?"

He shook his head. "From the time I was able to walk I wanted to fly," he said. "When I was seven, on our farm near the Rhine in Westphalia, my father taught me to fly the 1913 Fokker Spider monoplane he'd restored. When I was ten and attending boarding school in Bonn, I switched to a Bucker two-seat biplane at a nearby field.'' Hausen smiled. ''But I always saw beauty from the air turn to squalor on the ground. And like you, when I came of age, I decided to help people.''

''Your parents must have been proud,'' Hood said.

Hausen's expression darkened. ''Not exactly. It was a very complicated situation. My father had quite definite ideas about things, including what his son should do for a living.''

''And he wanted you flying,'' Hood said.

''He wanted me with him, yes.''

''Why? It isn't as though you turned your back on a family business.''

''No,'' Hausen said, ''it was worse. I turned my back on my father's wishes.''

''I see. And are they still furious?''

''My father passed away two years ago,'' Hausen said. ''We were able to talk shortly before his death, though much too much was left unsaid. My mother and I speak regularly, though she hasn't been the same since his death.''

While he listened, Hood couldn't help but think back to Ballon's comments about Hausen being a headline grabber. Having been a politician himself, Hood understood that good press was important. But he wanted to believe that this man was sincere. And in any case, there wasn't going to be press coverage in France.

A politician's Catch-22, he thought wryly. *No one to report on our triumphs if we succeed, but no one to report on our arrest and humiliation if we fail, either.*

As Hood was about to return to the cabin, he had an urgent summons from Stoll.

"Come here, Chief! Something's happening on the computer!"

There was no longer a frightened tremolo in the voice of Op-Center's technical genius. Matt Stoll's voice was thick, concerned. Hood made his way quickly across the soft white carpet.

"What's wrong?" Hood asked.

"Look what just hacked its way into the game I was playing."

Hood sat beside him on the right. Nancy moved from her seat on the other side of the cabin and sat on Stoll's left. Stoll pulled down the window shade so they would have a better view. They all looked at the screen.

There was a graphic of a vellum-like scroll with gothic-style printing. A white hand held it open on the top, another on the bottom.

"Citizens, hear ye!" it read. *"We pray you will forgive this interruption.*

"Did you know that according to the Sentencing Project, a public-interest group, one third of all black men between the ages of twenty and twenty-nine are in prison, on probation, or on parole? Did you know that this figure marks a ten percent rise from just five years ago? Did you know that these blacks cost the nation over six billion dollars each year? Watch for us in eighty-three minutes."

Hood asked, "Where did this come from, Matt?"

"I have no idea."

Nancy said, "Don't break-ins usually occur through interactive terminal ports or file-transfer ports—"

"Or E-mail ports, yeah," Stoll said. "But this break-in isn't originating at Op-Center. This scroll came from somewhere else. And that somewhere else is probably very well hidden.''

''What do you mean?'' Hood asked.

''Sophisticated break-ins like this are usually done through a series of computers.''

''So can't you just follow the trail backwards?'' Hood asked.

Stoll shook his head. ''You're right that these boobs use their computer to break into another, then use that one to break into another, and so on. But it's not like connect-the-dots where each stop is a single point. Each computer represents thousands of potential routes. Like a train terminal but with hundreds of tracks leading to different destinations.''

The screen cleared and a second scroll appeared.

''Did you know that the unemployment rate among black men and women is more than double that of white men and women? Did you know that an average of nine out of the ten top records of the country this year were performed by blacks, and that your white daughters and girlfriends are purchasing over sixty percent of this so-called music? Did you know that only five percent of the books in this country are purchased by blacks? Watch for us in eighty-two minutes.''

Hood asked, ''Is this appearing anywhere else?''

Stoll's fingers were already speeding over the keyboard. ''Checking,'' he said as he typed ''listserv-@cfrvm.sfc.ufs.stn.'' ''This is a group that discusses Hong Kong action films. It's the most obscure E-mail address I know.''

After a moment, the screen changed.

''I happen to think that Jackie Chan's potrayal of Wong Fei Hong is the definitive interpretation. Even though Jackie's off-screen persona is visible in the char-

acterization, he makes it work."

Stoll said, "It's safe to say the interlopers only went after the gamers."

"Which makes sense," Nancy said, "if they're going to be offering hate games to that market."

"But they wouldn't be offering them aboveboard," Hood said. "I mean, one wouldn't find their ads in the Internet Yellow Pages."

"No," Stoll agreed. "But word spreads quickly. Anyone who wants to play would know where to find them."

"And with the Enjoystick providing an extra kick," Hood said, "kids who didn't know any better would certainly want to play."

"What about laws?" Nancy said. "I thought there were restrictions on what you could send through the Internet."

"There are," Stoll said. He returned to the scrolls on Multi-User Dungeon and sat back. For the moment, his fears were clearly forgotten. "They're the same laws which govern other markets. Child pornographers are chased and caught. Advertising for hit men is illegal. But rattling off facts like these, facts you can find in any good almanac, is not illegal. Even when the intent is clearly racist. The only crime these people have committed is breaking into other people's rooms. And I guarantee this message will be gone in a few hours, before network officials can get close to locating them."

Nancy looked at Hood. "You obviously think this is Dominique's doing."

"He has the capability, doesn't he?"

"That doesn't make him a criminal."

"No," Hood agreed. "Killing and stealing do."

Her eyes held his for a moment, then dropped.

Apparently oblivious to the others, Stoll said, "There are touches on this scroll which remind me of the game in Hausen's office." He leaned forward and touched the screen. "The shading under the curl at the bottom of the scroll is blue, not black. Someone with a background in publishing might have done that out of habit. During color separations, deep blue shadows reproduce richer than blacks. And the molded colors of the vellum, giving it a solid look here"—he touched the still-scrolled section at the top—"is similar to the texture of the deer skin in the forests of the other game."

Nancy sat back. "You're reaching."

Stoll shook his head. "Of all people, you should know the kinds of flourishes designers put in their games. You probably remember the early days of video games," Stoll said. "The days when you could tell an Activision game from an Imagic game from an Atari game because of the designers's touches. Hell, you could even tell a David Crane game from the rest of the games at Activision. Creators left their fingerprints all over the screen."

Nancy said, "I know those early days better than you think, Matt. And I'm telling you *Demain* isn't like that. When I program games for Dominique we leave our personal vision at the door. Our job is to pack as many colors and realistic graphics into a game as possible."

Hood said, "That doesn't mean *Demain* wasn't behind the game. Dominique would hardly produce hate games which looked like his regular games."

Nancy said, "But I've seen the portfolios of the people who work up there," she said. "I've been sitting here thinking about their graphics. None of them work like this."

"What about outside designers?" Hood said.

"At some point, they'd still have to come through the

system," she said. "Tested, tweaked, downloaded—there are dozens of steps."

"What if the entire process were done outside?" Hood asked.

Stoll snapped his fingers. "That kid Reiner, Hausen's assistant. He said he designed stereogram programs. He knows computers."

"Right," said Hood. "Nancy, if someone did design a game on the outside, what's the fewest number of people who would see the diskettes at *Demain*?"

She said, "First of all, something that dangerous would not come in on diskettes."

"Why not?" Hood asked.

"It would be a smoking gun," she said. "A time-encoded program on a diskette would be proof in court that Dominique was trafficking in hate games."

"Assuming they didn't erase it once it was uploaded," Stoll said.

"They'd keep it until they were sure everything went off as planned," Nancy said. "That's how they work here. Anyway, an outside program like that would have to be modemed to a diskless workstation."

"We've got those, Boss," Stoll said. "They're used for highly sensitive data which you don't want copied from the file server—the networked computer—onto a local diskette."

Hood was at the limit of his technical know-how, but he got the gist of what Stoll was saying.

Nancy said, "The only people who have diskless workstations at *Demain* are vice-presidents who deal with information about new games or business strategies."

Stoll erased the program on his laptop. "Give me the names of some of those high-ups who have the technical chops to process game programs.''

Nancy said, ''The entire process? Only two of them can do that. Etienne Escarbot and Jean-Michel Horne.''

Stoll input the names, sent them off to Op-Center, and asked for a background report. While they waited, Hood addressed something that had been roiling around inside him ever since he'd spoken with Ballon. The Colonel had been less than enthused about Hausen's participation. He'd called him a headline-grabber.

What if he were worse than that? Hood wondered. He didn't want to think ill of someone who seemed a good man, but that was part of the job. Asking yourself, *What if?* And after listening to Hausen talk about his Luftwaffe father he was asking himself, *What if Hausen and Dominique weren't enemies? Hood only had Hausen's account of what had transpired in Paris twenty-odd years ago. What if the two were working together? Christ, Ballon said that Dominique's father had made his fortune in Airbus construction.* Airplanes. *And Hausen was a goddamned pilot.*

Hood carried his thinking a few steps further. What if Reiner had been doing exactly what his boss wanted? Making Hausen look like a victim of a hate game in order to sucker Op-Center, Ballon, and the German government into an embarrassing incursion? Who would ever attack Dominique a *second* time if the first assault turned up nothing?

Stoll said, ''Aha! We've already got some potential rotten apples here. According to Lowell Coffey's legal files, in 1981 M. Escarbot was charged by a Parisian firm with stealing trade secrets from IBM about a process of displaying bit-mapped graphics. *Demain* paid to settle that case. And criminal charges were filed and then dropped nineteen years ago against M. Horne. Seems he received a French patent for an advanced four-bit chip which an American company said was stolen from them. Only they couldn't prove it. They also couldn't find the person who supposedly ripped off the . . .''

Stoll stopped reading. His white face turned slowly toward Hood, then toward Nancy.

"No," she said, "there aren't two Nancy Jo Bosworths. That was me."

"It's okay," Hood said to him. "I knew all about it."

Stoll nodded slowly. He regarded Nancy. "Forgive me," he said, "but as a software designer m'self, I just have to say that that's very uncool."

"I know," Nancy replied.

"That's enough, Matt," Hood said sternly.

"Sure," Stoll said. He sat back, tightened the seatbelt which he'd never unbuckled, and turned around so he could look out the window.

And then Hood thought, *Damn everything.* Here he was rebuking Stoll when what he should have been doing was wondering about Nancy showing up in the park the way she did. And when he happened to be with Richard Hausen. Was it a coincidence, or could it be that all of them were in this thing with Dominique? He suddenly felt very unsure and very *stupid.* In the rush of events, in his eagerness to stop Dominique from getting his message and his games to America, Hood had utterly ignored security and caution. What's more, he'd allowed his group to be split. His security expert, Bob Herbert, was roaming around the German countryside.

It could be that he was making more of this than there was. His gut told him he was. But his brain told him to try and find out. Before they got to *Demain,* if possible.

Hood remained beside Stoll while Nancy had returned to her side of the aircraft. She was unhappy and not attempting to hide it. Stoll was disgusted and not trying to hide it either. Only Hood had to keep his feelings to himself, though not for long.

As Elisabeth came on the intercom to announce the final descent into Toulouse, Hood casually borrowed the laptop from Stoll.

"Want me to boot up Solitaire?" Stoll asked, referring to Hood's favorite computer game.

"No," Hood said as he switched the machine back on. "I feel like Tetris." As he spoke, Hood typed a message onto the screen. *"Matt,"* he wrote, *"I don't want you to say anything. Just put me on-line with Darrell."*

Stoll casually touched his nose, leaned over, and entered his password and Op-Center's number. The disk drive hummed as the prompt said, *"Processing."*

Stoll sat back when the prompt said, *"Ready."* He turned his head toward the window, but kept his eyes on the screen.

Hood typed his personal transmission code in quickly, then wrote:

"Darrell: I need every detail you can get on the life of German Deputy Foreign Minister Richard Hausen. Check tax records from 1970s. Looking for employment by Airbus Industrie or by a man named Dupre or Dominique of Toulouse. Also want details of postwar life and activities of Maximillian Hausen of the Luftwaffe. Call me when you have anything. Shoot for 1600 hours EST today at the latest."

Hood sat back. "I suck at this game. What do I do now?"

Stoll reached over. He transmitted the E-mail message. "You want to save any of these games?"

"No," Hood said.

Stoll typed in :-) then erased the screen.

"In fact," Hood said, shutting off the computer, "I want you to take this machine and throw it out the window."

"You should never play video games when you're tense," Nancy said. She looked across the cabin at Hood. "It's like sports or sex. You've got to be loose."

Hood handed Stoll the computer. Then he walked over to Nancy and buckled himself in beside her.

"I'm sorry I got you into this," he said.

"Which 'this' do you mean?" she asked. "This little raid or this whole stinking, lousy business?"

"The raid," he said. "I shouldn't have imposed on our . . ." He stopped to search for the right word, settled reluctantly on "friendship."

"It's all right," Nancy said. "Really it is, Paul. A big part of me is tired of running and of depending on *Demain* and on the whole expatriate life that you have to be drawn to to enjoy. What was it that Sydney Carton said on the way to the scaffold in *A Tale of Two Cities?* 'It is a far, far better thing that I do than I have ever done.' This is far, far better than the things I've done till now."

Hood smiled warmly. He wanted to tell her not to worry about the scaffold. But he couldn't guarantee her fate any more than he could swear to her allegiance. As the plane landed gently on the soil of France, he only hoped that the worry on her face was for her future and not his.

FORTY-NINE

Thursday, 2:59 P.M.,
Washington, D.C.

Hood's wireless transmission was received by Darrell McCaskey's executive assistant Sharri Jurmain. The FBI Academy graduate E-mailed it to McCaskey's personal computer and to Dr. John Benn of Op-Center's Rapid Information Search Center.

The RI-Search Center was little more than two small, interconnected offices with twenty-two computers run by two full-time operators and overseen by Dr. Benn. A former librarian with the Library of Congress, the British-born bachelor had been an embassy researcher in Qatar for two years when the Arab state declared its independence from Britain in 1971. Benn remained there for seven years before moving to Washington to stay with his sister when her diplomat-husband died. Charmed by Washington and by Americans, Benn remained behind after his sister returned to England. He became an American citizen in 1988.

Benn's proud, singular skill, acquired during his otherwise uneventful years in Qatar, was quoting obscure lines of dialogue from English literature. Even with the help of Usenet groups, no one at Op-Center had ever correctly identified a single one of Benn's characterizations.

Benn was taking an early tea and pretending to be Mr. Boffin from Dickens's *Our Mutual Friend* when Hood's E-mail request came through. It was heralded by a synthesized electronic voice calling out, "I will arise and go now" from Yeats's *The Lake Isle of Innisfree,* followed by the identification number of the person making the request.

"Once more unto the breach, dear friends, once more," Benn said with a flourish as they swung to the number one screen. He and his assistants Sylvester Neuman and Alfred Smythe immediately recognized Stoll's "greeting," the :-), his "smiley face" lying on its side. In one of his more paranoid moments, Stoll had arranged with them that if he were ever being forced to transmit data, he would input :-(, a frowning face.

The team went to work efficiently gathering the information.

For a biography of Deputy Foreign Minister Richard Hausen and any information on his father, Smythe went on-line and executed FTPs—File Transfer Protocols— to acquire data from *ECRC Munich, Deutsche Elektronen Synchotron, German Electro-Synchotron, DKFZ Heidelberg, Gesellschaft für Wissenschaftliche Datenverarbeitung GmbH, Konrad Zuse Zentrum für Informationstechnik Konrad Zuse Center,* and *Comprehensive TeX Archive Network Heidelberg.* Neuman used three computers to enter gopherspace on the Internet and accessed information from *Deutsches Klimarechenzentrum Hamburg, EUnet Germany,* the German Network Information Center, and *ZIB, Berlin auf Ufer.* With the help of an aide to Matt Stoll, Deputy Assistant Director of Operations Grady Reynolds, they hacked into tax, employment, and education records of the former Federal Republic of Germany and the German Democratic Republic. The records of many Germans, especially the former East Germans, existed as hard copy only. However, the educational and financial history of politicial figures would have to have been put on disk for filing with various government commissions. Moreover, many large corporations had scanned their books onto computer. Those, at least, might also be available.

Darrell McCaskey's office, which had dominion over contact with other agencies, put them on-line with the FBI, Interpol, and various German law enforcement agencies: the *Bundeskriminalamt* or BKA, the German equivalent of the FBI; the *Landespolizei*; the *Bundeszollpolizei* or Federal Customs Police; and the *Bundespostpolizei*, the Federal Postal Police. The *Bundeszollpolizei* and the *Bundespostpolizei* often caught up with felons who had managed to slip past the others.

As the two assistants word-searched data and retrieved blocks of information about Hausen, Dr. Benn wrote it up in essential, digestible chunks. Since Hood had requested a phone call, Benn would read it to him. However, the data would also be stored for downloading or hard-copy printout.

Reading the information which came in, and rereading the original request, he wondered if Hood had got things quite right. There seemed to be some confusion about which Hausen had done what during his career.

Nonetheless, Benn continued to work quickly in order to meet the deadline Hood had imposed.

FIFTY

Thursday, 3:01 P.M., Washington, D.C.

All requests for information from the RI-Search division were automatically given a job number and time-coded by computer. Job numbers were always prefixed by one, two, or three digits which identified the individual making the request. Since requests were frequently made by someone in a dangerous situation, other individuals were automatically notified when those requests came in. If anything happened to the person in the field, their backup would be required to step in and finish the operation.

When Hood asked for data from RI-Search, Mike Rodgers was alerted by a beep from his computer. Had he not been present, the signal would have sounded once every minute.

But he was there, eating a late lunch at his desk. Between bites of microwaved hamburger from the commissary, he examined the request. And he began to worry.

Rodgers and Hood were unalike in many ways. Chief among the differences was their worldview. Hood believed in the goodness of people while Rodgers believed that humankind was basically self-absorbed, a collection of territorial carnivores. Rodgers felt that the evidence was on his side. If it were not, then he and millions of soldiers like him wouldn't have jobs.

Rodgers also felt that if Paul Hood had doubts about the Hausen clan, there must really be cause for concern.

"He's going into France to search for a terrorist group with Matt Stoll as backup," the General said to his empty office. He looked at his computer. He wished he could input ROC and have the Regional Op-Center, fully staffed and with Striker personnel on hand, on site in Toulouse. Instead, he typed in MAPEURO.

A full-color map of Europe appeared. He overlaid a grid and studied it for a moment.

"Five hundred and forty miles," he said as his eyes went from Northern Italy to the South of France.

Rodgers hit ESC and typed NATOITALY.

Within five seconds a two-column menu was on-screen, offering selections from Troop deployment to Transportation resources, from Armaments to Wargame simulation programs.

He moved the cursor to Transportation and a second menu appeared. He selected Air transport. A third menu offered a listing of aircraft types and airfields. The Sikorsky CH-53E was free. The three-engined chopper had a range of over twelve hundred miles, and it had room enough for what he was planning. But at 196 miles an hour, it wasn't fast enough. He moved down the list. And stopped.

The V-22 Osprey. A Bell and Boeing vertical takeoff and landing vehicle. Its range was nearly 1,400 miles at a cruising speed of 345 miles an hour. Perhaps best of all was the fact that one of the prototypes had been turned over to the Sixth Fleet for testing in Naples.

Rodgers smiled, then escaped from the menu and called up his phone directory on-screen. He moved the cursor to NATO Direct Lines and selected the Senior NATO military commander in Europe, General Vincenzo DiFate.

Within three minutes, Rodgers had pulled the General away from a dinner party at the Spanish Embassy in London and was explaining why he needed to borrow the chopper and ten French soldiers.

FIFTY-ONE

Thursday, 9:02 P.M., Wunstorf, Germany

"Stupid cripple!"

Herbert had heard some strong epithets in his day. He'd heard them being thrown at blacks in Mississippi, at Jews in the former Soviet Union, and at Americans in Beirut. But what the young sentry shouted as he stalked toward Jody was one of the dumbest invectives he'd ever heard. Weak as it was, though, it still pissed him off.

Herbert snatched the flashlight from his chair and took a moment to glance into the driver's side of the car he'd followed here. Then he scooted to the side lest someone shoot at his light. He watched from the darkness as the sentry reached Jody and she finally stopped walking. Then Herbert pulled the Skorpion from under his leg.

Jody and the sentry were about ten yards from Herbert and twenty-five yards from the line of neo-Nazis. Beyond them, the rally continued undisrupted.

Jody was standing directly between Herbert and the sentry.

The boy asked something in German. Jody said she didn't understand. He shouted to someone behind him for instructions about what to do. As he did, he stepped slightly to the left. Herbert aimed the Skorpion at the boy's right shin and fired.

The brawny youth went down with a shriek.

"Now we're both crippled," Herbert muttered as he stashed the gun in a worn leather pocket on the side of the chair. He rolled quickly toward the passenger's side of the car.

The crowd fell silent and the line of neo-Nazis hit the dirt well behind the wounded man. The rise in the terrain made it impossible for them to fire from where they were—though Herbert knew they wouldn't stay there for long.

As Herbert rounded the car he yelled to Jody, "Do your thing and then let's *go!*"

The girl looked at him, then looked across the field of white faces. "You didn't beat me," she yelled in a strong voice. "And you won't."

Herbert opened the passenger's side. "Jody!"

The girl looked down at the wounded boy, then ran back.

"Get in the driver's side," Herbert told her as he started to pull himself in. "The keys are still in the ignition."

Some of the ralliers had begun to shout. One of the neo-Nazis in the line had gotten up. She was holding a gun. She aimed at Jody.

"Shit," Herbert said and fired through the window. Jody screamed and clutched at her ears. Hebert's shot struck the German in the thigh and she was thrown backward behind a splash of blood.

Herbert got back out of the car and into his wheelchair and covered her retreat from behind the open door. Jody got into the car, started the engine, and gunned it. The young woman was no longer composed. She was shaking and breathing heavily, exhibiting a classic post-stress breakdown.

Herbert couldn't afford to lose her. "Jody," he said, "I want you to listen to me."

She began to cry.

"Jody!"

"What!" she screamed. "What, what, *what?*"

"I want you to back the car away slowly."

She was gripping the wheel and looking down. The mob was roiling like ants behind the prostrate front line. In the distance, Herbert could see the speaker talking with a woman. It was only a matter of time, maybe just seconds, before they were attacked.

"Jody," Herbert said patiently, "I need you to put the car in reverse and back away very slowly."

Herbert knew that he wouldn't be able to get in the car without lowering the gun. And lowering the gun, they'd be attacked. He took a quick look back. As far as he could tell in the dark, the terrain behind him was clear for several hundred yards. His plan was to let the open car door move him and the chair backwards, allowing him to keep the gun trained ahead as they retreated. When they were a safe distance away, he'd pull himself in and they could drive off.

That was the plan, anyway.

"Jody, are you listening?"

She nodded, sniffled, and stopped crying.

"Can you drive us back slowly?"

With painful slowness and uncertainty Jody put her hand on the gearshift. She started to cry again.

"Jody," Herbert said calmly, "we've really got to go."

She moved the lever just as the front tires exploded.

The car left the ground as they blew up, chewed apart

by a burst of gunfire from somewhere ahead. The open door flopped back, slapping Herbert toward the rear of the car. A moment later gunfire from a semi-automatic began eating into the open door. The crowd had parted to make a path and a woman was holding the weapon under her arm. As Lang had said—was it only that morning?—*"This can only be Karin Doring."*

Herbert rolled back. He opened the rear door, got behind it, and fired a burst from around the side. That kept the front line pinned down though it didn't stop the woman. She was coming as inexorably as winter.

Jody was crying. Herbert saw the guns in the backseat. He also saw something else there, something he could use.

He fired another few rounds at the mob, then said, "Jody. I need you to cover me."

She shook her head. He knew she had no idea what he was saying.

Bullets slammed into the front door. *A couple more bursts and they're goin' right through,* he thought. Then they'd penetrate his door and after that they'd penetrate him.

"Jody!" Herbert screamed. "You've got to reach through the partition, take the guns from the backseat, and shoot. *Shoot,* Jody, or we're dead!"

The young woman was squeezing the wheel.

"*Jody!*"

She continued to cry.

Desperate, Herbert turned toward her and put a round into the seat beside her thigh. She screamed and jumped as feather-light padding flew up, then drifted down.

"Jody," he repeated. "Take the guns and shoot Karin Doring or she will goddamn *own* you!"

The student turned to him, wide-eyed. Apparently *that*

she understood. Turning determinedly toward the back, Jody stretched through the open partition and grabbed the two guns.

"Release the safeties," Herbert said, "the little latches on the—"

"Got them," Jody said.

He looked at her as she sniffed back tears. Then he watched as she fired a burst at the windshield, leaned back against the seat, and kicked out the shattered expanse of glass with a yell.

"Amazing," he said under his breath. "Gauge your fire!" he cautioned as he leaned into the car. "Conserve ammo!"

He kept an eye on the front line of neo-Nazis as he picked up the six sparkling water bottles and put them in the leather pouch of his chair. As Karin Doring neared, the line grew bolder and one of the men rose.

"*Bastard!*" Jody screamed and shot at him.

The shot went wide, but the German dropped.

Herbert shook his head. *I've bred myself a little killer here,* he thought as he twisted the bottle caps from two of them and spilled the contents onto the ground. When they were empty, he rolled back a few feet and used his Urban Skinner to cut a section of gray tubing from the left wheel of his chair. Even Karin Doring wouldn't be able to walk through a wall of fire.

Bullets scudded across the hood of the car and ricocheted off. Jody threw herself to the far left. Obviously realizing she'd trapped herself against the door, she dropped to her right side. A moment later bullets ripped through the car and buried themselves in the backseat.

"Jody," Herbert yelled, "push in the cigarette lighter!"

She did, then ducked back down. Herbert knew she

wasn't going to be getting up again.

Karin was about three hundred yards away. Apparently sensing that they were safe, the other Germans began moving forward.

By this time, Herbert had opened the gas tank and was siphoning fuel into the bottles. Bullets began striking the car with greater frequency. Flashes rose from different parts of the crowd. In about half a minute, he and Jody were going to be Mr. and Ms. Frankenstein in the hands of angry villagers.

He heard the click of the cigarette lighter. Jody wasn't going to be able to help him. Rolling forward quickly, seeing far too much firelight through the perforated front door, Herbert reached through the front passenger's side and pulled up some of the stuffing from the bullet-ridden seat. He set one of the bottles on the floor and jammed the stuffing into the other. Then he snatched the cigarette lighter from the dashboard, touched it to the padding, watched as nothing happened.

And realized with horror that the damn stuff was flame resistant.

With an oath, he pushed the padding in partway. Then he dropped the lighter into the bottle and threw it with a high, arcing stiff arm. He prayed the wadding would fall.

It did. The Molotov cocktail exploded in mid-flight, showering the front of the mob with flaming droplets and shards of glass. Screams rose from where the burning splashes struck flesh or eyes.

Jody looked up from the seat. Her fear was replaced by amazement. Her gaze shifted from the fireworks to Herbert.

"I'm out of bombs," he said as he pulled himself in. "I suggest we move."

Herbert shut the door as best he could as Jody backed the limousine away. Ahead, Karin Doring pushed through the crowd, firing after the car. Other guns joined in.

"Oww—"

Herbert looked to the left as Jody moaned. She slumped toward him. The car slowed, then stopped.

He leaned over, saw that she'd been hit in the shoulder. Outside the rib, it looked like, under the clavicle.

She was panting, her eyes pressed tightly together. He tried to shift himself so her arm was resting on his shoulder and there was no pressure on the wound. As he moved himself and her, he saw the cigarette pack in the pocket of her blouse. He quickly removed it, and his heart jumped when he saw the matches tucked in the cellophane wrapper.

Laying Jody down on the seat, he scooted to the right, picked up the second bottle from the floor, and nestled it between his thighs. Karin had cleared the mob and was reloading her semi-automatic. Herbert pulled out his handkerchief, jammed it in the bottle, and struck a match. He touched it to the fabric, which flamed and disintegrated faster than he had expected.

"Either they don't burn or they freakin' immolate you," he said as he leaned out the door and chucked the bottle toward Karin.

The glass cracked audibly as the gasoline spread. A flame sparked, spread, and rose up. Like organ music, Herbert thought.

He turned immediately to Jody. She was holding her shoulder. He knew that the area would pretty much have gone numb, and the worst pain she would feel was when she moved.

Herbert folded his chair and pulled into the car,

largely so he could have the phone if he needed it. He wasn't sure if the phone in the limousine had survived the gunplay. Then he helped Jody up.

"Jody," he whispered, "I need you to do something. Can you hear me?"

She nodded once, weakly.

"I can't step on the gas. You'll have to do that for me. Do you think you can do that?"

She nodded again.

He wedged himself behind her slightly and took the wheel. He looked ahead and caught glimpses of a man holding Karin back from charging through the curtain of fire.

"Jody? We don't have much time. I'll take care of you, but we have to get out of here first."

She nodded again, licked her lips, and gasped as she extended her leg. Jody's eyes were shut, but Herbert watched as she felt around for the gas pedal.

"There," he said. "You've got it. Now push."

Jody did so, gently, and the car started back. His right arm across his chest, his hand on the steering wheel, Herbert turned around. He guided them along the rough-hewn path, through the trees, as the orange glow of the fire flashed dully on the rear window.

Bullets clanged against the front of the car, but with less force than before. They were shooting through the fire, blindly, as somebody shouted for everyone to calm down.

Chaos on Chaos Days, Herbert thought with some satisfaction. *Feuer stopped by fire.*

The ironies would have been delicious if he had time to savor them.

The car continued to move backward. The steering was awkward and they jerked on the broken front wheels and slammed the occasional tree as they retreated. Soon, the camp was just a glow reflected against the low-lying clouds of the evening sky. Herbert was beginning to think that they might actually get out of the woods alive.

And then the car died.

FIFTY-TWO

Thursday, 9:14 P.M., Wunstorf, Germany

Karin Doring coolly brushed away the fiery beads of gas which rained down on her. Her mind was on the cowardly behavior of her followers, but she refused to allow that to distract her. Like a fox, her eyes were on her prey. She watched the retreating car through the flame and smoke, through the rushing, tumbling mass of her followers.

Clever man, she thought bitterly. No headlights. He was backing away, driving by the dull glow of his braking lights. And then those lights went off. The SA dagger dangled from her belt hook by its metal clasp. The gun she held would be for the man. The dagger: that was for the girl.

Manfred grasped her shoulder from behind. "Karin! We have wounded. Richter needs your help to restore—"

"I want those two," she sneered. "Let Richter deal with the bedlam. He wanted to lead. Let him."

"He can't lead our people," Manfred said. "They won't accept him yet."

"Then you do it."

Manfred said, "You know they'll only march into Hell for you."

Karin rolled her shoulder to throw off Manfred's hand. Then she turned on him, her expression feral. "Into Hell? They scattered like cockroaches when the American turned on them. They were beaten back by one man in a wheelchair with only an hysterical girl to help him! They shamed me. I shamed myself."

"All the more reason to put the incident behind us," Manfred said. "It was a fluke. We let down our guard."

"I want revenge. I want blood."

"No," Manfred implored. "That was the old way. The wrong way. This is a setback, not a defeat—"

"Words! Bullshit words!"

"Karin, listen!" Manfred said. "You can rekindle the passion another way. By helping Richter lead us all to Hanover."

Karin turned. She looked through the flames. "I have no right to lead anyone while those two live. I stood by Richter and watched as my people, my soldiers, did nothing." She spotted a pathway through the shrinking fires and picked her way through the thinning smoke. Manfred lumbered after her.

"You can't chase a car," Manfred said.

"He's driving without headlights on a dirt road," she said. She broke into a slow jog. "I'll catch him or I'll track him. It won't be difficult."

Manfred trotted after her. "You're not thinking," he said. "How do you know he's not waiting for you?"

"I don't."

"What will I do without you?" Manfred yelled.

"Join up with Richter, as you said."

"That isn't what I mean," he said. "Karin, let's at least talk—"

She began to run.

"Karin!" he yelled.

She enjoyed the explosion of energy and the breathless dodging as she moved through the trees and across the uneven terrain.

"Karin!"

She didn't want to hear anything else. She wasn't sure how much her supporters had failed her and how much she had failed them. All she knew was that to atone for her role in the debacle, to feel clean again, she had to wash her hands in blood.

And she would. One way or another, tonight or tomorrow, in Germany or in America, she would.

FIFTY-THREE

Thursday, 9:32 P.M.,
Toulouse, France

Hood was looking out the window as Hausen guided the jet to a careful, easy landing. Hood had no doubt about where they were headed. A bright spotlight mounted high on the small terminal shone down on a band of eleven men clad in jeans and workshirts. A twelfth man was dressed in a business suit. As he watched the young fellow check his watch repeatedly or brush down his hair, Hood could tell he wasn't a lawman. He didn't have the patience for it. Hood also knew right off which man was Ballon. He was the one with the bulldog expression who looked as though he wanted to bite someone.

Ballon walked over before the plane had come to a complete stop. The man in the business suit scurried after him.

''We didn't even get bags of peanuts,'' Matt Stoll said as he undid his seatbelt and drummed his knees.

Hood watched as Ballon—and it was the bulldog he'd picked out—ordered his men to roll the stairway toward the jet. When the copilot finally opened the door, it was waiting.

Hood ducked through the door. He was followed by Nancy, Stoll, and Hausen. Ballon glanced at them all, but his gaze lingered harshly on Hausen. It snapped back to Hood when he reached the tarmac.

"Good evening," Hood said. He held out his hand. "I'm Paul Hood."

Ballon shook it. "Good evening. I'm Colonel Ballon." He pointed with his thumb to the man in the business suit. "This is M. Marais of Customs. He wants me to tell you that this is not an international airport and that you are only here as a favor to myself and the Groupe d'Intervention de la Gendarmerie Nationale."

"Vive la France," Stoll said under his breath.

"Les passeports," M. Marais said to Ballon.

"He wants to see your passports," Ballon said. "Then, hopefully, we can be on our way."

Stoll said to Ballon, "If I forgot mine, does that mean I get to go home?"

Ballon regarded him. "Are you the man with the machine?"

Stoll nodded.

"Then no. If I have to shoot Marais, you're coming with us."

Stoll reached into his jacket pocket and withdrew his passport. The others produced theirs as well.

Marais looked at each in turn, checking the faces against the photographs. Then he handed them back to Ballon, who passed them to Hood.

"Continuez," Marais said impatiently.

Ballon said, "I'm also supposed to tell you that, officially, you have not entered France. And that you will be expected to leave within twenty-four hours."

"We don't exist but we do," Stoll said. "Aristotle would have loved that."

Nancy was standing behind him. "Why Aristotle?" she asked.

"He believed in abiogenesis, the idea that living creatures can arise from nonliving matter. Francesco Redi disproved it in the seventeenth century. And now we've disproved Redi."

Hood had returned the passports and stood watching Marais. He could tell from the man's face that all was not well. After a moment, Marais took Ballon aside. They spoke quietly for a moment. Then Ballon walked over. His face was even unhappier than before.

"What is it?" Hood asked.

"He's concerned," Ballon said. He looked at Hausen. "He doesn't want this very irregular situation to receive any publicity."

Hausen said coolly, "I don't blame him. Who would want to advertise that they are the home of Dominique?"

"No one," Ballon replied, "except, perhaps, the nation which gave us Hitler."

Hood's instinct in any confrontation of this type was to mediate. But he decided to stay out of the way of this one. Both men had been out of line, and he felt he could only make enemies by interfering.

Nancy said, "I came here to help stop the next Hitler, not make cracks about the last one. Anybody care to help?"

Shouldering past Ballon, Marais, and the other members of the Gendarmerie, Nancy headed for the terminal.

Hausen looked at Hood and then at Ballon. "She's right," he said. "My apologies to you both."

Ballon's mouth scrunched as if he weren't quite ready to let the matter go. Then it relaxed. He turned to Marais, who appeared deeply confused.

"À demain," he said sternly, then signaled his men to go on. Hood, Stoll, and Hausen followed.

As they walked briskly through the terminal, Hood wondered if it had been coincidental that Ballon had selected the salutation "See you tomorrow," which in French also reflected where they were going.

Ballon led the group to a pair of waiting vans. Without undo fuss, he made certain that Stoll was comfortable between Nancy and Hood. Ballon got in front, beside the driver. There were three other men in the rearmost seat. None carried arms. Those were in the second van, along with Hausen.

"I feel like the botanist on HMS *Bounty,*" Stoll remarked to Hood when they were under way. "He had to transplant the breadfruit they were after and Captain Bligh really looked out for him."

"Where does that leave the rest of us?" Nancy said with a scowl.

"Bound for Tahiti," Hood said.

Nancy didn't smile. She didn't even look at him. Hood had the impression of being on the Ship of Fools, not the *Bounty,* Without the romanticism of memory to obscure it, he remembered now, vividly, how Nancy would regularly get into moods. She'd go from sad to depressed to angry, as if she were sliding down a muddy slope. The moods wouldn't last long, but when they came over her things could get nasty. He didn't know what scared him more: the fact that he'd forgotten them or the fact that she was in one now.

Ballon turned around. "I spent what was left of favors owed to me getting you into France. I had already used up most of them obtaining the search warrant to enter *Demain.* It expires tonight at midnight but I don't want to waste it. We've been watching the plant for days by remote video camera, hoping to see something that would justify entering. But so far, there's been nothing."

"What do you hope we'll find?" Hood asked.

"Ideally?" Ballon said. "Faces of known terrorists. Members of his terrible New Jacobin paramilitary force, a resurrection of the league which did not hesitate to murder old women or young children if they belonged to the upper classes."

The Colonel used a key attached to his wrist to open the glove compartment. He handed Hood a folder. Inside were over a dozen drawings and blurry photographs.

"Those are known Jacobins," Ballon said. "I need a match with one of them in order to go in."

Hood showed the file to Stoll. "Are you going to be able to see a face clear enough to make a positive ID?"

Stoll flipped through the pictures. "Maybe. Depends on what someone's standing behind, whether or not they're moving, how much time I have to do the imaging—"

"Those are a lot of conditions," Ballon said irately. "I need to place one of these monsters inside the factory."

"There's absolutely no leeway in the warrant?" Hood asked.

"None," Ballon said angrily. "But I won't let poor resolution allow us to pretend an innocent man is a guilty one just so we can go inside."

"Gee," Stoll said. "That doesn't put too much pressure on me, does it?" He returned the folder to Ballon.

"That is what separates professionals from amateurs," Ballon noted.

Nancy glared at Ballon. "I'm thinking that a professional wouldn't have let these terrorists get inside. I'm also thinking that Dominique has stolen, possibly killed, and is ready to start wars. But he gets the job done. Does that make him a professional?"

Ballon replied evenly, "Men like Dominique disregard the law. We don't have that luxury."

"Bull," she said. "I live in Paris. Most Americans are treated like shit by everyone from landlords to gendarmes. The laws don't protect us."

"But you obey the laws, don't you?" he asked.

"Of course."

Ballon said, "One side operating outside the law is still just that. A rogue force. But both sides operating outside the law is chaos."

Hood decided to get in the middle of this one by changing the subject. "How long until we reach the factory?"

"Another fifteen minutes or so." Ballon was still looking at Nancy, who had turned away. "Mlle. Bosworth, your arguments are sound and I regret having spoken harshly to M. Stoll. But there is a great deal at stake." He looked at all of them. "Have any of you considered the risks of success?"

Hood leaned forward. "No, we haven't. What do you mean?"

"If we work surgically and only Dominique falls, his company and its holdings can still survive. But if they fall, billions of dollars will be lost. The French economy and its government will be seriously destabilized. And that will create a vacuum similar to those we have seen in the past." He looked past them toward the van behind them. "A vacuum in which German nationalism historically has flourished. In which German politicians stir the blood." His eyes shifted to Hood. "In which they look with greed at Austria, Sudetenland, Alsace-Lorraine. MM. Hood and Stoll, Mlle. Bosworth—we are on a tightrope. Caution is our balancing pole and the law is our net. With them, we will reach the other side."

Nancy turned to look out the window. Hood knew she wouldn't apologize. But with her, the fact that she'd stopped arguing meant the same thing.

Hood said, "I also believe in the law and I believe in the systems we've built to protect it. We'll help you get to the other side of that tightrope, Colonel."

Ballon thanked him with a small nod, the first appreciative display he'd shown since they arrived.

"Thanks, Boss," Stoll sighed. "Like I said, that doesn't put too much pressure on me, does it?"

FIFTY-FOUR

Thursday, 9:33 P.M.,
Wunstorf, Germany

When the car died, Jody had lifted her foot from the
gas pedal, lay back on the headrest, and shut her eyes.

"I can't move," she panted.

Herbert turned on the overhead light and leaned toward her. "Sweetheart," he said softly, "you have to."

"No."

He began pulling wads of cotton-soft padding from
the car seat. "Our car's dead. We will be too if we don't
get out."

"I can't," she repeated.

Herbert moved the collar of her blouse aside and gently dabbed at the blood on her wound. The hole wasn't
large. He wouldn't be surprised if the bullet was a .22
fired from some homemade piece of crap by one of the
kids in the crowd.

Stupid punks, he thought. *They'd puke at the sight of
their own damn blood.*

"I'm afraid," Jody said suddenly. She started to
whimper. "I was wrong. *I'm still afraid!*"

"It's okay," Herbert said. "You're asking too much
of yourself."

Herbert felt bad for the kid, but he couldn't afford to
lose her. Not now. He didn't doubt for a moment that

Karin would be coming after him, alone or in force. The caduceus of Nazism had to be coated with the blood of the conquered to serve as an emblem of power.

"Listen, Jody," Herbert said. "We're close to where we started, about a mile from the main road. If we can get there we'll be okay."

Herbert turned to the glove compartment and opened it. He found a bottle of acetaminophen inside and gave two to Jody. Then he reached into the backseat, retrieved one of the water bottles, and gave her a drink. When she was finished, he let his hands drop behind the seat. He was feeling for something.

"Jody," he said, "we need to get out of here."

He found what he was looking for. "Sweetie," he said, "I've got to fix the wound."

She opened her eyes. "How?" she asked, wincing as she shifted her shoulder.

"I've got to take the bullet out. But there's no tape for a bandage or thread for a suture. When I'm done I'm going to have to cauterize it."

She was suddenly more alert. "You're going to burn me?"

"I've done it before," Herbert said. "We have to get out of here and I haven't got the horsepower to do that." He said, "What I'm going to do will hurt, but you're hurting now. We've got to fix that."

She lay her head back.

"Hon? We don't have time to waste."

"All right," she rasped. "Do it."

Holding his hands low where she couldn't see, he lit a match and held it to the tip of his Urban Skinner to sterilize it. After a few seconds he blew out the flame and used his fingers to gently open the wound. The back of the shell glinted in the yellow light of the car. Taking a deep breath, Herbert placed his left hand over her mouth. "Bite me if you have to," he said as he raised the knife.

Jody groaned.

The trick to treating a bullet wound was not to cause more damage removing the shell than it caused going in. But it had to be removed lest it work its way around the tissue, ripping it or even fragmenting itself as they fled.

Ideally, the surgeon would have forceps or tweezers to remove the shell. Herbert had only the knife. That meant he had to get under the bullet and pop it out fast, lest her writhing drive the blade this way and that.

He studied the wound for a moment, then put the tip to the opening. The bullet had entered at a slight left-to-right angle. He would have to go in the same way. He held his breath, steadied the knife, then pushed it in slowly.

Jody screamed into his hand. She struggled hard against Herbert, but he pinned her with his left forearm. There was nothing like pushing around a wheelchair to build the upper body.

Herbert pushed the blade along the bullet. He felt its end, angled the tip of the knife beneath it, and used the Skinner like a lever to ease the shell out. It emerged slowly, then tumbled down her body.

Herbert tucked the knife into his belt and released her. He grabbed the matches.

"I need four or five seconds to seal the wound," he said. "Will you give me that?"

Her lips and eyes pressed shut, she nodded briskly.

Herbert struck a match and used it to set the rest of the matchbook on fire. The matches would be hotter and faster than if he heated the knife and used it to close the wound. And seconds mattered now.

Once again pressing his hand to her mouth, Herbert pressed the heads of the matches to the bloody wound.

Jody tensed and bit his hand. He knew this pain and knew it would grow worse as the moisture in her skin evaporated. As she dug her teeth into him, he fought his own pain and bent toward her ear.

"Did you ever see Kenneth Branagh in *Henry V*?"

One second. The blood boiled off. Jody's hands shot toward Herbert's wrist.

"Remember what he told his soldiers?"

Two seconds. The flesh began to sear. Jody's teeth sliced through the meat of his palm.

"Henry said that one day they'd point to their scars and tell their kids that they were tough cookies."

Three seconds. The wound sizzled. Jody's strength seemed to evaporate. Her eyes rolled up.

"That's you," Herbert said. "Except you'll probably have plastic surgery."

Four seconds. The edges of the wound knit together under the heat. Jody's hands fell back.

"No one will ever believe you were shot. That you fought with King Bob Herbert on St. Crispin's Day."

Five seconds. He pulled at the matches. They broke from the burned flesh with a slight tug. He dropped the book, then brushed away the embers which still clung to her skin. It was a small, ugly job, but at least the wound was closed.

He removed his hand from her teeth. His palm was bleeding.

"Now we'll both have scars to show off," he grumbled as he reached for the passenger's side door. "Think you'll be able to walk now?"

Jody looked at him. She was sweating and her perspiration glistened in the car light.

"I'll make it," she said. She didn't look at the wound as she pulled her blouse over it. "Did I hurt your hand?"

"Unless you have rabies I'll be fine." He opened the door. "Now if you'll help me with the chair we can get the hell out of here."

Jody moved slowly, tentatively as she came around the car. She was more confident with each step and seemed her old self by the time she reached him. She struggled slightly to get the chair out, then held it open for him.

Pressing his hands on the car seat, he hopped in.

"Let's go," he said. "Due east. To the left."

"That's *not* the way I came," she said.

"I know," Herbert replied. "Just do it."

She started pushing. The chair seemed to snag on every exposed root and fallen branch. Far behind them, in an otherwise still and silent night, they heard crunching.

"We're never going to make it," Jody said.

"We are," Herbert said, "as long as you keep going in this direction.

Jody leaned into the chair and they moved slowly through the dark. And as they did, Herbert told the young woman one thing more he needed her to do.

FIFTY-FIVE

Thursday, 9:56 P.M., Toulouse, France

Leaving the vans behind, Ballon, Hood, Stoll, Hausen, and Nancy crossed the Tarn by foot across the high-arched brick bridge. Streetlights placed every twenty yards or so provided enough light for them to see—and, Hood knew, enough light for them to be seen.

Not that that mattered. Dominique would have assumed he was being watched in any case. Their approach would probably not cause him to take any extra precautions.

Upon reaching the former *bastide,* the group stopped. They sat beside a thicket on the narrow stretch of grass which sloped toward the river.

Muttering the entire time, Stoll entrusted his computer to Nancy while he unpacked the T-Bird.

"You're sure we're not doing anything illegal," Stoll said. "I'm not going to end up starring in *Midnight Express II* and getting caned."

"We don't do that in France," Ballon said. "And this is not illegal."

"I should've read the warrant on the plane," Stoll said. "Except I don't read French, so what difference would it've made?"

The computer scientist hooked the shoebox-like device to the fax-machine-sized imager. He pointed the front at the building and used a button on the imager to activate the laser line scanner. This scanner would clean up the image, removing blur caused by air particles which scattered the light.

Stoll said, "Colonel, you got any idea how thick those walls are?"

"Half a foot in most places."

"Then we should be okay," Stoll said as he squatted and switched on the terahertz generator. Less than ten seconds later the device beeped. "But we'll know now for sure in half a minute."

Still squatting, Stoll leaned over and waited for the color picture to come from the imager. The paper emerged at a rate equivalent to a moderately slow fax machine. Ballon watched expectantly as the glossy sheet curled out.

When the machine stopped, Stoll tore off the paper and handed it up to Ballon. The Colonel studied it in the light of a small flashlight. The others moved closer.

Hood's spirits plummeted. On the strength of this they'd be going nowhere very soon.

"What is this?" Ballon asked. "It looks like a swimming pool."

Stoll's knees popped as he rose. He looked at the image. "It's a picture of wall which is a lot thicker than six inches," he said. He studied beam-back data on the bottom of the paper. "It got 6.27 inches through the wall, then stopped. Which means it's either thicker than you thought or there's something on the other side."

Hood looked at Nancy, who was frowning. Then he looked at the five-story-tall edifice. There were windows, but they were shuttered. He was sure there would be radio-reflective materials on the other side.

Ballon threw the paper down angrily. "*This* is what we came here for?"

"Ya pays yer money and ya takes yer chances," Stoll said. He was obviously relieved. "I guess we should've known it wouldn't be as easy as hacking into government computers."

Even as he said it, Stoll obviously knew he'd made a mistake. Ballon turned the flashlight on him. Hood regarded the computer whiz.

"Can you break into computers?" Ballon asked.

Stoll looked at Hood. "Yes. I mean, I have. But that's highly illegal, especially—"

"We tried to get into *Demain*'s computers," Ballon said, "but Dominique wasn't on-line anywhere we could find. I had some of our best people working on the problem."

Nancy said, "That's because you probably didn't know what you were looking for. Did you find any of his games?"

"Of course," said Ballon.

"Then they were probably in there. Hidden inside MUDs. Multi-User Dungeons."

"Hey," said Stoll. "I was fooling around with one on the plane."

"I know," Nancy said. "I saw the commands you were typing. Also, the other message you sent."

Hood grew warm with embarrassment.

"It's like reading lips," Nancy said. "With enough experience you can read keyboards. Anyway, when we program games we always put in secret doorways to other games. I hid a game of Tetris inside Ironjaw, a game I wrote for *Demain*."

"That was yours?" Stoll asked. "That was awesome!"

"It was mine," she said. "No one ever reads the credits at the end. But if you did, you'd have found Tetris. All you had to do was highlight the correct letters sequentially in the fictitious names Ted Roberts and Trish Fallo."

Hood said, "How the hell would anyone ever think to do that?"

"They wouldn't," Nancy smiled. "That's what makes it so much fun. We leak the information through fan magazines and on-line bulletin boards."

Hood said, "But no one would ever think of looking for an activation code in an innocent adventure game."

"Right," said Nancy. "But that's exactly what it takes. A simple activation code. A program in somebody's computer in Jerkwater Township, U.S.A., could unleash a hate game across the entire Internet."

"Why didn't you say anything about this?" Hood asked.

"Frankly, it didn't occur to me until now," she snapped. "I didn't think of somebody sneaking hate games into the world through role-playing programs. Why didn't Matt think of it? He's your computer maven!"

"She's right," Stoll said. "I should've. Like the old joke says, you go hunting for elephant, sometimes you forget to look in the refrigerator."

Hood didn't remember the old joke, and didn't care right now. He said, "So the hate games are hidden. Where do we look for them?"

"And even if we find them," Hausen asked, "can we trace them back to *Demain*?"

"It's tough to say where to look for them," Stoll said. "He could have had the program passed around like a football—The Scorpion Strikes to The Phoenix from

Space to Claws of the Tiger-Man.''

''Would the hate game program have to come to rest in a *Demain* game?'' Hood asked.

''No,'' said Stoll. ''Once it was planted, it's like a virus. Timed to go off at will.''

''So there's no smoking gun,'' Hood said.

''Right,'' said Stoll. ''Even if you could stop the program from being launched, which is debatable since he'd probably have a backup somewhere, there wouldn't be any fingerprints on it.''

Ballon said disgustedly, ''That doesn't help me. Not a bit.''

Hood looked at his watch. ''He's going on-line now,'' he said. ''Nancy, are you sure you don't know *anything* more about this? About his M.O. or about the programmers and how they work?''

''If I did, Paul, I'd have told you.''

''I know. I was just thinking maybe something slipped your mind.''

''It didn't. Besides, I don't do the finishes on these programs. I write the parameters, the outlines, and other people color them in here. Paid big bucks and sequestered and loyal to the boss. When we do things like the extra game in the credits, that's more or less an afterthought. This is way out of my area.''

Everyone was silent for a moment. Then Stoll clapped his hands once and dropped to the grass. ''I know how to do it. I know how to *get* that bastard!''

Ballon crouched beside him. ''How?''

The others moved around them as Stoll unwrapped the cables for his portable computer. He attached the machine to the T-Bird. ''The programmers work like painters. Like we saw in Mr. Hausen's office, they take stuff from the landscape around them and use it in the games. It's dark now, so we'd have a problem eyeballing scenery. But if I take terahertz pictures of the trees and the hills and everything else, the chemical compounds appear as visual data. That'll give us the shape of things down to leaves and boulders. If we feed those into the computer—"

"You can run a video comparison program to see if any of the images match up," Nancy said. "Matt, that's brilliant!"

"Damn right," he said. "With any luck, I can handle the whole thing here. If I need more juice, I can download to Op-Center."

As Stoll worked Hood watched, confused but trusting his associate. And as he stood there, his phone beeped. He stepped toward the river to answer.

"Yes?"

"Paul?" said the caller. "It's John Benn. Can you speak?"

Hood said that he could.

"I have a full report for you, but here is the gist. Maximillian Hausen, father of Richard Hausen, worked for Pierre Dupre from 1966 to 1979. His title was Pilot and then Senior Pilot."

"You said 1966?" Hood said.

"I did."

That was before Richard Hausen and Gerard Dupre went to school together. In which case, it was not likely that they met at the Sorbonne, as Hausen had said. They almost certainly knew each other before that. Hood glanced back at Hausen, who was watching Stoll. The question which bothered Hood was not so much when they met but whether they were still in contact now. Not as enemies, but as allies.

"There's more," Benn said. "Apparently, Hausen the

Elder was a loyal Nazi who continued to meet in secret
with other ex-Nazis after the war. They belonged to the
White Wolves, a group which plotted the creation of the
Fourth Reich.''

Hood turned his back on the group. He asked quietly,
''Was Richard a member?''

''There's no evidence one way or the other,'' Benn
said.

Hood was glad to hear that, at least. ''Anything else,
John?''

''Not at present.''

''Thank you,'' Hood said. ''This is all very helpful.''

''You're welcome,'' Benn said, ''and have a good
night.''

Hood clicked off, then stood for a moment looking at
the dark waters of the Tarn. ''I hope that's possible,''
he said under his breath as he turned and headed back
to the others.

FIFTY-SIX

Thursday, 10:05 P.M., Wunstorf, Germany

Jody moved as quickly as her sandbag-heavy legs and aching shoulder would permit. It was amazing, she thought, how she had always taken so many things for granted. A healthy body, for one. A walk through the woods for another. Pushing or sometimes pulling a wheelchair with someone in it made the exercise a much different proposition.

Add the fact that someone was chasing her, someone she could hear but couldn't see, and every aspect of the experience became more vivid still.

She stumbled, got up, pushed, groaned, and leaned against the wheelchair. She relied on it nearly as much as it relied on her. And then she heard the woman's voice shout from behind her.

"Don't move another foot!"

Jody stopped.

"Lift your arms."

Jody did.

"Take two steps to your left and remain facing away."

Jody obeyed. She listened as Karin Doring walked forward. The German was breathing heavily. Jody started as the woman put three bullets into the back of the wheelchair. The dead body fell forward.

"God—*god!*" Jody gasped.

Karin circled the girl. Even in the dark the terrified young woman could see her angry expression. She also saw the SA knife.

"You dared come to my camp as you did!" Doring screamed at her. Her voice was angrier than it had been earlier in the day. She kicked the wheelchair out of her way. "You dared to challenge me, to insult me!"

"I'm sorry," Jody said, trembling. "You—you would have done the same, wouldn't you?"

"You are not me!" Karin said. "You've paid no dues!"

Suddenly, three shots flashed in the trees. Karin lurched but remained standing as they struck her in succession. She looked up as Bob Herbert stirred in the lower branches. Karin dropped to her knees, blood oozing from the wounds.

Herbert dropped his gun to the ground, then lowered himself from the branch. He hung there from his powerful arms. "Right about now I'll bet she's glad she's *not* you, Karin."

Karin struggled to keep her eyes open. She was shaking her head slowly, trying to raise the gun. It dropped to the ground. A moment later, she followed it.

Jody refused to look at Karin. She kicked away the body of the dead policeman they'd placed in the wheelchair. Then she ran over to Herbert. He dropped into the seat. Jody leaned against the tree.

"You had to do it and you did it like a pro," Herbert said. "I'm proud of you." Herbert started to reach for the gun he'd dropped. "Let's get the hell—"

Before he could finish, a hulking figure screamed and charged at him from the dark. His knife raised high, the enraged Manfred Piper brought the knife down hard toward Herbert's chest.

FIFTY-SEVEN

Thursday, 10:06 P.M., Toulouse, France

After putting the phone back in his jacket, Hood made his way back up the grassy slope. Though the group was still standing beside the trees, Stoll had moved a few yards away, toward the bridge. There, he had an unobstructed view of the river and the opposite bank.

As Hood approached, he heard Ballon talking to Nancy.

"... if they do see us, they can go to Hell. I don't care. It was the same when I walked in on my former wife and her lover. Not liking what you see won't make it go away."

"That wasn't what I asked," Nancy said. "I asked if you hope that someone from *Demain* sees us. And if they do, what you think will happen."

"We're on public land," Ballon said. "If they see us, they can do nothing. In any case, I don't think Dominique will pick a fight. Certainly not now, with his games downloading."

Hood stopped beside Hausen. He was about to take him aside when Ballon walked over.

"Is everything all right?" the Colonel asked.

"I'm not sure," Hood said. "Matt, have you got everything under control?"

"More or less," Stoll said. He was sitting with his legs straight out. The computer was resting on his knees and he was leaning into it, typing furiously. "What's the word for anal?"

Ballon answered, "*Fidele* is retentive—"

"I'll accept that," Stoll said. "Our boy is certainly *fidele*. The first game came on promptly at ten. And I mean promptly: 10:00:00. I saved it on the hard drive. I've got the T-Bird covering about thirty-eight degrees with each picture, so I should have a complete sweep in about ten minutes."

"And then?" Hood asked.

Stoll said. "I have to start playing the game and get to different screens, different landscapes."

"Why don't you download it to Op-Center?"

"Because what I'm doing is just what they'd do," he said. "I'm writing a small modification to the Match-Book program so it can read images from the T-Bird. Then it's in the lap of the gods. If I don't screw up too much, the background images will keep scrolling along. I'll get a *ping* when there's a match." Stoll finished typing, then sucked down a deep, deep breath. He booted the game. "I can't say I'm going to enjoy this thing. It's a lynch mob."

Nancy had walked over while he was speaking. She knelt behind him and gently put her hands on his shoulders. "I'll help you, Matt," she said. "I'm pretty good at these."

Hood regarded them for a moment. The way she'd touched Matt made him jealous. The way her hands floated down and came to rest like falling flower petals filled him with longing. And the way he was feeling filled him with disgust.

Then, with perfect timing, Nancy turned slowly and

looked at Hood. She moved slowly enough so that he could have looked away if he'd wanted. But he didn't. Their eyes hooked and he tumbled right into them.

It took the thought of Hausen to snap Hood from Nancy's spell. His unfinished business with the German was more pressing.

"Herr Hausen," Hood said, "I'd like to talk to you."

Hausen looked at Hood expectantly, almost eagerly. "Of course," he said. The German was obviously excited by what was happening, but for which side?

Hood put his hand on the German's shoulder and led him toward the river. Ballon followed several steps behind. But that was all right: this involved him too.

"That call I just had," Hood said. "It was from Op-Center. There's no delicate way to ask this, so I'll ask it directly. Why didn't you tell us your father worked for Dupre?"

Hausen stopped walking. "How do you know that?"

"I had my people look into German tax records. He worked as a pilot for Pierre Dupre from 1966 to 1979."

Hausen waited a long time before answering. "It's true," he said. "And it was one of the things Gerard and I argued about that night in Paris. My father taught him how to fly, treated him like a son, helped teach him to hate."

Ballon stopped beside the men. His face was just inches from Hausen.

"Your father worked for this monster?" the Colonel said. "Where is your father now?"

"He died two years ago," Hausen said.

"There's more, though," Hood said. "Tell us about your father's political affiliations."

Hausen took a long breath. "They were corrupt," he said. "He was one of the White Wolves, a group which kept Nazi ideals alive after the war. He met with other men regularly. He . . .'' Hausen stopped.

''He what?'' demanded Ballon.

Hausen composed himself. ''He believed in Hitler and the goals of the Reich. He viewed the end of the war as a setback, not a defeat, and continued it in his own way. When I was eleven''—he breathed deeply again before continuing—''my father and two of his friends were coming home from the movies when they attacked a rabbi's son on his way home from synagogue. Afterwards, my mother sent me to boarding school in Berlin. I didn't see my father until years later, after Gerard befriended me at the Sorbonne.''

''Are you trying to tell me that Gerard went to the Sorbonne just to become your friend and bring you back?'' Hood asked.

''You must understand,'' Hausen said, ''I was a force to be reckoned with from an early age. What my father had done revolted me. I can still hear him calling me to join them, as though it were a carnival sideshow I mustn't miss. I can hear the young man's moans, his attackers's blows, the way their shoes scraped against the pavement as they moved around him. It was disgusting. My mother loved my father and sent me away that night to keep us from destroying one another. I went to live with a cousin in Berlin.

''While I was in Berlin I formed an anti-Nazi group. I had my own radio program when I was sixteen and police protection a month later. One of the reasons I left the country to go to school was to get away from the death threats. I was never insincere about my convictions.'' He glared at Ballon. ''Never, do you understand?''

''What about Gerard?'' Hood asked.

"It isn't much different from what I told you earlier," Hausen said. "Gerard was a rich, spoiled young man who learned about me from my father. He viewed me as a challenge, I think. The White Wolves had failed to stop me through intimidation. Gerard wanted to stop me through argument and intellect. The night he killed those girls he was trying to show me that only sheep and cowards live inside the law. Even as we fled he said that the people who change the world operate by their own rules and make others live by them."

Hausen looked down. Hood glanced at Ballon. The Frenchman was angry.

"You were involved in those killings," said the Colonel, "yet you did nothing except to run and hide. Whose side are you on, Herr Hausen?"

"I was wrong," Hausen said, "and I've been paying for it ever since. I would give anything to go back to that night and turn Gerard in. But I didn't. I was scared and confused and I ran. I've been atoning, M. Ballon. Every day and night, I atone."

Hood interjected, "Tell me about your father."

Hausen said, "I saw my father twice after the night he attacked the Jewish boy. Once was at the Dupre estate when Gerard and I fled there. He asked me to join them and said it was the only way I could save myself. He called me a traitor when I refused. The second time was the night my father died. I went to his side in Bonn and with his dying breath he called me a traitor again. Even on his deathbed I wouldn't give him the acquiescence he sought. My mother was there. If you'd like, you can call her on Mr. Hood's telephone to confirm it."

Ballon looked at Hood. Hood continued to look at Hausen. He felt the same way he did on the jet. He wanted to believe in this man's sincerity. But there were lives at risk and despite everything Hausen had said, there was still the hint of a doubt.

Hood took the phone from his pocket. He punched in a telephone number. John Benn answered.

"John," Hood said, "I want to know when Maximillian Hausen died."

"The suddenly ubiquitous Nazi," Benn said. "That'll take a minute or two. Do you want to hold on?"

"I do," said Hood.

Benn put him on hold. Hood regarded Hausen. "I'm sorry," Hood said, "but I owe this to Matt and Nancy."

"I would do the same," said Hausen. "But I tell you again, I despise Gerard Dominique and the New Jacobins and the neo-Nazis and everything they represent. If it hadn't smacked of Nazism itself, I might have turned in my own father."

"You've had some difficult choices to make," Hood said.

"That I have," said Hausen. "You see, Gerard was wrong. It takes a coward to operate *outside* the law."

John Benn came back on. "Paul? Hausen the Elder died two years ago next month. There was a short obituary in a Bonn newspaper—ex-Luftwaffe pilot, private pilot, etcetera."

"Thanks," Hood said. "Thanks very much." He hung up. "Again, Herr Hausen, I'm sorry."

"Again, Mr. Hood," said Hausen, "there's no need to—"

"Paul!"

Hood and Hausen looked at Stoll. Ballon was already running over.

"What've you got?" Hood asked as they followed Ballon.

"*Bupkis,*" he said. "I mean, however I poke and prod

it, my machine isn't fast enough to do an analysis before 2010. I was about to call Op-Center for help when Nancy found something better."

She rose and said to Ballon, "In other *Demain* games you can skip to the next level by pausing the game and pushing the arrows on the keypad in a certain sequence—down, up, up, down, left, right, left, right."

"And?"

"And we're already on level two of this game," she said, "without having played level one."

"Would Dominique really have been stupid enough to put the same cheat codes in one of these games?" Hood asked.

"That's just it," Nancy said. "It's already in the computer. It has to be removed, not put in. Somewhere along the line somebody forgot to delete it."

Ballon was standing very tall and looking toward the factory.

"How about it?" Hood asked the Colonel. "Is that good enough for you?"

Ballon snatched the radio from his belt. He looked at Matt. "Did you save the game on your computer?"

"The jump from level one to level two has been copied and stored," he said.

Ballon turned on his radio and put it to his mouth. "Sergeant Ste. Marie?" he said. *"Allons!"*

FIFTY-EIGHT

Thursday, 10:12 P.M., Wunstorf, Germany

Manfred attacked with the knife stabbing down toward Bob Herbert in his wheelchair.

For someone who can stand up, defending against a knife attack is relatively simple. You think of your forearm as a two-by-four. You extend it downward or upward and catch the attacker's forearm with your forearm. Then you pinwheel that two-by-four of yours, use it to redirect the attacker's momentum up and away, in and away, or down and away. At the same time you step out of the way. This enables you to prepare for the next slash or stab. Or better still, since you've probably exposed their side or back by maneuvering them away, you have the chance to beat the hell out of your opponent.

If you're in close or underneath your attacker, you still use your forearm for defense. Only now you bend your arm at the elbow first. Forming a "V," you catch the attacking arm firmly with your forearm. Retaining forearm-to-forearm contact you redirect the arm up, down, or to the side, just as you did with a straight-arm defense. The only difference is that you must block closer to your wrist than to your elbow. Otherwise the knife may slide down your forearm, slip under the elbow, and stab you.

Because Manfred was bringing his arm down, with his full weight behind the knife, Bob Herbert had to bend his elbow to stop him. He raised his left arm up, his forearm across his upturned forehead, his fist tight to strengthen the arm. As he met and stopped the attacking arm, he hit Manfred's exposed jaw with a hard right jab. The raging German barely seemed affected by the blow. He drew his blocked arm back, cocked it to his right, and slashed toward the left, toward Herbert's chest.

Herbert dropped his left forearm, made a ''V,'' and blocked again. Somewhere behind him he heard Jody scream. But Herbert was too focused, too determined to keep the brute away to tell her to run. More soldiers died in hand-to-hand combat because they were distracted than because they didn't know what to do.

This time, Manfred refused to be stopped. Though his arm was blocked, he bent his wrist. His hand moved as if it were independent of the rest of him. He pointed the blade toward Herbert, the knife-edge pressing against his flesh. Herbert was one second away from having his wrist slashed.

He bought himself another second by pushing his left arm toward Manfred to relieve the pressure. While Manfred adjusted to put the knife back in position, Herbert reached his free right hand over his blocking left. Grabbing the knife hand, he dug his thumb between Manfred's tight thumb and index finger and wrapped the rest of his fingers around Manfred's fist. Dropping his blocking forearm to get it out of the way, he twisted Manfred's fist clockwise, hard and fast.

Manfred's wrist snapped audibly and the knife dropped to the ground. But the relentless Manfred was on it in an instant. Holding it in his left hand and howl-

ing with anger, he surprised Herbert by driving his knee
into his gut. Herbert doubled over in his wheelchair and
Manfred fell on top of him. Pinning Herbert back with
his body, the German leaned over him, raised the knife,
and plunged it into the back of the chair. The blade tore
audibly through the leather as Jody screamed at the
German to stop.

Manfred stabbed again, snarling ferociously. Then
again. Then there was a loud pop and he stopped stabbing. He reached for his throat.

There was a hole in his flesh, a hole put there by a
bullet fired by Jody from Karin's gun. Blood leaked
from the two branches of his common carotid artery, just
below the jawline. The knife fell from Manfred's hand
and then Manfred fell from the wheelchair. He twitched
for a moment and then was still.

Herbert turned and looked at the young woman's dark
silhouette against the darker sky.

"Oh, God," she said. "Oh, God."

"Are you all right?" Herbert asked.

"I killed someone," Jody said.

"You had no choice."

She began to whimper. "I killed a man. I killed
someone."

"No," Herbert said. He wheeled around and headed
toward her. "You saved someone's life. Mine."

"But I . . . I shot him."

"You had to, just like other people have had to kill
in wars."

"A war?"

"That's exactly what this is," Herbert said. "Look,
he didn't give you any choice. You hear me, Jody? You
didn't do anything wrong. Nothing."

Jody stood there sobbing.

"Jody?"

"I'm sorry," she said to the body. "I'm sorry."

"Jody," Herbert said, "first of all, would you please do me a favor?"

"What?" she said numbly.

"Would you point the gun to the side?"

She did, slowly. Then she opened her hand and dropped it. Then she looked at Herbert as though she were noticing him for the first time. "You're not hurt," she murmured. "How did he miss?"

"I never go anywhere without my Kevlar-lining," he said. "Multi-layered bullet-proofing in the back and seat. I got the idea from the President. The chair in the Oval Office is lined with it too."

Jody didn't seem to hear. She wavered for a moment, then followed the gun to the ground. Herbert rolled to her side. He took her hand and gave it a gentle tug. She looked up at him.

"You've been through a lot, Jody." He helped her to her knees. Then he pulled a little harder and she started to get back on her feet. "But you're almost at the finish line. The home stretch, from here to the Autobahn, is a little over a mile. All we have to do . . ."

Herbert stopped speaking. He heard footsteps in the distance.

Jody looked at him. "What's wrong?"

Herbert listened a moment longer. "Shit!" he said. "Get up. Now."

She responded to the urgency in his voice. "What is it?"

"You've got to get out of here."

"Why?"

"They're coming—probably to check on the others." He pushed her. "Go!"

"What about you?"

"I'll get out of here too," he said, "but right now someone has to cover the retreat."

"No! I won't go alone!"

"Honey, this kind of stuff is what I'm paid to do. You're not. Think about your parents. Anyhow, I'd just slow you down. I'm better off digging in and defending us from here."

"No!" she yelled. "I'm not going alone."

Herbert realized that there was no point arguing with the young woman. Jody was scared, exhausted, and probably as hungry as he was.

"All right," he said. "We'll go together."

Herbert told Jody to retrieve the gun he'd used up in the tree. While she did, he wheeled over to Karin's body. He picked up her gun, then used his flashlight to search for the SA dagger she'd been holding. He slid it under his left leg, where it would be handy, then checked Karin's gun to make sure it still had a few rounds left. Then he went over to Manfred's body. He took the German's knife and felt for other weapons. There weren't any. He took a moment to examine the contents of Manfred's windbreaker pockets under his flashlight. Then he rejoined Jody, who was waiting several yards from the bodies.

Most of the time Bob Herbert felt like someone from *Wheelie and the Chopper Bunch,* a cartoon show he used to watch when he was in the rehab center. It was about a freewheeling hero in a souped-up stunt racer. Now, for the first time since he lost the use of his legs, Herbert felt like Rambo. A single-minded man with a mission and the will to enforce it.

Over a half-century before, a black man, Jesse Owens, had embarrassed Hitler by outracing his Aryan athletes in the Olympics. Tonight, Karin's angry pursuit had shown just how much Jody's survival had undermined her authority. Now, if a man in a wheelchair managed to escape these tough guys, it could very well end the myth of the Nazi superman. Certainly among this group.

FIFTY-NINE

Thursday, 10:41 P.M., Toulouse, France

Hood didn't know what to expect as they marched toward the fortress which had become a factory. As his own small group crossed the ancient walkway behind Ballon and his men, he wondered how many besieging armies had come this way over the centuries. How many of them had enjoyed success and how many had met with disastrous failure.

There was very little discussion of what they would do once they got inside. Ballon said that his intention had always been to find evidence tying Dominique to the New Jacobins, then arrest him. His men had been trained to do that. However, Hausen and Hood had persuaded him to let Matt and Nancy take a look in the computers to see what they could find there. Lists of New Jacobin members or sympathizers perhaps, or maybe more evidence linking *Demain* to the hate games. Either one would help to bring Dominique down.

There was also very little discussion about what Dominique might do to prevent all this from occurring. The man not only commanded a terrorist army, he himself had killed. He would probably go to any lengths to protect his empire.

Why not? Hood asked himself as they neared the main

entrance. Dominique would probably find himself above the law. Since the crippling rail strike of 1995, France had been reeling from public sector labor disputes and crippling unemployment. Who would dare take on a big employer like Dominique? Especially if he claimed that he was being harassed. Even Ballon's superiors would have to acknowledge that their man was a fanatic. *And that was if they were inclined to be charitable,* thought Hood.

An iron gate had been added to the perimeter of the *bastide.* The only concession to the modern day were small, black video cameras which looked out from the tops of the arabesque designs on top. There was a large red brick booth behind the gate, designed in the style of the edifice. As the group approached, two men emerged. One was a uniformed guard, the other a young man in a business suit. Neither seemed surprised by the arrival of Ballon's party.

"Colonel Bernard Benjamin Ballon of Le Groupe d'Intervention de la Gendarmerie Nationale," Ballon said in French as he reached the gate. He withdrew a leather wallet, unfolded a document, and held it open on his side of the gate. "This is a search warrant, executed by Judge Christophe Labique in Paris and countersigned by my commander, General Francois Charrier."

The man in the business suit extended a manicured hand through the gate. "I am M. Vaudran of the law firm Vaudran, Vaudran, and Boisnard. We represent *Demain.* Show me your warrant."

"You understand that I'm only required to present the document and explain the purpose of my visit," Ballon said.

"I will take it and read it and only then will you be admitted."

"The law says you can read it while we search," Ballon informed him. "You *are* familiar with the law? You may have it as a keepsake once we're inside."

Vaudran said, "I must show it to my client before I can admit you."

Ballon glared at him for a moment, then held the document up to the camera on top of the gate. "Your client sees it," he said. "This is a warrant, not a request. Open the gate."

"I'm sorry," the attorney said, "but you need more than a piece of paper. You need cause."

"We have that," Ballon said. "Proprietary elements have appeared in both *Demain* computer games and a hate game on the Internet called Hangin' with the Crowd."

"What kind of elements?"

"A level-select code. We have it on computer. You are entitled to see it before a trial, not before a search. It's all in the warrant. Now, M. Vaudran, open the gate."

The attorney regarded Ballon for a moment, then signaled his associate to return to the booth. The guard shut the wooden door and picked up a telephone.

"You have sixty seconds," Ballon yelled to him. He looked at his watch. "Sergeant Ste. Marie?"

"Yes, sir!"

"You have charges to blow open the lock?"

"Yes, sir."

"Prepare them."

"Yes, sir."

The attorney said, "You realize what you're doing, I hope?"

Ballon continued to look at his watch.

"Careers have been ruined by lesser mistakes," Vaudran pointed out.

"There's only one career at risk," Ballon said. He
looked directly at the attorney. "No. Two." He looked
down again.

Hausen had translated the exchange for Hood, Stoll,
and Nancy. As Hood stood watching, he wondered what
they were going to accomplish by this operation. Dominique had surely seen them outside and had concealed
or destroyed anything incriminating. He was probably
using these last minutes to make sure he hadn't forgotten
anything.

Less than a minute after leaving, the guard was punching a code into a panel in the booth. Ballon marshaled
his men at the gate. A moment later the attorney had
gone toward a side entrance of the main building and
the French officers were inside. They marched up to a
large golden door. One of the guards followed and
opened the door by inputting a code in a box on the
jamb. Ballon handed him the warrant before entering.

As soon as Balloon's men were inside, they lined up
at ease inside the front door. Ballon explained that if he
found any material they wished to remove, the men
would be called to collect it and carry it to the van. Hood
guessed that they'd done this so often in drills they could
do it blindfolded. In the meantime, they were told to
watch the exits and make sure no one left.

Ballon and his party continued into the factory. They
crossed a hallway which, if this were a tour and he were
a tourist, would have caused him to linger and stare at
the spectacular arches and intricate tableaux carved in
the stone.

Ballon's voice brought him back to the reason they
were here.

"This way," the Colonel said softly but imperatively when they reached the end of the long corridor.

Ignoring the eyes of other guards who had also obviously been advised to let them pass, the quintet walked through a short passageway with small, barred windows to the door which led to the programming rooms of the *Demain* factory.

Hood hadn't expected to see employees wandering about at night. But there weren't even cleaning crews afoot. Just the occasional guard, who ignored them.

Despite the addition of lights, alarms, cameras, and modern flooring, the edifice retained its ancient character. That is, until a guard admitted them to the computer room.

The former dining hall had been turned into something which resembled the National Reconnaissance Office. The walls were white and the ceiling lined with recessed fluorescent lights. There were glass tables lined with at least three dozen computer terminals. A vacuum-formed plastic chair was attached to the floor at each station. The only difference between *Demain* and the NRO was, again, that there were no people. Dominique wasn't taking any chances. The warrant was due to expire in just over an hour. If no one were there to answer questions, it had to slow them down.

"This is some playroom," Stoll said as looked around.

Ballon said to him, "Start playing."

Stoll looked at Hood. Hood nodded silently. Stoll took a breath and looked at Nancy. "Got a preference?" he asked.

"It doesn't really matter," she said. "They're all hooked to the same master computer."

Nodding, Stoll sat down at the nearest monitor, jacked

his portable computer into the back of the computer, and powered up.

"They've probably dropped inhibitors into the system," Nancy said. "How do you plan to get past those to the master system? I can probably help you with a few, but it will take time."

"We don't need a lot of time," Stoll said. He slipped a diskette into his B drive and booted it. "I always carry the Bulldozer program I wrote. It starts with my fast-acting Handshake Locator, which works on finding the mathematical keys to undo encryption. It doesn't have to hit them exactly. If one-through-six and eight-through-ten don't work, it doesn't bother trying seven. Once Handshake learns some of the language, which only takes a few minutes, Bulldozer rolls in and searches for menus. Once I get those, I'm in. And while we look at the data here, I'll be dumping everything into Op-Center's computers."

Ballon squeezed Stoll's shoulder, shook his head, and put a finger to his lips.

Stoll drove his palm into his forehead. "Sorry," he said. "Loose lips sink chips."

Ballon nodded.

As Nancy gave Stoll some passwords to try, Hausen wandered over to Ballon.

"Colonel, what are we going to do about Dominique?"

"We wait."

"For what?" Hausen asked.

Ballon faced the German. He moved close to his ear. "For Dominique to get nervous. As I indicated to M. Stoll, Dominique is certainly observing us. Hopefully, we'll find something in the computer."

"And if we don't?"

Ballon said, "I have you."

"Me?"

"I'll ask M. Stoll and Ms. Bosworth to send out a message on the computer: your account of the murders in Paris. In either case, we will cripple Dominique." Ballon grinned. "Although there is a third possibility. Dominique has waited twenty-five years for you. If he fears that you may finally reveal secrets about his past, the temptation will be great not to let you walk out that door."

"You really think he'd send his New Jacobins against us?"

"I've ordered my men to stand back," Ballon said. "If Dominique thinks he can get you before they can move in, he'll surely be tempted. Once he does that, I'll get all of you out and bring this place down." He winked charmlessly. "As I've said, I've waited a long time for Dominique as well. I intend to have him."

Ballon withdrew then to watch what Stoll and Nancy were doing. Hausen remained where he was, as though he were bolted to the hardwood floor.

Hood was standing beside Stoll. He could tell from Hausen's expression that all was not well. The normally impassive face was taut, the brows dipped in concern. But he decided not to ask Hausen about it. The German liked to think things through before speaking. If he had anything to share, he'd share it.

So Hood just stood there, silently watching with a mixture of fear and pride as the fate of the world was decided by a perspiring young man at a computer keyboard.

SIXTY

Thursday, 5:05 P.M.,
Washington, D.C.

When data began coming into Eddie Medina's computer from Matt Stoll in France, the young man took off his coat, sat back down, and told his evening replacement, Assistant Deputy Operations Support Officer Randall Battle, to notify General Rodgers.

Battle did, just as Stoll's :-) signature faded. It was replaced by a screen which announced a big file called *L'Operation Ecouter.*

Rodgers had Battle send the material to his own computer. Then he too watched the feed with Darrell McCaskey and Martha Mackall.

First up was a note from Stoll.

Eddie: I don't want to eat up too much line-time with notes. Bulldozer cracked the *Demain* files. Primaries were erased but backups weren't. I'm going to download everything from this file.

Following the note were photographs of people who served as models for characters in the game. After these came test segments showing white men chasing black men and women. White men raping a black woman. A black man being torn apart by dogs. Then there was a note from Stoll.

Real games being hatched from a nest somewhere

else. Point of origin well hidden.

There were different angles of black men and women hanging from trees. A bonus round in which a kid raced against a clock while he used black boys on swings for target practice. Martha was stone-faced. McCaskey's lips were rolled tight, his eyes narrow.

Ed—I must've set off an alarm of some kind. People running all around. Our French escort Colonel Ballon has got his hand full of gun. I'm supposed to get down—bye.

The images continued to come in for a few moments longer but Rodgers wasn't watching them. He had switched to an alternate computer line, and within seconds had been patched through to the cockpit of the V-22 Osprey.

SIXTY-ONE

Thursday, 11:07 P.M., Toulouse, France

"Get away from that keyboard!"

Using his left hand, Colonel Ballon pushed Matt Stoll to the floor and then pressed a button on his radio as the gunmen entered. In his right hand was his own weapon. It was the only weapon of any kind among the five of them.

Squatting on the floor beside the others, Hood counted twelve . . . fifteen . . . a total of seventeen men passing by the door and taking up positions along the corridor wall. Except for the high windows which would require a small ladder to reach, that door was the only exit.

Hausen was lying face-down between Hood and the crouching Ballon. "Congratulations, Colonel," he said. "Dominique has swallowed your bait."

Hood knew he'd missed something which had passed between the men. Not that it seemed to matter at the moment. Certainly Ballon didn't seem to care. Alert and cool, he was preoccupied with watching the new arrivals.

In the quick glimpse he'd had of the gunmen, Hood made them out to be a ragtag bunch. They were dressed simply, in several cases shabbily, as if they didn't want to stand out in the street. And they were holding a variety of weapons. Hood didn't need Ballon to tell him that these were New Jacobins.

"I guess these guys are the kind of evidence you were looking for, huh," Stoll said anxiously.

"Levez!" one of the men shouted as they trained their weapons around the room.

"He wants us to get up," Ballon whispered. "If we do, they may shoot us."

"Wouldn't they have shot us already?" Nancy asked.

"They would have to come in for that," Ballon said. "They don't know which of us might be armed. They don't want to take casualties." He leaned toward them and said more quietly, "I've signaled my men. They will be moving toward us, taking up positions."

"By the time they're ready it may be too late," Hausen said.

"Not if we keep concealed," Ballon said, "make the enemy come to us. We're prepared for this."

"We're not," said Nancy.

"If it happens that you're caught in cross fire," Ballon said, "and my men don't see you, shout *'Blanc,'* 'White.' That will let them know there are unarmed personnel."

Hausen said, "I'm going to give these animals a chance to shoot. Let's see what they're made of." With that, he stood.

"Herr Hausen!" Ballon hissed.

The German ignored him. Hood didn't breathe. He could only hear his heart thudding in his ears as he waited to see what happened.

Nothing happened for a long moment. Finally one of the New Jacobins said, *"Allons donc!"*

"He wants Hausen to leave," Ballon told Hood.

"This room or the building?" Hood asked.

"Or maybe this mortal coil?" Stoll added.

Ballon shrugged.

Hausen began walking forward. His courage impressed Hood, though a part of him couldn't help but wonder if it was courage or confidence. The confidence of a collaborator.

Ballon was also waiting. When Hausen was through the door, his footsteps stopped. They listened, heard nothing. He was apparently being detained.

The New Jacobin called for the rest of the people to come out. Hood regarded Ballon.

"You've dealt with these terrorists," Hood said. "What do they do in situations like this?"

"They beat up or murder people in *every* situation," Ballon said. "Mercy is not a word they understand."

"But they didn't kill Hausen," Nancy said.

"Maintenant!" shouted the New Jacobin.

"Until they get our weapons, they won't," Ballon said.

"Then we should get Nancy and Matt out of here," Hood said. "Maybe they can get away."

"And you," Nancy said.

Ballon said, "It's probably worth a try. The danger is that they may use you as hostages. Shoot you one by one until I come out."

"How do we prevent that?" Nancy asked.

"If that happens," Ballon said, "I'll signal my men by radio. They're trained for situations like that."

"But there are still no guarantees," Hood said.

The New Jacobin shouted again. He said he would send his people in if everyone else didn't come out.

"No," Ballon agreed, "there are no guarantees. But if that happens, they'll have to put each hostage in the doorway so I can see. And if I can see, I can shoot. And if I shoot, whoever is holding the hostage will go down. Then you had all better run.''

Hood envied the Frenchman his gall. From Mike Rodgers, he had learned that that was what it took to run an operation like this. He himself wasn't so confident right now. His thoughts were with his wife and children. He was thinking about how much they needed him and how dearly he cherished them. How it all could end here because of one wrong word or a misstep.

He looked over at Nancy, who was wearing a sad half-smile. He wished he could make it all up to her, his part in the turns her life had taken. But there wasn't much he could do right now, and he wasn't sure there would be a later. So he just smiled at her warmly and her own smile broadened. For now, that would have to do.

''All right,'' Ballon said to the others. ''I want you to get up and walk slowly toward the door.''

They hesitated.

''My legs aren't moving,'' Stoll said.

''Make them,'' Hood said as he rose, followed by Nancy and very reluctantly by Stoll.

''Here I thought we were the good guys,'' Stoll said. ''Do we raise our hands or just walk? What do we do?''

''Try and calm down,'' Hood said as they made their way between the banks of computers.

''Why do people always say that?'' Stoll asked. ''If I could, I would.''

Nancy said, ''Matt, now you're getting on my nerves. *Can* it.''

He did, and they walked the rest of the way in silence.

Hood watched the New Jacobin who had spoken, the man closest to the door. He had a thick black beard and mustache and was dressed in a gray sweatshirt, jeans, and boots. An assault rifle was tucked under his arm. He looked like he wouldn't hesitate to use it.

The three were quiet until they walked through the doorway. Hood saw Hausen facing a brick wall, his hands pressed against it, his legs spread. One of the men was pointing a pistol up against the base of his skull.

"Oh, shit," Stoll said as he entered the small, dark corridor.

The three Americans were grabbed by two men each and pushed against the wall. Guns were placed against the backs of their heads. Hood moved his head slightly so he could see the man in charge. The New Jacobin was cool, standing sideways so he could see his prisoners and also look into the room.

Beside him, Nancy was trembling slightly. To her right, Stoll was trembling even more. He was looking down the corridor as though weighing an escape.

"We have a search warrant," Stoll said softly. "I thought this was all legal."

The leader barked, *"Tais-toi."*

"I'm not a commando," Stoll said. "None of us is. I'm just a computer guy!"

"Quiet!"

Stoll's mouth closed audibly.

The New Jacobin leader studied them for a moment and then turned back to the doorway. He shouted for the last man to come out.

Ballon yelled back in French, "When you let the others go, I'll come out."

"No," said the New Jacobin. "You come out first."

Ballon didn't answer this time. Clearly, he intended to leave the next move up to the enemy. And the next move was for the leader to nod toward Hausen. The New

Jacobin standing behind the German grabbed his hair.
Nancy screamed as the man walked him toward the
door. Hood wondered if they were even going to give
Ballon the chance to come out, or if they were just going
to shoot the German and throw his body in and threaten
to throw someone else in next.

A gunshot popped from somewhere in the darkness,
toward the door which led to the main corridor. It took
a moment of searching before Hood could see that with
all the shouting and shuffling, no one had heard Ballon's
men remove the ornate knob from the door. They had a
clear shot at everyone in this corridor.

The man holding Hausen had fallen. He was squeezing his right thigh and crying. Hausen seized on the moment of confusion to run toward the door, in the
direction from which the shot had come. None of the
New Jacobins fired. Obviously, they feared being cut
down if they did.

Hausen opened the door and disappeared. There was
no one on the other side. They must have seen him coming and taken cover.

Hood didn't move. Though the man behind him was
looking away, he still felt the pressure of the front sight
and muzzle on the top of his neck.

Perspiration trickled down his armpits and along the
sides of his chest. His palms grew clammy against the
cold brick wall and he promised himself that if he survived this he'd not only hug each member of his family
for a good long time, but also Mike Rodgers. The man
had spent his life surviving situations like these. Hood's
respect for him suddenly grew very, very deep.

As he was thinking that, his hands began to vibrate.

No, Hood thought. *Not just my hands.* The old bricks

themselves were beginning to tremble. Then the sky outside the barred windows brightened. The air itself seemed to rattle. And the New Jacobin leader shouted for his men to finish the job and leave.

SIXTY-TWO

Thursday, 11:15 P.M., Wunstorf, Germany

The footsteps were gaining on them. But as Herbert wheeled himself through the woods, he wasn't thinking about them. He wasn't thinking about anything except what he had overlooked in the pressure of escaping from the camp. The key to survival, to victory.

What the hell was that name?

Jody grunted as they moved slowly through the dark. Herbert almost asked her to get behind him and kick him.

I can't remember.

He would. He had to. He couldn't let Mike Rodgers win this one. Rodgers and Herbert were both fans of military history, and they had debated the point many times over. If you had a choice, they had asked each other, would you rather go into battle with a small band of dedicated soldiers or an overwhelming force of conscripts.

Rodgers invariably favored greater numbers, and there were strong arguments for both points of view. Herbert pointed out that Samson beat back the Philistines using only the jawbone of an ass. In the thirteenth century, Alexander Nevsky and his poorly armed Russian peasants repulsed the heavily armored Teutonic knights. In the fifteenth century, the small band of Englishmen who fought beside Henry V at Agincourt defeated vastly superior numbers of Frenchmen.

But Rodgers had his examples as well. The brave band of Spartans were defeated by the Persians at Thermopylae in 480 B.C.; the Alamo fell to Santa Anna; and then there was the British 27th Lancers cavalry, the "Light Brigade" which was cut down in its self-defeating charge during the Crimean War.

Add to the list of the doomed Robert West Herbert, he thought as he listened to the footfalls and cracking twigs. *The guy who didn't have the goddamn brains enough to write down the name that could have saved them.* At least he would die in good company. King Leonidas. Jim Bowie. Errol Flynn.

Thinking about Flynn helped him stay loose as he psyched himself up to make a stand against all these enemies. He only hoped that Jody would run. The thought of fighting to save her gave him extra adrenaline.

And then, because he wasn't thinking about it, the name he'd been trying to remember came back to him.

"Jody, push me," he said.

She had been walking beside him. She stopped and got behind him.

"C'mon, push," he said. "We're going to get out of this. But we'll need time."

Jody put her tired back and wounded shoulder into the effort. Herbert reached for his weapon.

Unlike Flynn's doomed Major Vickers, Herbert was going to hold the enemy off. Though unlike Samson, he wasn't going to use the jawbone of an ass to do it.

He was going to use a cellular phone.

SIXTY-THREE

Thursday, 5:15 P.M., Washington, D.C.

The call was put through to Rodgers as he was waiting for an update from Colonel August.

Bob Herbert was on a cellular phone. Rodgers switched on the speaker phone so Darrell, Martha, and Press Officer Ann Farris could hear.

"I'm in the middle of a dark forest somewhere between Wunstorf and a lake," Herbert said. "The good news is, I've got Jody Thompson."

Rodgers sat up straight and triumphantly drove a fist into the air. Ann jumped from her chair and clapped.

"That's fabulous!" Rodgers said. He shot McCaskey a look. "You've done it while Interpol and the FBI are still asking questions and pissing off the German authorities. How can we help you, Bob?"

"Well, the bad news is we've got a bunch of Nazi wannabes on our butts. You've got to find me a phone number."

Rodgers leaned toward the keyboard. He alerted John Benn with an F6/Enter/17. "Whose number, Bob?"

Herbert told him. Rodgers asked him to hold on as he typed *Hauptmann Rosenlocher, Hamburg Landespolizei.*

McCaskey had swung over to take a look. While

Rodgers sent the number over to Benn, McCaskey jumped to another phone and called Interpol.

"This Rosenlocher is a burr in the fur of the head Nazi," Herbert said, "and he may be the only man you can trust. From what I overheard he's in Hanover, I think."

"We'll find him and get him over to you," Rodgers said.

"Sooner would be better than later," Herbert said. "We're pushing on, but we're losing ground to these guys. I can hear the cars. And if they find the bodies we left in our wake—"

"I read you," Rodgers said. "Can you stay on the line?"

"As long as Jody holds out I can," he said. "She's dead on her feet."

"Tell her to hang on," Rodgers said as he switched to the Geologue program. "You too." He brought up Wunstorf and looked over the terrain between the town and the lake. It was just as Herbert had described it. Trees and hills. "Bob, do you have any idea where you are? Can you give me any landmarks?"

"It's black here, Mike. Far as I know, we may even have done a W.W. Corrigan."

Wrong Way Corrigan, Rodgers thought. Herbert didn't want Jody to know they might be headed in the wrong direction.

"Okay, Bob," Rodgers said. "We'll get you a fix on everyone's positions."

McCaskey was still on the line with Interpol, so Rodgers called Stephen Viens himself. Even with light-intensification capabilities for night surveillance, Viens told him that the NRO satellites would require up to a half hour to pinpoint Herbert exactly. Rodgers pointed out that their lives might be at stake. Viens said, not dispassionately, that it would still take up to a half hour. Rodgers thanked him.

The General studied the map. They were really out in the boondocks. And if Herbert could hear the pursuers, it was unlikely a car or even chopper could get to them in time.

Rodgers looked over at McCaskey. "Have we got anything on that police officer yet?"

"Working."

Working. Rodgers always had a visceral reaction to that word: he hated it. He liked things to be done.

He also hated giving bad news to people in the field. But bad news was better than ignorance, so he got back on the line.

"Bob, NRO is trying to spot you. Maybe we can keep you moving away from the enemy. Meanwhile, we're still looking for the officer. Thing is, even if we find him it doesn't look like you're any place easy to get to."

"Tell me about it," Herbert said. "Goddamn trees and hills everywhere."

"Would it be better if you tried to flank the enemy?"

"Negative," Herbert said. "The terrain is rough here, but it looks rockier on either side. We'd literally be crawling." He was silent for a moment. "But General? If you can at least find Rosenlocher, there is one thing you can try."

Rodgers listened while Herbert extemporized. What the intelligence chief proposed was creative, ghoulish, and unlikely to succeed. But in the absence of anything else, it became their marching orders.

SIXTY-FOUR

Thursday, 11:28 P.M., Toulouse, France

There were ten closed-circuit surveillance cameras tucked two-atop-two in a closet in Dominique's office. Before the building had begun to rumble, he was sitting in his leather chair, calmly watching the activity in the corridor and in the computer room.

The stupidity of these people, he'd been thinking as he watched them break into his system and find themselves cornered. Dominique would have been content to let them go if they hadn't gotten pushy and broken into his secret files. Ms. Bosworth didn't have that degree of skill, so it had to have been the other man who did it. Dominique hoped that man lived. He wanted to hire him.

Even when the French commandos closed in on the New Jacobins in the corridor, Dominique wasn't concerned. He had sent word for other men to surround *them.* He had made certain that fully half of his hundred New Jacobins would be on the premises tonight. Nothing must go wrong with the downloading of his games.

Dominique wasn't concerned about anything until the building began to shake. Then his high forehead wrinkled and his dark eyes blinked, batting away the reflection of the TV screens. Using the control panel built into his top desk drawer, he switched to external views of the compound. On the river side the black-and-white screen was awash with white light. Dominique turned down the contrast and watched as an aircraft settled down, its navigation lights burning brightly. It was an airplane whose engines had tilted into the vertical so it could descend like a helicopter. The parking lot had cars scattered here and there so the aircraft was unable to land. As it hovered fifteen feet up the hatch opened. A pair of rope ladders were unwound and troops climbed down. NATO troops.

Dominique's mouth tensed. *What is NATO doing here?* he roared inside, though he knew the answer. It was a newly defined mission designed to get him.

As twenty soldiers fell in on the asphalt of the parking lot, Dominique rang Alain Boulez. The former Paris police chief was waiting in the underground training area with the reserve force of New Jacobins.

"Alain, have you been watching your monitors?"

"Yes, sir."

"It appears NATO has nothing better to do than to attack member nations. See that they are turned back and notify me aboard *Boldness*."

"Absolutely."

Dominique called his Operations Director. "Etienne, what is the status of the uploading?"

"Concentration Camp is finished, M. Dominique. Hangin' with the Crowd will be out there by midnight."

"I need it faster," Dominique said.

"Sir, this was preset when we hid the program in—"

"Faster," Dominique said. He switched off and punched up the pilot of his LongRanger helicopter. "Andre? I'm coming down. Ready *Boldness*."

"At once, sir."

Dominique clicked off. He stood and looked out at

his collection of guillotines. They appeared ghostly in the glow of the TV screens. He heard one gunshot, then others.

He thought of Danton about to be beheaded, saying to his executioners, *"Thou wilt show my head to the people: it is worth showing."* Yet even if the plant fell, the games would be uploaded and he would be free. He would fall back to one of the many national and international facilities he'd designated as backup sites. His plastics firm in Taiwan. His bank in Paris. His CD-pressing plant in Madrid.

He shut down the TV screens, donned leather gloves, and walked briskly from his office toward the elevator. He was not retreating, he told himself. He was simply moving his headquarters. What a waste, he thought, if this first wild skirmish should claim him as a victim.

The elevator took him to an underground passage which led to the landing field behind the factory. He entered the code in the door at the end. When it popped open, he snatched a New Jacobin pistol from the gun rack, then climbed the steep steps. The LongRanger helicopter was already warming up. Dominique walked along the tail boom assembly, ducked under the spinning rotor blades, and was greeted by one of his official *Demain* guards, who came running over.

"Dominique, your factory guards are still not involved in this action. What do you want us to do?"

Dominique replied, "Disassociate me from the New Jacobins. Make it seem as if they've come here uninvited to send the foreigners back home."

The guard asked, "How can I do that, *monsieur*?"

Dominique raised his pistol and shot the guard in the forehead. "By making it seem as if you resisted them," he said as he dropped the pistol and hopped from the boarding step into the cabin.

"Let's go!" he said to the pilot as he entered the spacious cabin. He pulled the door shut.

The flight deck was to his left. The copilot's seat was empty. In the main cabin, there were two rows of thickly cushioned seats. Dominique sat in the first one in front, beside the door. He didn't bother to buckle himself in as the helicopter rose.

The pounding drone of the chopper seemed to rattle away his facade of equanimity. Dominique scowled angrily as he looked back at the *bastide*. The VTOL had begun to move toward the field from which he'd just taken off. The craft took up a large section of the field as it set down. The NATO soldiers were no longer in the parking lot. Dominique could see flashes of gunfire through the windows and in the compound.

He felt violated. The soldiers were like Visigoths amok in an English church, destroying wantonly. He wanted to scream at them, *"This is more than you understand! I am the manifest destiny of civilization!"*

The helicopter crossed the river. Then it circled back toward the *bastide*.

Dominique yelled to be heard over the rotor. "Andre, what are you doing?"

The pilot didn't answer. The chopper began to descend.

"Andre? *Andre!*"

The pilot said, "You told me over the phone that you followed all my moves. But you missed one. The one where I came up to your pilot and hit the poor fellow with twenty-five years of anger."

Richard Hausen turned and regarded Dominique. The Frenchman felt ice shoot down his back.

"I took off to make room for the other craft," Hausen said. "Now you're going back, Gerard. Back twenty-five years, in fact."

For a moment, Dominique considered an appropriate response. But only for a moment. As in Paris those many years ago, the idea of debate was pushed aside by the stench of Hausen's sanctimony. Dominique hated it. Just as he had hated it when Hausen had defended those girls.

Losing control of the delicate balance between danger and need, between reason and desire, Dominique threw himself at Hausen with an inarticulate cry. He grabbed the German's hair from behind and pulled his head back, over the seat.

Hausen screamed as Dominique yanked down hard, trying to break his neck. The German released the control stick and began clawing at the Frenchman's wrist. The chopper nosed down instantly and Dominique fell against the back of the pilot's seat. He released Hausen, who was thrown against the systems display.

Groggy, his forehead bloodied, the German struggled to get his bearings. Pushing off the windshield, he managed to find the control stick.

The chopper came out of its dive. As it did, Dominique slid around the pilot's seat. The headphones had fallen to the floor and he picked them up. With an eye on the control stick, Dominique slipped the cord around Hausen's neck and pulled tightly.

SIXTY-FIVE

Thursday, 5:41 P.M.,
Washington, D.C.

Mike Rodgers was studying a map of Germany on the computer when Darrell McCaskey looked over with a thumbs-up.

"Got him!" said McCaskey. "Hauptmann Rosenlocher's on the line!"

Rodgers picked up his phone. "Hauptmann Rosenlocher," Rodgers said, "do you speak English?"

"Yes. Who is this?"

"General Mike Rodgers in Washington, D.C. Sir, I'm sorry to be calling so late. It's about the attack on the movie set, the kidnapping."

"*Ja?*" he said impatiently. "We've been following clues all day. I've only just arrived—"

"We have the girl," Rodgers said.

"*Was?*"

"One of my men found her," Rodgers said. "They're in the woods near Wunstorf."

"There's a rally in those woods," said Rosenlocher. "Karin Doring and her group. We believe Felix Richter may have gone there as well. My investigators were looking into it."

"Your investigation was compromised," Rodgers said.

"How do you know that?"

"They tried to kill my man and the girl," Rodgers replied. "Hauptmann, they've been running for hours and there isn't time to get help to them. A large group of neo-Nazis is closing in on my man. If we're going to save them, I need you to do something for me."

"What?"

Rodgers told him. The Hauptmann agreed. A minute later, Op-Center's communications expert Rosalind Green was making the arrangements.

SIXTY-SIX

Thursday, 11:49 P.M., Wunstorf, Germany

The phone beeped in the dark.

The man nearest it, young Rolf Murnau, stopped and listened. When he heard the muffled beep a second time, he turned his flashlight to the left. Then he walked several paces, through closely knit branches. His flashlight beam formed a cone of light on top of a body. From the broad shoulders, he could tell the body was that of Manfred Piper. Beyond it lay Karin Doring's body.

"Come here!" Rolf shouted. "My God, come quickly!"

Several men and women ran over at once, their flashlight beams crisscrossing as they approached. Several gathered around Manfred's body and looked down as the phone rang a third time, then a fourth. Several others ran over to Karin Doring.

Rolf had already bent beside the body. The blood had formed a large, dark blot on the back of Manfred's jacket, with tendrils reaching down the sides. Rolf turned the body over slowly. Manfred's eyes were shut, his mouth open and lopsided.

"She's dead," a man said from Karin's side. "Damn them, *dead*!"

The phone rang again and then again. Rolf looked up

into the beams. "What should I do?" he asked.

Footsteps crunched toward him. "Answer it," Felix Richter said.

"Yes, sir," Rolf said. He was numb from the loss of his leaders, his heroes, as he reached into Manfred's jacket. He removed the phone. After a moment of feeling invasive, then ghoulish, he flipped open the unit and answered.

"*Ja?*" he said tentatively.

"This is Hauptmann Karl Rosenlocher," said the caller. "I want to speak with whoever is in command of you animals."

Rolf looked up at the light. "Herr Richter? He wants to speak with the commander."

"Who does?" Richter asked.

Rolf said, "Hauptmann Karl Rosenlocher."

Even in the dark Rolf saw Richter stiffen. More and more of the neo-Nazis were gathering as word spread of the deaths. Groups formed around Karin and Manfred as Richter stood there.

Jean-Michel arrived as Richter took the phone. Slowly, the German brought it to his mouth.

"This is Felix Richter."

"You know my voice," said Rosenlocher. "I want you to hear this voice."

A moment later a young woman said in English, "I told you you didn't beat me. You'll never win, any of you."

Richter said, "Child, we will come after you."

Rosenlocher came back on. "No you won't, Herr Richter. She's safe with me, along with the American who got her out. He called for me to collect them. As for you, this is one fire you won't be escaping."

Richter's eyes peered through the dark woods as he motioned several men over. He covered the mouthpiece. "Guns," he said. "Get ready with your guns!"

The men raised their weapons.

Richter said, "I'll meet force with force of my own."

"It won't do you any good," Rosenlocher said slowly, confidently. "This fire is from within."

"What are you talking about?"

"How do you think the American got to your camp tonight?" Rosenlocher asked. "He's one man in a wheelchair. Or is he?"

Richter peered into the dark.

"You were infiltrated, Herr Richter," said Rosenlocher. "My people are with you now. They helped him."

"You're lying," Richter said tensely.

"They've been with you all day," said Rosenlocher. "Watching. Preparing. Helping the American. You've lost key personnel tonight, haven't you, Herr Richter?"

Richter wasn't able to see very far in the thick night. "I don't believe this, and I don't believe you."

"Come after me. Perhaps a firefight will ensue. People will be firing into the dark. Who knows who will fall, Herr Richter? From which side will the bullet come?"

"You wouldn't dare murder me," said the neo-Nazi. "The truth will be discovered. You'll be ruined. There are laws."

Rosenlocher said, "Karin ignored them when she attacked the movie set. Do you think the public will care, Herr Richter? Will they really care when they learn that cold-blooded murderers were slain?"

Richer said, "You won't win, Hauptmann. If I terminate this chase or leave now, you can do nothing!''

"It's out of my hands," said Rosenlocher. "I'm only calling to say good-bye. That, and to let you know I will not be among those who mourn."

The Hauptmann hung up. Richter threw down the telephone. "Damn his blood!"

"What is it?" someone asked.

Richter shook a fist and glared at his accomplices. "Hauptmann Rosenlocher says that we have been infiltrated by members of the Hamburg *Landespolizei*."

Rolf said, "Here?"

"Here," Richter said. He looked around. "Of course he's lying. It's idiotic, insane!" He thought aloud, "But why lie? He has the girl and the American. What does he gain?"

"Maybe he wasn't lying," one man said nervously.

Richter looked at him. "Do you want me to call off the pursuit? Maybe you are one of his men!"

"Herr Richter!" shouted another. "I have known Jorgen for years. He is true to the cause."

"Maybe the policeman is lying," said another man.

"Why?" Richter asked. "What does he gain? Fear? Dissent? Indecision? Panic?" He roared gutturally, *"What does he gain?"*

Jean-Michel said from behind him, "Time."

Richter spun on him. "What are you talking about?"

"The Hauptmann gains time," Jean-Michel said smoothly. "We find the bodies, stop to take care of them, then stand around trying to figure out who may or may not be a traitor. And as we do, Rosenlocher puts more distance between himself and us."

"To what end?" Richter asked. "He has what he came for."

"Does he?" asked Jean-Michel. "I don't think the

American and the girl have had enough time to reach the Autobahn. Perhaps the cripple had a phone with him and called the Hauptmann.'' The Frenchman came closer. "You did, after all, give a speech in which you named your worst enemy.''

Richter glared at him.

Jean-Michel asked, "It isn't difficult to generate a conference call, to make it seem as if Rosenlocher, the American, and the girl are all together.''

Richter shut his eyes.

"You made the kind of mistake a leader cannot afford to make,'' said Jean-Michel. "You told the American how to beat you, provided him with the name of the one man he could trust. And now you may be giving that enemy the chance to weaken you with an old psychological game.''

Richter bent slowly at the knees. Then he shook his fists at the sky and screamed, "Get them!''

The Germans hesitated.

"We should take care of the bodies,'' said one man.

"That's what the Hauptmann wants you to do!'' Richter screamed.

"I don't care,'' said the man. "It's the right thing.''

Rolf was in turmoil, buffeted by grief and rage. But above all, there was duty. He turned his flashlight around and started out. "I'm going after the Americans,'' he said. "That's what Karin Doring and Manfred Piper would have wanted, and that's what I'm going to do.''

Several others followed wordlessly, then more and more of them joined in. They moved quickly to make up for lost time and also to burn off their anger.

But as Rolf picked his way through the woods, tears

rolled down his cheeks. The tears of a little boy who was still very close to the surface of the young man. The tears of someone whose dreams of a future with *Feuer* had just turned to ash.

SIXTY-SEVEN

Thursday, 11:55 P.M., Toulouse, France

Colonel Brett August's primary job with NATO was to help plan maneuvers. Though his specialty was infantry assaults, he had been fortunate to work with experts in aerial and nautical attacks as well. One of the men with him, Airman Boisard, had worked on aerial extractions in Bosnia. August enjoyed working with men like him to see which maneuvers could be transplanted, mixed, and mutated to surprise the enemy.

For the *bastide,* however, he had decided to go with a simple, proven two-by-two assault. Two men advance while two men cover, then the two covering men move in while the forward pair covers them. Even if eight or ten or twenty men were going in, four men were always responsible for each other. It enabled the assault to remain tight, focused, and to strike with laser accuracy. If a man fell, the squad switched to a double-leapfrog assault. The rear man moves to the middle while the front man covers, then moves to the front while the rear man covers. That way, he isn't accidentally shot by his own teammate. If two men fell, the remaining two went in leapfrog. If three men fell, the last man hunkered down and tried to keep the enemy pinned down.

Twenty-two NATO troops entered the *Demain* factory

under August's command. One man caught a slug in the hand, another in the knee. Among the Gendarmerie personnel, only Colonel Ballon was hurt with a bullet in the shoulder. Three of the twenty-eight New Jacobin terrorists died and fourteen were wounded.

August would later testify before a special committee of the French National Assembly that the casualties among the New Jacobins occurred because they fought too hard and too chaotically.

"They were like chess players who knew the moves but not the game," he would read from a statement he and Lowell Coffey II prepared. "The terrorists charged from the factory without a plan, divided their forces, and got chewed up. When they retreated into the building and tried to regroup, we closed in. Finally, after they'd been flanked, they attempted to punch their way out. We tightened the knot until they surrendered, and that was that. The entire operation, from first shot to last, took twenty-two minutes."

It had seemed much longer to Paul Hood.

When the massive V-22 Osprey had descended on the compound and the New Jacobin leader had ordered the execution of his captives, gunfire popped not only from where the doorknob had been removed. It also came from a hole which had been cut in the pasteboard of the false ceiling and from a window to which one of the Gendarmerie officers had rappelled. It was a perfect triangulation and it accounted for three of the New Jacobin wounded: the three men who had been ordered to execute Paul Hood, Nancy Bosworth, and Matt Stoll.

As soon as the men fell, Hood threw himself atop Nancy and Matt dove for the ground. Ballon received his wound as he ran out to cover Matt.

The prisoners were ignored in the madness which followed, as the New Jacobins scrambled to escape what had become a shooting gallery and get out into the open. They were back within ten minutes, trying to hold off the attackers. But by that time, Hood and his companions had retreated to a kitchenette, where Nancy cleaned and bandaged Ballon's wound as best she could and Hood struggled to keep him down. Despite the pain, the Colonel was anxious to get back into battle.

Stoll stood aside, admittedly sickened by the blood and distracting himself with self-congratulatory palaver for having noticed the doorknob being removed and attempting to distract the New Jacobins with "my 'I'm just a computer guy' riff." Like the New Jacobin before him, Hood told Stoll to be quiet.

Two NATO privates were the first ones into the kitchenette. By then, the corridor had been secured and a medic was summoned to take care of Ballon.

Hood, Nancy, and Stoll were evacuated to the Osprey. August and his French interpreter had set up command headquarters beside the cockpit. After receiving a report that the team had secured the first floor and was moving to the second floor, he introduced himself. Then his attention turned back to the interpreter, who was on the radio as the NATO team closed in on the executive suites.

Hood wanted to know if either team had found Dominique or Hausen, and he was desperate to talk to Rodgers. He was concerned about Herbert and wanted to know how he was faring. But it would have to wait. At least they were all safe.

Stoll had already made himself comfortable in the Osprey cabin. Hood was about to invite Nancy inside when a light appeared in the sky. It was star-small and moving east to west. Suddenly, it turned toward them and grew larger, accompanied by the distinctive beating of a helicopter rotor.

August also looked up.

"One of yours?" Hood asked.

"No," he said. "It could be the one that took off before we landed. We assumed some top-level instigators were getting out."

Suddenly, a Gendarmerie officer approached from the edge of the field. A man in shirtsleeves was draped over his shoulder.

"*Sous-lieutenant!*" the officer called to the interpreter.

He placed the groaning man on the ground beside the Osprey and talked with the Second Lieutenant. After several moments, the French officer turned to August.

"This man is a pilot, sir," he said. "He was warming up the helicopter for a M. Dominique when a blond man hit him."

"Hausen," Hood said.

The helicopter began to spiral down. It was obvious that it was falling now, not flying.

August told everyone to get down and cover their heads. Hood lay on top of Nancy, though August remained standing. The Colonel watched as the chopper leveled itself out at about two hundred feet, then pulled back toward the river.

August asked, "Who's Hausen, Mr. Hood?"

Hood stood. "A German politician and a flier. He hates Dominique, the man behind all this."

"Hates him enough to risk his life stealing a chopper?"

"More than enough," Hood told him. "I think Hausen would take himself out just to get Dominique."

"Himself, the chopper, and everyone underneath,"

August said. He continued to watch the helicopter. It swooped off to the north in an arcing climb, then leveled off again. "I've seen this before, old rivalries getting out of control." The Colonel turned to the interpreter. "Are Manigot and Boisard still on the first floor?"

The Second Lieutenant got on the radio and was given an affirmative. "Still on cleanup, sir," he said.

August said, "Tell them to report back here at once. You're in charge."

"Yes, sir," the officer said, saluting.

August looked up at the cockpit and moved his index finger in a circle, over his head. The pilot saluted and fired up the vertical engines.

"Colonel, what is it?" Hood asked.

August ran toward the stairs which led to the cockpit. "Somebody wants that chopper to land and somebody else doesn't," he said. "If we don't get aboard it's going to do neither."

"Get aboard?" Hood shouted.

But the two NATO commandos arrived quickly and climbed on board, and the thunder of the powerful engines precluded an answer. Stoll jumped out of the Osprey's cabin. Hood and Nancy backed away, and less than two minutes after the helicopter had first been sighted the huge VTOL was airborne.

SIXTY-EIGHT

Friday, 12:04 A.M., Wunstorf, Germany

The police car raced along the Autobahn at over one hundred miles an hour. Hauptmann Rosenlocher was looking to his left, past the driver, watching for any sign of activity. He was running without a siren, the driver flashing his toplights briefly at anyone who happened to get in the way. One man sat silently in the backseat. He wore the blue uniform of the *Landespolizei*. Along with his commander, he was watching the road.

Behind Rosenlocher's car were two other cars, designated Two and Three. Each one carried six men of his fifteen-man tactical force. Five of the men were armed with .30 M1 carbine rifles used for sniping. Five had HK 53 submachine guns. All carried long-barrelled Walther P1 pistols. All were watching for the young woman and the man in the wheelchair.

The silver-haired, craggy-faced officer wondered if Richter had bought the bluff. Rosenlocher himself didn't have any experience in these PSYOPS, psychological operations. His expertise was in riot control and undercover operations. But General Rodgers assured him it had worked for one of his colleagues in a situation in 1976 involving the Croatian hijackers of a TWA jet over Paris. And what General Rodgers had said made sense.

Most revolutionaries, especially new and insecure ones, could be convinced that there were traitors in their midst. Often, there were.

The officer's phone rang. *"Ja?"*

"Hauptmann Rosenlocher, it's Rodgers. We've finally got all of you on satellite. Bob and the girl are about three kilometers north of you, headed toward the Autobahn. The neo-Nazis were stopped but now they're moving again. It'll be close as to who reaches them first."

The Hauptmann checked the odometer, then leaned toward his driver. "Go faster," he said softly.

The baby-faced driver grunted.

"Thank you, General," said Rosenlocher. "I'll call back the moment I have something to report."

"Good luck," said Rodgers.

Rosenlocher thanked him again, then peered ahead. The shotgun was in a rack on the back of his seat. He reached around and grabbed it. His palms were as sweaty as always before he went into action. Though unlike most situations, he ached for this one to develop into "a shooting war." He cherished any excuse to strike at the brutes who wanted to destroy his country.

"A little bit faster," he said to the driver.

The driver pursed his lips and leaned into the gas pedal.

The night sped by. The other cars sped up. And then he saw two pale figures amidst the dark foliage on the left side of the road. They ducked back quickly.

"That was one arm of Richter's team," the Hauptmann said. "I can smell those bastards at one hundred twenty miles an hour. Slow down."

The driver obliged. Seconds later, two people struggled from the woods. A man in a wheelchair with a young woman behind him.

"Stop!" Rosenlocher said.

The driver touched the brakes and pulled over as Rosenlocher picked up his radio. The other cars also slowed.

"Two and Three," he said to the other cars, "you see them?"

"We see them in Two."

"We've got them in Three."

The Hauptmann said, "Two, you cover the south flank. Three, you pull up and take the north. I'll bring them in."

The three cars stopped twenty meters apart on the side of the road. The drivers remained behind the wheels as the police officers emerged on the passengers' sides. In the event of casualties, they would race to the hospital in Hanover. The officers in Two and Three moved south and north. In the dark, they set up a skirmish line behind the railing at the side of the road. If they or the Americans were fired upon, their orders were to shoot to kill.

Rosenlocher was the first one over the guardrail. He was less than thirty meters from the edge of the woods, where Bob Herbert and Jody Thompson were rushing to outrace their pursuers.

Rosenlocher raised the shotgun. He aimed at the area behind the woman where he saw movement.

"Come!" he called to Herbert.

Jody continued to push. She was panting and stumbling but she wasn't stopping.

Rosenlocher watched the others. He saw faces in the headlights as traffic passed. Young faces. Some were angry, some were frightened. He knew that all it took was one misstep, for whatever reason, to cause this situation to get out of hand. He hoped that self-preservation would win out and no one would lose his cool.

He could see the Americans' faces clearly now. Herbert was intense as he turned his wheels. Jody was sobbing as she half-pushed, half-leaned on the chair.

Rosenlocher concentrated his aim on a clutch of young men who had emerged from the woods. Bold men, obviously, willing to sacrifice their lives to make a statement. After a moment, however, he knew that they weren't going to attack. Rosenlocher didn't see Karin or Manfred. He didn't know why they weren't here, but he did know that without the head the body wasn't going to think. And without the heart it wasn't going to act. Whatever these ruffians were capable of doing to lone adversaries, they weren't willing to take on a trained force.

Herbert and Jody reached his side. As instructed earlier, the drivers of Two and Three got out to help Herbert over the fence. There was no sense of urgency, no panic. Just a workman-like efficiency which was a hallmark of Rosenlocher's squad.

As the police officers remained at their posts, the drivers helped Herbert and Jody into the first car. When they were safely inside, the men at the rail peeled off from the outside, one at a time. They went back to the passengers' sides of the cars, where they covered the other men as they returned to the cars.

When everyone was safely away from the guardrail, Rosenlocher turned his back on the woods and walked to the car. He half-expected to die. There was always one coward in every crowd of terrorists or thugs. He kept his head erect. Cowards were intimidated by men who refused to be. By men who didn't fear. As he walked, he was completely aware of every sound, every step, knowing that each could be the last he enjoyed.

When he reached the car he walked to the passenger's side and quietly instructed his men to get inside.

They drove off without incident.

Rosenlocher instructed his driver to go directly to the hospital. The man punched on the siren.

Sitting in the backseat of the police car, Jody fell against Herbert's shoulder. She began crying big, heaving sobs.

"My arm hurts," she cried.

"Hush," Herbert said.

"Everything hurts. Everything."

Herbert cradled her head. "We're going to get you taken care of," he said softly. "You're going to be okay. You're safe. You performed like a real hero."

She clutched him around the shoulder. Jody's breath and her tears were warm against his neck. He held her even tighter, so proud of her that his own eyes misted over.

Rosenlocher said softly, "Are *you* all right, Herr Herbert?"

"Yes," Herbert said. "Very."

"Your friend the General was correct," Rosenlocher said. "He told me all I had to do was buy you a few minutes. 'Loosen the noose and Bob will slip out.' "

"Sure," Herbert said, "slip right from the gallows into quicksand. Thanks for hauling us out, Hauptmann. You're gonna be on my Christmas card list for a long time."

Rosenlocher smiled. He turned around, picked up his car phone, and asked his dispatcher to put him through to General Rodgers in Washington.

The shotgun was between his legs. As he waited, Rosenlocher felt the weight of it against his right knee. It had taken a war to bring Hitler down. Once the police had transported Herbert and the girl to safety, they would return and track down the rest of these thugs. It would be ironic after all these years of chasing Felix Richter, after training for assaults and firefights, if the new Führer fell without a shot being fired.

Ironic but fitting, Rosenlocher thought. Perhaps we have learned something after all. If you confront tyrants early enough you'll find that all of them are dressed in the Emperor's New Clothes.

Rosenlocher savored that thought as he had the pleasure of passing the telephone back to Bob Herbert so he could tell his superior that the mission had been accomplished.

It had indeed.

SIXTY-NINE

Friday, 12:16 A.M., Wunstorf, Germany

Felix Richter watched the members of his hunting party straggle back.

"Where are the Americans?" he demanded.

Rolf was among the first people to return. He looked at the bodies of Karin and Manfred. Their heads and shoulders had been covered by windbreakers. They reminded him of dogs which had been run over in traffic. He looked away.

Richter walked up to him. "What happened?"

"The police were waiting," he said. "There was nothing to do."

Richter screamed, "Is that what Karin Doring would have said? That there was *nothing* to do?"

"Karin would have been there doing it," someone yelled back, "not waiting for us to come back. Karin wasn't a *talker*."

"I never said I was Karin Doring—"

"No," said Rolf, "you're not. And I'm leaving."

Richter stepped in front of him. "Listen to me. All of you. You can't let the legacy die because of a setback. We owe it to those who came before us to fight on."

Several people stopped to pick up the bodies. Others waited for them.

"Don't let this end!" Richter said.

The men moved past him to join those who were still waiting at the camp. Rolf followed the flashlight beams which carved through the dark. Were these meager things the spotlights Richter had spoken of, the ones which were supposed to shine across their symbols and accomplishments?

"This is a setback, not a defeat," Richter said. "Don't let them stop us!"

The men continued to walk.

Richter repeated the lines verbatim, his voice rising as he tried to reignite the fervor of the rally.

Jean-Michel said from behind, "They don't care about your distinctions, Herr Richter. They only know that they've lost their heart. If you're clever and determined, perhaps you'll get some of them back. But now it is time to go home."

Jean-Michel looked toward the beams of light and followed, leaving Richter alone in the dark.

SEVENTY

Friday, 12:17 A.M., Toulouse, France

The Osprey hung over the field like a storm cloud, dark and rumbling, its navigation lights flashing lightning. Colonel August stood in the cockpit, behind the pilot, as the craft rose to one thousand feet.

The LongRanger was nearly three miles downriver, moving southeast. The helicopter still lurched and roller-coastered now and then, though less frequently now. It was like a bronco resigning itself to being broken. Only August didn't want it resigning itself *too* fast. Legally, he suspected, he wouldn't be able to justify what they were about to do unless the chopper was out of control and a threat to people on the ground.

"Approximate speed one-two-five miles an hour," the pilot said as they watched the LongRanger recede.

The Osprey nosed down slightly, the props tilting forward as it moved ahead. At speeds of up to 345 miles an hour, the VTOL would overtake it quickly. However, the crew chief wasn't ready yet. He and his three-man team were in the cargo bay readying a two-thousand-pound hoist with a two-hundred-foot cable. The cable was used to pick up or deposit cargo in areas where the Osprey couldn't land.

August had told them to get the hoist ready. When he

told them why, Manigot and Boisard jokingly requested that they please be court-martialed and jump right to the execution instead. The end result would be the same.

But August didn't believe that. He told them what he told everyone in his command. If a job is planned correctly and executed by professionals, it should go as smoothly as getting out of bed in the morning. And while there were always intangibles, that was what made the job exciting.

The Osprey soared ahead in its helicopter configuration. August was not so much concerned with speed as being able to track the chopper. If the pilot decided to change course abruptly, August wanted to be able to adjust accordingly. The Colonel had also ordered his radio operator to maintain silence. The less information the LongRanger had about who was on board or why, the less likely he was to dig in his heels. There was nothing more antagonizing than a faceless, voiceless adversary.

The pilot adjusted the Osprey's altitude so that it was flying one hundred feet higher than the LongRanger. He bore down on the helicopter, sweeping east or west as it moved with the river. Obviously, whoever was at the controls knew how to fly but not how to navigate. He was following the river to get away.

The Osprey closed the gap, bearing down like a storm, fierce and unstoppable. The LongRanger pushed itself but wasn't able to pull away. In less than two minutes the Osprey was on top of it. The LongRanger tried to move aside, but each time it did the larger aircraft moved with it.

All the while the hoist crew worked quickly to ready their equipment. When it was finally done, the crew chief radioed the cockpit.

"Senior Airman Taylor is ready, sir," said the pilot.

Colonel August pulled on gloves and nodded. "Tell him to open the bay. I'm coming back."

The pilot acknowledged the order as August opened the cabin door and crossed the fuselage. Wind tore through the cabin as massive gears churned and the underbelly door opened. The canvas covering the ribs of the fuselage whipped violently on both sides.

August moved quickly despite the wind. Once a team was primed it was a bad idea to keep them waiting. Waiting was to energy like cold was to heat: it sapped it.

August arrived as the men were checking the hooks on their parachutes. "We ready to go?" he asked.

The men answered in the affirmative.

August had outlined the plan when he had first boarded with Manigot and Boisard. Taylor was going to lower Manigot fifty feet straight down, just beyond the horizontal stabilizer to the crosspiece halfway between the main cabin and the tail assembly. There was enough room behind the main rotor blades to accomplish that. The only real concern they had was a five-to-eight-second period when the airman or the cable above him was directly behind the main rotor. If the LongRanger slowed or angled up or down during that time, Manigot or the cable could be sliced to pieces. If the chopper moved at all, Manigot was to release the cable immediately, parachute down, and the mission would be aborted. Otherwise, once both men were on the tail boom, they would make their way to the landing skid and enter the cabin.

At least, that's how it was supposed to work. They'd done simulations of chopper-to-chopper transfers. But those helicopters were hovering. Now that he was standing in the open doorway, looking down at their target, he realized that he couldn't risk sending his men from one moving vehicle to another.

He was about to abort when something happened to the LongRanger.

SEVENTY-ONE

Friday, 12:51 A.M., Toulouse, France

Richard Hausen was lying on the floor of the cockpit, rubbing his throat, wondering why Dominique hadn't finished him off. Then he heard the sound of a pursuit aircraft. He felt the vibrations. Someone was on their tail.

He knew they weren't going to shoot Dominique down, and the only way to stop him was if they boarded the LongRanger.

Even in his pained state the German didn't know whether or not that could be done with a moving helicopter. But he knew it would be easier if the LongRanger weren't moving, if Dominique couldn't evade them.

Hausen blinked hard to clear his eyes and then sought the automatic hover button on the control panel. Finding it, he threw himself against Dominique, pushed the button, and pulled the Frenchman to the floor of the cabin.

SEVENTY-TWO

Friday, 12:52 A.M., Toulouse, France

The Osprey shot over the hovering LongRanger and August ordered the pilot to turn back. The Osprey swung around and hovered directly over the LongRanger.

August looked down from the open hatch. Both vehicles were steady, though he had no idea how long the LongRanger would remain so. He wondered if Dominique might be trying to draw them out.

No, he thought. Dominique didn't know whether their intentions were to board or pursue. Moreover, the Frenchman wouldn't be able to see them from the cockpit. He would have no idea if he'd succeeded in drawing out any or all of the team. August's gut told him that Dominique wasn't the one responsible for the hovering. It was probably Hausen.

Manigot, Boisard and Taylor were all looking at the Colonel, waiting for the command.

There was no gain without risk, and those who feared risk had no business wearing a uniform. The Colonel had a mission and he had the men.

"Go!" he said.

Taylor pressed the button on the hoist to lower Manigot quickly. The cable played out at 3.2 feet each second and he was on the stabilizer in fifteen seconds. Once

Manigot had hooked himself to the crosspiece, he attached the cable, then signaled with a flashlight. Boisard slid down quickly and cleanly. Once he was secured to the other side of the crosspiece, Manigot unhooked the cable and Taylor withdrew it at once. The weight of the heavy hook at the end worked like a plumb bob to keep the cable from blowing back into the tail rotor.

August watched in the dim light from the open hatch of the Osprey as Boisard unwound the rope from his belt and slipped it through the steel loops on Manigot's belt. Then Manigot released himself from the crosspiece and started shimmying along the top of the tail boom.

Suddenly, the LongRanger dove. It wasn't a wild ride, like before: it was a purposeful attempt to get away. It caused Manigot to slide toward the mast of the rotor head. Only his quick reflexes stopped him from being tossed into the spinning hub as he grabbed onto the exhaust pipe just aft of the assembly. Boisard held onto the stabilizer, literally dangling forward as the helicopter dove.

August got on the radio and ordered his pilot to pursue. Then he squinted into the dark, watching for the men to jump.

They didn't. Both men were proud but they weren't reckless: if they could get off they would. They were probably worried about jumping off and landing in the rotors.

Frustrated by the distance and the blackness and the wind, August held on to the open hatch as the Osprey threw itself after the LongRanger. Finally, the LongRanger steadied again and August turned to Senior Airman Taylor.

"Lower that thing again!" he yelled. "I'm going down!"

Taylor said, "Sir, we have no idea if the chopper will remain stabilized—"

"Now!" August barked as he pulled a parachute from the equipment locker and slipped it on. "I'm going to hook 'er to the tail boom. When I get to Boisard, we're going to drag this sucker home."

"Sir, we're tested for two thousand pounds, and the chopper is—"

"I know. But as long as the helicopter rotor is turning, it won't be deadweight! Tell the pilot to stay with him, no matter what. I'll flash you twice when I've hooked her, then you radio the pilot to turn around!"

Taylor saluted, then moved toward the controls with a confidence he clearly didn't feel.

Like its namesake, the Osprey tore relentlessly through the sky. As it did, the cable unwound and August was lowered at an angle toward the chopper. He torqued around the cable as he descended, twisting around several times before he was able to grab the stabilizer. Crawling to the opposite side from Boisard to keep from unbalancing the aircraft, he hooked himself to the boom and then latched the cable around it as well. It slid back, smacked up against the tail fin with a clang, and held there.

August had his fish. But he didn't signal the Osprey. He had something else in mind.

Looking forward, he began shimmying along the boom toward Manigot. The headwind was devastating as he inched ahead. As he neared the cabin, the LongRanger suddenly righted itself and swung off toward the east. The Osprey got a late start keeping up. The cable played out and the LongRanger shuddered violently as the cable grew taut and the hoist held.

August slid from the top of the tail boom to the side.

He looked up to make sure that Manigot was okay, and then he looked down. His legs were less than two yards from the skid. They were two dark, windy yards, but the tips of the skid were directly below him. If he released himself, he'd have to pass them on his way down.

He tucked his arms at his sides and chucked all his rules about planning. This was one of those things like a shot from the key: either you made the basket or you didn't.

He removed his gloves and let them drop. He undid the metal clasp which held him to the line which girdled the tail boom. He waited for the LongRanger to stabilize again, and then he dropped.

August reached out at once. Free of the chopper, he was blown backward. But not so far backward that he couldn't reach the rear strut of the skid. He hooked it with his left arm, quickly reached over with his right, and struggled to pull himself over. The wind was intense and he hung down at a forty-five-degree angle, slapping against the baggage compartment as he fought to haul himself in.

Now he saw the pilot look back at him. There was someone between the seats of the flight deck, on the floor, struggling to rise. As the pilot turned away, he tried to throw the chopper into another dive. The cable held, both vehicles shook, and then the pilot looked back again. This time, though, he was not looking at August but at the cable.

Slowly, he began backing the helicopter up. With a flash of terror, August realized what he was trying to do. He was attempting to use the rotor to cut the cable. If he couldn't get away he was going to take everybody down.

August scrambled feverishly to drag his leg up over the skid. As soon as he was standing, he reached for the cabin door and literally yanked it open. He hurled himself into the passenger compartment. With two strides he was in the open flight deck. Stepping over the semiconscious man on the floor, August cocked his arm into a tight jujitsu chamber, with the elbow waist-high, straight back, and punched the pilot in the side of the head. With piston-like speed, he hit him a second and third time, then pulled the dazed man from the seat.

Dropping into it, August held the control stick steady while he turned to the man on the floor.

"Hausen? Get up! I need you to fly this damn thing!"

The German was groggy. "I . . . I tried to steady it for you . . . twice."

"Thanks," August said. "Now c'mon—"

Slowly, Hausen began to drag himself into the co-pilot's seat.

"A little faster, please!" August shouted. "I have very little idea what I'm doing here!"

Wheezing, Hausen flopped into the seat, dragged a sleeve across his bloody eyes, and took the stick.

"It's okay," the German said. "I . . . I have it."

Bolting from the pilot's seat, the Colonel angrily threw Dominique into the cabin, then went back to the open door. He leaned out. Boisard was manfully making his way to Manigot.

"We're secure in here!" August yelled. "When you have him, undo the cable!"

Boisard acknowledged and August ducked back inside.

"You okay up there?" the Colonel shouted to Hausen.

"I'll be fine," the German said wearily.

"Keep it steady until you get the word," August said. "Then we'll head back to the factory."

Hausen acknowledged. Bending over Dominique, August picked him up, plunked him into a chair in the cabin, and stood in front of him.

"I don't know what you did," August said, "but I hope it was bad enough so that they put you away forever."

Dazed and bleeding, Dominique managed to look up at him and smile. "You can stop me," he said through loose teeth, "but you can't stop us. Hate . . . hate is more bankable than gold."

August smirked. And punched him again. "There's interest on my account," he said.

As Dominique's head rolled to his right, August went back to the open hatch. His arms shaking from exhaustion, he helped Manigot inside. When Boisard was finished unhooking the cable, August assisted him in as well. Then he closed the door and fell heavily to the floor.

The sad thing was, the bastard was right. Hate and hate-mongers continued to flourish. He used to fight them. Used to be pretty good at it. Still was, he had to admit. And though it took a while for his brain to catch up to his heart, he knew that when he landed he had a call to make.

SEVENTY-THREE

Friday, 12:53 A.M.,
Toulouse, France

The men of the Gendarmerie had secured the factory by the time the Osprey returned. The New Jacobins had been rounded up and handcuffed. They had been separated into groups of two and placed in office cubicles guarded by two men each. Ballon believed that martyrs and heroes were either exhibitionists or wind-up toys. They were less likely to do anything if no one was there to see or provoke them. The quick collapse of the New Jacobins reinforced something else which Ballon also believed. That they were cowardly pack animals with no stomach to fight when left on their own or faced with equal or superior numbers.

Whatever the truth of the matter, there was no further resistance as local police vans were summoned to cart the captives away. Ambulances were also called, though Ballon insisted on being treated at the site and remaining there until the Osprey and LongRanger had returned. Along with the others, he'd watched the distant struggle. Until the Osprey pilot radioed that Dominique had been taken, no one knew what the outcome had been.

When the Osprey landed, followed by the Long-Ranger, Colonel August personally took charge of Dominique. They exited side by side, August holding

Dominique in a forearm lock. The Frenchman's forearm was facing up, resting on August's. His elbow was tucked into August's armpit and his hand was turned up and back toward his body. If he tried to escape, August would simply bend the hand toward his body, causing excruciating pain in the wrist.

Dominique didn't try to escape. He could barely walk. August immediately turned him over to the Gendarmerie. He was placed in a van with Ballon and four of his men.

"Tell Herr Hausen he can *have* the headlines," Ballon told August before they drove away. "Tell him I will write them myself!"

August assured him that he would.

The Osprey pilot had called ahead for the NATO medics. Though the cuts and bruises Boisard and especially Manigot had suffered were mostly superficial, there were a lot of them. And Manigot had fractured two ribs.

Hausen was in the worst shape. In an effort to remain conscious and focus his energy during the flight back, he had talked to August. He said that Dominique had tried at first to strangle him. And each time Hausen had rallied and tried to wrest control of the helicopter, Dominique had kicked or beaten him again. As soon as the helicopter landed, Hausen slumped over the control stick.

Hood entered the LongRanger so he could be with the Deputy Foreign Minister until he was evacuated. Hood sat in the pilot's seat beside the German as they waited for the NATO medic to finish with the assault casualties.

Hood called his name. Hausen looked over and smiled faintly.

"We got him," he said.

"You got him," Hood replied.

"I was willing to die if I could take him with me," Hausen said. "I . . . didn't care about anything else. I'm sorry."

"No need to apologize," Hood said. "It all worked out."

The American got up and stepped aside as a medic and her assistant arrived. She examined the wounds on Hausen's neck, temple, scalp, and lower face to make sure there was no need for hemorrhage control. Then she checked his eyes and heart rate and made a cursory spinal examination.

"Mild neurogenic shock," she said to her assistant. "Let's get him out of here."

A stretcher was brought over and Hausen was carried from the LongRanger. Hood walked out behind them.

"Paul!" Hausen shouted as he was lifted down the steps.

Hood said, "I'm here."

"Paul," Hausen said, "this is not finished. Do you understand?"

"I know. We'll get that regional center going. Take the initiative. Now don't talk."

"In Washington," Hausen said as he was placed in the ambulance. He smiled weakly. "Next time we meet in Washington. Quieter."

Hood smiled back at him and squeezed his hand before they shut the door.

"Maybe we ought to invite him to a budget hearing," Matt Stoll said from behind him. "This'll seem like a day at the beach."

Hood turned. He squeezed his associate's shoulder. "You were a real hero tonight, Matt. Thanks."

"Aw, it was nothing, Chief. It's amazing what you

can do when your ass is in danger and you've got no choice.''

"Not true," Hood said. "A lot of people panic under fire. You didn't."

"Bull," Stoll said. "I just didn't show it. But I think you've got other unfinished business. So I'm just going to tiptoe away and have a nervous breakdown."

Stoll left. Nancy was standing directly behind him, in the shadows.

Hood stared at her for a moment before he walked over. He wanted to say that she'd performed like a hero too, but he didn't. She'd never warmed to slap-on-the-back compliments, and he knew that that was not what she wanted to hear from him.

He took her hands in his. "I think this is the latest we've ever been out."

She laughed once. Tears rolled from her eyes. "We were old fogies back then. Dinner, reading in bed, ten o'clock news, early movies on weekends."

Hood was suddenly aware of the weight of his wallet inside his jacket and of the two ticket stubs inside it. She wasn't. She was staring into his eyes with love and longing. She did not intend to make this easy.

He rubbed the backs of her hands with his thumbs, then moved his hands to her shoulders. He kissed her on the cheek. The warm salt of her tears made him want to move closer, hold her, kiss her ear.

He stepped back.

"There are going to be inquiries, a lot of commissions and court dates. I would like to get you an attorney."

"Okay. Thanks."

"I'm sure someone will pick up *Demain*'s assets when this is all cleared up. My staff has muscle in all kinds of places. I'll make sure you're involved. Until then, Matt will find things for you to do.''

"My savior," she said dryly.

Hood grew annoyed. "This isn't fun for me either, Nancy. But I can't give you what you want."

"Can't you?"

"Not without taking from someone else, someone I love. I've spent most of my adult life growing up with Sharon. We're intertwined in ways that are very special to me."

"Is that all you want?" she asked. "A relationship that's special? You should be *delirious*. We were. Even when we fought we had passion."

"Yes," Hood said, "but that's over. Sharon and I are happy together. There's a lot to be said for stability, knowing that someone will be there—"

"For better or worse, richer or poorer, in sickness and in health," Nancy said bitterly.

"That," Hood said, "or even just showing up at the movies."

Nancy's mouth turned down. She blinked several times without looking away. "Ouch," she said. "Direct hit."

Hood was sorry to have hurt her, but at least he'd found the strength to say what needed to be said. It felt bad but it felt right.

Nancy finally turned away. "So," she said. "I guess I should have gone back to town with Colonel Ballon."

"The local police are on the way," Hood told her. "They'll see that we get a ride."

"You're still a blockhead," she said with a brave smile. "I meant he's single. It was a joke."

"Gotcha," Hood said. "Sorry."

Nancy took a deep breath. "Not as sorry as I am. About everything." She looked at him again. "Even

though this didn't work out the way I wanted, it was
good to see you again. And I'm glad you're happy. I
truly am.''

She started to walk away, swaying as she had when
he'd seen her at the hotel, her hair snapping this way,
then that. Hood started after her. Without turning
around, she held up her hand like a police officer stopping traffic and shook her head.

Hood watched her go, his own eyes dampening. And
when she had disappeared into the crowd of police and
medics he smiled sadly.

The date, at last, had been kept.

SEVENTY-FOUR

Monday, 9:32 A.M., Washington, D.C.

Hood, Stoll, and Herbert were welcomed back to Op-Center with a small party in the Tank, the high-security conference room. When they arrived, the senior staffers were already gathered with trays of coffee, croissants, and crullers.

"We bought out all of the French and German-sounding pastries in the commissary," Ann Farris pointed out as she welcomed Hood with a cheek-to-cheek air kiss.

Ed Medina and John Benn had spent the weekend building a small tableau of toy soldiers representing NATO, Hood, and Herbert. They were defending a fort labeled "Decency" from a horde of disfigured soldiers pouring from a troop transport labeled "Hate."

The bruised but unbowed Herbert was touched. Stoll lapped it all up. Hood was embarrassed. Rodgers stood cross-armed in the corner, out of Hood's limelight, a hint of envy in his expression.

When prompted to speak, Hood perched himself on the corner of the conference table and said, "All we did was what people like General Rodgers and our Striker personnel do all the time."

"Run amok abroad," Lowell Coffey suggested, "and make the diplomats earn their pay?"

"No," Stoll countered. "Fight for truth, justice, and the American way!"

"Where're my pom-poms?" Ann Farris asked.

Hood quieted the twenty-odd people gathered in the office. "Like I said, we only followed the example that our Op-Center colleagues have set for us. Speaking of which, Mike—you want to make the announcement?"

Rodgers shook his head and extended his hand toward Hood. Hood wanted to drag him over, force him to share in this triumph. But self-promotion was not in Rodgers's lexicon.

Hood said, "Over the weekend, General Rodgers finalized plans for Colonel Brett A. August to come to Washington to take command of Striker. Colonel August was the man who actually collared Gerard Dominique, and he's going to be a great strategic and personal asset to our team."

There was a smattering of applause and upthrust thumbs.

"As I'm sure you've all noticed," Hood went on, "this weekend the press was full of the fall of Dominique and the implications of *Operation L'Ecouter*. I saw a lot of editorials about the way the prejudices and suspicions of otherwise good people were going to be manipulated, used to destroy lives and societies. I hope the warnings don't die with the headlines. Ann, we'll have to talk about that. Let's see if we can work up some kind of educational program for schools."

She nodded and smiled proudly at him.

Hood said, "The evidence Matt dug up on the *Demain* computers is safe with French prosecutors. Since there were international elements to the crime, representatives of the U.S., Germany, and other nations will be on hand to make sure that Dominique doesn't wriggle away. I would also like to congratulate Matt and his team. Yesterday, they traced the launch site of the hate games here in the U.S. to a bank computer in Montgomery, Alabama. They were planted there over the Internet so they could be launched as close as possible to the place where Rosa Parks refused to give her bus seat to a white man in 1955. Dominque believed in history. Too bad he didn't learn a damn thing from it.''

Rodgers said solemnly, ''As Samuel Taylor Coleridge said, 'If men could learn from history, what lessons it might teach us. But passion and party blind our eyes.' ''

Hood said, ''I think we opened a few eyes in Europe, especially thanks to Bob.''

''And Jody Thompson,'' Herbert said. ''I'd be under a pile of rocks if it weren't for her.''

''Yes, and Jody,'' said Hood. ''We've been told that the Chaos Days celebration in Germany fizzled after what happened. A lot of the younger people became disillusioned and went home early.''

''Poor babies,'' said Martha. ''Wanna bet they'll be back?''

''You're right,'' said Hood. ''We didn't put an end to hate. But we *did* put them on notice. At ten o'clock, I'm meeting with Senator Barbara Fox—''

There were scattered boos.

Hood held up his hands. ''I promise you that she won't leave here without rescinding the budget cuts she's threatened. Actually, over the weekend I was thinking about how we could use additional money for a new division operating either as part of Op-Center or independently. A Web Patrol or Net Force to watch over the information highway.''

''Why not call it Computer CHiPs?'' Stoll asked. ''Or how about Information Highway Patrol?''

There were several loud groans.

''What?'' he said. ''Net Force is better?''

"It'll get taken seriously by Congress and the press," John Benn said, "and that's what counts."

"Speaking of Congress," Hood said, "I don't want to keep Senator Fox waiting. I want to thank everyone for this welcome home, and I especially want to thank General Rodgers for the support you gave us overseas."

Hood left then, followed by respectful applause and a few cheers. On the way out, he patted Rodgers's shoulder and asked him to join him. They left the Tank together.

"Is there anything we can do to make Colonel August feel welcome?" Hood asked as they walked back toward his office.

"Only one thing I can think of," Rodgers said. "I'm going to head into D.C. at lunchtime to see if I can find a model of Revell's Messerschmitt Bf 109. We used to build kits as kids and that was the big one we missed."

"Expense-account it," Hood said.

Rodgers shook his head. "This one's on me. I owe it to Brett."

Hood said he understood, then asked Rodgers if he wanted to attend the meeting with Senator Fox.

Rodgers declined. "Once a week is enough. Besides, you've always handled her better than I have. I just don't have the touch."

Hood said, "I just tried doing what you do for a living, Mike. You've got the touch all right."

"Then it's settled," Rodgers said. "If we can't persuade her, we put her in a helicopter in cuffs."

"It works for me," Hood said as his assistant, "Bugs" Benet, poked his head from his office down the hall. He informed the director that the Senator had just arrived.

With Rodgers's good wishes following him down the hall, Hood hurried to meet Senator Fox at the elevator.

The woman arrived with her two assistants and a sly expression.

"Good morning, Paul," the Senator said as she stepped out. "Have a restful weekend?"

"When my wife wasn't yelling at me for nearly getting killed, yes."

"Good." They began walking down the hall. The Senator said, "As for me, I wasn't resting. I was trying to figure out how I'm going to lop off heads working for the man who just saved the free world. Did you plan that, Paul? Just to make my life difficult?"

"I can't sneak anything past you, can I?" he replied.

"It'll sure play on *Larry King Live,*" Senator Fox said. "Especially a man in a wheelchair saving Ms. Thompson. That was not only miraculous, it was a PR dream. And the press is positively loving her. Especially since she's been turning down offers to sell movie rights to her ordeal unless she can direct it. Smart cookie."

The group reached Hood's office. They stopped outside.

"Helping Ms. Thompson was Bob's and Mike's doing," Hood said. "Not mine."

"That's right," she responded. "Preserving the melting pot, stopping our cities from being torn apart by riots, ending the career of the world's next great despot. That was all you did. Well, I'm still determined to make cuts, Paul. I owe that to the taxpayer."

Hood said, "We should talk about this in my office. But we should really talk about it alone. There's something I want to tell you."

Fox said, "I have no secrets from my associates. They may not be high-maintenance like your team, but they're mine."

"I understand that," Hood said. "Still, I'd like to

have a moment or two alone with you.''

Senator Fox said without looking at her aides, ''Would you mind waiting here? I'll be right back.''

Neil Lippes and Bobby Winter declined Hood's offer to wait in an office. After Senator Fox stepped inside, Hood shut the door.

''Have a seat,'' Hood said as he walked to his desk.

''I'll stand, thank you,'' she replied. ''This won't take long.''

Hood decided to remain in front of the desk, not behind it. He had a personal loathing for theatrics and wanted to make this as clean and direct as possible. But he knew he had better be close to her.

He picked up a manila envelope from the desk. He held it toward her but didn't let go.

''This was delivered over the weekend via the German diplomatic pouch,'' Hood said. ''It's from Deputy Foreign Minister Hausen.''

Hood waited. He'd gone to Matt's condo on Sunday and had him run a computer analysis to make sure. There was no doubt. Though he'd been dreading this moment since the package arrived, he had to go through with it.

''I'm listening,'' Fox said.

Hood said, ''Years ago, Gerard Dominique and Richard Hausen were students together in Paris. They were out one night. They'd been drinking.''

Fox's naturally ruddy cheeks lost some of their color. Her dark eyes fell to the package.

''May I?'' she asked, holding out her hand.

Hood gave it to her. She brought it toward her, holding it in both hands. She pressed it between her thumbs and index fingers, moved them from side to side trying to feel what was inside.

''Photographs,'' she said.

Hood came closer. He said gently, "Senator, please sit down."

She shook her head and put a hand into the envelope. She selected a photograph without looking. She looked at it.

The color snapshot showed a girl standing on the top of the Eiffel Tower, hazy Paris spread behind her.

"Lucy," the Senator said. Her voice was choked, barely audible. She put it back and then hugged the envelope to her breast. "What happened, Paul?"

Hood watched as tears filled her eyes. She blinked them away and crushed the envelope tighter.

"Dominique attacked them," Hood said. "Hausen tried to stop him. We found these photographs in Dominique's office at *Demain*."

The Senator's eyes were shut. Her breath was shallow. "My baby," she said. "My Lucy."

Hood wanted to put his arms around her. Instead he just watched her, aware of the inadequacy of any words or gestures he might offer. He was also aware of the political icon becoming flesh. And he knew then that whatever might come between them in the future, she could never entirely retreat from him. Not after what they'd just shared.

The Senator obviously knew it too. She relaxed her arms and looked at Hood. Then she took a cleansing breath and returned the envelope to Hood. "Would you mind keeping these for a time? After twenty-five years, you've given me—well, it's the buzzword of the nineties," the Senator said, "but you've given me closure. I'm just not ready yet to deal with the grief again. I suspect there will be a lot of that in Dominique's trial."

"I understand," Hood said. He laid the envelope behind him on the desk. He remained standing so she wouldn't have to see it.

The public Senator began to return almost at once. Her eyes cleared, her shoulders straightened, her voice became stronger.

''So. You know that now I can't make cutbacks,'' she said.

Hood said, ''Senator, I didn't do this for political favors.''

''I know. Which is even more of a reason why I have to fight for you. I was being snippy when I arrived, but Op-Center has proven its worth. So have you. Coming from most of the people I know, this moment would have reeked of manipulation. Washington isn't a training ground for real intimacy but you created it here today. And I do believe, Paul, with all my soul, that we have to get behind our worthy people as well as our worthy institutions.''

She offered her hand. Hood shook it.

''Thank you for today,'' she said. ''I'll call later so we can arrange another meeting. Let's figure out how we can satisfy the budget watchdogs and you.''

''I warn you,'' Hood smiled, ''I may need more money. I've got an idea for a new agency.''

''That may be the way to *get* more money,'' the Senator said. ''Cut from Op-Center, give it back with extra for a different agency. It's smoke and mirrors but everyone's happy.''

Senator Fox showed herself out, ignoring her aides' questioning looks as she marched them toward the elevator.

Hood went around the desk and sat down. He put the envelope in a drawer. Then he took his wallet from his jacket pocket, removed the ticket stubs, and tore them up. He put them in an envelope and tucked them in the drawer.

After twenty-five years, Hood felt that he had closure as well.

ABOUT THE CREATORS

Tom Clancy is the author of *The Hunt for Red October, Red Storm Rising, Patriot Games, The Cardinal of the Kremlin, Clear and Present Danger, The Sum of All Fears, Without Remorse,* and *Debt of Honor*. He is also the author of the nonfiction books *Submarine, Armored Cav,* and *Fighter Wing*. He lives in Maryland.

Steve Pieczenik is a Harvard-trained psychiatrist with an M.D. from Cornell University Medical College. He has a Ph.D. in International Relations from M.I.T. and served as principal hostage negotiator and international crisis manager while Deputy Assistant Secretary of State under Henry Kissinger, Cyrus Vance, and James Baker. He is also the bestselling novelist of the psycho-political thrillers *The Mind Palace, Blood Heat, Maximum Vigilance,* and *Pax Pacifica*.

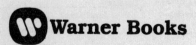